2017

★

2 0 1 7

★

Olga Slavnikova

Translated from the Russian by
Marian Schwartz

OVERLOOK/DUCKWORTH

NEW YORK • LONDON

This edition first published in hardcover in the United States in 2010 by
Overlook Duckworth, Peter Mayer Publishers, Inc.
New York • London

NEW YORK:
141 Wooster Street
New York, NY 10012

LONDON:
90-93 Cowcross Street
London EC1M 6BF
inquiries@duckworth-publishers.co.uk
www.ducknet.co.uk

A portion of this work originally appeared in *Subtropics*, no 7 (Winter-Spring 2009).

Grateful acknowledgment to the National Endowment for the Arts
for a major grant in support of this translation.

Cataloging-in-Publication Data is available from the Library of Congress

Book design and typeformatting by Bernard Schleifer
Manufactured in the United States of America
FIRST EDITION
2 4 6 8 10 9 7 5 3 1
ISBN 978-1-59020-309-5 US
ISBN 978-0-71563-910-8 UK

Translator's Acknowledgments

Many people and institutions have been instrumental in bringing this translation to the American reading public, for which I want to express my deep gratitude.

Natasha Perova, the pioneering editor of *Glas: New Russian Writing*, introduced me to Olga Slavnikova's work and published an excerpt from a previous version of the novel in 2003, in a volume entitled *Nine of Russia's Foremost Women Writers*.

The National Endowment for the Arts provided a major grant in support of this translation. Without it, I would never have been able to take the necessary time to complete the novel.

David Leavitt, editor of the fine literary journal *Subtropics*, published an excerpt from this translation in 2007 and has been a champion of both Slavnikova's work and mine.

As he has in the past, my dear friend and colleague R. Michael Conner shared his long experience and invaluable counsel on geological terminology.

My agent, Peter Sawyer, of the Fifi Oscard Agency, and before him Fifi herself, have been unfailing supporters of this translator's sometimes obscure endeavors.

Most of all, I want to thank the author for writing such an amazingly fresh and exciting book about Russia..

Part One

★

1

★

ON JUNE 7, 2017, KRYLOV WAS SUPPOSED TO BE AT THE TRAIN station at seven thirty. He had no idea how he'd overslept, and now he was loping between winding puddles that reminded him of Matisse dancers in extended poses who had confused right and left. Krylov's arms were wrapped around a camel's hair sweater crammed into a plastic bag. He had to give the sweater back to Professor Anfilogov, to replace one that had been irreparably damaged by moths: in the north, which it was going to take the expedition three weeks to reach, spring was only just coming into its own, and under the drunken spruce trees, in the shelter of their broad black shawls, the stony snow, strewn with needles, was still white. As Krylov raced across the plaza in front of the station, his sneakers smeared the oozy mess that had fallen from the bird cherry trees. He glanced at the gray tower with the square clock, where the arrow, like a blind man's cane, had ticked and just missed the Roman IV, and realized he would make it—with time to spare.

Krylov was so much lighter than the rest of the train station crowd, which was sorely weighed down by the baggage it was dragging, he was practically skimming past a pile of oilcloth valises when his attention was captured by a gossamer-wrapped woman. The stranger shone through her thin, gauzy dress and was silhouetted in a sun cocoon, like a shadow on a dusty windowpane. Scurrying between Krylov and the stranger were a great many people wholly absorbed in their own baggage. No one saw anything around them but the arrivals and departures board, half erased by the sun, where, at irregular intervals, lines that had outlived their usefulness crackled to pieces, only to leap out with the names and numbers of the arriving trains (delaying the final piece for a split-second, as if they were composed of mistakes). The stranger shared the general obliviousness. She straightened the square glasses on her face with her splayed fingers as she spoke rapidly to someone Krylov couldn't see, who was resting his creased carry-on bag comfortably on his sneakers. It took Krylov a few minutes to realize that this someone was in fact Vasily Petrovich Anfilogov, who was not disguised in any way but who had grown a tobacco stubble, which after the couple of months of the expedition would become his usual bushy beard. Vasily Petrovich noticed Krylov as well and beckoned to him with an imperious sweep of his arm meant to reveal the flashy watch under his cuff.

They mingled greetings, and the practical Kolyan ran up, presenting Anfilogov with a fan of baggage-claim tickets. Even so, there was still a hell of a lot of baggage underfoot, so Krylov quickly loaded up, slinging the canvas straps over his shoulders and carelessly (letting anonymous hands do the passing) entrusting his light but cumbersome package to the stranger. Lanky Kolyan, smiling with wet steel teeth, slipped carefully into the straps of a backpack he personally had sewn, where the pride and joy of the expedition rested heavily: a Japanese motor purchased instead of a dentist's services. Anfilogov tossed his raggedy cap jauntily on his head and led his small brigade through a dank tunnel occupied by a camp of Asian beggars who had come to make money and had already set out what looked like boxes of chewing gum under the scattered rain-coins (professionally sensing precisely where the roof leaked).

At last they stepped onto the platform. The train hadn't pulled in yet, and the open expanse of rails and cables was empty, like a drawing lesson in perspective. An indefinable but amazingly precise human figure mounted the steps of the pedestrian bridge schematically drawn above the ravishing morning clouds, trying her best with her childish gait to help her baggage cart along. Kolyan, whose eyes were watering like crazy, was trying to smoke and yawn simultaneously, and smoke was pouring out his covered mouth like from a damp stove. Anfilogov, perfectly composed, profiled in the hubbub of the platform, reminded Krylov of the romantic criminal he in point of fact was.

"If you would be so kind, then, be ready to work in mid-September," he addressed Krylov, shifting to that dry, staccato tone that had won him a bad name among easily wounded university bosses. "Buy the rest of the equipment. You can spend all the money. We'll make up for it with interest."

From the way Anfilogov lowered his voice, Krylov understood that what he said was not meant for the stranger, who was standing a little ways away, with gooseflesh on her bare arms, hugging the package. The woman obviously bore some connection to Anfilogov —amorous rather than familial or work-related—but Anfilogov made no effort to clarify their relationship. Krylov had still not had a proper look at her. A cursory glance had taken in vaccination scars like oat flakes, a tiny patent leather purse, and a pink, mannish ear, behind which unconscious fingers kept tucking a lock of hair cropped short. Standing close to the stranger, Krylov for some reason lost his sense of his own height and couldn't tell whether he was in fact taller or not. This woman seemed wholly self-contained. Meanwhile, she must have been initiated somehow into the expedition's secret and purpose because an anemic flush spread across her cheeks, spilling under her glasses, and the general excitement, which the men hid behind their practicality and usual bravado, played inside her like a matte light.

Now Krylov was wishing Vasily Petrovich and Kolyan would just leave. He wanted to be seeing them off so that he could finally move on to awaiting their triumphant return—all the more triumphant for being so predictable—with their stash of amethyst druses to distract envious eyes. At last he heard a low, ragged whistle, and the top of the locomotive pulling its train cars came into view, getting bigger and bigger, until it filled one of the long voids of perspective. The train swooped in, its brakes hissed, and the lady conductors with their pale legs glided up in the open doors as the train slowed. While

Anfilogov, Krylov, and Kolyan were hoisting the baggage into the train car, dragging it down the sun-striped corridor, periodically getting stuck, and arranging everything, taking turns on the bare brown leatherette bench in the cramped compartment, the stranger stood down below, and between the shadowy train cars a slanting sliver of sun, like a rifle with a blindingly bright bayonet, crossed her closely planted, untanned legs.

From time to time Krylov stole a peek at the woman through the dirty window mottled with the dried traces of either Chelyabinsk or Perm rain, like bird droppings. Once in a while the train shuddered and a gasping spasm rolled from its head to its distant tail, and then Krylov imagined the shadowy cars had rustled a little, like large flags touched by the wind, and the sunny sliver spilled over and, uncontainable now, streamed out. An oncoming train that had filled the little station backed off to the left, hooted, expanded, and broke away, revealing a cold expanse the size of a steel lake, humps of boulders scattered with rusty needles, and deep blue mountains to the horizon.

In fact the train was still waiting. The professor tapped his nails on the thick glass, looking out at the stranger, who ran up at his signal. Standing on tiptoe, she pressed her long, precisely delineated palm to the window. Anfilogov put his own there in response, and Krylov was amazed at how similar these hands were: there was something Latinate in their lifelines and a wonderful elegance to their finger bones. Without waiting around for any more instructions or parting words, Krylov quickly climbed down from the car. He was definitely in a bad way—doubtless the effect of a sleepless night. Everything he had seen was amazingly distinct and had left an extraordinarily sharp stamp on Krylov's mind. No sooner had he jumped the two iron steps to the platform than the dusty train gave a shudder of relief, spilled what was left of the water in its pipes on the rails, and slowly moved off past the row of well-wishers, as if counting them off. Striding after it, picking up his pace with it,

Krylov drew even with the stranger, who was waving at the windows slipping away, until finally the train's tail popped up, like the back of a playing card.

At first it seemed an accident that they were staying even. There was only one exit—that same tunnel, where Krylov managed to shake off a nine-year-old Asian child hanging onto his companion, a wretch with lustful male eyes whose sticky paw had already nearly crept into the stranger's defenseless bag. On the front steps of the train station, where they should have parted, since they hadn't been introduced, Krylov suddenly felt he simply couldn't face the solitude of the day, which was still as fresh and radiant as if the sun's warmth had just dissolved its minty, sleepy haze but which already held nearly its fill of the heavens' void. Running his worn shoes over the crumbling steps, Krylov ventured a joke. The woman looked around inquiringly and stumbled, pushing her glasses up. Right then on the station plaza a brass band, the likes of which had never been seen before, struck up a tune. A rotund gentleman with a cross-shaped emblem on his jacket lapel, an emblem repeated by the tasseled party standards, strode out like a pigeon before a rank of quasi-military men, whose various thicknesses and slouches made them look like pickles.

Struck dumb, Krylov, who heard only the sound of his own plugged-up brain, took the stranger's elbow and tried to smile. The woman freed herself with a gentle shrug, and without looking at the band or the rank, set off quietly in the opposite direction, as if testing the strength of the invisible thread that connected her to Krylov. Where she was heading, everything looked brighter and better than in the other three corners of the world: a small pharmacy was bedecked with elegant, gift-wrapped medicines; a small fountain on a wet pole looked like a toy windmill, sparkling cheerfully in its watery web; and the many empty streetcars at the last stop swayed, creating their own special dimension of rocking, windows, and reflections in windows, and the passengers stood there stock-still, their eyes screwed tight by the sun. Afraid that if he didn't start after her immediately the woman would simply unwind him, like a spool of thread, down to some naked core, Krylov hurried in her wake, and fell in step, quickly finishing his interrupted joke. A cagey smile was his reward.

"Actually, I've liked that joke since I was a kid, too," said the woman archly, stepping slowly across the wobbly slabs, which squelched with the dampness of the flowing fountain.

"I know lots of others," Krylov hastened to inform her.

"All my favorites, I bet," the woman remarked.

"Then I'll tell each one four times."

"Are you always so talkative?"

"No, just when I'm hungry. Hey, have you had breakfast? Look, that cellar over there, it must be a café."

"It's not a café, it's a travel shop."

"You mean they don't sell anything edible here?"

"They do, but it all tastes like it was made the day before yesterday. I don't advise it."

"That's okay. Once I survived an entire month on canned food that was all eighteen years old. Just imagine: you open a can and instead of meat there's a piece of dry peat. I cooked a jelly out of the cubes and paper, and it swelled up."

★ ★ ★

It was a very odd, very long day. The whole city and May had just shed their petals, which lay like tissue paper in the warming puddles. The sweet, faint smell of decay and damp tobacco mingled dolefully with the bold green smells of the fully opened leaves, which were cold to the touch. For a long time each one felt that the other was leading the way; each was merely following the stranger's whim. At the slightest misstep, afraid of getting separated, they concentrated on finding their line of equilibrium, which sometimes led them right into the street. They were looking out for each other's movements;

sometimes their arms bumped, and then each felt as if they had accidentally touched a bird in flight.

Probably only from a great height—where a small advertising blimp hovered, dusty in the sunny thickness of the air—could you begin to understand and read the tentative curve their movement described through the city. But they didn't understand anything. They just kept turning up in places, often unfamiliar ones. They found themselves at an outdoor marionette show, where marionettes in pretend shoes that looked like bread crusts looked as if they were trying to break free from the strings of their stooping master; the very few spectators were absorbed not so much in the content of the play as the progress of that struggle. They were drawn through a small political rally, which filled the neighborhood with marching verses. Led more and more downhill, they gradually approached the city's river with its park pond, deep as a belly, where all the things that fell into the river, including drowning victims, accumulated and stewed. Here, below, they roamed cross-country—over fresh ditches with stone abrasions and old gray slopes sparkling and slippery from broken glass. Here they couldn't keep moving identically as before, so they demagnetized. Each scrambled separately—and the stranger, skidding comically on her heel, slid down the pitch straight into his clumsy male embrace. Krylov immediately let go of her slippery ribs, but he had felt the round heft of a jumping hemisphere and beneath it, like in a pocket, a trembling heart the size of a baby mouse.

Later, faced (fated?) with this experiment on himself, Krylov tried to figure out what had actually held him back at that fateful train station plaza. After all, it would have been easy to separate, and as evening fell he would have recalled their chance meeting over a beer at his workshop, enjoying the bliss of the semi-dark, which was like a caressing fur after the harsh light of work. However, instead of going and working on his important order, Krylov, like a high school senior, played hooky with a faded beauty who raised a ticklish draft in him.

The reason probably lay in the special excitement, the alteration of his destiny that awaited Krylov in the event of the expedition's success. What did he care about the agate cabochons, the assortment of rejected stones fit for the street vendors? For months he had lived with an incomprehensible hunger. Night after night Krylov's bed was sprinkled with crumbs, like the sands of a desert spread out around him. In short, in his daily rut a hole had formed that he had to fill. At night, Krylov dreamed of big money—the kind of money that would last far beyond his lifetime, settling its possessor in a comfortable eternity. But he ended up getting something very different from life. How the substitution came about, Krylov and the woman simply could not understand.

That day, after setting off on foot from the station, they wandered through the streets like tourists. Hunger and anonymity imparted a special ease to their shared, increasingly coordinated gait, and they got better and better at staying together. In an open-air café in the park, where Krylov and his companion stopped for a bite to eat, a faded Sunday menu lay on the little red formica tables, although the calendar said it was definitely Wednesday. In the lazy park, though, it was always Sunday, and across the pond, swathed in an oily light, a dingy white swan glided in its own wave, as if on a plate; at the shooting gallery shots clicked; and on the woman's neck a spot of sun, flickering, fastened itself to her vein, like an improbable cartoon vampire. Relaxed in the pale sun, which had warmed the wobbly formica a little, the stranger informed him, at last, that her name was "Tanya, let's say." It wasn't her real name; he could tell from the slight hitch in her confident voice. Joining in the game, Krylov introduced himself as "Ivan," to which the freshly named "Tanya" chuckled delicately, taking a sip from her plastic cup of synthetic juice.

"You can call me Vanya. Then we'll rhyme," Krylov proposed.

"Tanya-Vanya? Kindergarten stuff," the woman shrugged, frowning at the pizza plunked down in front of her on the table by the long-legged young waitress in red shorts. "Why don't I try to guess your profession instead?"

"College history teacher!" Krylov reported so quickly and loudly that now all the waitresses, who depicted a sports team—the current fashion—looked at the couple at the far table, and the fat, watchful manager with tomato-red lips stuck his head out of the storeroom. "Another pizza with mushrooms for each of us," Krylov shouted out, and that calmed them down right away. The manager dragged himself into his office, and the long-legged waitress passed the hard ball on a string with the café's logo to her colleague and stuck two plates with the thick premade circles into the microwave.

"You're going to eat those yourself," said "Tanya," smiling and frowning. "Do you want to know my profession?"

"Not really. I'd rather you told me whether you're married."

"Yes. So, you mean my profession doesn't matter?"

"Hardly at all. Especially for a woman."

"Are you waiting for me to get mad? Don't hold your breath."

"Usually ladies object to comments like that. Especially the ones who function as furniture at work."

"I function at work as a gray mouse. I graduated from the university, and I work in my specialty, which I acquired in a four-month course. Just unlucky, I guess."

"There's lots of that going around now. The television is the friend of the unemployed."

"You're not one of those political activists, are you? They're crazy and they hand you completely dopey leaflets on the street."

"Do I look crazy?"

"Forgive me, but you look a little like an intellectual."

"No, word of honor, I'm not crazy."

What Krylov could never figure out later was the unremarked disappearance of the sweater package, which never was passed on to Anfilogov. When he was walking behind the stranger across the station plaza he had definitely had the package, which kept thudding against his legs; later, in the chilly park, where it was June in the sun but the solid shadow had a May chill to it, Krylov was about to suggest to the shivering woman that she at least throw the sweater over her shoulders—but at the time "Tanya" had the package, a fact "Ivan" was embarrassed to point out. Later they wandered down steep paths, which would occasionally turn into concrete steps sealed with rough plaster; once they came across a booming band shell, where well-dressed old women were waltzing, dragging their puffy legs across the boards, to a hoarse accordion, and a little farther on they were held up by a packed group of young people with shaved heads clapping steadily and handing out free posters. Farther on, in untended weeds more characteristic of a public outhouse, they discovered a small movie house made appealing by the cheapness of its tickets and the touching old-fashioned quality of its sturdy columns, over which the white plaster seal of the USSR reminded them of Caesar's bald pate. However, the next few shows were for kids—an old cartoon about the Star Pirate—and they both realized it would be simply unbearable to wait four hours for the old comedy.

"We are both grownups, after all," said "Tanya" in an angry, slightly dejected voice.

By then the package was gone for good—maybe left in the rickety taxi where they'd kissed and gasped, as if the air were being pumped out of the cab, and they kept popping up in the rearview mirror, which the narrow-shouldered, slicked-down driver kept righting, as if pouring off its contents. Anfilogov's apartment, where Krylov wasn't supposed to feed the unfinicky, nickeled fish for two days, greeted them with the daytime gloom of its only room, which was stacked to the ceiling with thousands of dark, inosculating volumes; from the outside, the other side of the tightly closed curtains, which were full of hot sunny color, a flock of pigeons was clawing hard at the metal. The narrow professorial cot was unmade.

"For the first and last time," "Tanya" whispered hoarsely, and "Ivan" whispered something into her hot, bitterish ear, too, tugging at the zipper on her dress, which he couldn't get unstuck.

After undressing each other, they tromped around in the checked scuffs they'd happened to pick out by the front door—one clumsy pair for the two of them. When "Tanya" pulled her multi-layered gauze over her head, her glasses slipped down and got tangled up, and they had to be picked out of her dress, like a butterfly from a big floppy net. Despite her sham proficiency, she was thoroughly spooked, not having been touched in a very long time. Her nipples were big and soft, like overripe plums, and on her narrow, slightly sagging tummy there was a scar that looked like a thread of cooked noodles. On her skin, which resisted "Ivan's" lips with a tiny puckered wave, he kept encountering spots that burned as if they'd been rubbed with a medicinal ointment, as if she were really not very well. The moment "Ivan" succeeded in bringing her to her first weak climax, "Tanya" let out a muffled cough, and her temples became swollen and damp. Later, when "Ivan," after her whisper-short time in the shower, went to rinse off, too, he saw that the mirror hadn't even fogged up from her bathing.

They fell asleep instantly, completely forgetting when they dropped off; the sagging hammock of the professor's cot was barely big enough. Later they admitted to each other that the first time they hadn't felt anything special; it was sleeping spoon-fashion that had evidently brought about the decisive change. They lay there chastely and closely, like twins in their mother's womb, and truly did start looking more and more alike. The room's summertime semi-dark, without the negative intervention of a lamp at the transition from sun to night, was amazingly pure. All the dishes in the room were empty but seemed full; the dull, congealed crystal of the cut glass on the desk, the size of a half-liter tin, seemed to be reading the newspaper under it through a magnifying glass. The decorative fish no longer saw the glass wall of the aquarium as a solid barrier and swam freely about the room, their tiny maws nibbled at the offal of scattered clothing, and their insides looked like dark tangles, which would occasionally isolate a fat thread hanging in the air. The blanket had slipped off; almost simultaneously, struggling to retain the last grains of their winding, all the clocks in the house went off. In their sleep, the quotation marks fell away from their invented names; at half past five, when the streets deepened and a band of sunlight passed over the roofs, like a gilt fillet around a glass's rim (while in the grubby train carrying him northward, the professor suddenly sat up on his shifted mattress and pressed his hands against his angular face), they both surfaced from their dreams as other people and felt that this time was by no means the last.

★ ★ ★

They began meeting but in secret, because according to the normal logic of things, what had happened to them was impossible. Why him? Why her? They were surrounded by hundreds, thousands of people to whom nothing like this ever happened.

Krylov was probably not at his best. His eyes, which were too beautiful for a man, as his ex-wife used to say, envying their cornflower blue color and their wonderfully curled, feathery-thick eyelashes, now pulsed red, bloodshot, and his rusty stubble soon made his chin look like yesterday's schnitzel, no matter how often Ivan shaved. His steady clients—half of them respectable, elderly Jews, self-described failures, and half of them wiry rock hounds who smelled of the forest—were worried that the maestro was unwell, which was how they explained the condition of this man who had placed himself in the hands of fate.

Tanya and Ivan had apparently been stricken in earnest by that ancient and virulent disease that no medicine in the world has ever vanquished. The hostile environment couldn't kill the virus off straightaway, and now they kept reinfecting each other with each kiss and the nomadic love they made in rooms rented by the day in tourist hotels. The vaccines life had inoculated them with didn't help, either. All those lonely women of a certain type (a tic over one eyebrow, a dramatic shawl) with whom Krylov had readily shacked up for half a year or a couple of weeks at a time had not given him any immunity. As for his relations with his ex-wife, whom Krylov had managed to divorce but not leave, they lent his life an unbearable sadness and had never inspired the surges of soundless inner music Krylov was dancing to as he moved through the blurry world between home and workshop.

Their illness nonetheless required protection, a bell jar. A propitious confluence of circumstances—the encounter at the train station and immediate departure of Anfilogov (whose apartment was immediately snapped up by his student niece, a tenacious girl with a luminescent manicure and swivel hips that Krylov barely managed to dodge)—had given them a chance to make a clean break with real life, where they were both ordinary people. Neither had any doubt that they had only one, not very sound basis for their reality, and if they started digging around too casually they would discover common acquaintances and events that pertained to them both. In no case were they to look for each other in the real world because that would mean *coming at it from the wrong side*. Both knew that there was only one way into the place where they exchanged tenderness, moisture, and animal warmth (and something on top of that, something transmitted not directly but as if via a satellite hovering constantly overhead), and this was their big secret.

They knew almost nothing about each other—and guarded against knowing. At the very beginning, Tanya let slip that she worked as a bookkeeper in a small publishing house. Ivan found this touching and unusual for some reason, although the owner of the gemcutting workshop where he worked (he also owned a couple of stores which, in addition to his cheap *legal* jewelry, were stacked to the ceiling with second-hand clothes that stank of disinfectant) had bookkeepers as well: two middle-aged women with boyish bangs and hair chopped off at the nape. Krylov swore at these ladies because when they filled the kettle in the one and only shared bathroom they detached the hose that fed the workbenches and let the water spill out on the floor, and as a result the grinding wheels would heat up and a puddle would collect next to the hose, flooding the far corner where the tile was broken. Many times Krylov had asked his boss to put those messy ladies in one of his stores, nearer the dresses, but the tubby little man, who was overgrown with musty wool and who cherished his joyless tranquility, would merely point wordlessly to the catacombs of goods that occupied every storeroom and that looked like circus costumes for trained apes.

Now, each time he saw the bookkeepers, Krylov thought of Tanya and gave them a dreamy, diffuse smile—and in response he suddenly began receiving homemade pirozhki on fine china with a crown monogram from some restaurant he'd never heard of. In a scary way, both ladies instantly became prettier, and their downcast eyes, framed in thick silver, reminded him of champagne corks. He now would find the unfortunate hose mostly reattached and spritzing the mirror, but his materials no longer suffered from dry abrasive.

Too much information about each other could have affected their reality, made it too human. Krylov had no intention of loving his sundry neighbors through Tanya. The only thing that interested Krylov (he couldn't help it) was Tanya's *husband*, who had first been mentioned in the red plastic café and whom Ivan's efforts had transformed into an exaggerated, nearly relentless figure. From certain oblique but unquestionable signs Krylov realized that Tanya was not seeing anyone else. Each time she freed herself from her baggy skirts and peasant tops with the knotty lace (it didn't take long for Ivan to know all her summer things and the minor quirks of their harassing fasteners), she would be slightly stiff—stale, in a way. To help her catch up to today, he had to literally wake up her long body and massage the blood pooled under her cold skin, whose goose bumps reminded him of sleet. A lifetime of experience, however, suggested to Krylov that there are marriages without physical intimacy, especially those fouled in a complicated net of moral obligations, having become a nearly indissoluble symbiosis.

Feigning indifference as he steered the conversation to the sensitive topic, he tried to assemble an avatar of his invisible enemy. From Tanya's reluctant answers (her eyes always dimmed then, and her glasses glinted angrily), he compiled a positive, but grim image utterly devoid of life. This man, had he existed in reality, would have had to be kept in a box and run off the electric power grid. Tanya stuck to her story about her marital situation, though, and turned to stone the moment Ivan tried to make her admit her lie. If they had this difficult conversation in bed (and Ivan, tactless and impulsive as only a truly ill man can be, summoned up that specter even when they were all alone), Tanya would turn abruptly to the wall and immediately find something interesting in the paper herbarium of the neutral wallpaper, allowing Ivan to study her untanned shoulder blades just as steadily. Temporarily mollified, Ivan would beg her forgiveness, kiss the Latinate "N" on her palms, and catch her chilly smile with his lips as if it were a stream of drinking water.

All Ivan's insistence led to was the husband, defended from his attacks with rash obstinacy, becoming more and more ideal. As he lost human authenticity, he gained more and more positive qualities, preeminent among which was a maniacal domesticity. Ivan was indignant at the thought that at the very moment he was holding Tanya that indomitable rogue was having a grand time vacuuming the rugs or chopping boiled beets for salad. He saw that no matter how sincere her impulses for him, through some logical twist of mind he didn't get, Tanya was faithful to her mechanical doll.

Ivan was even more perturbed by the fact that he himself was unfaithful to Tanya and didn't know what to do about that. She, meanwhile, did not ask questions. The only thing that reassured him was that the husband, if he did exist, was obviously not a rich man. Testimony to this was not only Tanya's modest wardrobe but also her few pieces of jewelry, dark and small, like thorny weeds with dingy seeds. In them Ivan's unerring specialist's eye determined imitation diamonds made of cubic zirconium and crystal.

"Could you go with me somewhere far away?" Ivan once asked, his arm around Tanya, near an iron parapet behind which an invisible nocturnal pond squelched like a hot water bottle.

"I could fly to the moon with you."

"But there's no air on the moon."

"Are you sure we're breathing air right now?"

Ivan took a deep breath. The smells of the sludgy bottom rose from the water; the small white inflorescences beside it, swarming in the darkness, exuded a faint vanilla scent; coming from somewhere was the smell of grilled meat, music, and loud conversation.

"It's a quote from an old movie," Tanya said conciliatorily, huddling in her cotton print against the damp breeze.

Nonetheless she had expressed what they were afraid to say. Everything around them was unreal. The two cut-crystal glasses that were the Economic Center glowed dully, and the moon shone overhead like an elevator button.

"Can we go any farther away than we already are?" Tanya said softly, and Krylov had nothing to say in reply.

★ ★ ★

Krylov knew that a war over a woman, no matter how little she valued material goods, meant economic war. Fortunately, poor Tanya lacked that multilayered polish of opulence that turns a person into his own depiction and brings his everyday appearance maximally close to the photographs in the glossy rags that feed the public their weekly dose of society gossip. These rags, actually, pursued the couple from hotel to hotel, lying like frayed butterflies around their rooms—and sometimes Ivan would pull a flimsy drawer out of a piece of furniture and suddenly come across a photo of his former spouse beaming her killer smile, responding with this standard flash to the camera's attacking flashes.

Tamara liked to have her picture taken in her emerald necklace, whose split stones Krylov had only recently repaired. At the thought of how many times he had fastened that necklace on Tamara's bent neck, Krylov felt his heart ache, slowly. He realized (in the meagerly lit hotel pencil box, under the barely warm shower, which encircled his body with a limp rope of water) that the secret he and Tanya were shielding from the world left Tamara with her position as the principal woman in Krylov's life. All his other occasional girl-friends—always beauties with aplomb, always with some bizarre defect, like a big navel resembling a candle end, or toxic armpits—fell under her chilly tutelage and, unable to withstand the comparison with her, quickly dropped Krylov. Sometimes Tamara seemed to be picking up on signs of life in him—the very life that was slipping away from this radically rejuvenated woman who had *everything*, but was connected with this "everything" solely by right of ownership. A thin layer of emptiness had formed between Tamara and reality, and it clothed her like a beautiful dress. Krylov remained for Tamara the last battlefield where she might encounter women like herself, who would make her feel more alive than any man could.

Tanya was a through-the-looking-glass creature. Krylov couldn't imagine bringing her to Tamara's suburban home, where at any time of day or night you couldn't see anyone in the lit windows, but in the unlit rooms you might bump into anyone at all, from a youthful poet curled up asleep to a State Duma deputy attempting to move a bottle of cognac by the power of the firm stare under his swollen brow. In this world, Tanya was by definition absent. Therefore, the world of which Tamara was the legitimate center did not change a bit with Tanya's appearance.

The expedition's result was supposed to resolve this tug-of-war of many years between Krylov and Tamara over who could get along without the other first. The people around them thought they'd split up over the difference in their success and social status. But proud Tamara would never have stooped to a base comparison of incomes. Unlike many women in business, Tamara didn't even try to set her husband up as an executive—Director of the Analytical Center for the Study of the Doughnut Hole, or Chairman of the Regional

Committee for the Defense of Domestic Insect Rights—such as made serious people smile quietly but justified wearing a brand-name tie. She had given her husband every opportunity to be himself, that is, in society's understanding, a simple craftsman. She had guessed that Krylov's *feel for stone* had made him a representative of the forces secretly behind the gem-filled Riphean lands, that is, a representative of a power in some sense more legitimate than a governor's.

Krylov preferred not to recall the event that had provoked their divorce four years before. Although it had not led to a final split: their relationship persevered and during their infrequent intimacy Tamara would do everything she could to make time disappear. There was nothing left to do but separate. Krylov had to have a *separation* from Tamara. The private event, which no one had recognized or witnessed, was for him more real than the memorable appearance before the district judge, who divorced them behind closed doors, time and again confusing Krylov with Tamara's very proper bodyguard, who was pruned like a hedgerow.

But Krylov did not have the freedom to put an end to what related only to the past. Having his own money promised him freedom and the right to be in charge of himself. Up until recently, Krylov hadn't known what exactly to do: leave Tamara forever, giving her in parting some neutral, very expensive gift; or arm himself with a bouquet of her favorite pink roses, as heavy as apples, and arrive in full dress to ask for her hand. Now, of course, his choice had been made—or rather, there was no choice left.

Had it not been for Tamara's existence, Krylov might have considered his relationship with Tanya a continuation of his one continuous life. But there had been Tamara, and life had to be split into two unequal parts: he had to finish one and start the other. At the same time, he couldn't know which of the parts would end up bigger and which more important. This obvious inequality held a secret, perhaps the most important in Krylov's fate.

2

★

THE RIPHEAN MOUNTAINS, WINDSWEPT AND BLANKETED BY SMOKE that passes through hundreds of gradations of gray, look like decorative park ruins. There's nothing left for a painter to do amid this ready-made lithic beauty. Every landscape, no matter where you look, already has its composition and basic colors, a characteristic correlation of parts that combine into a simple and recognizable Riphean logo. The picturesqueness of the Riphean Mountains seems intentional. Horizontals of gray boulders green with lichen and softened by slippery pillows of rusty needles are intersected by verticals of pines huddled in tight groups, and like everything in the landscape, they elude simplistic uniformity; overall it seems to have been constructed according to the laws of the classic opera stage, with its unwieldy sets and choristers facing the stalls. The Riphean waters are also distributed for picturesque effect. Some streams, poisoned by industry, have the workaday appearance of a pipeline accident, but others have retained the architect's intent. Their banks, as a rule, are cliffs; the dark and fissured layers of slate look like stacks of printing spoilage whose dark layers probably contain illustrations; the pink-spotted cliffs seem stuck with pieces of cellophane, and their pebbles, which retain as one the idea of a cube, pour abundantly from the fissures. Each bend in a stream reveals new likenesses of what was just seen, which is why the banks seem to be moving rather than the water, which itself seems to be straining to retain the reflection of the sky and the silvered clouds.

The sky reflected in Riphean waters is much bluer than it is in reality because of the summer's northern chill, which even on hot days can make itself felt in a gust of wind in the vicinity of the deeply frozen bedrock. Gentle lizards bask on heat-retaining outcrops of gold-laden quartz; these are the Riphean's friends, living pointers to subterranean riches. The same is true of the tiny dark vipers that rest among the rocks in glistening ringlets; at the slightest disturbance one will tense like an arrow laid against a bow-string, but usually they slither away peaceably into a stone fissure, leaving behind a light rustling in the bitter green grass.

The lakes in the Riphean Mountains are numerous and huge. Their large, amazingly empty, glassy surfaces serve as a mirror not so much for material objects as for the weather. The slightest changes in the atmosphere are reflected as incorporeal images having no counterpart on shore, melting into dark oil and becoming solid at some indeterminate point. Often you can't see the boundary between water and land. Sometimes atmospheric specters are not just reflected but seen above the lake surface quite distinctly. This Martian television is best observed from high up, where the boats near the cottage shore look like seed husks. Some lakes are stunningly clear: at a perfectly still midday, the sun-net on the sloping bottom achieves the perfection of gilt on porcelain; the fisherman in his sun-warmed flatboat, smelling of fisherman's stew, sees the distant clump of bait and the dark backs of the big perch through his own shadow.

In the Ripheans' bountiful southern reaches, where the homely forest strawberry, whose fruit looks like nodules but is amazingly aromatic, grows and the garden strawberry sometimes gets as big as a carrot, the lakes take up even more of the beautiful space. Looking down, you can't always tell what you're seeing more of, water or land; they envelop, blend into each other. There are islands all over; one, like a cup, will hold another irregular oval of shining water, though this is not a part of the mother water world but its own internal lake, fed by its own springs, and inside it is yet another little island: a decorative cliff with a scattering of pebbles, like a broken piggy bank. From a cliff leading to the edge of a neck of land, circles of water, land, and stone seem once again to spread out over the entire expanse; the place erases the boundary and distinction between the named geographical location and the unnamed object, like the burly birch on the tiniest island whose stiff little leaves shimmer in the wind as if it were adorned—to supplement its own weeping mane—with tinsel-rain.

The Riphean range is in one of those enigmatic regions where the landscape directly affects people's minds. For the true Riphean, the land is rock, not soil. Here, he is the possessor of a profound—in the literal and figurative sense of the word—geologically grounded truth. At the same time his land is also fruitful. Just as the inhabitant of Central Russia goes out "into nature" to pick berries and mushrooms, so the Riphean drives his old jalopy out looking for gems; to him, a place without deposits and veins makes no sense. Far from everyone who grows up in the Riphean range later joins the community of rock hounds—unlicensed prospectors who, while having other professions, often intellectual ones, in town, structure their budgets around their illegal endeavors, which grow into a passion. However, virtually every Riphean schoolboy goes through a collecting phase; it's the rare family whose attic isn't strewn with fused cobbles and malachite scales covered with black oxides, quartz druses that look like the city's spring ice, and polished chips of all the common gemstones.

Meanwhile, the Ripheans' subterranean riches are not what they once were. Everywhere they go on the territory of known deposits, professional rock hounds and even ordinary tourists stumble across old mining pits. These might be flat holes long since grown over with wet bracken and made impassible by woolly-leaved wild raspberries; only the experienced eye would discern prospecting holes that date back to his great-grandfathers' day. Sometimes a hole in the ground that looks like an old man's toothless, sunken mouth leads the prospector to a mine from the century before last that looks like a low buried hut half crushed by a rock: cold larch braces flaking with dead, time-eaten splints, varnished on top with soot from the torches that stole the miners' sweet subterranean oxygen, and noises that emanate from the darkness exactly as if someone were scuffling over the damp grainy stone. Sometimes the mine is located not in a remote mountain corner but on the edge of a potato field where a small tractor jolts around. It's a common occurrence: from the substrate leading to the prosaic collective gardens, another diverges, fainter, and quickly climbs the slope, and from the slope the view opens out onto an old surface mine that surrounds, bezel-like, a strangely harmonious volume of air, like a tear of emptiness. You can't tell right away that the surface mine is filled to a certain level with water. You can't see the water. The reflection of the quartz walls, one of them burning in the hot noonday and the other icy, is so detailed and perfect that your eye doesn't catch where the real cliff leaves off and its reflection begins. This marvelous symmetry is accomplished by the mirrored image of the reflected sky with the dots of birches leaning into it. You have to descend into the surface mine down a well-trodden, rustling path, one hand touching the wall that rises by your temple; sometimes a flat pink stone comes out in your hand like a book from a shelf, and when you throw it down, a raw, piping sound leaps up. Only from the fat watery circles do you discover where you shouldn't step; the water, like clay on a potter's wheel, does seem to be trying to turn into a vessel. But it doesn't. Slowly, after an almost endlessly long time, the disturbed perfection is restored—and suddenly the moment comes when the water disappears again right at your feet. Once again the viewer is left facing a stunning emptiness where the mountain was taken out. The sunny wall, amazingly vivid and finely detailed, seems lit from below by powerful electricity, and its sugar vein sparks.

Virtually everything that could be extracted from the top has been. The Ripheans' surface has been played out. The same can be said of the surface of the Ripheans' beauty. The nature logos that make it so easy to assemble the components of a recognizable landscape on canvas have always encouraged amateur rather than professional painters. Realism, be it a method of art or, more broadly, a way of thinking, has here been a characteristic of fundamentally *superficial* people, well-intentioned dilettantes who take the use of ready-made forms for a type of patriotism. In this sense, the Ripheans have been cunning. From the very beginning, there has been all the *ready-made* material you could ask for. As a result, a specific stratum of artists, poet-songwriters, collectors, and ethnologists formed who were seized by splendid impulses. These serious-minded fellows, who were old by the time they were thirty, who wore the ubiquitous sardine-gray jacket and carried various membership cards in their inside pockets, had the vague feeling something was expected of them by all this stone and industrial might, the loaded sky above it that kept transporting tons and tons of clouds without end—but they never got past the surface, which seemed to satisfy the demand for artistry and Riphean originality.

When an ecological crisis came that was as real as could be, it became clear that the true Riphean's thinking was fantastic thinking. The farther from the soil, the better! It turned out that an anchorite living in Lower Talda and studying Sanskrit expressed the essence of his little homeland more accurately than the peony-ruddy composer of songs for folk chorus. At exhibits of new artists who had ascended to the astral heights of modernism, the perpetual Riphean's darkened, heavy strokes disappeared from their painting for the first time, and the painting was purged; as a consequence, the new rich, who knew very little about it but were childishly drawn to clear colors, eagerly purchased their compositions, which looked like board games, drawn puzzles, and assemblages of young people's electronic toys. This outburst of unpatriotic, demonstratively un-local art in fact expressed a purely local quality of mind whereby the Riphean, being down-to-earth, simultaneously thought of himself as someone else.

At the same time, the authorities, who were clueless, kept up official encouragement of ethnographers and folk collectives. They saw progress in matching a scenic peasant chorister with the conventional Orthodoxy that befit him. The ardent tenor in the silk tunic really was hard to swallow; he looked too much like a Young Communist. The transference of sacred notions from the factory to the temple was a better fit with his elegant artificial world festooned with rowans and dahlias. The stage-gentlemen officers with guitars, too, felt better and even strode toward life, marching through the rust-colored cube of the city's commercial center in groups of ten or twelve. There was a return to roots observed everywhere. Young fathers with soft beards decorously spread on their chests drove through town in heavy black Volgas that looked like the province's old official ones—the worse for wear, of course. The churches whose ownership had been restored reminded him with their twirling cupolas of a parade of blimps—without the advertising, of course. At the appointed time their bells pealed above the city, spilling through the air like a thin, oily stream of sound.

★ ★ ★

All this had little or nothing to do with the spiritual life of a Riphean, who did put candles in front of popular icons and during the Blessing of the Water at Epiphany readily took a dip in a moon-lit ice-hole whose solid ice grabbed his wet soles like powerful glue. No matter how far from his ordinary place and life a Riphean's intellectual interests might stray (many rock hounds, in the licit part of their lives, worked in space research and defense), he always knew that the veins of ore and gems were the rock roots of his consciousness. The world of mountain spirits where the Riphean has always resided is a pagan world. It includes, specifically, UFOs three to fifteen meters in diameter as well as the silky green quasi-men that outsiders take for extraterrestrials. In fact, these are the locals: clever reptiles guarding semi-precious lenses.

From time to time, prospectors have caught a glimpse of the Great Snake, a subterranean reptile with the head of an old giant. Its head is bald and has dark, burnished spots; its lips are fleshy and mottled, too, and it has a broken nose the size and shape of a boot. The Great Snake travels underground as if it were underwater. Its body, stretching out in rings in front of the dumb-struck prospector, looks like a stream of thundering gravel being dumped from the back of a truck: dust rises, whitened bushes stir, and the ground turns gray in patches, forming a wrinkly trench—and it is along this trench that you should search for the alluvial and vein gold that royally fills the prospector's ruined trousers.

Sometimes a mountain spirit is hard to tell from a human. The Stone Maiden, also known as the Mistress of the Mountain, looks nothing like the beautiful actress in the fake blue eyelashes and green headdress who represents the Mistress in local theater matinees. The Stone Maiden can appear to a rock hound in the most ordinary guise—for instance, like the middle-aged vacationing schoolteacher stained with berries, besieged by mosquitoes, and carrying a pail of cucumbers; or like the woman at the little train station's snack bar with the starched tower of bleached hair and puffy, yearning eyes; or like the fifteen-year-old girl who has a breeze flying down the neck of her loose t-shirt as she bends over and works the pedals of her rickety bike. The Stone Maiden doesn't keep just to the remote parts of the forest and mountains by any means. She's no beast. She feels perfectly free to appear in the city with its four million inhabitants, which is standing without realizing it on top of mighty knobs of malachite, a kind of subterranean cabbage field, and thick gold veins in ribbed quartz.

In the narrow eddies of the urban population, the Stone Maiden is recognized only by whoever she has come to see. Suddenly, at the sight of a perfectly unremarkable woman, the rock hound's soul is strangely magnetized. Unfamiliar features and gestures suddenly compose themselves into a dear and desired face, and to the atheist it seems as if right before his eyes, out of ordinary matter, of which there is so much in a crowd, God has created a unique and miraculous being just for him, presented him with obvious proof of man's creation by divine sleight-of-hand.

It's not true that the Mistress of the Mountain needs gemcutting skill from a man. In reality, she, like any woman, needs love, but it must be real love of that special and genuine composition whose formula no one has ever been given. Any feeling has shadowy parts—sometimes it's a shadow itself. Lacking any basis for comparison or real expertise, the Stone Maiden's chosen one feels he has been granted much more than ever before. Doubts lay intersecting wrinkles on the chosen one's face, and the lifelines that an ordinary man sees in his palm and in some sense holds in his hand appear on his brow. The subject alternatively does and doesn't believe in the authenticity of his own emotion; one unsettled night, when his girlfriend's perfectly still body suddenly gets very heavy in her sleep and crushes her half of the bed, like a toppled statue, it occurs to the man that it would be easier to rip open his own belly than to open himself up and check on his own soul—at least the former is physically possible. Suicide over a happy love, over a fully reciprocated feeling, is not such a rarity in the Riphean capital. If you dig through the police files, you'll find quite a few puzzling suicides, when the deceased was found with a blissful smile on his petrified lips—that is, his mouth had literally turned to mineral, a hard stone flower, an eternal adornment on his sunken face. Somewhere nearby, in an obvious spot, lined up parallel to the furniture and room, there would be a document from the deceased—his suicide note, addressed to a woman and consisting for the most part of mediocre verse.

She whom the suicide addressed would have vanished completely, as if she had fallen through the earth. Descriptions of her, related by the deceased's family and neighbors, would prove so contradictory, it was a wonder how the powerful optics of their collective—and now even greater—dislike had distorted the suspect. Subsequently at the suicide's grave, on the tombstone on any warm day, people might see a pretty little lizard, perfectly ordinary at first glance. Only a specialist, had he been there, would have realized that the creature did not belong to any known species and would have exclaimed, "Impossible!" at the sight of the fern pattern on its back and its tiny feet, which looked like they were wearing black gloves. Many imagined they saw on its flat head the flash of a crown no bigger than a gold tooth; at any attempt to catch this rarity the lizard would first fall still, imitating the caution of the stealthy incoming hand, and then all of a sudden draw a lightning zigzag and vanish into nowhere, sometimes leaving behind for its pursuer its pointy tail revealing bare cartilage.

Sometimes, though, a Riphean would survive an encounter with the Stone Maiden. Never again did a man like that venture beyond the city limits or have anything to do with the gem business, and according to rumors he couldn't see himself in mirrors, as a result of which he lost his sense of self and would restlessly finger his own face, squeezing the solid parts hard and grabbing the soft flesh in thick folds. Whenever anyone addressed him, the poor man would immediately get distracted verifying his own presence and the presence on his person of appropriate clothing. The hesitation, which was accompanied by a survey of his buttons and a bow to his own trousers, was brief but so unpleasant to his interlocutor that a former rock hound who sincerely promised himself to henceforth lead only an ordinary, licit life could never get a career going. In rare cases, the Stone Maiden's lover would run off with her, taking none of his possessions, and laying out his money—sometimes wads of dollars in rubber bands—neatly in that same obvious place where his last letter would have lain had he killed himself. Experienced cops who had studied the M.O. of these kinds of disappearances called this spot the "mailbox."

Sometimes, if the relatives were especially insistent and refused to believe in the irrevocability of the event, the cops would manage to trace the first leg of his journey. For a while the police would work on a story about the standard runaway under the influence of drugs.

According to witness testimony, he and his girlfriend had acted as if they didn't know the city at all and every minute feared losing each other. All this was reminiscent of two butterflies dancing in the air, blindly following a bizarre curve—and then suddenly the moment came when one or the other sensed the hole they were seeking in space. The runaways' friends, who didn't know about his disappearance, would run into him sometimes on their illicit geological explorations: he would appear out of a ruddy darkness like you sometimes see under your eyelids or in the forest around a burning campfire; he would sit down to the shared meal and drink from the metal cup of Riphean moonshine, as strong as the whistle of a locomotive in your head. He would explain his gaiety and the lack of sleep on his gaunt, badly ground-down face by an unusual stroke of luck, and the team would explain his hasty retreat into solitude, where no one was sitting and where the corrosive, ashy smoke from the fire went, the same way. As they went to bed in their tents, the team would envy their friend; later, when they learned what had happened to him, they would silently raise their eyebrows and shake their beards. Who knows whether it was luck or its opposite that came to the man beyond the horizon of their ordinary shared life, beyond the limits of fate?

3

★

ᴇACH TIME, THEY ARRANGED ONE AND ONLY ONE RENDEZVOUS. HAD it fallen through, Tanya and Ivan would have had no way of seeing each other again, no way of finding each other in this city of four million without outside help.

Because the dimensionless summer was unbearably brief, each time morning came Ivan experienced the previous day's rendezvous as a loss. He took the banal fact that yesterday cannot be repeated and remains in the past with a painful literalness. This is doubtless how Krylov came to process each rendezvous in his memories and new episodes accumulated inside him that tore at his heart in his hours of solitude. However, there was one important reason why Tanya and Ivan had not given each other their addresses or exchanged telephone numbers (other means of communication like e-mail were forbidden, too). Each time they experienced each other (but not so much each other; both realized they were weak in the face of circumstances and their desires in fact meant very little), they were testing fate. If only Tanya and Ivan had been able to find some reason in or around themselves for what was happening to them! Then they might have figured out whether all this could vanish as suddenly and violently as it had begun. But for now they both required fate's daily sanction.

At first they met in the same place, next to the Opera, which, in their reinforced concrete city, was one of the few places to boast any beauty—sculpted medallions and garlands—though its boxy structure looked like a bulldozer. Here, by the circular fountain, was a favorite meeting place for young people. Time and again another couple would kiss in the fountain's spray and be off, while not far

away, on the benches, the university exhibit of unmarried girls lan-
guished, each with a fluttering book on a tanned knee, every other
one wearing fashionable sunglasses that looked like they'd been
filled with beet juice. Soon, though, the usual place bored them;
moreover, given the regularity of the afternoon hour when Ivan and
Tanya could get away from work, this fixed spot stripped the experiment of its essential purity.

That was when they bought two identical street maps with the
Opera lit in four tiers of tiny white lights on the front cover and with
the latest information on municipal transport and a subway map
reminiscent of a complex organic molecule. Now their rendezvous
were arranged like this: Ivan would name a street from the index at
the back, which was surprisingly long, half comprised of the clumsy
names of obscure revolutionaries that reminded him of what it felt
like to be going to visit his hard-drinking proletarian relatives; and
Tanya would add an address, citing a number at random. The next
time they would switch roles. Thus, they told their fortune on the
city. Neither of them knew in advance what the building, which was
held out to them like a ticket from a lottery drum, would turn out to
be. The irrationality of the scheme was heightened by the fact that
the maps themselves had been distorted back in Soviet times. The
industrial city's very proportions had been considered classified
information, and the distortions, like polio, affected the city's structure, conferring bizarre kinks on the streets and forcing the clumsy
streetcars to make abrupt turns and detach from the overhead power
lines.

The secrecy of the rendezvous themselves aggravated the situation; fate really did have to look kindly on the experimenters if they
were to have any chance of locking themselves away in some pathetic
matchbox for a couple of hours. Thus, fate joined battle with the
environment, which seemed bound and determined to offer Tanya
and Ivan the harshest options rather than the likeliest apartment
buildings. One day, the address they had chosen turned out to be a

brand-new private home behind a lattice fence on a burning hot, bare lot, like an elephant in an open-air cage at the zoo. While Ivan was marking time, trying in vain to make himself invisible among the popsicle-slim poplar saplings, the alerted guard checked his I.D. twice. A couple of days later, a random address led Ivan to a very rural street, or rather, what was left of a street, which ended in a huge foundation pit into which chewed-up bird cherry trees had been toppled, their leaves drowning in the clay. The address he was looking for—a dirty pink barracks with two mismatched porches— was barely clinging to the brink, where the soil had already rolled back like a droopy, worn-out mattress. Behind the long, accordion fence, which was black with damp, a wet dog panted and rattled its chain; and from the dilapidated window nearest Ivan, an ill-pleased female face kept an eye on him. This stranger loitering at their door must have upset the locals because a little later a tough-looking sort stripped to the waist sat down on the front steps and stared at Ivan, who found the man's flab and thick skull, which was covered with a black nap and a few white bald spots, even nastier than the crowbar playing in his paws.

During their wanderings through the industrial zones, adventures were not only possible but highly likely. Lounging on crates beside grated shops, gloomy as prisons, where alcohol was sold, were the local youth. Girls with froggy little faces and large dear pink knees were exactly like the ones Krylov had hung around with in his own proletarian adolescence. There was no point teaching these girls dances, for instance; on the other hand, their physical existence had a language-free irrefutability; unlike young ladies from educated families, each of them had a natural right to have one of the future men put at her disposal. As for the boys, they were on the puny side compared to the crew where Krylov had been the boss twenty years before. In these boys today, impudence was interlaced with fear; the young working studs were trying to pick out a decorative bitch. The dyed hair on their heads reminded Krylov of ocean creatures—octopi or actiniae. They were aggressive, though. Krylov was aware that due to the difference in age he was practically a dead man in their eyes. Passing another zone of youths, he tried not to react at all to their hard stares, which couldn't have risen higher than a meter and a half and nastily grazed his clothes, bag, and watch.

It was nothing short of a miracle that he had only one run-in. A gang sent its resident clown to cut him off—a fine-boned teenager with slender arms on which his jersey sleeves fluttered like red flags. This was a hero for name-calling, not mixing it up. Cupping his palms, he started shuffling and sniffing in front of Krylov, imitating an Asian beggar. Krylov didn't like hitting someone like that, but to his left the other fighters were lazily rising to their feet. The warriors were in no hurry, but Krylov had no time to lose. He struck cruelly at the little guy, who dodged the blow, as if his being had a huge hole in it, big enough for Krylov's small fist. Ahead, the narrow, thorny path ran into a wall covered with graffiti, where the letters were made for maximum resemblance to horrible monsters. But they didn't let Krylov get as far as the dead end. He shook off the first ones hanging on his shoulders like a coat, but the others were more persistent, and their rough hands slipped into his pockets, tearing them and the lining out. They smashed a can of red paint over his head, and he landed one on someone, and again, missed, suddenly was on the ground and with one swollen eye saw gray and black sneakers raining down on him like garbage pigeons.

In a few jerks, as if he were a climber on a cliff, he got to his feet, and the evening in his eyes was instantly replaced by night. Then it got light again, and Krylov saw Tanya, disheveled, with wet down on her temples and a cigarette in her trembling fingers. She was looking at Krylov the way a commander might look at a soldier from his broken army who for some reason was getting up alive.

"What happened to you? My God. Oh my God. I've been searching for you in the bushes for a whole hour!" Behind her glasses, Tanya's eyes burned with fury as her hands felt Krylov's aching ribs and touched his fat left ear, which had swollen up like a blood-filled parasite.

Through the heavy haze in his head, Krylov was distinctly horrified at Tanya's stroll through the local landscaping, in the twilight, in her light dress, which would taunt the monsters, who had obviously not gone to their houses to watch "Good Night, Young 'Uns."

"Are you all right? Is everything okay?" Krylov in turn grabbed Tanya by her smooth cold shoulders. "Why did you look in the bushes? Am I an alcoholic?"

"You tell me then. What else could I do? Where else was I supposed to find you?"

At this Krylov grasped that Tanya really did have absolutely nowhere else to look for him besides these trash thickets, in the area around the appointed building, on the ground or under it.

"Listen, maybe we could set this up some other way. What's the point of all this? Now don't get mad, please, calm down, think about it." Frowning, Krylov leaned toward her face, which echoed his grimaces like a small silver mirror.

The kiss was painful. Ivan felt the firm lath of Tanya's teeth, and his own, which were as wobbly as splinters. Pulling back, he was amazed at how badly Tanya's red lipstick had smeared.

"You don't understand! You just don't understand!" Tanya suddenly broke down and turned away, hiding her expression, which was something like despair. "We can't be like everyone else. I—can't! Nothing good ever came out of ordinary life for me. And nothing ever worked out for anyone on this side of a television screen. You can take my word for it!"

The unattractive spot under Tanya's nose oddly changed her, making her look like a fox. Suddenly Krylov grasped that this wasn't lipstick but his, Krylov's, drying blood.

* * *

The way of life Tanya and Ivan had chosen for themselves turned out to be not only dangerous—nowhere did anyone like the suspicious strangers—but unusually exhausting. Sometimes it took them all that remained of the evening to make their way back from the outskirts (like small towns that the megalopolis had swallowed but not digested completely, with their residual structure and their gypsyish flowerbed for a central square, usually as quiet as a hospital yard). Often, Tanya and Ivan never did get to a cheap hotel. Then their rendezvous consisted of agonizing kisses under the cover of rough bushes and of stupefying marches down a highway or paths like felled trees to senselessly distant bus stops. After a marathon workout like this, Ivan and Tanya didn't have the strength to want each other. All they cared about was grabbing a bite to eat in some modest diner—and then it would be time to go to their respective homes.

This monastic routine was not to Tanya's liking. Her need for physical contact was so strict, so insistent, that when luck was with them Tanya didn't mind the overcrowded third-class hotels full of traders from the Caucasus or the nasty, grimy sheets. She fasted stubbornly and never complained of weariness; her tender, bony arches, which Ivan would massage sometimes, marveling at the violin shape of this perfect creation of nature, had been worn down by her straps to wet calluses, which then looked like they'd been sprinkled with lime and broken shells.

Ivan was concerned and touched by the fact that all the special difficulties, including Tanya's refusal of multiple intimacies with him, had nonetheless in some higher sense been overcome for his sake, out of her feeling for him. However, he also sensed something excessive here. Besides the real Krylov, who could be ignored sometimes or even gotten angry at over little things, there seemed to be an imagined Krylov, too, an idea that pertained not to Krylov himself but exclusively to the woman who knew best how to handle him. It was this other man whom Tanya fed her selfless sacrifices. The Krylov who had had a part of himself taken away felt a strange emptiness.

A couple of times he tried asking Tanya cautiously whether she wasn't too tired. Of course she was tired. She had grown noticeably thinner and had stopped wearing high heels, preferring flats for their expeditions, which made her step rather duck-like. But to Ivan's questioning she energetically shook her head and latched on harder to his sleeve, as if to demonstrate her strength, which had not flagged from their dangerous and arduous journeys.

Ivan already knew that the most dangerous stage was hanging around the building once he'd found it, thereby provoking the local residents and worst of all the cops who protected that territory, so Ivan tried to make sure Tanya didn't have to wait for him. As close to five as he could manage, when the sun's light, still daylight, was growing heavy, and through the humid noises of his weary gemcutting the bells of the streetcar began to penetrate as it made its way down their side-street, Krylov aimed to flee the workshop. Sometimes he would cut the boss off in mid-accusation, obviously having gotten wind of Anfilogov's success. The stones the professor had brought back the previous year, which had sent Krylov into incomparable rapture, had gone out through channels absolutely beyond the fatman's reach. Nonetheless, the swindler had learned something—or, like a nervous aquarium fish, had felt the seismic shifts in Anfilogov's business. Now he was trying to provoke Krylov into telling him something, inventing gracious grimaces and even showing him a dark bottle of some kind of alcoholic castor oil, which, since he was not a drinker due to his health, he always carried around the way a suicide bomber carries around an explosive device. As if on purpose, the clients who wanted to find out when the agate insets would be ready for their idiotic dye-cast goods would also move in along about five. To get rid of these people, Krylov would climb through the thickly painted bathroom window and come crashing down in the pointy wild shoots of tiny ox-eyed daisies, where the dog excrement smelled like rotten fruit. Farther, around the corner, was the freedom of Tatishchev Avenue, down which the antediluvian streetcars raced, rattling like cases of vodka, while overhead, across the trestle, the sound of the express light rail stretched out like a double bass. The clock over the Old Passage, yellow and convex, the size of the moon, had always been ten minutes slow.

The city, however, created its own obstacles on Krylov's route: the sudden cancellation of transport routes, traffic jams that moved from light to light like mercury in a giant thermometer. As a result, occasionally Tanya did arrive first. When he finally caught sight of her standing in the shadow, Ivan was struck by how lost she looked: literally like a lost thing any passer-by might pick up. The sum of his losses, that is, the sum of their previous rendezvous, struck him hard, and Krylov picked up his pace. She remained motionless, although she had seen Krylov running. Only at the last moment did she take a very short step toward him—and immediately, with a bend characteristic of her alone, she pressed close and snuggled in, closing her eyes for the first kiss, which was complicated, like the touch of a blind man. Feeling as if the woman had sucked out half his brain, Ivan hurried to lead her away—while her eyes were still shut tight and she was languid—but afterward he would imperceptibly scope out the location, always cutting off danger in the form of double-breasted security guards next to iron gates of unknown ownership or their possible opponents—sullen thugs with shaved heads which seemed to have been set on their short necks more than once, creating messy folds on their napes.

It annoyed Krylov sometimes that Tanya herself was fearless. She remained utterly calm and headed where Krylov, had he been alone, scarcely would have. Then he admitted that his forty years did not make him a young man. Dark, untidy parks with vanishing paths, dumps with automobile carcasses as empty as suitcases, suspicious decaying cellars—all this made Ivan tense up. No matter how he tried to remember himself as the kid who gladly went anywhere that hinted of adventure, he couldn't drum up any enthusiasm for this. How old was Tanya? That he didn't know. She seemed young but at the same time completely ageless; her paleness created a haze, and gray hair, if any could be found in her coarse, icy-feeling hair, was completely lost in her natural gray aura. Tanya could have been thirty or fifty. He didn't like thinking just how old. Her perfect skull, which could be guessed through the tender fabrics much more distinctly than usual in a person, was not the image of death. Rather, it reminded him of a high-cheekboned pagan idol—and in some inaccessible way added to Tanya's attractiveness, letting him understand that inner beauty is not always spiritual, that what can be beautiful in a person may, for instance, be her skeleton. At times Krylov thought Tanya was in some—by no means Christian—sense immortal.

★ ★ ★

Sometimes Ivan would spot Tanya on the bus on his way to their trysting spot and would try to keep from being discovered for as long as possible, in hopes of suddenly penetrating to the place where Tanya existed without him, slipping into the world barred to him and seeing the real Tanya, who didn't suspect that he was already there, watching her from the thick of passengers being tossed around by the rough shakings of the bus floor.

He was forced to admit that the world where Tanya sojourned without him was wonderful. In it, people, including the people crushing Krylov in the bus, bore some relationship to Tanya; they might be or become her neighbors, relatives, co-workers; therefore Krylov, clutching the slippery handle, agonized over these glimpses of boundless loneliness. One time, Ivan suddenly imagined that the man sprawled out on the small bench next to Tanya, this man with a head as hard as a turnip, was her mythical husband inexplicably escorting her to her tryst in some bedroom district. Two stops later, though, the man jumped up, revealing a childish snub nose on a broad face with fat circles. He then tugged at his jersey and made his way to the doors, which he slipped through sideways, barely pulling his disorderly briefcase out behind him.

Rarely did Ivan manage to stay hidden all the way. Tanya's long eye would discover him, and her face would be exactly the way it was right after waking up from a hotel room nap. She would stretch and push her way through to him, and Ivan, wrapping his arms around her delicate ribs, would take little hops with her at the mighty speed bumps. Even so, instead of getting off at the next stop and hurrying off in search of a hotel, they would ride to the appointed place. It was as if they had to register with some third party who had actually been *designated*. Being together intensified the bizarreness of them doggedly seeking out the randomly chosen address, questioning occasional badly dressed and uncomprehending passers-by, but never entering the building they'd finally found. The inhabitants of the building, that is, the address's legitimate holders, were never anyone they might otherwise visit, and they shied away, hell-bent on not being overtaken on the way to their fortified entries; their tan, squarish soles matched the color of the clay characteristic of the outskirts of town.

Indeed, Ivan and Tanya never could figure out how to fill those few minutes they felt they should spend outside the building they had gone to such trouble to find.

"I feel as though you and I once lived here together," Tanya said as she examined another large prefab bloc of apartments, with balconies and without.

"We're suffering from a shared false memory," Ivan tried to joke, but that made Tanya sad, and she quietly picked up some bright piece of paper and a cork and crafted an origami doll.

Krylov noticed that the more he joked, the more visibly Tanya plunged into an odd sadness, as if they were saying farewell at a train station, parting forever, and there was nothing to fill the final pause before the train pulled out. The pauses in front of the conjured-up buildings they had found together were just like that.

Simultaneously, this was where they felt the presence of whoever had brought them together and watched out for them. They divined it in the mysterious image of the lonely bench, the lazy pink stars formed by the overlapping evening leaves, and the peel from a child's ball, that orange of emptiness eaten up some previous summer. Sometimes the long evening shadows, forming a line of italics under the straight and crude font of the street, promised an answer to the puzzles of things—like the answers printed at the bottom of the page in children's magazines. But sometimes the third party didn't show up and it made no sense to wait. Then Tanya would say they needed to mark the spot in some way, and she would toss a few coins onto the shaggy lawn.

This superstitious practice gave Ivan the idea of marking *her*. Ignoring the usual request of married lovers not to leave marks (actually, Tanya never did say this explicitly), Ivan would treacherously suck her pliable skin, leaving crescent-shaped bruises to swell up on her bloodless whiteness. These marks obviously went unnoticed, though; her husband apparently paid them no mind, and after a while the bruises would turn yellow and start to look like the nicotine stains you see on cigarette filters.

Dissatisfied with the effect, Ivan gave Tanya little presents nearly every time they met. There was also a cunning calculation in this: the cheating wives who loved the treasures and surprises they expected from Krylov—who did work with precious stones, after all—never knew how to legitimize the bracelet or ring he had given them; some of these items, which accumulated a bitter film of disuse, were rattling around in Krylov's worktable to this day.

Tanya, however, accepted calmly and with dignity the jewelry that Krylov got wholesale, over the workshop owner's bald head, from the skinny jeweler who worked for the firm. The settings for these knick-knacks were inexpensive, but Krylov chose the stones with taste: moss agates that the eye saw as soft March woods with soggy snow; agates with geodes where the blue amygdule was encased in quartz crystals like large grains of salt; picture jaspers with scenes of ancient volcanoes erupting; and brocade jasper, which made you think of the mystery of life as seen under a microscope. There were tiger's eye cabochons whose vertical pupils seemed to narrow in the light; incrustations of uvarovite, a saturated, chemical green; peachy cornelians with soft spots; a little bit of real silk malachite, distinguishable even to the lay eye from the Zairian stones that were as tired as linoleum. All this, mined straight from the *old* land that surrounded the concrete city, cost mere kopeks. Krylov bought the stones in their raw state, after which he himself cut, polished, and selected the stones and came to a quiet agreement with the alcoholic who couldn't seem to drink away the talent that rested in his hands.

As for Tanya, the stones seemed to be magnetized to her and looked *right*, warm and heavy on her chilly skin. Tanya was obviously not trying to hide her pieces of jewelry and wore them constantly, showing up for their rendezvous decked out like the Mistress of the Mountain. At the thought that these knick-knacks spent time where Tanya lived without him, a strange agitation gripped Ivan. Gradually, this provocation made way for some minor shamanism. Passionately wishing to obtain some knick-knack from Tanya's forbidden world (the way the Americans from NASA who launched the unmanned *Voyager-18* dreamed of images of Saturn), Ivan now looked upon his gifts as souvenirs in reverse. A few days before giving them to her, he would carry them around in his pocket, imagining they had already been *there*; so he would get an inversion of time, a castling of the future and past—which eventually revealed a recyclable resource. Krylov imagined the stones pinpointing Tanya's location for him, sending out faint radio waves that his tensed brain would detect and read.

"Here, take this, it's for you," Tanya told him one day, digging up a handful of something metal from her purse.

This happened downtown, where their lot had happily been cast. Nearby, drowning out the hum of Cosmonaut Boulevard, was the historic dam, whose waters spread the smell of blackened wood bathhouse rot and sprayed the air over the little tables at the shashlyk place and the wide flower beds that looked like children's paintings —even though they still had to get to a hotel with acceptable prices and an obliging management. What Tanya held out to Ivan across her plate of charred meat turned out to be a ring of keys: the unexpectedly heavy, jangling bundle consisted of a magnetic button—the kind that opens front doors—and four works of the locksmith's art, among which one, in the shape of a prerevolutionary "P," stood out and felt more solid than the rest.

"What's this?" Ivan asked, although he had guessed and his heart had leaped to his throat.

"The keys to my apartment," Tanya explained offhandedly, squinting through her glasses, now cloudy from the drizzle, at the dark waterfall and the perpetually wet monument to the city's founders, which from a distance looked like two tin soldiers.

"What about your husband?" Ivan asked, who couldn't resist, and at the sight of Tanya's dewy face, where the eyebrows went up but the eyeglasses slid down, he immediately regretted it.

"My husband is my problem,"

"But what if I learn your address?"

"You won't."

"Still, why are you giving me the keys? I can see they aren't extras. Someone's been using this set."

"Well, you know, just in case. Think of them as a souvenir."

Meanwhile, the endless summer, which seemed as round as the heavenly cupola it filled, was moving fast, and the money he had taken from Anfilogov for gemcutting equipment but had spent on hotel rooms and dinners in bars was dwindling even faster. Something had been damaged in Krylov's sense of self. The working hours spent without Tanya at the gemcutting shop had become tediously irrelevant. His soul was cramped, and he realized that in his condition he wasn't even making a living and was existing on loans: every day he was borrowing against the future. As he pulled another hundred out of Anfilogov's packet, Krylov tried not to test the envelope's thickness; nonetheless, there came a moment when just a few bills were left from the fat wad, not enough now even for his splitting machine.

Part Two

★

1

★

O N A RELIEF GLOBE, THE RIPHEANS LOOK LIKE AN OLD, STRETCHED out scar. There used to be a globe like that at the local history museum; its hollow bumps resembled a cardboard mask. You could spin the clumsy contraption caged inside four wooden ribs, and if you rubbed the globe's rough side hard it would make three or four turns with a plaintive creak, tumble across its own axis one last time, and land with South America on the bottom. There, underneath, some irritating widget would keep rattling for a while. Young Krylov's mother, in those days a thirty-year-old woman in high heels, had an old woman's job at the museum. She sat on a plain chair among the museum's marvels and kept people from touching the skeleton of the brown antediluvian mammoth, whose sole tusk looked like a broken ski with a splint jutting out in front.

But neither the globe nor the mammoth, to say nothing of the swollen cobra in green denatured alcohol, or the dusty TV-size dioramas on prehistoric themes, held any fascination for young Krylov. His imagination was drawn by the crystals, which rested in the display windows in cardboard nests lined with cotton wool. They also towered in the museum lobby, balancing out its patterned, wrought iron plangency with their absolute and intact muteness. The most powerful rock crystal, inside of which iridescent mealy stone-snow seemed to be melting, turning into water, was taller than twelve-year-old Krylov by its entire blunt fissured point. No less amazing were the black morions: two chunky druses, which looked as if they'd been chopped out of solid resin with an ax. In the smoky quartzes called Venus's hairstone, through their tea yellow, it was as if you were seeing bundles of iron needles, or the prickly leavings from a haircut at the barber's. The crystals' sides, if you looked at them from a specular angle, were cross-hatched here and there, the way they teach you to cross-hatch figures in drawing class, while others had polished patches, as if they'd been through major renovations underground.

The museum had other, nontransparent minerals, too. Visitors always took a special interest in the famous gold nugget that looked like the mummy of some tiny animal. The guide—Krylov remembered her black skirt and her heavy feet stuffed into stretched out scuffs—told the schoolchildren that sometimes a miner who dies underground petrifies and turns into his own statue. Afterward Krylov wasted no time clarifying whether or not this was so. It turned out that, indeed, under specific conditions organic remains can be replaced by sulfur-pyrite. There was no impermeable boundary between the mineral world and living nature. Young Krylov, who often showed up at the museum despite his mother's prohibitions, felt that he was closer to knowledge there than he was in his classes at school.

Conical crystals chopped off at the root and transferred to the plinths of rust-brown cloth possessed in full measure a quality that had bewitched young Krylov since his very first glimmers of consciousness: *transparency*. A person's earliest memories have an obscure and muddled origin. When later Krylov saw TV shows about the ancient emir's capital where he had spent his first years, he had the feeling not that he had once lived amid these huge glazed ceramics and crude, oxidized copper engravings, this Asiatic vegetation, but that he had dreamed it all. The dream of his early childhood was vibrant and trembled at the mere sight of marble-hard white grapes sprinkled with harsh Riphean snow at the fruit stand—and then dropped right back into his subconscious. The episodes accessible to the adult Krylov's memory consisted in part of his parents' stories and in part of restorations from his imagination; he couldn't seem to separate out the grains of what was genuine and what was unconditionally his.

Just one episode was steeped in an ammonia-like reality. All he had to do was wish to see it and in his mind an osier bush flashed above soap-green irrigation water, and in his hand he found a sliver of blue glass, curved, from a bottle probably, through which the flashes of sunlight on the irrigation canal looked like welding sparks (this is a later insertion). Something sticky was smeared along the edge of the piece of glass, and on his finger, buzzing and thick, there emerged, as if from a half-shut eye, a fat red tear. Who was that stout man *he knew*, who leaned over him, smelling of sweat through his clean, blindingly white shirt? He demanded that Krylov throw the glass away that instant, or give it to him, but young Krylov, smeared with blood, stubbornly held his find behind his back and retreated into the leafy shade, which was as hot as splashes of tea (this is a later insertion). He had felt it with unutterable clarity at the time: the blue sliver contained something that almost never occurs in the simple matter around us: *transparency*, a special and profound element, like water and sky.

Actually, it was dating from this episode that Krylov remembered himself. His attraction to the transparent, to the mystery of the gem, which subsequently inserted Krylov into the true Riphean mentality, must originally have been an emanation of the dry, flat Asiatic world, where water was especially valued and everything earthly under the red-hot sky was divided into what seemed fit for being ground into pigment, on one hand, and tintless monotony, on the other. Young Krylov perceived transparency as a substance's highest, most enlightened state. Transparency was magic. All simple objects belonged to the ordinary world, *this* world; no matter how cleverly they were arranged or how tightly sealed, you could open them up and see what they had inside. Transparency belonged to a world of a different order, and you couldn't open it up and get inside. Once young Krylov attempted to extract the orange glass-juice trapped in the thick walls of his aunt's vase and that was much better than the colorless water poured into the vase. One afternoon, on the balcony, on a carefully spread out newspaper, young Krylov struck the vase with a hammer, exploding its emptiness like a grenade in a war movie. The shards, though—some of them flew into the sneering sycamore or under his aunt's old tubs—were just as self-contained as the intact object. Choosing the very best bottom piece, with the densest color, young Krylov continued to smash it on the scraps of the now slivered and silvered newspaper until he ended up with a hard, completely white powder. The only color in the powder came from his, Krylov's, unanticipated blood, which looked like a chewed up raisin. Not a drop remained in the powder of the *transparency* for whose sake the experiment had been performed.

The experiment that ended in powder made a much bigger impression on Krylov than the fatherly beating that followed. He had learned that what is transparent is unattainable and, like everything precious, connected with blood. What he gleaned about stones at the children's library, where he choked on the paper dust (Krylov could barely remember a time when he couldn't read), confirmed his intuition's findings. "Great Moghul," "Excelsior," "Florentine," "Shah" —the names of the world-class diamonds were as much music to him as the names of world capitals are to romantics of another bent. Famous stones were the heroes of adventures on a par with D'Artagnon, Captain Nemo, and Leatherstocking.

Meanwhile, his mother and aunt had precious stones, too: large earrings on slender gold hooks, with pale blue stones that held more patterns than a cardboard kaleidoscope; and four rings. One, bent, had a gaping black hole, but in the others marvelous transparencies winked like cat's eyes. Young Krylov was as convinced of the high value of these objects as he was of the authenticity of the painting by Shishkin, "Morning in the Piney Woods," that hung in the living room of his neighbors, the Permyakovs, over their lumpy couch, whose imposing dilapidation arose powerfully in his memory when a few years later young Krylov was secretly researching the museum's taxidermied deer and wolves. Later, when he had done some reading, Krylov learned that the picture was in fact held at the

Tretyakov Gallery. It was hard for him to believe in the Tretyakov's reality and, consequently, Shishkin's painting itself vanished from reality. The world appeared to young Krylov as a string of copies without an original. Even after his disappointment in the reproduction, though, his belief in the precious stones kept in the shabby box covered in nettle-green velvet remained intact.

Young Krylov understood from the grownups' conversations that they all earned very little money. For some reason his aunt, considered a beauty, earned the least of all. She had a habit of puffing out her ribs, tensing the slender veins on her neck, and circling her waist with her hands so that the fingers nearly met in the crumpled silk of her shift; her hair, which poured smoothly down her back all the way to her waist, was piled up and hovered in the air like the striated smoke from his father's cigarettes. She was the first to lose her job. One day she came home walking—and looking—utterly *off*, and to all questions she turned to face the wall. The old Yuryuzan refrigerator, which looked like a Zaporozhets without wheels and which his mama and aunt had been planning to get rid of, chuckled with glee. To young Krylov, though, it seemed that both this refrigerator, and the worn red carpets, which in spots looked like colored batting, and the lack of a car of their own, which his father, *who was not a thief,* grumbled about on Saturdays behind his half-lowered newspaper—that all this was just a game because the family in fact kept treasures. The certainty never left young Krylov that everything transparent was worth insane sums, and stones in gold settings weren't just any old buttons. In essence, he saw them as magical objects. The very presence of these stones elevated his mother and aunt above ordinary working women with nasty-smelling kitchen hands into the ranks of titled ladies. He dwelled for a happy time in the confidence that should some calamity befall them, the stones would be sold to fairy-tale merchants in luxurious turbans that looked like white roses and would save the day.

★ ★ ★

They did not save the day. Everything changed. Nothing seemed real anymore but rather as if you were seeing it in a mirror in which you couldn't tell who was doing what or who was going where. Young Krylov still didn't have the right words but he did have a visceral sense of the disorientation of things; he noticed that many people on the street now seemed *off*. Others, who didn't speak Russian well, seemed to double in this mirror: in the courtyard, each time he ran into mocking Mahomet with his iron fingers, or Kerim with the blue-gray head from the seventh floor, young Krylov felt with his drawn-together shoulder blades that, while they were in front of him, they were simultaneously behind him. In the evenings, they turned off their electricity; everyone sat in the kitchen around the one candle, which melted as it burned into a warm puddle; in his book, which he managed to fit among the dirty dishes, black pictures stirred on yellow pages. His father, wiping his teacup with a greasy crust of bread, would tell the story for the umpteenth time about the man from his institution who had made certain "improper attacks" against him and cut him off on the street for no reason at all.

Strangers came to the Krylovs' apartment: two who looked liked they were from the market, wearing identical jackets that looked like they had been glued over a piece of warped cardboard. The strangers walked through the house, looking around cautiously and meticulously. One, with temples like pieces of gray coal under his skull-cap, asked Krylov's frightened mother something, his angry, effeminate voice rising from time to time to a quizzical whine; the other said nothing but seemed to be thinking, and the wrinkles on his forehead were exactly like the ones you get on the front of crumpled trousers. One day these two, whom his parents referred to privately as "the buyers," brought with them an utterly senile and bent old granddad whose body looked like a skinny dog in man's clothing. While the young men were crawling under the bed and in the closets—now without any ceremony whatsoever—the granddad sat on a stool, his bowed legs in their soft, dusty shoes folded in an impotent curl. Granddad looked absolutely nothing like the rich merchant whom young Krylov's imagination had created with a little help from the *Arabian Nights*. His robe, belted with a dirty cotton scarf, had been incinerated by the heat to shreds of brown batting, and his beard was like the threads from a torn-off button. When young Krylov happened to look into his eyes, where some kind of warm wax was accumulating, he felt—as clearly as if he had become *transparent* for a second—that this granddad didn't care what happened to him, or to these young men, or to the Russian inhabitants of this profane apartment, who to this granddad were no more than shadows on the unfamiliar walls around him. When they had completed this latest inspection, the strangers lifted the doddering djinni by his spread elbows and walked him off, adjusting to his small felt steps—and from the vestibule you could see the Permyakovs' door open across the landing and the anxious neighbors waiting inside. There were fewer "buyers" than "sellers."

The "move" dated from this time. By no means all the familiar items that disappeared *here* showed up later *there*, in the cold northern city where the trees' summer greenery functioned as a raincoat, in the tiny apartment stingily lit by windows the size of an open newspaper. In the same manner his aunt disappeared as well—the princess, his friend, the beauty with the round face that glowed in the dark—she vanished without a trace, and young Krylov understood from the muffled tone of the new apartment silence that in no instance was he to ask about her. It turned out that the precious stones were all gone, along with Mama's savings, to pay for the containers in which their furniture arrived, crippled and suffering from, now chronic, dislocation of the joints. The wardrobe where his aunt's colorful dresses once hung now had a tendency to come apart, the way the slick magician's painted box comes apart in the circus ring.

An adult might call the emotion young Krylov experienced disenchantment. In fact, it was a mixed sensation, like acute orphanhood while your parents are still alive. He recalled the morning of their departure, when the air was like chicken broth. The boys whistled for him to come outside, but he was in a new part-woolen suit, which made the grass and old roses by the front door seem part-woolen, too. He remembered both the reserved seats on the train, which was permeated throughout with the sadness of the long sunset lying low over the steppe, and the unfamiliar taste of crooked green apples bought at the station—a taste like cotton wool and medicine from the pharmacy. At the same time, he didn't think he would remember anything. Life split between "before" and "after." For a long time young Krylov couldn't get used to the idea that the summer here was so inauthentic, like the reheated leftovers of the previous year, when he had not yet been in this apartment or this yard, where no one ran around barefoot.

No matter how hard his parents tried to get it out of him why he had done *that terrible thing*, young Krylov preferred to keep his own counsel. You didn't see him asking why they hid the only photograph of his aunt as far away as possible, under the technical manuals from the nonexistent microwave and sewing machine, although he suspected foul play—a reluctance to look at the person they had for some reason abandoned. One evening, scarily close to his parents' return from work, he decided to poke around in the stiff drawer under the mirror, which was crammed full. Hastily tossing the uninteresting papers aside, afraid now that what he'd been searching for would not turn up among these scraps, he suddenly saw his aunt—taken in the same studio where they had taken him, standing as if she were a singer on stage, in front of folded drapery which young Krylov remembered as red but in the photo was brown. All at once his urge to steal from his parents the sole copy, which had no original, was superseded by another. Feeling the tears that had welled up press on his nose, Krylov ripped the photograph into sticky pieces, some of which ended up on the floor. Then he managed to unseal the damp ventilation pane and released his aunt from his fist, like a small bird, onto the dark October wind that was scraping its belly over the earth, trying to overcome the mass of air and withered leaves pulling it down and fly south. He didn't notice that some of the scraps fluttered back into the room and got tangled in his hair like confetti.

When his parents, tired from the bus, dragged themselves and their bags of groceries into the utterly quiet, unlit apartment with the electric drizzle on the uncurtained windows and the little criminal hiding in the dark toilet, all the clues were in evidence. Young Krylov couldn't remember another fatherly punishment like this one: the belt seared his clenched, trembling buttocks, and the pain made him wet himself on the clammy oilcloth his father had thrown down as a precaution on the *new* ottoman brought from the house. His mother, clutching her crushed beauty parlor hairdo, sat at the empty table in front of a solitary dish of marmalade and the remnants of some colored sugar—and remained sitting like that while the criminal, holding his trousers and upturning chairs, stumbled back to the toilet, where he kept tattered matches and smelly butts wrapped in paper behind the wastebasket.

★ ★ ★

Actually, what shook young Krylov at the time was not his parents' behavior but his newly discovered capacity to commit terrible crimes. He developed this capacity further in school and the yard, which was notorious for its drunken brawls, teen rumbles, and the giant puddle, shaped like a grand piano, that appeared spring and fall in an unvarying outline in the exact same spot. After the "move," young Krylov got out of hand, as they say. A ceasefire was in effect only on museum territory, where, if his mother didn't pester him too much, Krylov quietly did his homework in the staff room with the thick walls and sloping window, where the raspberry sun of the winter sunset sat like a loaf of bread in the oven, or the spring branches melted in the March blue. All the rest of the time he led an independent life.

Unlike the children of all his parents' old friends who had moved from Central Asia to cold Russia, Krylov was almost never ill in his new homeland. Never was he hit by the deep frosts, which transformed the industrial city into a dim, enchanted garden, or by the famous Riphean snow showers—cold oatmeal on water, which tasted of coal; in the fickle northern sun he tanned to an Asiatic blackness. In everything that had to do with health, the teen Krylov was the utter despair of his parents and at their slightest attempt to instruct he would storm out of the house before he could tie his army boots, the only ones he had, stolen at the wholesale market.

He and his thrill-seeking buddies would ride the freights that dragged past the long row of gray buildings, or he'd flatten pieces of scrap metal under train wheels, scrap that seemed to retain some of its terrible weight and quaking power, like the echo of the caboose, as if the freight train, making its groaning sounds, were retreating from him in both directions. With that same enterprising gang, young Krylov climbed the abandoned TV tower the Ripheans called the Toadstool. The town's main attraction, it had never been used for its original purpose and for a good ten years had been deteriorating in a striated mirage above the cubist apartment blocs and cellophane river, guarded by the police, but only very theoretically. There, inside the concrete pillar, which had holes like a whistle, the rusted stairs were rickety and some places were like a creaking swing. The wind up top, bursting through the cracks, instantly dried your sweat, making the thrill-seeker feel as if his whole body had been trapped in a sticky spider web. Despite the difficulties of the climb, though, the column was covered in graffiti just as solidly as any proletarian stairwell. At the very top, on the wind-lashed circular platform, which bobbed around like an airborne raft, he couldn't keep his feet at first, even in the relatively safe center; he felt like lying flat on his belly and not watching the skinny grating of the guard rail, buried by winding tendrils, ladle the sun-drenched blur, not watching the pink rag that was tied to it and ripped to shreds flap furiously.

Teen Krylov had already figured it out, though. If you wanted to be a real Riphean, you had to take risks—lots of them, and the more reckless the better. Standing at the very edge, feeling where the low wall stopped and emptiness began, just above knee height, like a cello bow passing across strung nerves, he was one of the few who could piss straight into the abyss, where his output scattered like beads from a broken necklace. When out-of-town base jumpers first showed up at the tower and started jumping over the side, flicking the long tongues of their parachutes like lighters, Krylov decided he was definitely going to jump, too, but it was not to be.

"Don't even think about it, buddy," a guy with kind, deeply set eyes that glistened amid his wrinkles and lashes like drops of dark oil told him. "You have to train for six months to base-jump. It comes down to a matter of seconds, get it? You could fuck yourself up good." The good man explained what exactly would happen to Krylov, using an expression of exceptional profanity while looking good-naturedly around the thrill-seekers' hangout, where an empty balloon drifted, drunk on the thin air and shining like a sixty-watt bulb in absolute sun.

"So I fuck myself up. So what? It's my right." Krylov wouldn't back down.

"See this parachute?" the good baser nodded over his shoulder. "It costs two grand. If you fuck yourself up, I'm not getting it back."

This argument convinced Krylov. The two grand figure made an impression. Krylov's activities outside the house now tended to be partly commercial in nature. He and his buddies, wearing loose Chinese-made Adidas sweats, shoplifted on a small scale from "their" supermarket, the Oriental, keeping cheeky outsiders off their territory. They prospected at Matrosov Square, formerly Haymarket, where the river lay on the sand like a woman on a sheet, and under the sand, in the black, foul-smelling muck that used to be cleaned off the bottom by the municipal cleaners, they'd find different coins, gold ones even, as small as a Soviet kopek, with a two-headed eagle the size of a gnat. Soon teen Krylov's mind had invented a kind of virtual bookkeeping. A parachute was two grand. A used PC—two hundred fifty. The new *World Coins* catalog—fifty-four. A headlamp for crawling through the vaulted shallow underground mines—eight hundred rubles. A sturdy Polish backpack—four hundred fifty. Not all—or even many—of his dreams could come true.

Teen Krylov adjusted to jumping from the Toadstool in his dreams. As he drifted off, his URL was a specific array of sensations—in particular, the image of a balloon being borne off, which tuned every nerve in his body to the four hundred meters of altitude, at which point the balloon reminded him of an astronaut stepping out for a space-walk. Not always, but often Krylov reached a state where everything was swaying, tossing, and whistling. As in real life the clouds' wet shadows floated deep in the golden abyss and were greedily collected by the city blocks, the way water collects pieces of sugar. In his dreams, Krylov broke away from the concrete by making a special effort with his tensed diaphragm; immediately, his ears and head felt like a jammed receiver. The paradisiacal two thousand-dollar parachute on his back just wouldn't open, so he had to dissolve in the wind as fast as possible and without a trace, which Krylov set about doing quite practically, surrendering utterly to the logic of his dream and its vibrating, vanishing words.

When he started earning some money, teen Krylov felt more grown up than he really was. He'd been through all the trivial agonies of a self-centered young oaf with a laughable father (by this time his father had become a toadying chauffeur for a piss-ugly boss and was driving a Mercedes, just like he'd always wanted), and things got much easier for him with his parents. His silence in response to their helpless cries now seemed perfectly natural, and from time to time he would even leave his school report in the kitchen, by way of impersonal information, a perfectly proper school report with good marks. Studying came easily to Krylov. What was worse was that his parents' mere presence kept Krylov from having a good read. They

obviously suspected him of hiding a porno magazine under his algebra textbook—not a Frederic Paul novel.

All in all, relations between teen Krylov and his parents consisted of endless suspicions. Imagining what they were imagining while
they waited up for their sonny boy at night under their stupid
kitchen lamp, Krylov admitted that no matter how hard he tried he
could never be as bad as that pair who had once conspired to give
birth to him thought he was. Looking at them, Krylov could more
readily have believed that he'd been conceived in a test tube. He was
perfectly well informed about where children came from, and he had
enjoyed the favors of Ritka and Svetka, two sisters one year apart
who never said no and who had rough kissers and soft asses. Krylov
could not possibly imagine his mother and father getting it together
to have him; and he really couldn't understand why they'd bothered.
Krylov's parents flattered him with their fears. No matter what happened in nearby neighborhoods—a fire at a kiosk that had stood
there ever since in the form of a hut of black and fresh plywood, a
burglary at the apartment of the hereditary dental technician who
had kept the secret of his family collections all his conscious life and
was now forced to keep it, except as someone else's—in everything
they saw the complicity of their son, who had no alibi. Their delusion was so strong that his father, who considered himself something
of a diplomat, even attempted to *win over* the dental technician, who
had parked his secondhand Zhiguli next to the Mercedes, but the
technician, who had the skull of an elephant, not a man's, on his
short body, reacted like a rape victim and clarified nothing.

In short, his parents believed that Krylov was to blame for every
crime committed in the vicinity. The image created by his parents'
imagination coincided with Ritka and Svetka's ideal—someone to
share, like all their boyfriends and their cheap dresses with the gold
sparkles and puff paint designs. They pictured this ideal as a tough
guy who thought life meant having control over everything that
moved and who was on friendly terms with a benign papa-thug,

whose thick shaved neck sported a gold chain as chunky as a tractor tire. All the gang—from the lookout with the shaved head, whom Krylov had only seen from behind, to puny Genchik, famous for his ability to send his bubbly spit flying several meters—possessed a common quality: a nauseating *soulfulness.* They took serious offense if something seemed amiss to them. Some fuzzy-eyed moron with a head no more complexly constructed than a gearbox could for some reason *remember* a guy and chase him down like a jackrabbit, becoming the ubiquitous godling of their home courtyards and garages as far as his victim was concerned.

These tattooed punks horsed around for a long time before installing their own general at the Oriental—Krylov's classmate, Lyokha Terentiev, who'd repeated two grades. Lyokha's close-set eyes studied intimidation and practiced on the other guys, provoking a rush of malicious energy in Krylov and an urge to crush not only Lyokha but the store he'd taken over as well. Actually, Lyokha himself, being both curious and clumsy, had overturned a rack of housewares, and the crash buried the unfamiliar object that had caught his eye under a heap of enameled cookware and detergents gurgling in plastic squeeze bottles. Ever since, the general, rather than working personally, had just shot the breeze with the guard while the guys, shielding each other from the surveillance camera, lifted expensive compacts and perfumes.

Krylov was all set to fight him for the business and out of pure rage beat up that big lug Lyokha in the boys room at school, somehow managing to jam this unzipped hulk under the sink right behind a wet pipe, where his head got stuck in an unnatural position. After they freed Lyokha's head by pouring vegetable oil over it and his paws grabbed onto the parallel legs of the girl mathematician who'd rescued him, after he'd worked himself free, Krylov actually felt guilty at the sight of Lyokha's tears smeared over his dirty, oily cheeks.

Lyokha wasn't long in being avenged, though, and they made things hot for Krylov. After a chat with the unpretentious enforcers, who had managed to fit eight into a rusty Zhiguli, Krylov's teeth were wobbly and salty for a long time, and his ribs on the right side felt like they had current running through them so that he couldn't take a deep breath. It became perfectly clear to him that mixing with tattooed punks cost too much. The gang was a freak of nature, a genetic phenomenon, and occasionally, when he watched the tiniest residents of the courtyard banging their toys on the bench and running away in their flannel booties from their pale mothers mincing after them, Krylov would suddenly catch a glimpse of *their* future man—as if he were marked from birth by some secret sulkiness, a concavity in his hard forehead, the corporeal weight of his raw being.

Because of Lyokha, Krylov lost a substantial portion of his income, but he had no regrets, particularly as the romance of the supermarket, with its predictable Chinese-Turkish assortment, had lost its allure by then. On the other hand, he had other interesting occupations the thugs couldn't touch. The thugs, whose main output was the physiological terror they produced in people, themselves went around full of that terror, like jugs, up to their ears in it, and so were incapable of pure and pointless risk.

The world was laid out for Krylov like one big amusement park. In his relations with the world he had worked out and followed his own rules of equilibrium. For instance, if some collector ripped Krylov off for a rare Soviet twenty, then Krylov, in turn, would rip off someone else, but only one someone, and not necessarily the same someone. What was important here was keeping it impersonal; the owner of a major collection of Soviet coins who looked an awful lot like and was known to all as Duremar could hang out right there, where the deals went down, but Krylov wouldn't come near him. Instead, he would carelessly show a worn prewar *lat* to a snippety old lady with a puffy powdered face who looked like an owl-moth and who had shown up for no one knew what dividend, and when he'd made an unfair deal would feel perfectly satisfied. Teen Krylov didn't want to hold on to anything extra, be it insults or the memory of all the people who had come and gone. He was like an ecologically pure contraption that returns to its environment precisely what it takes in. He thought that by maintaining this balance he was in some magical way protecting the world from collapse and preserving its substance. If someone lifted a book from his bag, he'd take one from a bookstall or the school library; if someone didn't return the head-lamp he'd lent, he wouldn't buy another, he'd pinch one from a subway construction worker, crawling through the gaps in the patched link fence behind which the dusty excavation site sputtered and boomed. For himself, Krylov made no distinction between the people who insulted him and the people who suffered at his hands. The "me versus everyone else" ratio was, of course, unequal, as it would be for anyone, not just a kid from the crummy projects who had the slimmest of social chances; but Krylov was not eager to admit any inequality.

★ ★ ★

In search of adventures for his own pathetic ass, teen Krylov tried to grasp the character of his new northern homeland, the essence of true Riphean-ness.

As in any Babylonian-type city, four-fifths of the capital's population comprised newcomers, refugees, ex-convicts, and the graduates of thirty or so functioning colleges. Natives were in the minority. Given this spontaneous growth of the inhabited environment it wasn't easy to understand what the city's primordial territory, the expression and symbol of the Riphean spirit, actually was. Especially since the city itself originally had not been inclined to create a center. The old merchant mansions adorned with thick wrought-iron lace on front balconies the size of beds had been put up without any consideration for their neighbors' style, as if they had no neighbors at all in fact. The city administration, experiencing a natural need for a proper center, responded by razing mansions and putting up new housing that combined the idea of a barracks and Peter the Great's Monplaisir. The Ripheans were offered a choice of symbols: the open-air geology museum, where the big chunks of jasper flushed out by the dam looked like pieces of stone meat shot through with quartz veins; a life-size model of a locomotive, invented here, that looked like a meat grinder; or the monument to the city's two founders, who stood in their stony German garb, their identical polished faces turned toward the black dam tunnel and waterfall, above which some hotshot, one of the ones who liked to dangle his legs over the abyss, had written in bright white waterproof paint, "There is no God."

In reality, the true symbol and expression of the Riphean spirit was the bluish Toadstool that loomed over the city, the largest of those irrational phenomena that seemed to have come about purely to arouse the Ripheans' principal instinct, which you might say was the instinct to climb something just because it was there, to conquer what you weren't supposed to, or, even better, were forbidden to. The Riphean's world was patently nonhorizontal and in this sense like an insect's. The Toadstool was their cult, and for the town's teens, it was an ant trail to heaven. The grown-ups could climb their 8,000-meter Himalayas, organize international (with only melancholy Finns participating) competitions for climbing the red sausage-like Riphean pines, and schedule crazy rallies over forest roads, which were nothing but raw steepness with boulders jutting out, and winter motorcycle races down the frozen river, which involved scooting nimbly under the vaults of the Tsar Bridge. Though what they were doing was much worthier of punks, the grown-up Ripheans nonetheless took it quite seriously, maybe because they held on inside to something solid, some cold, crystalline filler. Teen Krylov figured out early on that a true Riphean's soul possesses the quality of *transparency*: you could see straight through it but never get inside.

Soon he had a similar formation in his own chest that consisted of tiny spots and fissures of insult from his earliest childhood that he could no longer return to his environment. Krylov learned that when something irreparable happens, then at first it's interesting, like finding yourself in a movie. That's how it was when his father drank his boss's whiskey and drove the Mercedes into a silly but solid billboard. He was trapped by the air bags and got off with literally a scratch, whereas his boss had half his skull ripped off by a post that rammed through the car. Although the accident was the fault of a Moskvich that was never found and that skidded and clipped a line of cars (there were plenty of reckless drivers among ordinary engineers driving rusty old wrecks, not only among the new rich, on the Riphean roads), his father, as a consequence of the deceased's stature and the alcohol he'd drunk, was put behind bars. Krylov saw him for the last time in the courtroom and fixed in his memory his small, focused eyebrows and his patient pose of an ice fisherman. After that his father went away in a convoy and never came back, honestly serving out his four years but, like many in his situation, making his escape from reality.

The splendid Toadstool's dramatic demise made a much bigger impression on Krylov. Despite the special qualities of the reinforced concrete used in it, the 400-meter tower had deteriorated so badly as to be unsafe. Meanwhile, there was absolutely nowhere to drop it. During the years the Toadstool had adorned the low Riphean skies, around it were built, first, your standard nine-story apartment blocs and then prestigious housing complexes, and on the most dangerous, almost always windy side, there was a shopping mall that looked like a giant paradisiacal greenhouse. Delay threatened calamity, though, such as the Russian Emergency Administration had never seen. One fine summer noted for its mighty white rains, which rumbled in the drain pipes like anchor chains, the municipal administration summoned the will and the means and gave the go-ahead. Naturally, the Toadstool remained standing over the city all the next winter, sparkling like sugar and leading Ripheans into temptation to climb it with amateur radio equipment and drag a battery up for their broadcasting needs. Prices for suburban real estate went up like gangbusters, and insider realtors close to the mayor's office made a bundle.

The following summer, which, unlike the previous year's, was so dry the town stream turned to a coffee-like muck, military specialists took over the Toadstool. They spent two months evacuating the nearby blocks, which came to resemble a Martian city where dusty dogs ran in packs, while blasters drilled holes in the concrete, spread cables, and replaced the explosives looted the previous year. On D-day, it became obvious that these were pros at work: the air in town shuddered and the Toadstool was transformed into a neat pile of dust, like a candle that had burned down very quickly, plunging, halfway to the ground, into rising clouds of solid ash. Where it had just been, a blinding spot formed on the thin and cloudy amalgam. Even when the cumulus dust, thinning and translucent, rose to almost the full height of the vanished tower, the lambency didn't disappear; the dusty specter of a fatter Toadstool lingered in the air for days, settling on the wan leaves and broken glass that crunched under the feet of the returned inhabitants and that sobbed under the janitors' brooms, forming fragile, layered piles of trash. Even afterward, whenever the dust came up, it was like a faint impression being powdered in the air, or if the sun came out from behind a cloud at an unusual angle, the tower became visible; people saw it in a thick snowfall, as if it had washed the violet shadow with soap. Lots of Ripheans had trouble believing they'd ever physically been there, where now the wind roamed freely; drifting off to sleep with this thought, the punks and even college students who already shaved their soft beards flew in their dreams.

2

★

LIKE ANY REAL RIPHEAN, WHEN THE TIME CAME, YOUNG KRYLOV lit out for the mountains. He found out what it was like to hike with a backpack that gets heavier with every kilometer and smells more and more of canvas and sweat, exactly as if you were carrying an extra body of your own on your back. He found out what it was like to hammer test holes using someone's great-grandfather's chisels and hammers, and then chop the cold chunks up in the sun, letting stone chips fly like pointy stars.

Young Krylov even had some minor success: at home he assembled the standard assortment of newspaper-wrapped samples, and he even managed to sell a few pieces. He had one good find in the old tailings of an emerald mine that had been bought up whole by some Russian-Japanese firm and was lazily guarded by porky he-men in decorative camouflage. While the sportsmen, wishing to linger at their picnic, built a large fire, whose luxuriant smoke trailed off into the skies, the rock hounds calmly infiltrated. They had to be careful, though, climbing over the bare manmade inclines, which were held in place only here and there by a web of weeds: a man could be seen even without binoculars. Piles of angular rock that had been let drop over the decades ground tightly underfoot, but any loose piece could be the pedal that released a landslide. Nonetheless, the game was worth the candle: the poorly deciphered layer contained not only lightly fractured beryls, which the Russo-Japanese used for industrial purposes, but also gem-quality crystals. Krylov had the good fortune to dig up eight intact six-faceted bottles stuck in the layer of rock, and in their white and green veins he was thrilled to glimpse live zones of *transparency*. Even while fleeing the rangers through the booming pine forest, which resounded with their yells and shots, like an iron fence struck by a stick, Krylov continued to feel exaltation at this elucidated substance. His find yielded enough money to pay for his first year of university study and to buy his mother, who suffered from serious edema, a trip to a sanatorium. Still, Krylov couldn't shake the feeling that he'd parted with his find with indecent haste, as if he'd missed something in it; his intuition was correct and subsequently wholly vindicated.

It didn't take Krylov very long to realize that his luck wasn't all that great, worse than average probably, and the industry, though it didn't reject him altogether, would never feed him. It wasn't that he'd had no encounters with the mountain spirits, either. Like many others, he'd seen lesser phenomena in campfires, when the flame, after crumbling the fragile blazing coals like wafers, suddenly seemed to rear up on its toes and start dancing, turning the team's faces into a flickering movie. Later, in the ash-gray fire ring, they would find characteristic "bruises": solid patches of dark purple which led prospectors in the know to gold-bearing sand within a twenty-meter radius. Once, Krylov even observed a flying saucer—not such a rarity really. Something elliptical literally galloped across the night sky sheathed in a thin ripple of soapy clouds and then disappeared behind a high-tension tower, drowning in the tower's luminescence like a spoon in sour cream. But even apart from how the spirits behaved, among the rock hounds, Krylov felt like he belonged.

There was something of the little boy—even though he was at the university and had a prickly mustache—about the way he had latched onto those tough but good-natured aficionados who in their collective subconscious clung to the notion that only someone who has a conscience gets a gem. The secretive, nimble rock hounds, who stood out ordinarily only because of the particular sooty color of their tan and the white area on their jaw where they'd shaved their summer whiskers, which lent something apish to their faces, the rock hounds had found a way to exist independently of the authorities and the thugs. The authorities, focused on the big picture, preferred to turn a blind eye to small-time evil and even permitted one modest private firm to organize monthly mineral shows—whose true earnings might have amazed the tax agencies. In turn, the thugs had an inkling that somewhere in the forest lay real, unearthed money. This, of course, made the thugs take notice: they had divided up the turf with their fists down to the very last stall and then had suddenly discovered around them an irritatingly inaccessible terra incognita. But even they, with their identical heads as tough and hard as boxing gloves, realized that no matter how many times they descended upon nature, which scared them with its cold sameness in all four directions, they weren't going to find any gems. The few attempts to put the business under their control ended in failure. The rock hounds wouldn't subscribe to any extortion schemes the thugs understood, and the most zealous seller of protection, the ferocious general called the Wheel, was discovered one day beneath a prominent pine that looked like a hanger dangling wet winter caps, right at the cross-over from the northern tract—bearing no trace of violence but no signs of life, either. The autopsy showed that the small heart under his uninjured ribs had literally split in two, like an apricot. The culprits, naturally, were never found.

Krylov was drawn to the rock hounds. He realized that the gap between the millstones that ground the electorate into an endless stream of flour had to be defended not only by an economic conspiracy but also by a sustained spiritual effort, a constant churning of energy in a shared interior space and personal dues paid into the corporate moral capital. At the same time, Krylov observed substantial differences among the rock hounds. One man, for the sake of a single find, would process a full measure of stone and subsoil to the point that at night, eyes shut, he would still see the shovel taking dig after endless dig, letting the dark clumps fan out as they fell. Another could pass through a ditch someone had slaved over and abandoned, kick over a scratched rock that was sending him mysterious signals, and discover a crystal of excellent purity.

This difference was no accident; among the rock hounds there were a select few—though they were incapable of getting rich in a serious way. They probably dealt with the world according to the same principle of equilibrium that had been revealed to Krylov when he was a teenager: no one hurt them so much that they'd cash out and exchange their hard industry for a handsomer way of life. Krylov got to know a few of them pretty well. There was old Seryoga Gaganov, an adventurer and scoutmaster, a strict teacher for quirky pubescent boys with mediocre grades. There was Gaganov's friend Vladimir Menshikov, who was not only a lucky rock hound but also the author of a dozen different books, from the history of treasures to adventure novels. Farid Habibullin, a Tatar, practically the only one of the "old men" who was a professional mining engineer, looked the most oppositional. In town he always wore a wrinkled black tunic and cowboy boots and gathered his long hair streaked with lead gray into an uncombed tail. Habibullin's secret was his goodness. Possessed of the greatest talent for the fortuitous kick to a cobble, sometimes, with a quick glance of his yellow eye, he would show a young man where to poke while he himself walked away indifferently, his bowed legs describing fanciful figures, as if he were riding an invisible bicycle across the stone talus. Having completed his training as a young man with some very special troops, Habibullin may have been the only one of the brusque rock hounds decidedly incapable of punching someone in the face. In contrast, the lucky, good-looking Roma Gusev, a stocky sculpture of a man with mighty rusty curls, got into a fight nearly every week. Stone sober, never favoring the bottle, when Roma was a little late for work he could go through different yards and break in on a group of far-gone lushes who ruled the ragged bushes. In literally half an hour, the conflict's participants, their faces like a painter's palette, would have crawled over to the police booth, and Roma—puzzlingly, no less drunk than the rest of the group—would have set out in the same direction, muttering and licking his battered fists in the manner of a large tabby cat.

There were others besides these, too—solid, respected, welcomed rock hounds with the free-and-easy brotherly attitude accepted here, but nonetheless with a hint of gentle respect. Of course, Krylov realized he would never be like these men, that his place in rock hunting would always be well down the ladder. At the same time, something whispered to Krylov that he had in fact landed right where he needed to be. He was very important to the community, he just didn't know yet in what way.

* * *

The mystery was solved when Professor Anfilogov appeared and took up his place in Krylov's life. Krylov entered the History Department in memory of the ethnographic museum that was now decaying in the steamy basements of the municipal administration building and of the mammoth bones that had fallen apart again as if there had never been a restoration on a metal carcass in the cupola hall. Now the painted bone beams had entered into a new oblivion and had much less in common with a dead giant than when they had lain there, washed away, in the dense, dull, prehistoric sand. From this example Krylov learned that there had been an irrevocable spoiling of history, and he guessed that this kind of thing happened fairly often.

Professor Anfilogov lectured his novice humanitarians long and tediously on historical philosophy. Ordinarily the university administration, following their bureaucratic instinct, gave their blessings to bores, but they despised Anfilogov, and why they didn't toss him out on his ear was anybody's guess. The only way you could pass Anfilogov's exam was with a knowledge of his lectures, which couldn't be checked out of the library and which were a concentrated cocktail of sources whose recipe clearly involved a special trade secret. On the eve of the winter session, the department ephemeras, pale gentle truants on whom the boredom of Anfilogov's lectures acted like chloroform, made up for their absence with the most complex mimicry—but virtually all of them died in the icy examination room, where the professor sat in his jauntily set coat, drumming his white nails on the table. Anfilogov was arrogant and almost never looked at the person he was talking to. The professor's mind seemed rigged with a special timer that measured the precise length of any communication, regardless of his opponent desire; as soon as the device went off, Anfilogov interrupted the other person with his raised palm, which was covered with calligraphic lines that formed extremely insulting words in Latin letters. He himself, in turn, fit ideally into the academic hour; no sooner did he scrape the mottled pages off the podium than the electric bell went off in the hallway.

In essence, the professor was trying to provoke those around him to search for the bases of that feeling of one's own dignity that jabbed at their own sore spot. Some, the shy ones, were inclined to ascribe to the professor secret accomplishments, up to and including foreign medals; others no less cowardly declared Anfilogov an utter nobody. As for first-year Krylov, he saw the professor's nature as a *transparency* of the highest quality, an absolutely solid emptiness inside of which there was nothing resentful people could detect, but it itself existed in a crystallized form worth top price per carat. In secret, Krylov admired Anfilogov: his grotesque features, his thoroughbred profile—the whole bizarre Anfilogov appearance, which the observer's imagination seemed to help shape. At the same time, he realized perfectly that the professor had no need of any observer, least of all first-year Krylov. On the contrary, the ill-wishers around him needed the professor, if only to explain their need, and it was almost impossible to liken Anfilogov to the figure that appears when you tell fortunes on dripped wax or coffee grounds and testifies to or tells you about something. This made it sad to think about the disappearing generations of student synopses—the multivolume manuscript edition of Anfilogov's works, where the professor's original thoughts may have gotten lost, thoughts he had no desire to mull over for the moderately filled audience of bored moon-faces.

Naturally, lecturing to the ceiling as he did, Anfilogov didn't notice first-year Krylov, who preferred sitting in the balcony, in honor of his schoolboy memories. But he did notice him at the exam, when he pulled on his cheek with distaste and scratched "satisfactory" into the brand-new exam record. That spring, though, at Farid's apartment, where they brought the equipment before heading north and where in the morning a faded truck from some friendly topographers was supposed to show up, Anfilogov immediately fixed his gaze on his student in the crampedness of the six-square-meter kitchen, where the smokers were standing as if they were on an elevator. "Vasily Petrovich," the professor introduced himself anew, moving his narrow hand in Krylov's direction. Shaking it, Krylov felt its bony power and rough calluses. He'd never expected to see at Farid's this harmonious and agile Anfilogov, wearing an ironed checked shirt that looked like it had been overstitched with cotton wool and camouflage trousers held up by a well-polished belt; even less had he expected the professor to turn out to be the very same Vasily Petrovich (the elite just called him Petrovich) people said was on business terms with the Stone Maiden and impervious to her inhuman enchantment because he was impervious to enchantment in general. They also said Vasily Petrovich had more money than that other wholesaler who had skipped to Israel to cut the Riphean stones he had from the rock hounds.

Apparently Anfilogov, too, was planning a trip into the field. His serious backpack, which he'd placed next to the expedition equipment that filled the dark, mirrorless corridor, was the ideal backpack. A little later the professor addressed Farid, pointing to the confused Krylov with his eyes.

"This one going?"

"No. Helping," Farid answered deferentially as he stirred a thick layer of swollen pelmeni in a purple pot.

"And he's okay?" Anfilogov continued his questioning after a little while.

"Quite."

"I see," the professor took a drag on the lady's cigarette he'd taken from his chest pocket, something he never did at the university. "Making any money?"

"Mmm . . ."

Farid was shoveling food onto the cracked plates offered him on all sides, and the smokers, airing out the layers of tobacco smoke with the outside cold coming through the window, filed into the other room. Krylov definitely did not understand what had piqued Vasily Petrovich's sudden interest in his person. Downing his burning hot portion at the far edge of the table, which was bending not under the plates but from the elbows of the noisy crowd, Krylov, modest guest that he was, walked over to Farid's display cases and there for the umpteenth time fell under the spell of the sleeping substance, the futuristic architecture of the druses, which scarcely let in the muffled electric light, which was inadequate for the room. While Krylov was standing there, Anfilogov loomed up behind him for a minute, perfectly silent, and appeared in the glass, like a hologram trapped inside, with his sleek curved nose and distinct shirt checks; it seemed to Krylov that the professor was just about to tap him on the shoulder—but instead he moved away and disappeared.

★ ★ ★

Later Krylov decided Vasily Petrovich's curiosity about him was nothing special. Anfilogov liked people and knew how to organize them, choosing them for himself wherever he found them, on the basis of characteristics that for the professor were absolutes. A group had formed around him that was structured completely differently from the rock hounds. Even though the professor brought a lot of people together, he never got chummy; by introducing people, he became not a bridge between them but an impenetrable barrier. Subconsciously, everyone was well aware that before understanding each other they had to figure out Anfilogov—which was precisely what they could never do.

The professor's system was founded on an artistic conspiracy in which the professor had natural proclivities evidently akin to mathematical and to some extent musical ones. You could visit Anfilogov on business for years and assume your partners, whom you met regularly in the entryway, were the professor's neighbors. The pseudo-residents somehow looked more convincing than the real ones—downtrodden supernumeraries in that recognizable kind of clothing that says it's been produced in the same invariable form by the same factories for twenty years. This curious contrast, had anyone noticed, gave you a sense of Anfilogov's inner makeup: he was trying to control reality by replacing it partially with something transitory, fantastic even.

By gofering (delivering nearly empty envelopes containing tiny objects that poked through the paper, like thumbtacks, in their lower corner to an old foreign woman who looked like a pirate's parrot), young Krylov gained entrée to the professor's quarters; the proportions of his sole room, where the professor, aristocratically not recognizing kitchen seating, received his pupil, reminded him of a construction site office. This real estate obviously did not correspond to Anfilogov's financial means. The rumors meant nothing, of course, but at the professor's Krylov saw with his own eyes a wallet that had so many dollars in it that at first Krylov mistook it for a thick book. It was no stretch to conclude that Anfilogov was setting funds aside, probably for a future abroad.

Meanwhile, the professor's past, embodied in his beat-up iron cot, which looked like a pregnant dachshund, and his old-man dishes with the gray fillets where the gilt used to be, became more and more entrenched as a result of their owner's thrift. It was as if the decrepit cups and saucers, having survived their set, would never break or get lost, and the small change that had petrified on the bookshelf like a trilobite would never be spent. Something told young Krylov that the past *doesn't lose time* and soon no monetary levers would be capable of launching Anfilogov into a bright future.

Their conversation took place in a perfectly human if perhaps not intimate setting. The professor served his pupil very strong, resinous tea that turned bitter the moment it cooled. The host himself poured four spoonfuls of sugar into his outsize mug, but instead of stirring, swirled the drink around and slurped it in layers until he got to the thick sweetness at the bottom. When Krylov tried to do the same, he discovered that the bottom mixture tasted like fresh blood. Gradually he told Anfilogov the story of his childhood enthusiasm for famous diamonds and the magical crystals in the museum. The professor listened attentively, although he looked straight past Krylov, as if he were listening to the radio, not a guest in his room. In return (over the course of several months) the professor showed Krylov his legendary collection, which he kept not in display cases, like at Farid's, but in cardboard banana and cigarette cartons that buckled under the weight.

A glimpse of the first examples (the battered side of the box pulled out from under the cot broke away completely) told Krylov that he was looking at something very specific. By then he already knew something about the laws of crystal formation and their resemblance to living nature, which was expressed in their feeding and growth. Anfilogov's collection was a cabinet of curiosities—a collection of freaks in an altered habitat. Here Krylov saw products of all the unfavorable conditions and crippling events in the life of a crystal. The hellish tightness of subterranean cavities, the sprinklings of pyrite and other parasites that suffocate the mother crystal and provoke multi-headed growth, the super-immobility of the nutrient medium that produces "starved" skeletal forms that look like fish frames—all this brought into the world bizarre objects that only the loving knowledge of a specialist could serve as an explanatory mirror. Krylov looked at one grotesque druse after another where you could see the eternally frozen, tortured struggle of crystal embryos, the geometric tragedy in the crystal's milky haze; predatory crystals with their victim inside—replaced by a crystal-phantom left only in the form of a hologram, a transparent wedge; crystals with fissures, in various stages of regeneration, resembling swollen joints or viscously glued ice cubes. Krylov saw a petrified cinema that demonstrated the struggle between the oriented field of the crystal, its unimaginably slow rocket launch, accomplished in its own time, into space, and the chaos of *horizontal* events and ordinary time crumbled into small coarse bits.

It wasn't hard to realize how valuable Anfilogov's cabinet of curiosities was. Such expressive rarities were valued highly by collectors, so there was an entire fortune gathering dust under the professor's cot. The nature of the collection might make someone suspect the professor of a psychotic break, a gemological variation on sadism; however, to Krylov he seemed more like a medical man collecting instances of pathology while bearing in mind the ideal of health: the faultless, energetically optimal crystalline individual. In the struggle between order and chaos, Anfilogov was obviously on the side of order. Meanwhile, his freaks, preserved in deep pockets lined with soft nests of tissue paper, also had something inexpressively touching about them; the small zones of transparency in their stocky, Siamese, dystrophic bodies were like their incredible souls. Krylov managed to get his idea about the souls across to the professor. Anfilogov looked at his student with detached surprise, and for a while his eyebrows wandered over his forehead in perfect freedom.

"Show me your hands," he suddenly demanded in his examination voice.

Mechanically, in the same ritual gesture of an adolescent showing his parents or class monitor that his hands are clean, Krylov showed the professor his not very clean hands, where the lifelines were like the iris pattern on the wings of a cabbage-white butterfly. Anfilogov took a look and for some reason actually gave them a squeeze, feeling the tautest, most sensitive vein in his right wrist.

"That's just fine," he said at last. "Now I see. Oh, all right. It's time the young man got down to business. The day after tomorrow we're going on a little excursion. I hope you understand that I'm taking a nondisclosure statement from you. We'll see whether anything comes of it." After which the professor drummed rhythmic codes on different surfaces for a while, chuckling archly.

3

★

THE EXCURSION TOOK PLACE A WEEK LATER. ANFILOGOV LED KRYLOV, who was so excited he had put on his first hundred-dollar tie in his life, to a square earthen courtyard surrounded on all sides by sodden buildings from the century before last. In the entryway where Anfilogov graciously directed his excursionist, what remained of marble steps, now worn nearly straight through, led to the upper floors, but next to it was a steel door to a half-cellar equipped with an ordinary apartment doorbell. The professor pressed the button and looked around in amusement at Krylov, who had already rubbed his stiff jacket sleeve in the yellow lime.

The door was opened by a bouncy fatman on the top of whose head a tender bald spot shone like the moon in a curly cloud; none of the stuffy secondhand stores that later came to know the owner would have recognized their glum acquaintance in this fresh little man.

"Tax man?" the fatman slid his cheerful glance over the embarrassed Krylov, at which the professor spread his hands comically and sighed contritely. "I'm joking!" roared the little fatman, and without waiting for anyone else, he burst into laughter.

Very quickly, the little fatman locked the combination of locks behind the arrivals and skipped down the narrow iron staircase; at the very bottom, Krylov heard nagging, gnawing noises interspersed with a light tremor—the sounds of stone polishing. Then he felt an unpleasant vibration on his lips, like a fine and rough sound-dust, and he licked his lips nervously.

The place they had brought Krylov to, slapping him on the shoulder, was, as he immediately guessed, a private gemcutting workshop. He had never seen gemcutting before, and the contraptions at which two workers with identically protruding ears were cutting pieces of malachite scored with complex lines looked like pedal-operated sewing machines. Next to them, staying moist in a steel tub, grinding wheels and the items firmly fastened to them were spinning, sputtering like coals. It was warm in the room and damp, like in a cooling bathhouse, and the gemcutters were wearing sweaty T-shirts and canvas aprons, their wet, smoke-dried necks tensed as the effort of man and machine were applied to the piece. Amid all this, Krylov looked like a newly minted graduate. For some reason he had thought when he was getting ready to go with Anfilogov that he was being taken to get to know the old foreign woman better, that it would be somewhere sophisticated, fancy coffee with cinnamon, a kiss for the old woman's knobby hand, a conspiratorial conversation.

The next room differed markedly from the previous one. Here it was relatively clean. In front of the gemcutters in white, fairly fresh coats, equipment was laid out that reminded him of a cross between an antediluvian record player and a schoolboy's microscope. The worn discs spun, waltzing over the bald patches, and the faceted dies held to them by hand extracted a hissing, strangely hypnotic music. Around the "turntable" lay—and stood—many curious small objects; glancing over the nearest shoulder, Krylov saw in a box two half-cut, felinely lazy, golden beryls. He realized immediately what those "tacks" in the Anfilogov envelopes had been.

Meanwhile Anfilogov, silently parting his lips, which looked like they'd been elastic-taped together, was saying something in an impenetrable drone and nudging Krylov through a side door, where he found a small, smoking-cum-coffee room and the extremely slovenly makings for coffee or tea. Two gemcutters were concentrating in the corner over three dueling bottles of beer; many other bottles had been set on the floor, like captured chess pieces. They glanced simultaneously at the two men entering with their wet pink eyes and then exchanged looks and disciplinedly moved out, from which

Krylov concluded that the conversation between the partners was going to be financial.

Vexation battled inside Krylov with the foretaste of changes to come. He no longer regretted the abortive society event; a presentiment was ripening in him that he was being offered a chance to do something about his unfortunate inexperience here and now. Therefore he sat patiently, squeezing his toes in his inappropriate dress shoes and trying not to kick over the empty bottles. Meanwhile, the partners were indeed wrapped up in finances, every so often showing each other their calculators, which evidently came out with different numbers. The more cheerful Anfilogov became, the gloomier the little fatman got; he kept missing the little buttons with his curly-haired index finger. Finally, they finished their calculating, and money was handed from Anfilogov to his partner, bypassing the table and observation. Then the fatman, with the important look of a bream which has just had the hook taken from its mouth, turned his entire short body toward his young visitor.

"I guess you're not the tax man," he said resentfully, staring at Krylov's iridescent tie. "What makes you think your young friend has talent?"

"He has a feel for stone," the professor responded briefly, scratching the soft cellophane off a packet of lady's cigarettes.

"Can he do anything at all?"

"Not a damn thing," Anfilogov was unflappable.

"That's just great!" exclaimed the little fatman. "I'm not running a trade school here! I have people working for me with special training! Tremendous experience!"

"Nothing but old men," remarked Anfilogov, wiggling his eyebrows. "Not only that, they're drunks." He glanced expressively under the table, where there was a sudden loud crash of glass.

"Oh, all right, all right," the fatman spun around, avoiding the glass spilling underfoot. "But he's going to practice on your raw material!"

"Do you have any other?" Anfilogov asked slyly, delicately tapping his ash, like a bright little bird dropping, into a mossy sardine tin.

At this the little fatman squinted for a minute, there was a pause, and in it Krylov sensed that the man was worried and that it had been pointless today to put on this woolen suit. Warm droplets were trickling down, tickling his skinny ribs. Nonetheless, even here, behind solid doors, the hoarse sounds of production plugged up his hearing, and the arguing men, literally looking each other in the mouth, sounded inside out, each in his own balloon. For a while Krylov heard snatches, "Abrasive's expensive nowadays!" "The lease agreement . . ." "You never set me those terms . . ."

Suddenly, outside, an ear-splitting mechanical ultrasound switched off, thereby revealing itself. In the ensuing clarity, the offended fatman shuffled through his papers, and the quietly beaming professor coughed distinctly.

"Oh, all right, all right, you talked me into it," the workshop owner stated mournfully. "Only he has to practice without pay. I won't pay him a salary for four months."

Krylov did not like this at all, but he told himself, "We'll see about that."

Inhaling through his little mouth, the workshop owner reached for the bell on the soiled wall and somewhere on the premises it sounded like a fire alarm had gone off. The chubby door flung open, letting in an angry sound like a motorcycle racing past and also one of the beer-drinking gemcutters—a powerful, slope-shouldered muzhik covered with oily patches of sweat and with a large, saddle-like face.

"Come in, come in, Leonidich," the workshop owner, who had slumped on his chair and undone his belt, welcomed him with malicious glee. "Since you've stopped by, I have a new pupil for you."

Krylov half-stood and leaned forward slightly, depicting a half-bow.

"What for? I don't need one," Leonidich said in a surprising tenor without even looking at the proffered Krylov. Instead he looked at the beer bottles, his own and the other alternately.

"We have no choice, Leonidich, none at all," the little fatman responded in a Jesuitically kind voice, scratching his raised buttons. "My investor gave the order, and there's nothing we poor folk can do."

"Come now, Leonidich, please," the professor interposed gently. "The young man has talent, you'll thank me yourself later."

"Oh we're already very grateful," the gemcutter grumbled and glanced covertly at the grinning Krylov. "Well, let's go, let's get that suit of yours good and dirty so you don't put it on again."

★ ★ ★

Krylov's training was longer and harder than the professor had supposed. After lectures—and sometimes instead of them—he would pad over to the workshop, stubborn and unpaid; in the evenings his head, which had soaked up the grinding, polishing, and other noises he no longer heard, hurt like hell, like he had a bad flu. Krylov irritated everyone by talking so loudly, as if he'd gone deaf. His seriously diminished mother was insulted by her son's shouting; realizing that Krylov never had become a big-time criminal, she now spoke to him much more freely. To his own amazement, Krylov felt sorry for her. When she came home from work utterly beat (ever since his mother had been let go from the museum, long ago, Krylov had no idea where she worked from nine to five—and he never did find out), this woman, who was nearly an old lady by now, had struggled to take the shoes off her swollen feet, which looked like bear paws, and would rest for a long time in the hall on the low stool opposite the half-bad mirror.

"You yell at me like your father," she reproached Krylov. "You're like two drops of water."

At the workshop Krylov was saddled with the clumsy nickname "Taxman." "Where's that Taxman of ours?" "Taxman's cutting something." At first Krylov thought the reason for this was his uselessness to his boss, who depended on the professor and had been forced to accept the pupil to pay some additional "tax." The workers—who really were old men for the most part, at least Krylov thought they were, taking their red wrinkles for signs of pension age—took pleasure in sitting back, taking a shot at this "representative" of the ill-loved structures, "Taxman, get us some beer!" Soon, though, Krylov realized he was doing more good than harm: having learned the simplest operations, he deftly cut the material marked off by Leonidich and was better than anyone at cleaning the sticky tar off a half-faceted stone. Nonetheless, the fatman, who paid his gemcutters monthly according to some homemade register as fake as a thirteen-ruble bill, carefully avoided Krylov.

Krylov wasn't stupid, and he realized how much he could be asking for. A veteran of the Oriental Mart, not that long ago he would have slashed someone's face over the least kopek. Here, though, at the workshop, he oddly had no thought of money whatsoever. Entranced and strangely indifferent to his own life outside the half-cellar walls, Krylov could spend any amount of time at his stonecutting. When he ground away a "window" in a dirty, shapeless piece of rainbow quartz, all that interested him was what he saw inside: *transparency* in its natural state, a zone where the substance turned clear. Plunging the stone into the immersion fluid achieved a truly poetic effect: as it sunk in the oily substance, disappearing from view, the crystal was *bared* as only a transparent thing can be. What happened was what Krylov had not been able to achieve in smashing his aunt's vase on the newspaper shreds: the transparency opened up from within and slipped the bounds of its own vessel—the internal inclusions and fissures, sometimes like fragile metal insects, became visible right in the crystal glass, like in an X-ray.

Thus Krylov conjured, without a care in the world. Outside the workshop he didn't like the fact that his gofer spot under Anfilogov—and the little bit of pocket money, too, probably—had gone to the rather crafty, freckled Kolyan, whom he hadn't known before. His unconcern did not leave Krylov entirely, however, when he left the half-cellar. As he climbed into the courtyard (the winter was damp and snowless), he saw the green earth under the trees—although if you looked at the lawns, in between the cold trash shining in the sun, you wouldn't find a single live blade of grass where the mirage was, and the trees themselves, covered with some membranous vegetative perspiration, looked like malachite. Krylov guessed that things like this could take the place of money for a man, that there were quite a few things like that around. So he didn't vie with Kolyan, although he found his new friend's smile, accompanied by the sniffing of his insolent straw mustache, mocking.

"Taxman's" almost daily presence obviously irked the workshop owner. Krylov guessed that the fatman didn't much believe in his apprenticeship or special talents but thought that Anfilogov had foisted a snitch on him. They were leery of Krylov. Absorbed with his transparencies, he sensed that much more was going on behind him than in front of him, which was awkward and unpleasant, like going around in a suit he'd put on backwards. Dubious individuals snuck around behind his back, dousing him with sharp smells that were only intensified by the desire to go unnoticed. Put a cap of invisibility on a hard head like that and he probably would have stunk like an invisible garbage can.

Life at the workshop never actually stopped; Krylov's peripheral vision was constantly picking up spectral manipulations. In fact, he'd long since taken careful note of all his boss's business acquaintances—who were also fat, or at least inclined to chubbiness—a kind of living catalog, from slight pudginess (a face like a liter of milk) to a sport of nature. Accustomed to showing up at the workshop as if it were their home, these specimens would start hollering merrily first thing; even though their shout could barely be heard—each word was immediately wiped out by the production noises—the boss would get scared and with a wagging motion point the stealth "taxman" out to the visitor, who would immediately slap his splayed fingers over his talking; his alarmed eyes would blink, and looking as if he had a full mouth, he would slink behind the worried boss into the secluded smoking room.

The gravity with which the fatman treated his own secrets made him perfectly manageable, but his attempt to keep Krylov in this unpaid scut work came to naught. The merest raised eyebrow on Anfilogov, and asymmetrical Leonidich, whose sad eyes with the down-turned corners were streaked with an unhealthy gold and blood, allowed Krylov to work independently with inexpensive rock crystal.

Once all the excess had been amputated, the stone became ridiculously small; the piece left for graduated faceting reminded Krylov of a jelly-filled chocolate.

"Don't make them big. Make them precise," Leonidich taught him, and he ran the piece over the coarse abrasive, leaving just the "jelly." "Don't worry about the waste," he advised, squinting at the future piece, which shone opposite the little window as if it were its window, a small copy. And sighing he added incomprehensibly, "Don't worry about anything at all."

Leonidich was not Krylov's friend; in point of fact, teacher and pupil had a hard time adjusting to working side by side. Both were too angular, their elbows clashed, and each needed more individual space than any fatman. Nonetheless, Krylov liked his teacher—the fact, for example, that Leonidich shaved so carefully, smoothing his long cheeks to a chalk-white cleanliness. This was important in a workshop, where words were mostly lip-read; unlike the bearded and mustached gemcutters, whose speech rustled like fingers in mittens, Leonidich's narrow mouth, which looked lightly touched with chalk, moved perfectly distinctly, allowing Krylov to read what he said all the way across the room.

In the beginning, the apprentice made all the typical novice mistakes. Out of some morbid loyalty to what was transparent, Krylov laid out the defects directly under the surface of the stone—and then Leonidich would give a little wink and scratch a silvery scale across the polished surface with his nail. If he rushed, the apprentice might find that the polished stone had been scratched up, as if a cat had clawed it, by the sand of the coarse abrasive. Stones split, cracked under heat, and shrank askew in the resin. Krylov's hands seemed to be working somewhere very far from his head. Most importantly, he couldn't seem to get the diamond's proportions. His stones came out dull, "asleep," leaden. With multiple sighs, Leonidich would pick up the "button," reduce the height of the pavilion, and with light cauterizations to the circle bring out the facets: a flash, and the stone was shining and laughing. Krylov crammed the facet angles like his multiplication tables. Gradually he learned to do his work, except that it was coming out a little worse than Leonidich's. Anfilogov's notions about his talent just weren't panning out.

* * *

Six months later, Leonidich died, and Krylov received a strange legacy from his teacher, maybe because it had all happened in his presence. Leonidich always carried a dumb thing—a man's puffy leatherette purse covered in gold rings for the zippers and closures—and an ugly stranger who'd been hanging around in the dark courtyard took a shine to it.

That evening the gemcutters had had a good sit over a beer. It was a little after eleven when they tumbled out, humming, into the fresh lilac-scented air. The dusk of early July was transparent. You could still hear children's voices in the courtyard, and a chubby child, his curls dangling, was being pushed in a sleepily singing swing. Leonidich, who preferred to keep to himself when he was a little drunk, in the stupor of his own halting thoughts, was walking slightly ahead, as if letting his widely planted feet measure the width of the path, which seemed to lead nowhere and be just bright patches in the gray grass. No one had time to note which direction the murderer came from. Small, with a white Adam's apple, for a second he pressed up to Leonidich as if he were trying to hide behind him from his own slow mates—and then he jumped away with a twisted face, as if Leonidich had in some horrible way betrayed the trust of the little man who had clung to him, had done something unimaginable to him, so that the stranger's features looked like a dead fly on a white wall. The little man dashed off straightaway, Leonidich slowly turned around, and his knees buckled to one side as he sank to the other.

A woman's hysterical shriek rose from a distant balcony, and the gemcutters were swept up by a sudden wind, like an intoxication, each separate at first, and then suddenly thrown together into one heavy wave. Krylov didn't know how he came to be kneeling, help-less and drunk, over Leonidich. Leonidich hadn't died yet but had turned oddly away from Krylov, smiling, showing his dingy teeth. Thick blood was gushing from under his ribs, and the t-shirt on his belly looked like a lung—organic and gently blood-filled. Tissue-thin blanket covers wafted quietly overhead. With a red hand, Krylov ripped a terrycloth towel from a branch. The rough, ice-hardened towel very quickly became soft, warm, and very heavy, as only a rag that has absorbed as much blood as it can does. To Krylov, the towel seemed to weigh almost more than Leonidich himself, as if the dying master's life had seeped into the cloth—and so it was in reality.

Krylov felt nothing but detached interest, as if he were observ-ing events in a made-for-TV movie. After a short time, cars flew into the courtyard with cold flashing lights that were waning in the dusk, but neither the cops with their official faces nor the doctors walking around in white amid the jagged linen that had fallen from the branches could change a thing.

After Leonidich's death Krylov came to believe that a man's emotions are the fruit of his imagination. There was the black plas-tic body bag they bundled Leonidich in. There was the dark track from the removed body, like a doused campfire. Where were his emotions, though? Not a trace. Meanwhile, it turned out that Leonidich had a family. Everyone had assumed that Leonidich lived a solitary life in some bachelor lair where the front door had torn oilcloth upholstery and an ax hanging on the back. But they said their farewells to the gemcutter in a spacious apartment fitted from floor to ceiling with rows of venerable, well-worn books. His tow-haired children sat quietly in one of the long rooms, and under her mourning scarf, the darkened face of his widow, who was smoothly carrying heaping plates from the kitchen, was silver.

After Leonidich's murder everything seemed to take a step back. Krylov couldn't shake the feeling that the world around him had more to do with the dead man than with Krylov himself. At the same time he suspected that his presence at the unexpected death had changed him in some way. Right when Krylov was balancing Leonidich's blood—not yet dormant, still alive, still eager to flow and pulse—in his arms like a newborn babe, something jumped from Leonidich to him. Not to say that Leonidich was such an unusually talented gemcutter, but some immortal element of his that contained the necessary ingredients suddenly merged with the potential that slumbered in Krylov's subconscious.

Krylov quickly figured out that he had been struggling with the cunning ways of his equipment, whereas his true instrument was the *transparency* that refracted the light. It felt as if he had shifted the lever from his left to his omniscient right hand; four days after Leonidich's funeral he presented the fatman with his first independently cut oval diamond—which now possessed the very characteristic optical brilliance, as complex as a drawing of a bird's feathering, that made Krylov's diamonds instantly recognizable in every set Anfilogov spirited out via his clandestine and highly profitable channels.

Suddenly Krylov felt he had been set free from the facet tables. Now, the moment he put a piece of raw material up to the lamp reflector he understood its inner structure the way a mathematician understands a simple theorem; he could see the future piece lying inside, like the pit in a strangely skewed fruit—and immediately guessed the turns that would draw out its transparency. Color zonality was no problem for him—more a puzzle on the thickening of the clarified substance, so that behind Krylov's back people started saying the gemcutter was using some special treatment to color the stones. Krylov paid no attention whatsoever to tiny defects; the stone itself winked its motes out, like an eye. In its large inclusions and fissures he saw the history of the crystal's development, its own unique system of light-bearing nerves.

Once he had mastered the art of faceting and then carving, he never indulged in those venous, vegetative effects on oddball stones favored by Riphean craftsmen, who carved leaves and berries in them in naïve imitation of woods and gardens. Krylov chose only large, transparent crystals to work on and manufactured a collection of specters, many of which were virtual portraits of real people. Now he looked on a stone's defects as the emotional state of these transparent beings. He even had Anfilogov with a cloudy patch on his forehead, and several of the grotesquely fat men of his boss's acquaintance, and a little Leonidich, who looked like a wet icicle. One of the workshop owner's acquaintances, an imposing man with a bosun's beard and a face like a flounder in a bony bathing suit, took a look at the collection one day and immediately tried to lure Krylov over to Granite, his funeral business, tempting the gemcutter not just with money but with the creative possibilities, inasmuch as the firm was erecting illustrated lanes of criminal renown, with monuments in polished suits and burly colonnades amid the micaceous cemetery birches. The moment Anfilogov got wind of this, he invited his pupil over for some more tea-drinking. After examining Krylov closely across the table, the professor offered his protégé a cut—a percentage of every stone Krylov worked on from Anfilogov's personal stash.

Part Three

★

1

★

THE STORY ABOUT TO BE TOLD TOOK PLACE TEN YEARS AFTER THE events already described. Professor Anfilogov, understandably, was still around. He never did quit his permanent residence for some more pleasant country—maybe because he still hadn't amassed sufficient funds, but more likely because he didn't want to retire.

All his old things still served him well and were by now irreplaceable. The main thing Anfilogov had acquired in all these years was a round aquarium with quite ordinary fish which sometimes, due to his ignorance, pecked each other to death, sending up clouds and twitching their tails amid the tender underwater bushes. The professor kept his largest stones, whose light refraction was close to the index for water, in the aquarium: the stones vanished, a slight optical colic on the bottom's round, flat stones. The implacable fish got used to the huge whooshing object that made bubbles in the water; plucking out the raw treasures, the professor's paw, pasted with wet fur, left the fish's element unsettled and murky, like soup that's boiled—and only the water's indignant expression, which lasted several hours, might tell a potential thief that the aquarium served its owner as an optical safe.

Something may have happened in the world of mountain spirits. It had been several years since they had displayed any unease, scaring rock hounds with cold campfires where food that had just been boiling hot suddenly turned ice cold, covered by a layer of grease, or, more rarely, with a strange illumination that filtered out at night from secluded folds in the land, as if someone were secretly reading a very big book under the earth's blanket. Old forest back roads with ruts like breeding grounds for waterfowl, where peaceful ponds slept back to back, would be blocked off by the fresh trunk of a cracked aspen; sometimes a tree would suddenly fall a few paces from a walking man who had just barely caught the mounting leaf noise, as if someone had splashed water from a giant bucket.

Chinks had probably formed in the coarse, depleted surface layer of the Riphean world. Disturbing rumors went around among the rock hounds. Once again legends were revived about the native gold on the Kylva River, which a hundred years before had been rich with gold that had vanished overnight, making its presence felt only in the yellow metallic sheen of the river surface. Talk revived about kimberlite pipes in the northern Ripheans; diamonds started trickling in from there, small ones, but at least VS1 pure: Krylov recognized them by their characteristic "Cape" tint, as if a little iodine had been dissolved in the stone, and by the unusual sparkle of the resulting diamond, which literally doubled before your very eyes under shifting light angles. They had assumed that Makar-Ruz, a modest ruby deposit in the northern Ripheans, was merely a dim likeness of what was supposed to exist farther south, and more accessible. Every rock hound knew that a high-class ruby was worth more than a cut diamond of the same quality, carats, and purity, so the latest rumor had had an especially disturbing effect. Even the unflappable elite succumbed to the bracing fever that had diffused in the air.

Fifty-year-old Roma Gusev—no longer a menacing warrior but the sentimental grandfather of a six-month-old grandson, the driver of a frisky blue stroller with little bells—was the first to make the observation, which stunned many because it was so obvious. He commented that many of the Riphean places where the deposits anticipated by their geological "address" were clean gone had in recent years been acquiring a visible authenticity, a density of vegetative, animal, and fish life. The impression was as if hundreds of square kilometers had existed in the form of copies, with intentionally decorative cliffs and trash accumulating in the ferns. Now where there had been old clearings overgrown with small-time twisty foliage suddenly full-grown cedars had risen up with long needles extended in a fist like a luxurious pelt; tall elk with pensive faces crossed busy tracts in places they shouldn't have been. The rusty frames of abandoned equipment would suddenly disappear (returning a few hours later, though). In their place for a short time there would be visions: untouched hollows with languid, almost sleepy greenery drunk on lungwort; mysterious forest glades, gilded swamps, and mossy tree trunks like tenacious roots on chicken legs.

To prove that the phenomena did in fact exist, Gusev showed his comrades cedar cones impregnated with tar and insanely fragrant with life that had supposedly been picked up on the Kylva, where the rich primeval forests had been cut down long ago and gravel pits that looked like gigantic ashtrays collected dust on the lower bank. The cones weren't gold nuggets, of course; nonetheless Anfilogov heard Gusev out very carefully. Anfilogov's sole error was his presumptuous attitude toward the Riphean world. The professor perceived its beauty as a powerful but irrelevant irritant, a test of his nerves; he was appeased by *forgeries* of beauty that were for the most part acquired in the artificial urban environment. Nonetheless, the professor was prepared as always to set out on an expedition—to go where the usual Riphean logo disappeared and the scenes rose up that Roma Gusev had talked about with the old gleam in his mad, darting little eyes, as he squeezed the soft lumps of his fists—an old habit.

★ ★ ★

No one knew about the first expedition for gem-quality corundums; even Krylov was told that the professor was flying to Prague for a Slavic seminar. In the summer of 2016, Anfilogov and the inseparable and hardy Kolyan moved upstream along the bank of a cataracted river whose name they subsequently never told a soul. The river, boiling and thundering, unreeled like fabric from a flattened core on a shop counter. Like any stream in its position, it served the surrounding geological firmament like a small blood vessel carrying all the elements that comprised its banks. In the same way the river's bottom was the rock that made up the long, deep notch, which was gloomily overgrown with bluish spruce, with rare deciduous spots over its sunken slopes, and with the asymmetrical outline of the main mountain, which looked like a scowling brow. The work consisted of endlessly washing the sandy and rocky slurry. The water's harsh cold squeezed their rubber boots and fell on their necks and hot sweat, and stinging midges landed, despite their puffing and splashing. It was deserted; only one time, thoroughly drenched kayakers came galloping by in their diving catamarans, concentrating hard.

It was the eleventh day of their secret expedition. Kolyan, who had caught a cold and was armed with a wide aluminum mug, threw some coarse, soggy grain into it, added water, swirled the heavy suspension with a wet slosh and then poured the grumbling slush into the cloudy stream. The bottom of the mug was left with stripes of black basalt pebbles, brown granite chips edged in crimson flecks, and white and rust-colored grains of quartz with mica flecks. Lifting his mosquito net, Kolyan pecked at his catch and, not finding anything interesting, chucked it out. At that time, Anfilogov was roaming over the crunching pebbly shoal, sorting stones, which on top were hot and blue from the bright sky and underneath were damp and had a dark quartz ice. Gathering suitable samples in his sack (he looked for cheesy spots), the professor split them on a boulder that jutted its brow bullishly in the white stars produced by the professor's hammer. The muffled stone tapping skipped up vertically and seemed like the only sound in the whole white intense blue, with the windy noise of the water spread out below and the barely audible drone of Esmark's cod.

From a distance Anfilogov saw Kolyan suddenly freeze over his sluicing assembly, as if he suddenly intended to gobble up its sieved contents. But Kolyan skeptically examined the tiny fragment that had suddenly glittered in the loose sediment like a triangle of crimson fire. Assuring himself that this had to be his imagination, he cautiously plucked the stone out with his cold-crippled blue fingers. Leaving the curved saucer on a humpbacked stone, which the sleepy water embraced like a pillow as it fell over it, he freed his waterproof field watch from his sleeve and scratched it. A distinct white scratch formed on the tempered glass—and an odd feeling passed through Kolyan, as if were unreal above the knees.

Tugging at his stuffy nose, he rowed his boat-like boots toward the shoal, as the professor, utterly calm, walked toward him. He was vivid and small in the harsh sun, as if he were wearing silver chocolate wrappers.

"Vasily Petrovich! Look! Vasily Petrovich!" Breathless, Kolyan was showing Anfilogov the blinding watch face when he was still far away.

"So what? I see it's half past two," said the professor coldly, as he tried to quiet his straitened heart under his burning jacket.

"Just a sec, look here." Breathing from his warm, foolishly mustached mouth on the proffered sliver, he flicked it again: across the pale first line now lay another, fresh one.

"Aha," said the professor. And that sounded rather foolish as well.

"It's a corundum, Vasily Petrovich. A ruby even! Gem quality!" Kolyan cautiously unclenched his raw fingers, to which the vivid triangular crumb had stuck. Instantly a gust of wind carried the crumb off, and Kolyan, his soaking wet boots slapping, rushed for the shingle.

"A fine way to waste your time!" Anfilogov shouted from above, and Kolyan, spitting away his mosquito net, obediently got up from all fours. "You won't find it anyway," the professor said conciliatorily. "And there's no need. The corundum was brought here from upstream somewhere. We'll go up and take a look."

Anfilogov had had a piece of dolomite with a large corundum spot that looked like broken chalk loose in his pocket, softly striking his leg, since the day before yesterday. The professor hadn't told

Kolyan of his find, afraid of sharing his joy, as always, and hiding his heart, which all this time had responded to the weight of the sample with the same weight and angularity, as if there were two stones, one in his chest and one in his pants pocket.

All the next week the expedition moved upstream along the ever-diminishing river, which was rapidly releasing its spring water, which first pooled up, as in a spoon, in a small natural backwater, then darted away, as if forking over a glittering bend, onto the shallow, rocky slope. On the sandbars they were constantly finding white pieces of host rock scattered with corundums, from which they were able to take a few slightly fissured tabular crystals, valuable only as collector samples. However, the white veins in the leeward granite, sometimes glittering like sugar cubes, sometimes like an old mark on worn asphalt, turned up empty. Now and again the two men, bathhouse red from the bites of the flickering midges, would climb away from the river over the slopes and crawl through close-set spruce whose dried lower branches caught at their tough pants like files. Anfilogov was interested in the upper outcrops of bedrock granite; sometimes, after disturbing the felt-like moss with his miner's hack, he would see the same worthless veins, which ran, like mysterious paths, from bank to bank and then onward, into subterranean oblivion. The river continued to be a source of hope; where it flowed from and where the expedition was now heading, there was a blue and not always noticeable but at the same time terribly *memorable* fold in the horizon, as if something had been pushed up close together there, face to face.

Anfilogov had a sense that the events that had begun with the find of the first corundum spot were developing a definite rhythm; his dream was coming true (although at the last, or even any moment, it might simply not). Anfilogov was calm, even though he lived every minute with a heightened emotional pressure, which balanced out the pressure from the oversaturated outdoor environment. Kolyan was rushing desperately, as fast as he could, into the river's upper reaches, and he was willing to abandon anything he was doing halfway; often, in town, standing at the tram stop, he would keep glancing at his steel watch, which was decorated with memorable scratches. Anfilogov knew they shouldn't rush. He had gone over this exact same scenario in his imagination many times, from the first signal find to the semi-precious vein as rich as a vegetable patch, and just as many times his imagination had broken off abruptly, anticipating the crushing of his dream. Now that his dream was unfolding in real time, he had to maintain his awareness of reality and only reality, and not let himself get one step ahead of himself. He couldn't explain this to Kolyan, who had become feverish, a bundle of nerves. His internal haste had made him voracious; Anfilogov, however, having listened closely to the rhythm of events, ordered that they economize on food. Now at their halts the rock hounds made do with a thin broth that was half-dried soup or fat noodles with occasional slivers of tinned meat. Sometimes Kolyan was lucky and caught slender minnows dancing like moths on his line from the stream; the fish were so tiny that all that remained of them in the boiling ukha was their skeletons, which looked like safety pins.

The area they were entering possessed precisely the characteristics Gusev had described. On one hand, this was good, because it spoke to the accuracy of their route; on the other hand, the undaunted Anfilogov felt himself on the brink of a serious depression. Beauty was pouring over him from all directions. Anfilogov scooped it up when he wanted to make dinner, out of the smiling river; sunlight fell on Anfilogov through this beauty—through the branches, through invisible aerial nets—and the sun itself was transformed from the ordinary natural lamp you don't look at into the focus of the beauty, a radiant object that irritated the nerves. The locale was infected, not to say irradiated, with beauty. White nights had come here, to the north end of the Riphean range; the day faded infinitely, and the sky was like the nacre of an open shell—wavy, like pale mother of pearl. Then came a spectral, shadowless twilight, and the red tent turned an unusual, somehow cosmic purple, and the sleeping river frothed gently, like an infant in swaddling clothes. In spite of the infinite extension of time, air, and space, everything here, in the north, happened very quickly. One fine night, after the spring's waters had retreated to the river's banks, life blazed up everywhere. Overnight, the shoots of barely blossoming bird cherry trees went to sleep as if they'd been wound on curlers—and by four in the morning, when the sun was already beaming nonchalantly above the horizon, both banks were drowning in luxuriant white, and down the river, in its dropping rhythm, floated bands of stupefying bitter smells. Here the tiny-leafed birches, as transparent as dragonfly wings, threw out catkins, and luscious blobs of dust swallowed up by the channel bars slid over the water.

Anfilogov felt that all this was much too much for him; he, who had grown a solid but invisible shell on his face, felt as if he might start crying any minute. Never had Anfilogov felt so helpless. From time to time Anfilogov thought he was about to die in the face of this beauty, which was intangible but, nonetheless, adamant. For the first time he could understand those people who kept strictly within the confines of urban existence, the limits of the world that comes out of the human mind. Here, there was nothing manmade to intervene between Anfilogov and the elements acting on him, and he had neither book nor light for reading to fill the extensible time after his meager dinner—the hungry, soapy twilights with the river that would not die down but gleamed like a knife with traces of butter and soft rich crumbs.

★ ★ ★

On the twenty-third day, the expedition came out on a dark blue shoal as much like the spot where they had found the first transparent corundum as the footprint from a left boot is like the right; even the aerial outline of the peaks, with their blue petals of snowfields, was the same. Anfilogov experienced very strong déjà vu when he saw the granite boulder where a week before he had smashed the empty dolomite with a hammer. This time, though, on the boulder's brow was a big sloppy white mark—and the whole thing was definitely pointing to the natural fold on the frowning slope: a friable channel, run its length with clayey and sandy alluvium, with outcrops of fissured stone in which Anfilogov instantly recognized host rock strongly eroded by water.

The water had probably flowed down here in the spring, and now the stream was dry. The very first stone he picked up on the shoal was sprinkled like an Easter bun with corundum specks. It was amazing, but the stream evidently echoed the bends of the dolomite vein and for long years had done the work that the rock hounds now had to bring to a victorious conclusion with their miner's hacks and chisels. Anfilogov had virtually no doubt that he was looking at the very same "pipe" from which the alluvial placer of corundum traces flowed. His last doubts scattered when Kolyan dredged the mineral slush out of the riverbed and washed it in his capacious mug: four whole angular sparklets—the classic "blue blood" color, no less—turned his watch face into a spiky ice cube under which the blinded dial winked its second hand.

Meanwhile, according to Anfilogov's calculations, they had no more than a week to work the vein. They still had a ten-day—and in bad weather a good fifteen-day—trek down to the last outpost of civilization: a sleepy train station with a defunct store and scanty potato fields. If the professor hadn't sensed the latent rhythm of events and started economizing on time, the corundum shoal would have been the expedition's point of no return. Once they'd reached this spot—where the déjà vu behind each bush (probably explained by the extreme fulfillment of their dream)—the rock hounds would have had to return immediately with empty hands. Now they had a little wiggle room, provided by their reserve of tinned meat, condensed milk, and noodles. However, their success had to be better focused: here their artificially extended stay in this alien element could not last long, and the irritatingly real beauty—down to the last butterfly spread out on a boulder—was at the very top of the atmospheric column.

Although the expedition was still inside the same basin lightly encircled by the asymmetric mountains, Anfilogov could not shake the feeling that he and his fellow worker had in some way reached that unusual fold in the horizon, like a mismatched pattern glued together, that he had been seeing all these days in the river's upper reaches. "The edge of the world"—these were the words the professor might have used to name his sensation, even though he was standing with both feet on what was solid ground in all directions. The rock hounds wasted a precious half-day breaking camp and neatly concealing their supplies from the rodents rustling in the grass. The first blow of the miner's hack on the desolate rock broke off a piece that looked like raisin-studded farmer's cheese. The corundums, however, were not transparent: the densely sugary, rectilinear crystals did not hold a jewel gumdrop.

"Here's what I say, Vasily Petrovich. We're not going to get anything off the top," concluded a beaten Kolyan, who tossed and turned all night in their tent. Outside, a northern rain sighed and shifted like a passenger in the next compartment—the first in the whole time of the expedition.

Anfilogov, too, realized that they had to dig prospecting pits. In the morning the bowed spruce looked like dark umbrellas, saturated with damp, and the streambed, although still without water, had swollen noticeably. What was bad was that the trees on the slope were sparse and virtually everything was visible from the river. Any recreational kayaker could spot the fresh holes and become curious about their contents. Counting on his luck, Anfilogov chose a spot for the prospecting pit under cover of some small cliffs that the wind had turned into melted snowmen. However there, in the humid dark, they had as much luck as inside a turned-off refrigerator: the top, easily broken layer still taunted the frenzied Kolyan with stone raspberries, and under that they found bedrock, practically iron granite, which the miner's hack skipped off with a piping song, sending an electric arc through his shoulders.

They had to go back to the previous spot. But the vein, despite their original impressions, took a sharp turn. Only the fourth hole gave the expedition its first gem-quality stones: small, a little cloudy, not good for faceting but maybe for cabochons. Anfilogov had the feeling that somewhere close by, literally underfoot, lay true success, that the expedition was maybe a millimeter off.

The millimeter turned out to be a big one, though. The expedition lost a whole day waiting out a windy rain, which swept over their sagging tent in gusts and down the swollen river, where the water's fur seemed to stand on end at the uneasy element's blowing. After the rain, the prospecting pits were half-filled with dark, debris-filled water that had to be scooped out with the mug and bucket. Even without any precipitation, though, the fissured rock seeped moisture, which ran down the walls slowly, as if groping its way; overnight a bucket and a half of water collected in the prospecting pit. For some reason, the subterranean water was as heavy as molten lead, and when it splashed it left a dark spot in the grass that would not heal over.

The morning began with the whistle of a sugar-stealing chipmunk. Every morning Anfilogov knew for a fact that they had to leave that day, camouflaging their promising works until the next summer. Without a word to each other, though, the rock hounds would hastily eat a few spoons of floury skilly, unembarrassed about licking the sour mugs, and walk mechanically to their corundum servitude. They started in on yesterday's and the day before yesterday's like machines, as if magnetized by this strange spot, as if they'd been wound up; doing anything that was not part of this daily rhythm felt as if it would cost them much more effort than continuing to wield their hacks, burying all the weight left in their body in their blow.

Hunger crept up on them like a long French kiss. Anfilogov caught himself thinking that he had completely stopped thinking—about anything. The point when they met with success seemed to have been determined by a fateful error, and now the resources of food and life were dwindling to no purpose. "Just a little more, just a bit!" a nearly bent over Kolyan, who had been bitten under the eye by a spider, would yell to buck himself up. Periodically he would literally tear himself away from the hypnotic dolomites, bury himself behind a bush so that a grayling looking up wouldn't see the hunter's shadow through the water, and toss in a splint with a tuft of bear fur. Lured by the "fly," the graylings would soar out of the water like small northern sunbeams, but in the air their rainbow skins quickly turned pale; the rock hounds instantly tore the meat off the baked fish, down to their pink skeletons, taking turns dipping their sticky fingers into the salt tin and wiping the last sweet grain from its smooth walls.

"Once we get back, Vasily Petrovich, the first thing I'm going to do is learn to cook," mused a languid Kolyan by the damp hissing campfire. "As good as the Metropol! Cakes with roses and salads with mayonnaise. You don't think I can read a book? If only I had the ingredients."

Anfilogov, who had been left with a dead aftertaste in his mouth from the unsalted fish, well understood these culinary dreams. He himself now could have performed some magic with a good fillet, some spices, and wine; at the same time he knew that Kolyan wasn't really going to do what he said because in the last ten years he'd never learned to do anything. What Kolyan knew how to do he knew how to do by nature; as for Anfilogov, for all his experience as a businessman and rock hound, he was utterly incapable of wresting food from the wild taiga.

Meanwhile, the jokes were bad. The noodles had run out; what was left of the buckwheat groats was practically dust; and some animal had shaken out the last of the flour all over the tent, as if it had torn the cellophane with a steel fork. They hadn't had cigarettes in a long time. This didn't affect Anfilogov, who occasionally would smoke a slim Vogue exclusively for the sake of the perceptible haze in his brain, but Kolyan was miserable: he would dry rotting clumps of used tea on hardened newspapers and crawl on all fours in search of sharp grass and dry fibrous filler; this whole mess rotted poisonously in his little tubes of newspaper, as stiff as twigs; and sometimes they would flare up like a torch, singeing Kolyan's gray whiskers.

In point of fact, the rock hounds had nearly eaten up their return trip. Anfilogov knew that a man can go without food for a month and live. But that's if he's lying in a bed under the supervision of doctors and a strike committee. It was a different matter altogether to escape the taiga when thirty kilometers a day turned into ten, and later five. You just might not hold out, not coincide with your chance of survival. Anfilogov knew that hunger. Once it overtook you, it was capable of special effects: some wild spot might suddenly seem as familiar as your own summer vegetable patch. Just when you thought you were about to come upon inhabitation, you couldn't get out. Without himself knowing how, a man would eat a poisonous mushroom, which looked like the finest dessert skewered on his napkin-wrapped knife. Anfilogov knew that hunger is like hypnosis; now, waking, he could feel the first onset of this gentle trance. Every morning he thought he had decided to wrap up camp and was now doing so. Simultaneously, he felt utterly at home near his prospecting pits; hunger's kisses awakened in him a dreamy sensitivity, the desire for a woman, subtle and pale, with delicate bones that fit together into a perfect skeleton, with small teats, puffy, like children's tonsils.

2

★

THAT NIGHT, UNDER THE MUFFLED, MACHINE-LIKE SOUND OF THE rain, the professor dreamed that this woman had come to him. Naked and very skinny, she was as perfect as a Latin letter, a sample of a special human typeface. Tucking up her angular elbow, she lay on her back, and her belly was as white as a mug of milk. There was nothing special in the lizard-narrow creature, but all the beauty on the banks of the corundum river had been a preface to this body, to the maddening shadow under her breast, like a delicate half-moon. For some reason the woman was crying, her bright temples were wet, her eyes underlined with moisture, Egyptian. In his dream, these soundless tears aroused Anfilogov incredibly. At the same time he was aware that the woman was by no means a stranger to him; moreover, it was very definitely one of his distant relatives, a decent, ordinary young girl to whom Anfilogov occasionally slipped a little money and who, in thanks, dashed over to clean his inviolable apartment and once broke a delicate porcelain teacup that had lived a grand life.

Anfilogov awoke with an unresolved anguish in his loins. Tears had turned the hair under his creased cheek into a wet clump. Kolyan, sprawled out, was snoring, and his mouth gaped like a dark rabbit hole. The professor went down to the fogged-in river, where the distant bird cherry trees looked like bouquets in tissue paper. Having done the necessary with his cupped red hand, Anfilogov released a hot, luxuriant spot into the water, like the fortune-telling wax from an entire burned down candle. Then he splashed himself with fistfuls of icy water, and buttoning his pants, tried to clear his head. The beauty focused on Anfilogov was straining to achieve maximum concentration, but the professor's mind was working clearly. He understand all the hints and instructions that gave the Mistress of the Mountain away in the humanitarian girl. Even the arbitrary fact that the girl was Anfilogov's third cousin was inherent in this dangerous scenario because, according to the legend, the Mistress of the Mountain and her chosen one are seen by people as similar, like brother and sister.

This was simply too much! Anfilogov knew that there were plenty of ladies around who were much more attractive—even, if it came to that, some of his numerous female relatives. But at the thought of this schoolmarm of a woman, always dressed in crummy little sweaters and stupid jean skirts that looked like they'd been dyed with ink, his heart for some reason contracted.

After the chilling freshness of the early morning, it was as stuffy as a rubber boot in the tent. Kneeling, Anfilogov shook Kolyan, who was reedily gurgling some mosquito-y song.

"Huh? What's up? Hell, right away, I'm coming." Kolyan tried to open his cloudy, senseless eyes, opened and shut them, but just couldn't wake up.

"We're leaving today. Time's up. We've got a lot of work and a climb," Anfilogov said jerkily, dragging the twisted sleeping bag off Kolyan.

"What's wrong with you, Vasily Petrovich? Where the fuck are we going? Did you get up on the wrong side of the bed?" Kolyan tried to push the looming Anfilogov away and collapsed onto his back again.

"Where? Home! To the grocery store! You'll croak here, you idiot!" roared Anfilogov right in his small, drawn face.

"Na-a-ah. . . . Not on your life. . . . You're the one, Vasily Petrovich, you shouldn't . . ." wagging his wild head, Kolyan crawled out, got up on his shaky legs, and, as if testing which was shorter, meandered over to the wet, silver-gray bushes.

Anfilogov shrugged and dragged their two backpacks, which

were now compressed and covered with mouse droppings, out of the tent, left them there to air out, and unfastened the polyethylene fly, letting the yellow water spill onto the grass.

"I'm alive! Alive!" The shout came from the glistening bushes.

Anfilogov, trying to be unflappable, busied himself with the campfire, where the damp twigs would only smoke, not burn, and the homey stove-like smell of the campfire stirred his soul.

"I'm not croaking, Vasily Petrovich, see?" Kolyan, tottering, collapsed in the tent again, and the tent started rocking.

At last the fire was crackling, emitting blue, messy fumes, like an old engine, and the transparent water had begun to tremble in the sooty pot. Trying to figure out what to make the most satisfying breakfast possible from, Anfilogov headed toward the tent, and at the entrance his nose was struck by the smell of rotten flesh. Kolyan, kneeling in front of a savagely opened can, was chewing greasy tinned meat. At this Anfilogov realized he didn't know whether there was any tinned meat left. The hollow lightness of the sack when the professor, cursing softly, found it in the corner, left him with no illusions on that score. Kolyan, smirking in the half-dark with his glossy maw, held the can with the remains of his feasting out to the professor, but the crudely hacked lid, the sucker of congealed fat, and the putrid smell that wafted from the tin nearly made Anfilogov throw up.

Instantly, Kolyan's cheeks puffed out and he bent over completely. Anfilogov barely managed to pull him out, bowels gurgling, to the tent opening. Kolyan vomited tortuously, the unchewed meat coming out of him along with the bile of his many days' hunger. The liquefied tinned meat even spurted out of Kolyan's nostrils. At last, after long convulsions, he calmed down and, in tears, stretched out on his sleeping bag, which Anfilogov had thrown down near the quaking, almost extinguished campfire.

After making him drink some watery, almost yellow tea, Anfilogov forced Kolyan to swallow through his tears and snot another mug, into which he'd tapped the sugar dust from the empty box. Then, ordering his fellow worker to join him, he went off to camouflage the prospecting pits, which looked from the river and their camp like large dark anthills. It started to drizzle again. The sky seemed to be spraying its silver paint on the winking leaves, the moss, and the stiff bilberry bushes; the path that nonetheless was left trampled from the camp to the prospecting pits and now would give their work away to a close gaze was brighter than the dormant grass, and it reflected the raw boulders, as in a stream.

It was very quiet. The noise of the river reached them like a wind-blown stream. Suddenly Anfilogov imagined the sound change, as if the river had turned around. Simultaneously he noticed next to the first prospecting pit, which the rock hounds had long since abandoned due to the meagerness of the find, a woman's silhouette as if through tissue paper. The woman was standing under a deep umbrella, and he couldn't see her face, but Anfilogov recognized her by her slender legs and her laced boots sunk in the clay. The woman turned around very slowly and began walking uphill, where last year's leaves gleamed next to each birch, like next to a hairdresser's chair; before the creature vanished, without reaching the limit of visibility but simply dissolving in the thickening drizzle, and the birch branches whistled sharply a couple of times on the wet umbrella fabric.

Anfilogov stood there a moment collecting his thoughts. He was insulted that he was being taught an additional lesson, as if he were a little boy. Trying to walk decisively, feeling his heavy heart grow heavier with each step, he climbed up to where the Mistress of the Mountain had lingered a few minutes before. There, in the diluted clay, the traces from her heel prints were distinctly visible. Pretending as if nothing special was happening, Anfilogov descended into a hole with a small amount of scree that gurgled loudly into a large, dirt-filled puddle. Anfilogov had been planning, actually, to collect the tool he'd left on the wall—but when he grabbed the pick-ax, he mechanically struck a friable outcrop that had bothered him for some reason.

The piece of rock came off easily, like a spout off a pitcher. Unremarkable on the outside, inside it was the image of a hedgehog. Large crystals strained by their efforts at growing, stuck out crudely from the dolomite, and in the crack that had formed from the blow he could see others baked into the rock and burning a deep crimson. The next piece to come off was as red as a banged-up knee from the corundum. Behind it he discovered something absolutely incredible. Not believing his own eyes, Anfilogov let out a triumphant holler, which echoed weakly in the milky overturned space, like the far-off howl of a locomotive. He suddenly felt he couldn't hold onto the slippery pick-ax. Scrambling out of the hole over the icy, ragged rocks, Anfilogov kept shouting and felt the damp sky on his face, like an ether-saturated gauze mask. From far off he saw Kolyan running, dark in his silvery shroud, like a water-gauge on the rippling bright surface of the water. When Kolyan jumped up, plastered all over with some wet vegetative kasha, in his worn boots, Anfilogov felt a weakness come over him, as if all his blood had gone into the formation of the crimson fissure, this coagulated subterranean beauty.

What Kolyan accomplished once he had realized the dimensions of the find is something one rarely gets to see in life. He beat his chest against the stone wall and fell, slipping, into the clayey swill; he screeched; in the corundum hole he was like a wet fledgling in an eggshell. Anfilogov observed him seated on a slippery old log; he couldn't understand why this sadness had overtaken him. It felt as if as much of his soul had been ripped out of him as he had found in the corundum vein to which the woman's blunt boot tracks had led him. These distinct tracks on the difficult hillock, where Kolyan's boots left a greasy waffle, spoke to Anfilogov of his loneliness and his long waiting under the whispering drizzle that developed the landscape like a faded photograph of a watery path leading into emptiness; several times he thought he heard a recalcitrant umbrella shaving through the glossy spruces.

After a short time, Anfilogov had to shout to Kolyan not to

waste his strength on barbaric dances that had turned his clothes into a clinging peel. Coming to his senses, his insane eyes squinting toward the bridge of his nose and a cut on his forehead, Kolyan grabbed his tool. Before dinnertime, which no longer referred to a meal but merely to a time of day, he shattered the precious vein without letup, this paradisiacal subterranean tree, which to the rock hounds was one miracle after another; losing his balance over and over, thereby tumbling out of reality, he would fall into the puddle or spin around with his hack raised like a butterfly net.

As he took the crimson hunks up from below, Anfilogov wondered at their outlandish booty and then ceased to wonder at anything at all. Figures started lining up in his mind, the chains of business that now would have a serious load to withstand—but all this was an entirely other world and had nothing to do with the heart pangs that made the stones being cleaned out of the rock fade oddly right before his eyes. After "dinner"—ten minutes of sitting with bowed heads by the damp campfire—Kolyan, in his now dry, clayey armor with a Morse code of midges next to his protruding red ear, stretched out on his litter. Anfilogov set about sorting their booty, throwing out everything they had collected before. Of today's he packed away only what staggered the imagination; comparing stones, holding them between his thumb and pointer like coagulated, broken stars, he chose between the happiness of possessing them and survival on the hungry return trip, when every extra gram could be fateful. Nonetheless, he ended up with a considerable paper bag, which dragged down his framed backpack handsomely. He buttoned four crystals that on the larger scale of things would have been a sin to be let cut rather than preserved as witness to nature's incredible generosity into the pocket of his sweated-through checked shirt, and through the fabric their little angularity felt like a bird's foot on his full-to-bursting heart.

All the rest Anfilogov wrapped up in a warped scrap of polyethylene, and dragging it to the corundum pit, he dumped the raspy bundle into the jumbled vein, the way all the innards get tossed into the corpse's yellow belly after an autopsy. Leaning with exhaustion against the wall, from which groundwater was seeping like from a lymph gland, Anfilogov had the distinct feeling that his incredible find had made the place's attraction nearly insurmountable. The mysterious magnetism that had kept the expedition to the bank of the corundum river, the powerful force that each morning had put the starving muscles on their aching bones into motion, had now come so close that Anfilogov, shaking, felt a physical need to take up his work pose in front of the wrinkled corundum, red in the broken section, like crude coal. The vein demanded that the rock hounds die alive, that they burn the last calorie there was to burn in their human bodies and, emptied, remain here, so that they would always—with their dead sight—see this terrible beauty, this light mountain sketch, like a fold of transparent sky fabric, and the river, winding up under the precipice, and the dark, burnt-looking cliff granite. The obsession was so strong that time seemed to stand still for Anfilogov; deprived of the alternation of satiety and appetite, his biological clock had stopped, and the damp birds in the heavenly window opened from below seemed to be feeling out the solid air with a stuck feather.

Anfilogov was dragged out of his oblivion by a staccato splash. Of the clumps of clay that had been copiously spit out into the puddle, one turned out to be a snake: its rhombic head glistening, making long water ribbons with its invisible body, the creature was heading for the professor's chilled feet. Anfilogov immediately flew up, as if up a flight of stairs. His puckered hands swelled and ached, but his right hurt more. Bringing it to his eyes, Anfilogov saw that hanging from it, having latched on with its tiny maw, was a bat that had come from out of nowhere. There was something perversely attractive in this flimsy rag, in its tightly frowning little face, like a sinister velvety flower. The professor grimaced and tossed the creature away, and it hovered over the hole, emitting a silent SOS, and suddenly slipped from view; for a little while there was a curve in the air that looked like it had been chopped out by mad scissors, a dark hole.

There was an ulterior motive to all this, and it had to do with the Mistress of the Mountain. The forest where the specter had gone this morning had plunged into the damp whiteness, and the trees close by were distinct, but the ones that came after them looked like their unfilled-in shadows on a white wall. Distracted, Anfilogov tried to remember the name of the humanitarian girl. Irina? Inga? He thought it started with an "I." The names that collected in his mind seemed artificial. "Ekaterina," a distinct, honey-filled voice said at the professor's ear. Instantly the professor felt the charms of the corundum river recede and how much room there was everywhere. Pushing himself away from a moldering log, Anfilogov stood up and looked around. There, to the southwest, beyond the thick, furlike forests, beyond the modest, two-peak range, beyond the sleepy station with the closed store, beyond the three hundred kilometers of his humming railroad journey, in a city filled to the roofs with people figurines, there was a real woman for whom the professor was now experiencing a passionate and painful curiosity. He realized that the Mistress of the Mountain was herself dragging him out and back to life but he still couldn't imagine how he would be able to take advantage of this.

Things worked themselves out with amazing ease, though. To camouflage the prospecting pits, Anfilogov kicked down the clumps of dug clay that stuck out and immediately soaked up the ground moisture and swelled in lazy bliss, sealing the treasure; then he chopped down flexible young spruce that jumped under his ax and hid the blurred holes in the earth with a luxuriant deck of poison-green moss. After descending cautiously to the river, Anfilogov was satisfied that from the water the remains of their enterprise could barely be spotted.

The next morning the expedition, which now consisted of two millionaires, started on its way back. The wet air snuffled in stooped

Kolyan's throat and his half-empty high boots. Time and again he ran his bony hand over his back to feel the corundum sack, as solid as if it were frozen, in his backpack. Anfilogov, who was going second, had the feeling that there was someone left standing stock-still at the prospecting pit, watching the treasure's seekers leave, waiting for the expedition to drop from view. After many very approximately counted days—during which the expedition passed the first sandbar, spread with the rotted remains of blossoms, like old nets, and that rift, as indefatigable as a washing machine, beside which Anfilogov had discovered the first corundum—the professor retained the sensation that that figure had not budged once.

The rock hounds barely said a word to each other. Each plunged individually into the green images covered by leafy masses and sudden dark patches of moss. Now the beauty was only over-head, hanging in the branches, and the damp, stony path underfoot was not much to look at; perhaps because the rock hounds had over-done their prospecting pit digging, all the tottery slate slabs and granite rubble in the lean, stony dirt seemed to them just plain ugly, like a dump mercifully covered over with a thin layer of northern woods. They were moving slowly. The first apricot-speckled leaves were sliding down the river, which was now rushing in the same direction as their small detachment, and swollen branches floated by, sometimes collecting, with crablike cleverness, on the overwashed stones. All this color borne by the water gently drove the men drag-ging along the bank onward. Their bodies held absolute lightness. Only their baggage had weight—but it weighed so much that some-times they couldn't take even one step forward.

What was bound to happen did. At a spot where the corundum river, shivering under low bushes, fell modestly into a slow, naviga-ble stretch, the weakened Kolyan fell off a cliff. The water was deep at the bank, and at first on the water's surface Anfilogov saw some-thing like a dark scorch mark—his hat with its clinging mosquito net floating away. But inasmuch as Kolyan was almost incorporeal from hunger, and only the bag weighed anything, the corundum back-pack, whose straps were too big for him, quietly slipped off. Underwater, Kolyan felt as if his shoulders had sprouted angel's wings. Then he jumped up vertically into the noisy air, batted away the forelock that had stuck to his face, and realized his loss—and nearly went under again.

There was no point diving for the treasure, though: the large river's current was pressing in earnest and had probably dragged the loss under the planking of orange logs that had become detached from their raft and that had jammed the small inlet. Fortunately, of the two backpacks, Anfilogov's survived, and in it were two lighters that still worked, half a packet of stale biscuits, and an uncharged cell phone. Kolyan, however, who seemed blinded from his swim in the cloudy, pulpy brown water, wouldn't leave the spot where his hopes had died—and there was a prudently sober, out-of-body moment when Anfilogov seriously thought about leaving him, deadweight, sitting on the bank with that odd smile snaking in his beard, like an unsteady flame in the kindling of a damp campfire.

But their stores, even if divided in half, no longer promised sal-vation, especially when it came to the lighters and the last stuck-together matches; confronted with this simple reality, Anfilogov told himself he had expected nothing else. For some reason he didn't show Kolyan the choice stones warming in the pocket of his checked shirt. His secrecy could be explained by a reluctance to share—not the income but the happiness that lit up Anfilogov's entire return trip. Anfilogov felt that Kolyan would simply swallow the happiness with his gaping faintheartedness and still would not be consoled by the stones' perfection because his heart had drowned with the sack.

Kolyan spent the entire return trip talking to himself, cooing and smiling like a mother over her baby's cradle.

"We should come back here with divers, Vasily Petrovich," he said one day quite distinctly. "What do you think? Offer them a tenth. God knows people hire them for less."

"Fool," the professor replied good-naturedly.

"Vasily Petrovich, I want to buy a car," Kolyan continued, striding freely, swaying from side to side, sometimes making a sudden move back and stepping on the professor, who took no breaks carrying the backpack and tent. "A foreign car for fifty grand American. I've wanted it since I was a kid. Why not? I'll take a class. I'll learn to drive as well as anybody else. I'll take my car to see my sister in Solikamsk."

He babbled on like this, nonstop, for an entire day. The next day the rock hounds looked out from a high precipice and saw a dove-gray village, half deserted, with birches on the log huts and remains of fences mightily overgrown and knocked onto their sides. The shriveled old woman wearing a man's fur cap with earflaps and a soldier's waterproof cape, hacking away in a hummocky meadow with an ancient scythe, looked like death but fed the rock hounds frothing steamed milk that smelled of the cow's womb.

3

★

THEY'D BEEN HIDING BECAUSE THEY WERE BEING FOLLOWED. KRYLOV had noticed the spy during a downpour, when he and Tanya had taken shelter under a narrow overhang covered with twisted ropes of water. Dark figures of pedestrians caught by the downpour were sheltering everywhere and looked like groupings of unlit mannequins. For some reason, Ivan's attention was drawn to a plump man he could barely see through the white tons of rain going to the left and right. The man was standing half-turned in the ingenious little porch of some bank. There was something irritatingly familiar in the tight tilt of his head and his strange, almost inanimate stillness, as if he would have to leave a dark round imprint on the wall he was leaning against.

The rain let up and then vanished. Tanya was frozen and her teeth were chattering. Trying to divert her—her wet hem was sticking to her legs—into a neatly lit bar, Krylov saw, out of the corner of his eye, the man descend from the porch as if lost in thought.

Then the man moved away, pensively skirting the broad and complexly communicating puddles. Led away along this route in an unknown direction, he quickly was lost to view behind the newsstands, which looked amid the mirror flood like drowned barges. Ten minutes later, though, almost before the waitress could plunk a swollen menu down in front of Krylov and Tanya, the man nonchalantly appeared in the doorway. He bore a surprising combination of frank banality he was practically flaunting and a special, serious solidity to his corporeal makeup, as if the man worked with weights professionally and so had turned into a heavy, economically fashioned object. Without paying the slightest attention to the customers, the man went to the bar and hoisted half his butt onto a protesting swivel stool. He obviously was in no hurry to go anywhere. Krylov's unease mounted, as if he had a speck of dust in his brain. He just couldn't figure out how he knew this suspicious person, who had sat with his back demonstratively turned but who was nonetheless vaguely obtrusive, vaguely threatening, sipping at something, using his elbow to block off the well-dressed young woman next to him who was drinking through a straw—a butterfly with its proboscis— very quickly draining her cocktail.

Ivan knew the man's crushed wide shorts from somewhere, but he didn't know that silk, obviously new shirt with the long label dangling out of the collar. As soon as the young lady climbed down, leaving a sudsy little bottle, Krylov apologized to Tanya and took the seat the silk skirt had only just slithered off. He was hoping the man himself would recognize him and start a conversation. His neighbor, however, immediately turned away, and his entire look demonstrated how ill disposed he was to conversation. In front of him was a beer mug as big as a dumbbell from which he took loud, round swallows at automatically even intervals, each more economical than the last. The man gave off a thick carnal scent of heated wool that made the hair on Ivan's arms stand on end.

Nonetheless, the man was an unquestionable specter, a fleshy vision born out of the depths of Krylov's consciousness. The vision was independent, clearly able to order alcohol and buy new clothing in a store, yet in some way it was a parasite on Krylov's brain. Indeed, Krylov had guessed this immediately, as soon as he had seen the motionless silhouette, as close to him as his own shadow, through the blurry downpour.

"You don't have the time, do you?" he addressed the bloodless ear, which was covered with stiff blond hairs and seemed as if it could rustle like burdock and which was propped up on the man's fist.

The man pretended not to hear him.

"Do you have the time?" asked Krylov more insistently, over-coming his powerful reluctance to chat with the part of his own "I" that was concealed in this man.

"It's half past seven!" the man responded with surprising vol-ume and good cheer. At the same time he looked pointedly at the television, where the news was just starting, blazing up with a stereo inset, and in the corner of the screen the number "18:01" was pulsing.

Distraught, Krylov felt the onset of impotent vexation, while the man, apparently enjoying himself, was snorting into the short tuft of his mustache, wet from beer. Staring blindly at the television, Ivan felt as red and blurry as the flags on the screen where, on the threshold of the October Revolution's centenary, they were talking about restoring destroyed revolutionary monuments and a nice new Dzerzhinsky was hovering above his pedestal, wrapped in the embrace of the long-armed proletariat. For the umpteenth time, Krylov thought how age takes its toll on a man. If he were younger, he would have smacked him across his crooked face—just like that—and felt no need to explain. Now he was constrained by the need to be under-standable to the people around him. If he started a fight, everyone would look up and ask why, and to stay real he would have had to have a straight answer.

Unlike Krylov, the stranger obviously felt no need to have any-thing out with anyone. Just his back, in folds of fat and silk, and his canvassed butt bulging on the stool, showed the smoking tables a model of disregard for any and all questions. The man bore an impossibly familiar absurdity. It seemed to Krylov that not only had he met this man in real life, but he had dreamed him as well.

After that day, the spy picked up the habit of materializing in the evenings. Sometimes he made it by the beginning of their tryst, and if Krylov was late, the man would be waiting a few steps away from a displeased Tanya, his eyes cast down and for some reason holding wilted flowers. Sometimes he followed the classic surveillance method and accompanied the couple in his charge through the streets, stopping at shop windows and monitors for advertising firms, where search programs chirped when the spy hit buttons at random. He discovered the spy had a little car—an old Japanese model with a mud-splattered license plate and very noticeable signs of repair. Often Krylov noticed the hapless means of transportation parked at the bend in his side street. That meant its owner was some-where nearby but out of sight for now. Maybe he was blowing the foam off a beer in a nearby bar. Sometimes the car looked as if it had been abandoned for several weeks at least. The weightless and tena-cious shadows of rapacious crows roamed over its warmed hood, and homeless bitches with inflamed teats dozed in the shade of the red-hot wreck, blinking and shuddering. But the energetic owner would show up flushed to his ears, drive off the unwanted forms of life, and sit behind the wheel.

Either the spy was not a professional, or else discreet surveil-lance was not one of his mysterious assignments. He was provoca-tively noticeable and bold as brass. Evidently he loved new things, and the upper part of his short torso had the advantage over the lower: the spy's trousers were, as a rule, tattered and sack-like, while the man often spoiled himself with a designer jersey or a colorful shirt. This characteristic doubtless reflected the spy's way of life. The man's feet waded through all kinds of trash littering the streets, and his butt sat on whatever it found, but his torso was for show. In short, to the objects of his surveillance, the spy was a powerful irri-tant, and anything but invisible. His mustache looked like it had been drawn on by a graffiti artist provoked by all the blank space on his face. As if to confirm this, when the spy suddenly shaved off his jaunty adornment, it left a dark daub under his nose, like an erasure mark. There was always something embarrassing and tauntingly wrong about his appearance, a big loop sticking out of the collar of his slick jacket, or his meritorious trouser fly unzipped to reveal the white of his bunched up boxers, like a handkerchief crumpled in a pocket. The man was so disheveled as to be alluring; he left you dying to go up to him and tuck in the loop, scrape the dried spot off his sleeve, and polish his shoes.

The spy was mocking Krylov, whose hands were itching to do something to him. Through various spatial maneuvers he maintained a safe distance. Even driven into a corner—in buildings he preferred secluded niches, the kind a spider would like—the spy still wouldn't have let Krylov get close. His frown made him look like a man trying to move objects with his mind, and Ivan's feet started to feel as if the floor were beginning to slope. In front of the spy, next to his invariable beer mug, there always lay a notepad filled with information. This tattered object with its dog-eared yellow corners exerted a strong pull on Krylov. He was also drawn by a holster-sized, antediluvian cell phone that sometimes dangled from the spy's waist. Krylov would have taken great pleasure in digging through the memory of that phone, which gave out instructions into the man's broad ear while the man himself merely grunted, letting a stack of coins clatter through his hairy fingers.

Naturally, Krylov took advantage of one of those deserted narrow side streets paved with small potato-like stones and wrote down the scorching-hot Jap's local license plate, which told him nothing. Maybe he would try to track down the owner of these wheels with the auto inspection bureau through one of his acquaintances, but Krylov had never done anything like that and couldn't imagine where to start. The déjà vu experienced deep down in Krylov's brain at the sight of the spy drove him wild. He thought his memory was just about to click and a name pop up, or the circumstances of some long-ago meeting, but clarity never did come. The spy kept changing his shirts and remained incognito—and elusive.

The worst part was that the spy, while keeping careful watch over his charges, never expressed the slightest personal interest in them. He always looked bored. It was perfectly obvious that the man was doing a job and was probably working by the hour. Having gradually got a grip on his assignment and figured out his charges' schedule (which was predictable, despite the map's tricks and the city's rather frightening surprises), the spy adapted to cheating his employer a little. Without abandoning his surveillance, he would find time to skip off to the markets and emerge with a fairly large bag of groceries. He also left some dark winter things whose thick woolen cloth resembled scorched peat off at the drycleaner's; and several times he stopped in at the savings bank and pawn shop. Moreover, the man was mired in high-level negotiations with a garage over his warranty service and as a result was without his patched up Jap for a long time, so he carried his heavy purchases around by the sweat of his brow.

The spy's domestic cares spoke to the fact that he was not expecting anything momentous from his charges, such as a meeting with some unknown individual, a handover of documents, or anything else that happens in detective novels. This meant that nothing the watched couple did could impress the scoundrel, and no matter what the wrathful Krylov undertook, the spy met his deed with the same bored expression and indifferent eyes, which looked like firmly attached glass buttons.

He couldn't have come up with anything more insulting if he'd tried. The outside world, which Tanya and Ivan had torn themselves away from due to a lucky set of circumstances, had apparently presented them with a formal witness in whose eyes nothing was happening. By continuing his surveillance, the spy really wouldn't see anything he hadn't before. The couple's visit to shady hotels, where the spy waited patiently in one of the sagging armchairs for his charges to fill out the idiotic "visitor cards" at the reception desk, were no secret to him. Not only that, but the spy took the trouble to make sure they weren't renting the room to compile ciphers. One time Ivan, who had just that moment come, with sweat on his brow and a thumping in his chest, heard very clearly behind the thin wall, right where the narrow bed stood, the familiar ironic grunt. Thus the fleshy specter made a kind of threesome in their field bed. They could not get away from him.

★ ★ ★

The spy had penetrated absolutely everywhere; he had wiped the fairy dust off the secret that had arisen between Tanya and Ivan on the train station square.

It had become significantly harder to believe in what Tanya and Ivan felt. What had happened to them could not be proved. The field tests of fate that had made Krylov's boots fall to pieces like old bark —his second pair—had not yielded a conclusive result.

Holding his dead footwear, which had literally been gnawed by the earth's teeth, Ivan realized that this was his only material evidence of the intangible that had come to him at mid-life. Somehow he knew that the most objective things were the intangibles. Though the source of this knowledge was unknown, it demanded faith— trust, for starters—but Krylov, Riphean that he was, viewed trust as nothing but a condition of deception, that is, the condition of a lie. In essence, all he had were these lousy boots. The journey he had taken hand in hand with this woman was, in his case, a literally physical journey across the Riphean land, whose look and composition made it unlike any other land on earth. No matter how built up or paved over the Riphean land was, its crumbled stone teeth and the profound cold of its native rock could be felt through any sole. The land got to your nerves; over dry land it penetrated footwear like dampness. Here and there, under the burdock or concrete, you could catch a glimpse of its characteristic, almost pickled colors with its impregnations of quartz and granite, like an element in a reptile's pattern.

It may have been this land, this stone creature with the crumbled skeleton, that had compelled Krylov to turn his relationship with Tanya into an exhausting adventure. His small homeland demanded of its inhabitants constant, senseless risk and wouldn't let him trust in the mysterious something that happens to a man for a good cause, but rather incited him to turn his meetings into a simulacrum of leaps from the Toadstool. The specter of the killer tower, which in the years it had been in the Riphean air looked like it had been covered with galvanized metal, loomed over many of Tanya and Ivan's routes and sometimes could be seen even from the distant outskirts, no less solid than the real industrial smokestacks. The tests of fate the lovers devised were like risky Riphean entertainments as well, because they gave no answers to any questions. What did a middle-aged muzhik with bark in his beard and soot on his scratched belly who had climbed a pine faster than anyone else get out of it? Or a crazy motorcyclist racing in a vortex of pulverized ice who had *not* cracked his head open on the frosty arch of the Tsar's Bridge? What except what these desperate men—who tomorrow would have to scramble up a steep slope or dive at insane speed into a guttered ice tunnel, either saving their life or throwing off this troublesome burden—already had?

Now, for the first time, Krylov understood that each time a Riphean started off on an adventure, he began from the same invariable fixed point. This small point of departure known as ordinary life evoked in Krylov a perplexity mixed with bitterness, as if he had not been living in the world. The extreme Riphean spirit suddenly presented itself to Krylov as the place's curse. The world of the native Riphean, which Krylov was used to taking pride in, truly did look like the world of an insect instinctively crawling over tremendous obstacles. Why did people's beloved risk-takers, the flower of Ripheanness, have to rouse themselves to feel alive, the way people sometimes arouse themselves for sex with dirty pictures? Why did Ripheans, who knew how to fight for life in situations when the ordinary person would perish instantly, so readily disregard the result of their struggle and climb where it was most terrifying all over again? What made the fact that they were alive unconvincing? Krylov did not know the answer: he had ceased to understand the triumph of the insect flying like an iridescent bullet to its death.

He could not stop, though, and kept meeting with Tanya according to the scheme they'd worked out. So he wouldn't forget the next day's designated address, he put a fat dot on his copy of the atlas. With sadness he saw this atlas falling apart in his pocket and the ragged pages coming away from the binding. The more the rendezvous accumulated, the more acute Krylov's sense of loss. Never to live that again, never to return or explain anything to anyone.

The interesting question was Tanya's attitude toward the spy. She might have thought him a private detective, for example, hired by her ineradicable husband, to convince himself of his wife's infidelity. However, the figure of her spouse had begun to look more and more like a collective image compiled from several men who had criss-crossed Tanya's life. These former men probably had not collectively hired a spy to study the new guy better. If her spouse was in fact a real person—who may have had little in common with the product of imagination represented in the word "husband" and who like gas, filled the entire available space—then the only explanation for this persistent surveillance, which had yielded no new information for a long time, was paranoia or a healthy streak of masochism.

To Krylov's direct question as to whether she knew where the spy had come from or his purpose, Tanya replied with a grimace of displeasure, as if Krylov had said something incredibly stupid. But she wasn't hard on the spy. She considered him the third in their party and even urged Krylov to consider his domestic needs. Sometimes at her insistence they would wait for the spy if he were detained at the market or some repair shop, though once they didn't, having hung around for half an hour at the market entrance, next to the iron cages of melons gurgling in the blazing sun like heated hot-water bottles.

The ability to vanish was a special talent which the spy in all likelihood had been born with. When his shift was over, the man seemed to step politely aside, yielding his place in space to a suitable passer-by, and slip into a hole in the air, as if he were mocking the very idea of thinking about him logically. Although he did seem a figment of his imagination, Krylov realized he couldn't have invented him entirely. The spy ate and drank and left behind messy, beer-soaked still lifes. There was more than enough material evidence for his presence. Even after he had finished work and dropped out of sight, the man sometimes dropped his large unwieldy package, which evidently would not pass through the narrow gap in space.

It bothered Krylov that he couldn't determine when the man had first appeared. It seemed as though the spy had always been looming somewhere nearby, but Krylov, who had tensely anticipated danger from cops and crooks in cahoots with each other, for some reason hadn't noticed him. The spy's omnipresence, in turn, gave birth to the idea of his omniscience. Meeting the scoundrel's white, frozen-looking eyes, Krylov could find no corner in the past where he might have been safe from the spy. The spy's omniscience—imagined, of course, but all the more certain for that—transformed the man into a caricature of that Omnipresent Being whose intent Tanya and Ivan had subjected so tenaciously to verification. The blasphemous thought that a clown had been sent to them as a representative of the Highest Office weighed unpleasantly on Krylov's spirit.

Yet this was the only explanation for the spy's possession of certain information. Somehow the man knew the addresses of their rendezvous. He would turn up and wait modestly in the shadow of the appointed building, sniffing at his bouquet, which looked like a dead bird. Sometimes, if Tanya and Ivan got lost among the winding courtyards in search of the right address, he would make welcoming gestures from a distance and even blow kisses very fast, after which he allowed the arriving couple to familiarize themselves with the building, stepping aside like a real estate agent selling the residential tower or pigeon-infested shop stall.

Sometimes Krylov was inclined to view the spy as a reflex of the environment. His Riphean experience suggested that if someone starts running, someone next to him will invariably be tempted by the flashing heels to break into a chase, without the slightest reason, just because, out of a desire to catch up to and touch the moving object. In exactly the same way, if someone tries to get away, someone will pursue him.

However, common sense allowed only two possibilities: the uninvited guest could stay at the party either on the bride's side or the groom's. There was still some chance it was Tanya who was trailing this firmly attached spy, and Krylov had no intention of letting her out of his sight. If he was being honest, though, it was his fate that had someone in it with both the motive and financial wherewithal to hire a detective in order to learn more about Krylov's life than he cared to reveal.

Part four

★

1

★

ALL IT TOOK WAS ONE GLANCE AT TAMARA'S HOUSE, WHICH LOOKED like a small train station, or spending some time in her central office, where the imported Swiss air that came out of containers froze the nostrils like cocaine, to tell you that she could have hired a fancier spy, a good-looking guy with a strong chin and a sarcastic mouth, one of those copies bred from the Hollywood actor Nick Lacey, the sixteenth James Bond. She wasn't going to be happy with a fat guy who looked so little like an agent in the role of agent. She would have gone for higher quality—or at least something that *looked* like higher quality.

Tamara had always tried to do everything top of the line. She adhered to the principle that a person is what he looks like more consistently than many people did. When hiring staff, she set up auditions, which made life at her house and office resemble a TV series. Looking at her secretary—a prunish young spinster in a narrow suit with a pencil-line part in her smooth hair—anyone would have said she was the secretary. What set her senior manager apart from her junior manager was the polish of his standard face, his brand of accessories, and the more expensive shimmer of his double-breasted jackets. Nonetheless, a fat clown might have gotten a cushy job from Tamara. He might have been able to convince her of his exceptional abilities through some sleight-of-hand, like disappearing in the middle of her office and reappearing on one of seventeen model Alpine meadows where her ideal raw air, infused with the ideal combination of pine needles and grasses, was collected.

Tamara's possible motives for hiring a private detective to tail Krylov were complicated. Their marriage, which had broken up four years before and cast, a very long shadow, seemed to have progressed to a second stage. The play's main action, for which the first, with its simple joys and clear roles, had served as a prologue, had begun. Tamara insisted that a higher tie existed between her and Krylov than the one sundered by the civil court. Krylov, too, realized that their relationship had by no means ended the day of their divorce. He knew it would take time until their parting, and he had to earn it.

For Tamara, losing Krylov now would be as dramatic as a director losing his audience or a writer his reader. Krylov was her audience, the meaning of her work on the forms her life took. Without him, all this impressive show, from the sedate business negotiations to the celebratory receptions complete with string quartet and a baton beating out the music, the movement of forks and knives, would have been for *no one*—except maybe God, in which she had not the least belief.

In the time since his involvement with Tanya, who had changed Krylov's name as well as his heart, he had seen Tamara only three times. Two visits he didn't remember at all, but in late June he escorted her, battling boredom, to an art opening of he wasn't sure what: maybe modern sculpture, maybe the latest kitchen units. Actually, all his forays with Tamara were more or less the same. Krylov performed his manly social duty without a murmur; in the summer months, to his good fortune, his duty was significantly lighter. Sometimes Tamara called him at the workshop, knowing it made no sense to give Krylov cell phones, which felt to him like her electronic tags, and because he didn't want to be reached; he would toss the latest Samsung equipped with video conferencing into his littered desk drawer, there for anyone who wanted it to steal.

Subconsciously, Krylov perceived all her elegant, purposely sentimental presents as spying equipment—even if it was an amusing beer mug, say, or a sculpted candle, which preserved its virgin white silky wick forever. Krylov liked the fact that he was as impermeable as a smooth wall to Tamara's money and opportunity machine. This was not to imply anything against Tamara herself; it was just the sport of withstanding the pressure and weight, Krylov's characteristic struggle against the superior forces of his environment. At the same time, he was gentle with Tamara and from time to time felt guilty that he couldn't see her half-realized project through: to spend a lonely night in front of a lit candle, gazing at the teary vertical flame and recalling something romantic—Tamara's first hat, which they bought together at a cheap sale, or their vacation in Italy, the gondola's equine motion down a green canal, nights with a trace of tar, and dark wine.

If he really thought about it, all of Tamara's gifts contained a healthy dose of purely feminine, *innocent* banality, whereas Tamara herself, unlike the very good actors she hired, was the real deal. Every day a well-produced, well-paid scene played itself out, but she herself had no role in her own performance. As a result, her house conveyed a strange emptiness. Krylov was glad the house had been acquired when he, her divorced husband, no longer numbered among the proposed lodgers. Otherwise his soul would have ached at the thought that by picking himself up and leaving he had contributed to the desolation and lack of cheer in Tamara's personal quarters. She had two enormous bedrooms with tall windows and identical views from those windows of the red paths of a brand-new park. Her two home offices were showrooms of Microsoft's latest achievements, with fine lines of dust around the perimeter of each object. The space's twinness helped soften for its owner the fact that she lived alone, whereas in fact her loneliness was doubled, and the black maid, a classically plump woman with beet-red lips and a white turban, sighed sadly as she pulled the unwrinkled sheets, cold as snow, from the broad bed.

Among her own actors, Tamara invariably looked superfluous, as if a member of the audience had wormed her way onstage. Certain elusive markers made it obvious that she came from *life*. Unlike her *correct* staff, Tamara was not a typical businesswoman, that is, she did not emulate the Russian president's wife, Darya Orlova, a powdered old woman with a field marshal's face who wore epaulets, patch pockets, and a flawless pearl of maximum caliber. If she looked like anyone, it was a goddess—a tall Egyptian goddess with broad shoulders and a keen-eyed bird's head. She had a pharaoh's bearing and a tendency to right angles in her sitting, gestures, and relations with people. When Tamara rested her crossed arms on her shoulders, her large bosom seemed superfluous in that serious world fixed upon by the gaze of her luxurious eyes, which extended to her temples like sacred signs. In Tamara's strong and soft veins mixed Tatar, Russian, and Polish blood, with an unconfirmed—and illegitimate—addition of something Turkish or Iranian. The result of mysterious reactions for which that illegitimate admixture likely served as a catalyst could not be reduced to its ingredients: a woman of a new nationality, an Eve without an Adam who so far—and this was partly Krylov's fault—had not borne children.

Tamara's large body possessed an unfeminine physical strength. You could say this strength exceeded the human norm. The school where young Tamara and young Krylov had studied (Tamara was two classes ahead) had given birth to the traditions of Soviet pedagogy and maintained the practice of top students taking laggards under their wing so that the advanced students dragged the dunces through the difficult subjects. Tamara, who excelled more than many in mathematics, arrived at her result by the shortest route. Without wasting words on arousing consciousness, she cracked her patrons over their hard heads with stacks of textbooks. Sometimes she even broke noses, after which her tutees, snuffling, stopped objecting to the figures of elementary functions. Everyone respected the might of Tamara's thrashings, as if a gold slab lay in the palm of her hand.

There was, however, a second-year boy by the name of Zotov who had no desire to get what was coming to him for his backwardness in algebra. He was a thickset lad with a low forehead, as if someone had added an extra shovel of material to the crude object, and had a nagging thought on his oddly squeezed face. In fact, he could not think, a fact to which the hard-headed mathematician, in turn, had no wish to reconcile herself. Attracted by the clatter of falling chairs, Krylov peeked into the mathematics office just as Tamara and Zotov were rolling on the floor, trying to butt their proud heads. The fact that Krylov managed to jump on the dunce and give Tamara a chance to stick her charge's ugly face into a textbook let him feel like a man.

My God, how far away and alien poor Ritka and Svetka, the bunny sisters, who were quietly filling out their sexy outfits, quietly getting them dirty on the cellar's sunken couch, which was splashed with boys' sperm like pigeon droppings, were to Krylov now. Tamara let Krylov unbutton the top buttons of her navy uniform shirt and went to the movies with him, where they ate hot popcorn and kissed salty lips to the rumble of Hollywood blockbusters. The chinaberry that popped up everywhere was insanely pretty; its jutting thorns reminded him of a young girl's perky breasts. She didn't mind at all when Krylov broke off a huge cold bouquet right under the nose of the pale night policemen. Where had it gone, all that amazing new feeling that nothing could touch? Had Krylov foreseen that Tamara's way of getting results by the quickest means, without wasting time on installing the necessary drivers in other people's brains, would become the essence of her iron character? A crisis of extreme simplifications—this is what happened to her in mid-life, and not everyone can handle that. Now, once a week, she called Krylov at his workshop, sitting on the edge of her enormous bed made up in shimmering silk over which emptiness loomed.

★ ★ ★

Krylov's last telephone conversation with Tamara had completely slipped his mind. In the exact same way he could not recall their last meeting, whether he had gone to see her at her house on

Sunday or they had sat in one of those restaurants where each dish costs as much as a jewelry store purchase and where they fuss over a bottle of wine as if it were a newborn babe. Evidently, Krylov really was overflowing with what was happening to him, so that everything else splashed out. As a result the thread of contact had been lost, and as he dialed her number, Krylov suddenly wondered whether he had lost Tamara as well in one of his confused, waking dreams.

She answered immediately, however, and her voice was cheerful.

"Come over right now. I'm at the provincial hospital. I have to stop by the morgue with Papanin; they have those green gates with the canopy. We're working here setting up stands. I have television at seven, a live broadcast with Mitya Dymov. I've got two hours between the two, and I'm giving them to you. Let's go to the Plow and relax a little."

"I don't feel like nightclubs. You and I need to have a serious conversation."

"Don't worry so much. I'll get a separate room."

In the taxi—an ancient Plymouth, one of those heavy, strange rattletraps that are migrating to Russia in herds under the pressure of world ecological standards—Krylov marveled yet again that Tamara had no thought of ever parting from him. It was he, Krylov, who had parting on his mind, but Tamara sincerely believed that their relationship could and should go on for ever. Meanwhile, the Plymouth shuffled up in a crush of gravel and clouds of peppery dust to the green metal gates where a new electronic sign stood on a tall stand: "The Granite Company. Funeral Services of European Quality." The guard, who had been forewarned, pressed a button, the gates shuddered and moved aside, and the Plymouth crossed onto the territory of the Fourth Provincial Hospital, which looked sugar-coated and whose windows faced the little morgue, its black tar roof, and the hot rainbowed puddle from the summer rains.

Inside, Krylov saw Tamara immediately. She was directing the placement of a coffin. Animated, disheveled, wearing an elegant light-colored suit under which the dove-white cups of her bra were modestly outlined, she gestured to Krylov to wait. He sat down on a random chair and accepted iced tea from the pale secretary, who smelled sharply of deodorant. What was happening in front of him was perfectly in Tamara's style. The oak coffin placed on the podium —an expensive presentation model—was elegant, like a fine musical instrument; other coffins were being shown on the monitor as computer graphics, which Tamara's staff programmer was still manipulating, shaking his mane. Young women from the head office were running here and there dragging dried bumpy pine boughs with fancy decorations, like a New Year's tree. The woman who would be working with clients and selling them all this finery was fixedly paging through the prices. She looked around dazed from time to time, as if she had woken up in an unfamiliar place.

Krylov guessed from the extent of the work going on that he would have at least an hour's wait. Occasionally Tamara would give him a kiss on his damp forehead as she ran by. Sometimes a tall door would open at the end of the darkish annex, and behind it Krylov would catch a glimpse of several high zinc tables. On the table farthest from the entrance he saw a yellow corpse—a former woman with a round belly and legs stretched out like a frog's.

It was amazing how excited Tamara was about her relatively new business, which had begun a year and a half before with the purchase of Granite and had now expanded to multifaceted oversight over the four most promising municipal cemeteries. Observing her inspired direction of morgue improvements, Krylov saw with satisfaction that she had literally come to life; a natural flush played under her rouge. Business had done what the injections of rejuvenating chips swimming in Tamara's veins, like music in an archaic cassette tape, had not been able to achieve. Tamara's blood, which combined too many components, may not have read the program born by the invisible microcomputers, the woman of this *new* nationality may not have been susceptible to the procedures that had only just appeared in the most progressive beauty clinics. Tamara had flown back from Switzerland not so much rejuvenated as fluffed up, with information processes under her polished skin trying to turn biological time back and forming something like a subdural brain. Now, despite the recent treatments and the still noticeable thickenings on her enlarged face, she shone with life and blazed with a smile at which even the malcontent pathologist, who skirted the team of outsiders, responded with a yellowish grin.

"Even a corpse would smile at her," Granite's former owner, the aging man with a skipper's beard who had once tried to lure Krylov with the creative possibilities of criminals' necropolises, said about the new owner. Tamara, appreciative of his branching connections in three district administration, had kept him in the business as a junior partner. Dead or not (the makeup artists at Granite, by the way, were superb and could give frozen mouths a dreamy, feather-soft curve), Tamara contrived to derive joy for the relatives who had suffered this loss by applying almost forcible methods. During the firm's reorganization, Krylov had seen his fill of these relatives' smiles—uncertain and hurt ones—but also very ordinary, everyday ones. He had seen weepy women's eyes, which looked like water-filled ashtrays, suddenly shine with grateful insanity; he had seen apparently hale pensioners sob and bow in thanks, their medals dangling, stunned to be informed of the free coffin upholstery and hearse benefits.

Tamara really did do much more for her clients than demanded by the competition, which was, by the way, quite conventional. She had a magic touch for business. Before the criminal structures could gasp, Granite offices had opened up at nearly every municipal hospital, which naturally had their own morgues. The criminal structures, which rightly considered funerals to be a part of their production cycle, had questions on this score, but it was all over before it started, and the goons suddenly pretended they didn't exist.

Tamara, who up until then had been a standard participant in standard business activity (suburban construction, the building materials trade, an Internet store for loans and securities), suddenly acquired an individuality that no one had expected of her.

"I'm an enemy of death," she stated in an interview for the Riphean insert of Russian *Cosmo*. "I don't want death to extend beyond its natural parameters. The people burying their near and dear are alive. We work to make sure our clients have what they need."

"What would you say to people who are calling you a blasphemous bitch?" inquired a correspondent for all the glossy Riphean publications, a large young woman with a hairdo like a radish top known to her readers by the gentle name Alenka.

"I'd tell them to lay off," replied Tamara in Alenka's style. "All over the world, people have two expensive events: their wedding and their funeral. People spend the most money for perceptions, which should be positive. We're a funeral services company and are merely improving on what has always existed everywhere."

Her last statement, however, did not correspond to reality. Tamara had disturbed the Riphean capital specifically because she had altered the ritual. Single-handedly she had encroached upon the method of parting with the dead that played out one way or another for all modern city dwellers. It was a miserable method, but it offered rules that one could simply follow and feel that one had fulfilled one's final duty. No one had had the audacity to modernize an industry where all the props, whether expensive or cheap, were total kitsch. In no other human sphere could all these wax flowers, airbrushing, and gilt—in short, the worst kitsch Russian commerce had to offer—have held on. Forward-thinking people who would never have tolerated painted flowers and cushiony satin anywhere else, here did just what everyone else did, and without a murmur. Here they agreed to what was commonly accepted, just so they wouldn't have to come up with anything original—because coming up with something that might *improve* the loss of someone close to you was unthinkable. Only Tamara, that crazy bitch, had suddenly decided to improve everything, and rather than start with the form she took direct aim at the essence.

In the unhappiness—the ritual's chief substance—she implanted elements of happiness and did so in the simplest way possible: Granite ran a lottery. Clients who made a deposit could spin the transparent drum, where white balls bubbled like eggs in boiling water. Fairly often, a *lucky* number that the owner could use for a free tombstone with a hologram of the deceased or, for example, a funeral dinner for fifty people at the Riphean restaurant, rolled down the chute all nice and warm. Some Granite offices that were still not fully equipped used a deep velvet bag instead of the drum. Once a poor widow wearing a mourning dress hastily sewn from a coat pulled out the grand prize: a vacation to the Caribbean for three. The television often showed both the clients and the drum with the cheerful balls and asked for quick interviews with the lucky winners, to which some agreed; drunk from grief, they dissolved in thanks to Granite; others turned away brusquely. The Riphean capital's press subjected Tamara's activities to harsh comment, and journalists exercised their wit, quite happy with the foolishness of their subject and the easy chance to demonstrate their freedom from moneybags.

Like Tamara's other schemes, the morgue lottery really did look like a farce, except that Tamara wasn't stupid. None of the cutting journalists understood her metaphysical objective. No one sensed, for instance, how her attempts differed from Mitya Dymov's "Decedent of the Year"—an energetic operation with two-seater graves and garlands of dancing girls that were like a friendly caricature of Tamara's firm, although in fact Mitya catered assiduously to the governor and, accordingly, with his characteristic childlike smile, was rude to the federal viceroy. In short, an atmosphere of cheerful scandal and quiet latent dislike had thickened around Tamara. She took it very hard when the boiling water of lottery happiness scalded the happiness of bared souls.

Her experiments were not without danger. Often the results were opposite to what she had intended. Some client could linger with inviolable calm and pedantically discuss the points of the contract with the operator, but no sooner did she get a coffee grinder from the firm than she had a fit of hysterics. Once, the father of a small boy who had perished in a fire, a very pale man with a blank look, himself groomed as if he were the deceased, hair for hair, suddenly rushed to Tamara, who had personally given him a box of some kind. Evidently, Tamara lost it, or the inconsolable father was insanely strong, but he managed to come crashing down on the rug with her, under the clattering wreaths. There the madman, taking advantage of the fact that security had gone off for a smoke, tried incoherently to crush her long-legged body, as if trying to drown it in his own grief. The confused shouts tore security from the bathroom, and the madman was dragged off with the help of two volunteers, who did not spare their funeral suits. They helped a disheveled Tamara get up. She had lost her left shoe, and her hairdo from the Europa Salon had slipped to one side, like a lacey hat. But she didn't head straight for the ladies room. Limping on her one remaining boat, she pulled the crushed box over the mixer the man had thrown aside and handed it to him, saying, "Take this. You need it"—which was the truth.

Tamara's truth was concrete; actions that shocked the public symbolized nothing. However, the hundreds of appliances the firm had given away were already in use in modest kitchens and were now covered with the film of daily life—permanent beet juice stains, coffee dust, saucer circles. Herein lay a lesson, inexpressible by any other means, that people were afraid to understand.

But Tamara continued to insist. A report about the fate of a widow who had gone to heaven did not stop her. For a while, an old Russian woman in a coat of heavy fat was a sight at a Caribbean paradise; a lonely dark spot on the long mirror of the beach, far from the noisy human rookeries, she spent days doing nothing but gaze at the gentle sea mist, perhaps searching for motionless spots like herself, grains of sand like her in the mollusk flesh of emptiness. Who knows what thoughts were born in her head, which was wrapped in a white kerchief? Soon after, a tropical hurricane came up that was shown on the world news programs, and there, amid the swaying palms and flying native huts, an amateur camera caught a clumsy figure lifted into the air. First it was taken for a cow, but when it was blown up it turned out to be human. There was no more news about the widow or the three other Russian tourists; however, Tamara refused to see a warning sign in this death-by-paradise.

She was apparently expecting some kind of miracle from her work. Once Krylov found her doing something resembling laundry. Tamara was rummaging in a polished oak coffin, slowly studying this parcel box as if she were trying to plunge up to her elbow in the next world and bring back something that had drowned there. The expression on her handsome face made Krylov shudder. It was exactly the same as on Granite's clients when they frowned and reached into the velvet lottery bag.

★ ★ ★

Right now Krylov was observing the restructuring of one of the firm's main bases. A new operator, a heavy but handsome brunette with a hairdo like a mound of turf, had evidently presented the standard destined to replace the diversity of employees at hospital morgues and thereby express Granite's philosophy. Any of the operators who could not squeeze herself into this maternal outfit and give herself a chignon and the same kind of turned-up nose as the new woman was threatened with dismissal under some clever point of her labor agreement. Krylov tried to imagine what exactly had driven the firm's psychologist to take this new woman as the model operator. Maybe her abundance of vital juices, their weight and density, evoked associations with the bounty of the earth where the cold client was going as he left his inconsolable relatives. As a new element in the world of appearances, the world of likenesses without originals, the woman was the image of a prosperous peasantwoman, which, considering the specifics of the farming at Granite, suited the firm's general spirit and its positive nature perfectly.

Lost in thought, Krylov nearly missed the new staff's appearance onstage. Granite's former owner stumbled through the sun-blurred glass door. He was pale from the heat, and there was a wire of some kind running from his wrinkled ear, which looked like a dead potato, to his trouser pocket; a dark circle around his left eye looked just like a panda's.

"You're late, Peter Kuzmich," noted Tamara coldly, tearing herself away from her monitor. "I've been waiting for you to take over from me, but you appear to have fallen asleep somewhere."

"I had a gypsy problem, Tamara Vatslavna!" Granite's former owner barked like an artillery commander, in a strange voice, probably having been listening to his MP3 player. "Those gypsies are swine. Apparently they didn't gild the earrings!"

"What earrings? What are you talking about?" Tamara was suddenly cautious, holding onto her purse.

"The earrings on the monument! The wife of one of our barons is lying there in North!" the sprightly old men kept shouting, stumbling to the rhythm of the music. "They gilded the bracelet, the ring, and the pendant, but they thought the earrings, they were just her curls."

"What's happening now?"

"They took it back to the workshop to gild them!"

"All right, then." Tamara looked at her cell phone, which had announced an incoming message to the tune of Mozart. "That's odd. The broadcast's been canceled today. Something's not ready. On the other hand I have my wine club; our sommelier is an orphan without me. So don't worry, Krylov. I won't take up your whole evening. Come, let's sit for an hour or so."

On the front steps, Tamara took Krylov's arm, and he felt the usual wave from her tottering gait on his right.

"It's awful, isn't it?" she said plaintively. "Kuzmich has a shiner, but where did he get it? You try and try and still you're surrounded by cretins. Russia is great, but there's no one to work."

"You might ease up a little, too," said Krylov. "It's going to end with someone especially inconsolable strangling you. Sacrificing you like a pagan."

"Well! Thank you for the prediction!" Tamara laughed, bumping her mighty and smooth hip into Krylov, like the side of a boat.

"Don't laugh. I'm serious." Krylov felt, as always, that Tamara's astringent perfume was keeping him from concentrating on what he was saying. "You realize perfectly well you're asking for trouble. Why do you have to do everything differently from everyone else? Who are you trying to impress? Mitya Dymov?"

"My dear, if I didn't go asking for trouble, as you kindly put it, I'd be working as a flunky for Mitya right now."

"Maybe you'd be better off being a flunky for Mitya," noted Krylov philosophically. "Right now you're doing great, but no one knows how things are going to develop."

"You're a pain, Krylov," parried Tamara. "A pain and a chauvinist."

Krylov did not object to this. Once again, as if nothing had happened, the homey grace of a family quarrel descended upon them, a quarrel they carried to her car like a shared banner.

Tamara's Porsche, a new lady's model with swan outlines on its silver chassis and long door-wings, was shining coldly on a scrap of asphalt melted by the sun to the softness of bilberry jam. A young homeless woman wearing a rotten pink dress and a filthy, vegetable-orange jacket, was applying makeup to her bloated eyelashes in front of the rearview mirror.

"Not again," said Tamara with a sigh, getting out her laser key. "Why do these train wrecks like putting on their makeup in front of my car so much?"

"Because your car's beautiful," suggested Krylov, slowing his step so as not to frighten the awkward creature. "The train wreck is attracted to what's feminine. They're feminine, too, if you look closely. Ribbons and beads. They'd never agree to be exactly like their men."

Meanwhile the homeless woman, noticing the approaching owners, picked her tattered bag up off the grass, tossed her grubby cosmetics into it casually, and moved off with a strange, swishing walk that combined sexuality and wine. In her you felt the charm of the rightful owner of all of civilization's discards, a particular garbage chic that young bottom dwellers sometimes have who have decided once and for all to remain women but not human beings.

"That silly slut couldn't be more than eighteen," said Tamara with a strange sadness, watching the young girl walk away, having crossed the lawn along a fragile trajectory, like a butterfly's line of flight in the grass.

"She looks like an old woman," commented Krylov, thinking about how the currents of youth one could sense through the dirty sunburn and the alcoholic puffiness were somehow like the effect Tamara bought in Lausanne for thousands of euros.

In the amazingly even cold inside the car you couldn't imagine flies flying; the seatbelt, which rose like a cobra in response to the passenger's weight, pinned Krylov elastically in the leather seat. The car floated along like an attentive TV camera filming panoramas shot through with sun like a dark blue varnish; through the Porsche's tinted windows all the windows in the buildings seemed black, and the leaves on the trembling trees were the color of a dove's feather.

Tamara, an invariably focused driver, did not take her eyes off the road mostly, but her eye, shining through her tousled locks, did dart over to Krylov from time to time.

"I hope you've worked up an appetite," she said, waltzing lightly on the turn with a spectral van, and Krylov guessed that she was again anxious in his presence. There had never been anything like that when he and Tamara were married; nor had there been on their first dates, which had been overshadowed by her sacred lack of experience and honest simplicity. Now that they were divorced, no sooner were they left alone than Tamara's voice cracked and her hands became damp, smelling strongly of mint.

"Let's have a cup of coffee somewhere," Krylov suggested, not at all eager to go to the Plow, with its enormous piebald blini and imbecilic waiters in their traditional Russian shirts.

"Stop it. You're my guest," Tamara passed a huge black ATV in the right lane like a pro. "Personally, I'm simply dying of hunger. I hope we're having dinner in fifteen minutes."

There was a traffic jam up ahead, though. Vast numbers of cars were dragging along at a meter every ten minutes, while beggars scurried between them, sticking to the Porsche's windows like blue vampires. Tamara, cursing like a lady, turned on some pleasant music, the kind she always knew how to choose to suit the moment. This was one of her comfortable habits that for some reason evoked an instant distaste in Krylov. A lanky beggar with an emaciated infant who looked like a third plaster hand and who was hanging at her breast would not back off, having taken a fancy to Tamara's car. In response, Tamara focused harshly on the back bumper of the pushy Lada trying to wedge into traffic and left Krylov to his own devices, which was just fine, because Krylov realized that he was in no way prepared for a conversation with Tamara.

2

★

ER DIRECTNESS WAS EXTREMELY AWKWARD FOR CONVERSATION; it seemed impossible to extract from her circuitously whether it was she who had hired the spy. Her motive could in fact be only one: Tamara wanted to be a part of Krylov's fate and arrange his temporary personal life—temporary until he ultimately reunited with her.

Part of this, undoubtedly, was her unexpiated guilt over that cute young man to whom Tamara had suddenly acquired obligations Krylov could not understand. The young man at the time wore a feathery beard and fine shoulder-length tresses that swayed at the slightest breeze. He was shy and wide-eyed and embarrassedly fought pimples, which looked like the remains of pea soup. Lots of people thought the divorce was due to Tamara's drastic haste, in the context of which her romance with the future star, recognized in hindsight as a social event, made perfect sense, and the gemcutter-husband, who suddenly became jealous and filed for divorce, looked like a comic figure and was justly dismissed. In fact, after Tamara landed in the trap of the cow-eyed boy, who had rendered her space habitable with the innocence of a stray cat, she honestly pursued the situation's logic and herself initiated all the procedures.

She was frankly miserable over the young man who played on her computer and walked around the house in her angora sweaters. Krylov never laid a hand on the clumsy creature, who smiled at him in a cowardly and insolent way, as if Krylov were the teacher whose chair had a tack on it. Nothing he did could drive the usurper from their conjugal bed, where he had once basked like a butterflied chicken and now every evening, at the children's hour, headed off for bed, wishing everyone goodnight and grabbing whatever book caught his eye off the shelf. He addressed Tamara familiarly; he walked into the dining room holding her hand and over his food shied away from the maid, who had disapprovingly taken away his sauce-drizzled plate. For reasons never made clear, this foster child had nowhere to stay. That is, there was nowhere to send him. The ruins of his rusty suitcase with the sunken lid, held together by stiff straps, stood modestly in the hall and evidently held all his worldly possessions.

In essence, what happened to Tamara was what happens at least once to every woman over thirty. Her tragic honesty stood between Krylov and the young wretch like an iron wall. Additionally, Tamara got mixed up in a nasty business originally connected with enrolling the youth in certain private courses. She made calls and went places daily, smearing her pursed lips with bright lipstick. She paid for the courses herself but still couldn't get free. Krylov held on as long as he could, spending the night in the guest room. He just couldn't speak frankly to Tamara after driving out that parasite, who had been so clingy and so easily upset if he didn't get a pat on the head. Krylov was a grown man and could have told Tamara that there were lots of boys like this one and that every woman gets mixed up with one at least once, that life didn't end there, including her life with Krylov. But Tamara wouldn't discuss it and demonstrated one thing only: her determination to pick up the tab.

In other words, the young man outlasted Krylov. But the moment Krylov moved in with his mother, to that same tiny apartment with the ramshackle windows and all the dead midges on the dingy shades that emitted meager electricity, literally a week later the boy simply left Tamara for a woman producer he had managed to strike up a conversation with at a party for a women's magazine and by setting forth his views about what made people tick got all the way to her house. A servant was sent for his rusty suitcase. The woman producer, who looked like an overweight top student and had hatchet ears on her square masculine head, lost four kilos out of sheer happiness and then an equal number out of fierce longing.

So began the destructive and glorious path of the young man who soon became the famous Mitya Dymov. For a while he was the domestic charge of a venerable writer, the director of a television channel, several actresses, and finally he managed to enchant Pavel Petrovich Bessmertny, who was head of the Gold of the Riph financial and industrial group, a solid and positive man with a general's brown mustache who had never suspected his own nontraditional passions when suddenly he found his destiny. For a while, Mitya performed onstage singing "light" music about summer vacation and sweet Natashka. He was filmed in a young adults' series as a tough carjacker, for which he pumped some serious iron. And at twenty-six he started trying to look younger than his age. Thanks to Bessmertny's money he looked like a high school boy, and his capricious upper lip, which was rimmed, like a butterfly, in rare silk, was a masterpiece of the plastic surgeon. Ultimately, Mitya was drawn into television. His elegant shows were sort of like mental garbage cans and addictive for gossip lovers. Persons of the male and female persuasion adored Dymov. "I have forgiven him a great deal," one lioness or another in an oval décolleté would say significantly, thereby raising her own ratings. High school girls entered the fray for Mitya, healthy girls in tight T-shirts and shorts who never wore underwear on principle and with crew cuts stormed Mitya's office and smashed bottles on his car. Having grown rich under Bessmertny, Mitya was now keeping someone himself, or so people said. The official story was that he was donating his fees to an orphanage. Moreover, he regularly gave subsidies to three or four actors who had not been particularly lucky in their field and went around as if made up for tragedy—and who supported, in turn, a few gentle beggar boys, who sat meekly at a separate little table and went halves on each portion of ice cream while magnanimous Mitya, having made the date in the stylish café, discussed theater and film with the paterfamilias.

Meanwhile, Dymov had not left his gigolo habits behind. He demanded gifts and got them by the score (lots of them went to the beggar boys, who tremulously wore designer jewelry and colorful boots on ladies' heels, which made their cheap, dark little suits look like cardboard. Mitya liked to say that all his belongings fit in one suitcase. That would be the same rusty suitcase with the rotted-out corners that had traveled with Mitya to every rich home he had ever lived in—and was never once opened during his career. Bessmertny himself didn't know what it held. From time to time, in Mitya's absence, the infatuated oligarch would enter Mitya's clothes closet and with a pounding heart study the withered monstrosity. A light smell of decay came from a dark crack with rough edges (the baked zipper had separated here and there, like stitches from an operation sewn in iron), and sometimes he thought he saw something white. Once, Bessmertny used ice tongs to pull an old beaver-lamb mitten out of the crack, but it flew apart instantly, like a dandelion. The object was so touching that the oligarch nearly cried. He was whiskerless now, with a bare and good face that was beginning to flow over his stiff collar.

Tamara, who had gained status as Dymov's discoverer, comported herself with queenly dignity. None of those swine made a peep when Krylov, in his synthetic sweater, which had shrunk in the wash, and his hands, scratched by bits of stone, kept showing up at her parties. Krylov was greeted like an old friend who had traveled the world. The maid spoke to him with exaggerated respect. Several sarcastic smiles that slithered through the group of guests were squashed like slippery wood-lice.

Dymov, in turn, also wanted to be friends with Tamara. This darling easily dropped people—but was deathly afraid of being dropped. The idea of losing anything at all gave Mitya a panic attack: after plucking at his shirt or brooch, he could turn all his elegant and untidy belongings upside-down digging through them and cancel a broadcast or very important meeting. He would not be consoled until he got back the trifle that had slipped away, which had suddenly become irreplaceable, no matter what the despondent Bessmertny, cooing, promised his fledgling. If the item disappeared without a trace, Mitya was left in a state of depressed anxiety, as if a small but very black hole had been revealed in his universe. Tamara's absence in the solid circle of Dymov's admirers constituted not just a little hole but a big one. Mitya tried this way and that to worm his way into Tamara's favor. He invited her to the fashionable Scorpion Club with its exotic striptease based on Dostoevsky plots, and to the formal, pseudo-British-style St. James, where all the waiters were bald and wore side-whiskers. Now and then Tamara would accept his invitation—exactly as often as it took to make her refusals not look like a message. Never once did she ask what had happened that icy wet March night when the pleasantly inebriated Mitya had latched onto the producer. Tamara was the only person to whom the perplexed Dymov sent five-kilo bouquets wrapped in silver paper with an ambiguous note pinned inside.

She behaved as if she had clean forgotten both Mitya's residence in her apartment and her own efforts on Mitya's behalf, which only Bessmertny was able to bring to their proper conclusion. This kind of memory loss could not be credited, therefore Dymov did not trust Tamara. From time to time he felt acute animosity for Tamara. At night, lying next to a naked Bessmertny, whose groin, which looked like a cobwebby gray attic corner, gave off the sharp smell of patent ointment, Mitya sobbed softly at his insult and loneliness.

His show, "Decedent of the Year," arose as a result of complicated inner motivations that had to do with Tamara, half of which Dymov didn't understand. Everyone, however, remarked on the special inspiration that descended upon Dymov in the studio, which was decorated with solid tombstones and laser spangles.

★ ★ ★

"I know what you're thinking about," Tamara said after her silver Porsche had shaken off the beggars and her nervous neighbors in the traffic jam and jerked to the freedom of First Circle Boulevard. "Dymov."

"That's right," Krylov admitted, caught by surprise. He knew that Tamara had moments of insight when she seemed to see Krylov's thoughts through his skull.

"I remember that it's all my fault." Tamara's voice held excessive pathos, and Krylov guessed that her insight had been killed by pretense.

Simultaneously, he was enraged.

"Yes, I would have forgotten him a long time ago if that ugly face didn't loom up on the television every Sunday, Wednesday, and Friday! Actually, I don't like the idea of you appearing on 'Decedent of the Year.' He needs you for something in that idiotic program. I think he's cooking up some dirty trick. Don't you think so?"

"I think his whole program is a dirty trick," Tamara replied, her eyes riveted above the steering wheel to the racing lane marker. "But I have no intention of sitting this out. I'm going to go and defend my ideas and my business. No matter what you say on the subject."

Meanwhile, the smooth Porsche passed a mustard-colored apartment house where Ivan and Tanya had met the previous week and plunged deep into Pushkarsky Lane, where evening shadows already lay and hung here and there like unfurled sails. Another four minutes of leisurely driving and they would reach the Plow, one of the most expensive and idiotic Russian clubs in the capital of the Ripheans' land. Now Krylov felt frozen through from the air-conditioned sedan as he tried and failed to plan in his mind for the conversation ahead.

"So you wanted to talk to me about Dymov?" Tamara asked, as if offhandedly, braking at the light and looking closely at the little old lady in the doll's dress mincing on the green light, accompanied by her stippled pet dog.

"No, remember you were the one who told me over the phone about the broadcast. I hadn't known."

"Then what?"

"Listen," Krylov protested. "Let's go sit quietly and I'll collect my thoughts."

"Fine, fine, I'm sorry," Tamara said hastily, suddenly flushing to her roots.

She had already parked by the carved wooden gates where a decrepit farm implement had been nailed that bore traces more like the remains of a nag's skeleton than the plow it pulled. A bucket-faced oaf in costume was hanging around the gates.

Tamara went ahead, a strapping goddess with a human body and a falcon's head. In a ringing, festive voice she greeted the maitre d', who was wearing a tight, cranberry red caftan, and waved delightedly to some gentlemen who were toasting her with sweating glasses of vodka. Smiling and bowing, the maitre d' led the new arrivals to the most desirable booth. The waiters, flying like silk roosters, nimbly served four kinds of kvass; also, knowing Mrs. Krylova's desires, they brought a bottle of Beaujolais and delicately lit a beribboned beeswax candle.

Like the candle, Tamara's gentle face filled with warmth and her eyes sparkled. Krylov already had an idea about the reason for this animation, this excitement, which made Tamara drink the young wine in greedy gulps. The mysteriousness of the topic of the impending conversation had cruelly deceived her. She had decided—or the idea had arisen in her unbidden—that Krylov had finally matured to the point of proposing to her.

It was not the first time this had happened. Krylov knew the fateful signs—the joy, the straight schoolgirl back, and the stars under her eyelashes. Each time, Krylov had to steel himself so that he didn't say what people wanted so much to hear from him. He accepted this torture at least once every six months. *Another mess,* he told himself, pretending to take an interest in the menu, of which six or eight pages lettered in a rough, fairy-tale style were given over to vodka.

What was he supposed to do with Tamara's loyalty? In all the four years since their divorce and the parasite's departure for the producer she had never once had a lover. If Krylov didn't spend the night once in a long while, when he was in a certain mood, in one of her two imperial beds, she wouldn't have had any sex at all. No one but Krylov was allowed into these palatial bedrooms. Tamara herself never accepted anyone's invitations to dine in an intimate setting. In the wealthy society where people bought themselves sensations more than objects, Mrs. Krylova's position seemed almost scandalous. Tamara kept people from enjoying life. No one—least of all Krylov—could understand why Tamara didn't like the handsome actor Shaforostov, who distinguished himself from all other representatives of his profession by his intelligence, or the Italian Count Riccardo de Cosi, who had taken up residence in the Riphean capital because of her and who nearly froze to death when his rented Volkswagen broke down on the way to Tamara's residence on a spectral ribbon of highway gripped by the spirit flame of a ground blizzard.

Life offered Tamara every kind of bald and full head, every mustache and beard, every bearing and status you could imagine. The fact that she chose none of this for herself raised suspicions of perverted inclinations. For a while people were saying—and even hinting in the skuzzier magazines—that Mrs. Krylova suffered from necrophilia. Jealous widows organized a demonstration, calling on wives and mothers not to give their loved ones' bodies to Granite. The rally was led by the spouse of the writer Semyannikov, who was still very much alive, although he was a rather tame and skinny old man whose bony forehead had fine gray hairs plastered to it. Mrs. Semyannikova had moved vigorously into politics and looked accordingly: that is, she was large, plain, nearly neckless, and had an angry head sitting firmly on her shoulders. Tamara had had to deliver an envelope of money in compensation to Mrs. Semyannikova, but even without that the rumors wouldn't have kept up for long. Tamara was the embodiment of corporal and spiritual health. She was *normal* and so made people perceive all her actions as normal. In general, her frank loyalty to Krylov touched everyone—Krylov himself most of all.

But here she was sitting across from him, the soul of naturalness and warmth. A marvelous woman who was not to blame for the fact that after so many years her feelings had not dimmed. Krylov's nerves flared up when a skillet in which white mushrooms were sizzling and jumping as if they'd been stung was suddenly plunked down in front of him.

"Shall we eat first?" Tamara suggested in her musical voice as she spread a cross-stitched napkin in her lap.

"You see, I've been having some trouble. A lot of trouble," Krylov spoke in a muffled voice, trying to change the subject in the only possible, if not very honest, way.

"Is that so?" Tamara's hands froze in the air.

"This guy has been following me for about a month," Krylov informed her, looking straight at the tablecloth. "I have no idea what he wants from me. He's fat and ridiculous, but nimble. He won't let himself get caught."

He rushed but described the spy as carefully as he could—his shirts, his skunk-like manners. Since Tanya was absent from the story, he had the feeling that something significant was lacking in his description of the spy. Meanwhile, a thick flush came over Tamara's cheeks and descended to her neck, like sediment.

"You must have thought I hired a private detective to watch you, right?" she asked archly, hitting the nail on the head. Her insight had returned, and now across from Krylov sat a completely different woman: straight-backed, broad-shouldered, frozen in the throne pose of an Egyptian queen on an oaken chair as big as a porch and upholstered in crimson velvet.

Krylov himself, seated in the same kind of absolutely unmovable item of furniture, felt trapped. He already regretted his candor.

"You thought that because of that one single time when I watched you from the car, right?" Tamara inquired coldly, not allowing herself the slightest tone of reproach.

But in the first place, that was not the one and only time. More than once, more than twice, Krylov had come out of his workshop and seen her late model black Mercedes parked a little ways off, looking odd among the few grubby, rusted out Toyotas and Zhigulis. When he noticed his ex-wife, Krylov took a few steps toward the Mercedes. But Tamara, wearing her Nina Ricci sunglasses, her unfamiliar mouth looking like she had drawn it without a mirror, waved at him to walk on by. Krylov obeyed, reluctantly. Naturally, Tamara was spying on him. What had she hoped to discover? A young lady waiting for Krylov on a bench, perhaps? But in the black stalls near the entryways and along the perimeter of the guttered sandbox sat only old women—and they in turn kept the Mercedes in their collective field of vision, flashing their cloudy little eyes at Tamara.

Secondly, when it came to young ladies . . .

"You see, I'm not waiting," Tamara interrupted Krylov's thoughts. "I'm not waiting for you to understand a few of my motives. You know sometimes it's hard for me to invite you over. You're always so busy, you could be running a major corporation. It seems anyone can see you just like that, without any pretext—anyone but me. Doesn't that seem unfair to you? How many times has it happened that you promised to call and didn't? You don't remember? I do. In the last four years—two hundred eighty-three times. Tell me, did I bother you very much when I parked a little in your courtyard? Did I take away some part of your life?"

Yes, Krylov thought, mechanically stabbing the fluffy deluxe blin generously coated in black caviar with his fork. If Tamara had her way, she would surround Krylov on every side: dress him, shod him, feed him, hang him with expensive electronics, and top it off with an icing rose from a cake. Indeed, what could he reproach her for? Just her reluctance to see that the main goal of a Riphean man was not to fit into society—including female society—in a nice way. His main goal was to remain an outpost unto himself.

Yes, there was a time, a few years ago, when the uncut gem-quality stones were running low and his orders were miniscule, and Tamara had instantly made money and fed Krylov. That is, the very substance of which Krylov's body consisted had been earned by her. Tamara didn't understand—or, on the contrary, she understood all too well—that ever since then Krylov had done everything in his power to flush the old toxins from his organism and get busy replenishing his cells.

"You remember, I never allowed myself to get in the way of your *other* intimate relations," Tamara continued, raising her even voice ever so slightly, literally half a jot. "You could always come over on a holiday with your latest girlfriend. Why would I spy? I could see everything anyway. Not only that, I myself introduced you to attractive women."

That was the very worst kind of spying. Tamara had never had girlfriends before. After the divorce they turned up out of nowhere: lightly dressed, with long, slender legs, capable of drinking one cup of coffee for two hours straight and smiling silently. These women did not look like Tamara's business partners, or like characters from her Bohemian crowd—which meant they weren't. They had first names but no last names: Marina, Inessa, Katya, Monika, Kristina. The casting principle was obviously being followed simultaneously. All these young ladies had very smooth hairdos that flowed over their heads like water creatures, high-set eyebrows, and round child-like eyes, gray or blue. Their correspondence to the presumed model made it clear that they were on the job. Krylov always suspected that Tamara, with her straightforwardness and tendency to act in the simplest and crudest manner, had hired the girls through some agency, he hoped a model agency, and especially for him, Krylov. Therefore he would take any excuse to ditch the "girlfriend" foisted on him for the company of the bartender, observing from afar as the invited model sparkled, lonely, in the middle of the living room, like a New Year's tree.

Actually, sometimes the young ladies got what they wanted, creating a situation that gave the man no way out. Contact with their long bodies and contact with their pretty seal-like heads were such different processes that sometimes Krylov doubted whether the next Natasha squeezing him with her muscular hips realized that she was she. Actually, this may have been a case of her professional training showing: to be just a body when a body was what was required. Krylov realized that Tamara was controlling him through these women—not so much making up for Mitya by giving him ten women as she was playing the vampire and invading a realm where former wives were not supposed to go.

In order to avoid the live traps awaiting him in the cozy nooks of her home, Krylov sometimes showed up with his own samovar, as they say. The women he brought were mainly clients on the prowl for inexpensive diamonds from his illegal stash. Or some aging classmate who looked a lot like his own mama and was perfectly free for the next two hundred evenings might suddenly turn up out of nowhere. Tamara welcomed the surprise guest with exceptional kindness and proceeded to keep her close, introducing her to one imposing man thinly coated in the highest quality grease after another, as well as to post-lipo women who were very gracious and had already begun to mummify under their golden tan. They all smiled at the guest with even rows of implants and said a few pleasant words. Extremely flattered, the guest would drink too much of the unfamiliar champagne too quickly and start chirping like a sparrow in an April puddle. All this would end in terrible tears—and, of course, with a breakup with Krylov. What was most insulting was that the women Krylov found for himself, away from Tamara's efforts, looked even more alike than the young ladies she hired. No matter how Krylov maneuvered he invariably ran into the same type: a dull brunette with a mane of hair that smelled like cigarettes, a secret neurotic and bore.

3

★

WHILE KRYLOV WAS TORTURING HIMSELF WITH THESE THOUGHTS, the goateed maitre d' of the folkloric drinking establishment had already peeked into their booth several times, disturbed by the fact that his important guests had yet to touch their food.

"Did I guess right? Do you think it was me?" Tamara asked, breaking Krylov's stream of consciousness, which she may have scanned across the cold goose- and apple-adorned table.

"I'm sorry," Krylov said flatly, and he girded himself for a new onslaught of her iron arguments.

Instead, Tamara suddenly softened.

"You're so silly," she said, making a sad and tender face. "If I'd put a detective on your tail, you wouldn't even have noticed. The same way you don't notice a lot of other things from me."

"Listen," Krylov couldn't resist spilling his thoughts to someone. "This person who's spying . . . I have the nagging feeling I've seen him somewhere, even that I knew him well at some point. It's like having an itch in your brain—you want to sneeze so badly, but you can't. Just when I think I'm about to remember, I can't." He fell silent, tilting his head to one side because the answer flickered again somewhere under his skull to the right, but it died out immediately, leaving behind the now familiar mental asphyxia. He took a gulp from his mug of pink kvass, which clunked him in the nose like a hefty fist. Krylov wiped his face and suddenly added, "This man . . . It's as if fate were following me around. It's as if I were going to kill him, or he was going to kill me. That's the kind of hallucination it is."

Looking up, he expected to see Tamara's trademark ironic grin, which scared her sleek managers to death. But Tamara remained grave, and her eyes beamed softly, like saucers of dark oil.

"Not likely it's a hallucination," she said thoughtfully. "You have to trust your sensations. Sometimes they report interesting news. But I realize you're hiding something from me."

"Everyone hides something," Krylov responded with a challenge.

"You and I are having a material conversation now," Tamara pulled him up sharp. "No matter how important what you're not telling me is, what I'm going to tell you now is much more important. You and your Anfilogov have a special kind of business. The issue is not whether it's legal or illegal. The problem is that you want to go it alone. I mean all your friends who used to come over when we were renting that little place on Kuznechnaya and then stopped coming over. I want you to be clear about one thing: today, everyone belongs to someone, and you're doing everything in your power not to. All people and all businesses are part of a single world molecule. This molecule is a lot simpler than the most primitive human individuality. Simpler than that homeless woman putting on her makeup today next to my car. Simpler even than my office manager, who sincerely believes that if you mix forty-proof vodka and eight-proof beer you'll get a forty-eight-proof drink. Even inside the molecule the upper levels are much more primitive than the lower ones. You can't even imagine how crude, coarse, and simple-minded the functions are at the highest stages of power, where I've only had a peek."

"You're right, I can't," Krylov agreed, recalling with a shudder the *intelligent* eyes of the big shot officials and financiers whose hands he'd had occasion to shake. Now these people seemed like flies caught in a spider web, living and breathing canned goods such as certain types of insects store away for their progeny. "On the other hand, though, rock hunting hasn't done anybody any serious harm yet," Krylov added judiciously. "And we have people making their living with bloody calluses. I've been through it myself!"

"Lord! Not glory to labor again!" Tamara exclaimed, flinging her napkin on the table. "Any pickpocket is more legal than you.

Any murderer is more *understandable* than you, with your crude miner's hacks and your flying saucers. The structure of the molecule I'm explaining to you has nothing to do with the state's laws and the laws of economics the way they're taught us. It's international. The only rules that exist for it are its own. And the people who aren't integrated into it don't exist either. You and your friends are blank spots on humanity. You and I are lucky. We were born in a gorgeous place where nearly half the population wishes it wasn't! There's nothing surprising in the fact each of you is looking for a means of verifying whether he's dead or alive. You're not good for anything but landing on the moon. Why do you think the world is letting you remain as you are?"

"I had no idea you took all this so much to heart," Krylov was taken aback.

"What do you know about my heart?" Tamara responded sadly, quietly straightening the knives and forks around her untouched plate. "When you and I were an official family, I could look on these independent occupations of yours as a hobby. Now you're on your own with no one to protect you and nothing to justify you. In open country, outside the law. All alone with the fact that you don't exist. Wait, don't keep me from saying what I've wanted to for a long time. In fact, I understand quite a lot. I assure you, the funeral business opens your eyes to certain things. Actually, I've long suspected. . . . You have your own special rights. Regardless of who was born here and who came here, you're autochthones, and all the rest are colonists. This beautiful location has in some way itself reproduced you—for its own, absolutely nonhuman needs. I heard my fill by your side about the Snake and the Mistress of the Mountain. I don't know what kind of creatures they are, but everything that happens to you can be read as the story of your relations with them. On the other hand, the molecule I was telling you about possesses instincts. Believe me, it's dangerous. It doesn't tolerate blank spots, even if the terra incognita is only on the soles of your outrageously muddy boots. So what you say about that fat spy and destiny following on your heels may not be so far from the truth."

"You're amazing," Krylov said dully.

He himself realized that the spy's appearance was humanity's reflex to a person's behavior. Here, then, is where we all live. A gorgeous spot. Terra incognita. It is this quality of obscurity that the autochthones busy searching for rock treasures value in their small homeland. Pathfinders live by this quality to a much greater degree than they do by the sale of their loot on the black market. Obscurity is their daily bread. In this sense, autochthones always reside nowhere, in their own nonbeing. The obscurity of the Riphean land is inexhaustible, the mountain spirits immortal.

"Let's take our head out of the clouds," Tamara said wearily. "I see two possibilities: either the amateur detective is working for your and Anfilogov's local competitors, or else it's representatives of the international market showing their concern—the Israelis, for example. Let's say you came across something major and were planning to supply not the raw materials but cut stones, which the gemcutting business could not possibly like. Then they would probably knock you over the head. That is, you personally and your workbenches and even your legendary artistry are no competitor for that industry. But if a unique find were suddenly added to your skills, then you would definitely be an extra cog."

"That's interesting." Krylov grinned, feeling a sudden surge of life-giving adrenalin filling his blood. "Well, just let them try. First I'll be running away from them, and then they'll be running away from me."

"What nonsense!" Tamara said angrily.

"Sorry, that was stupid," Krylov said irritably. "If those fat-asses want to knock my block off, then I can't stand up to ten of them."

"Whether you like it or not, you have me," Tamara declared calmly, but her voice held an insult so suppressed and so longstanding that Krylov was pricked by remorse. "I look at your amateur business from a position you can't. In the last three or four years, the market for precious stones has been unstable. The Diamond Club is supporting diamond prices by brutal, artificial measures. Some deposits—in South Africa and Brazil—are being strictly conserved. No one has any interest in finding major new deposits of gem-quality stones. I'll tell you something else. Today the technology exists—it has to do with weak ultrasound, but I don't really understand it—that allows them to take pictures of the entire contents of the earth's crust from a satellite. That is, they can see right through our dear Ripheans like a silk stocking stuffed with presents. They can assess the ground reserves of gem-quality diamonds within one or two tenths of a carat. What does that mean economically? It means that tomorrow I can calmly throw the Liz Schwartz necklace I paid fifteen thousand euros for yesterday into the garbage. Now you have to understand what your whole way of life is today. You dig the earth and split rock until you're sweating blood just to reach a crystal—meanwhile they can see you and the crystal from above. You're a muddy wildling nobody needs. Because they've figured out a way to synthesize any mineral very cheaply. The cubic zirconiums that fill the jewelry shops by the Metro are a thing of the last century. You can decorate your New Year's tree with them. The crystals grown right here, by the way, in the Riphean branch of the Russian Academy of Sciences, are not likenesses but absolute examples of diamonds and corundums. Stones of any size, color, and purity. You can decorate New Year's trees with them, too, and give them to children for toys. Naturally, if you allow the use of technology created five blocks from where we're sitting right now."

Under the table, Krylov's left knee had started vibrating very lightly, shuddering like a wind-up alarm clock. The washout from the adrenalin was hard and cloudy. Krylov imagined Anfilogov and Kolyan being photographed from a satellite using weak ultrasound. He imagined them walking far below, like two transparent minnows in the middle of thickly cast ruby lures.

"Hasn't it ever seemed odd to you that the world has so changed in the last ten years?" Tamara continued, frowning pensively at her undrunk wine. "Think about 2008 and 2009. So many things were new then: cell video, bioplastics, super-thin monitors, holographic videos, the first chips in medicine and cosmetics, even in laundry detergent. And then all came to an abrupt halt. Do you have any idea why? It turned out that an economic bomb is worse than an atomic bomb, and it can be created not only by physicists but by any smart guy who comes along in any field of science. Today, humanity is holding in a secret pocket a fundamentally new world in which it is incapable of living. Because in this new world most types of activity—yours, for instance—are pointless. Of the eight billion Homo sapiens, seven and half aren't needed for anything. The specialists most in demand will cost more than they produce. It will be cheaper to feed them than to keep their jobs. On the other hand, if these new achievements are lost, no one will survive anyway. Everything will lose its value, currencies will crash, and I'm not even talking about the stock markets. Chaos will ensue, and the best solution will be war: refined, anonymous, and nearly silent. Only war will be able to absorb and spew out super high-tech technologies, so that the surviving monsters can exert themselves fully on the radioactive tillage, just as the Bible says we all should."

"Forgive my stupidity," Krylov spoke cautiously, not understanding whether he did or didn't believe in a secret pocket where humanity had hidden its deliverance from the biblical curse. "Of course, you are much better informed than ordinary mortals. You've basically told me that we can feed, dress, and put in good houses everyone who is living in poverty now."

"We can, only why?" Tamara smiled. "There's no technical problem with feeding tens of thousands of voters five loaves of bread. Some politicians have even tried to do just that. It's a good thing the structure we've chosen to call the world molecule put a stop to them in time. The sins of highly placed officials, specifically, greed and the thirst for power, have never let anyone into heaven—though maybe into Armageddon. Sins are our salvation until we all die."

"A more than cynical point of view," Krylov commented.

"Just don't remind me that I'm a woman and a gentle creature! That's not your place!" Tamara jumped at that. "Are you suggesting the values of humanism? Humanism has collapsed. It's not even an idol; it's last year's snowman. There will never be any humanism again. But let's assume we do manage to feed the hungry and by some miracle don't get burned. What are these full bellies and shod feet going to do with themselves, existing in the form of albuminous bodies for a hundred and fifty years apiece? Have you considered how much about human beings is human? Twenty years ago, there was a devaluation of all creative achievements. Are we supposed to start liking poetry again? For me, personally, words written in a column remind me of arithmetic, not poetry. It's as if you were supposed to subtract one from another or, at best, add them up. What about the poets? Where are they now? They've been fired. I have one author of poems, Vitenka Astakhov, the village idiot. He looks like a poet because he walks around in sandals and wool socks in winter, can sleep at any time of the day or night, and has never once in his life earned a kopek. Sometimes I give him a little something for vodka. But I, a serious, successful person with property, would never admit that that frozen scarecrow might say anything I should listen to with respect."

★ ★ ★

"Hey, aren't you late for your wine club?" Krylov, who had long wished to be left alone, reminded her.

"I'm late already," Tamara replied cold-bloodedly. "Since I am, I'll probably go to the office. As for your problem, I'll give the assignment to my chief of security. My boys will suss out who this fatman is and who's behind him fast."

"No!" This was exactly the turn of events Krylov had feared. "You answered my question, and I learned everything I wanted to know. Please, don't do anything extra."

"Why not?" Tamara was surprised.

Both fell silent because the goateed maitre d', pining with tenderness for his high-level guests, had brought and respectfully served Tamara a decorated box with the check. While she was getting her credit card out of her purse, Krylov realized the full horror of his situation. In fact, he realized where his girlfriends had come from since the divorce. Formally free, he had become for Tamara the only dimension where she could encounter her own kind in order to wage a war to extinction. Now Krylov himself had arranged the decisive encounter. He could already imagine wending his way to the formal dinner Tamara gave every year in honor of the city's patriotic holiday and seeing Tanya there, invited through some distant acquaintances and wearing a pathetic evening dress from some Chinese stall.

At long last, the goateed maitre d', powerfully hindered by his caftan in his bodily displays of servility, got the hell out.

"Listen, I'm asking this favor," Krylov followed an arrogant Tamara in rising from his crudely set chair. "I really don't like the idea of someone else tailing me in addition to that fatman."

"I only wanted to help," Tamara replied coldly. "But as you like."

With a sigh of relief, Krylov thought privately that Tamara's help, including her presents, was always beside the point and pointless. But she had never known how to really help, the way close friends do, even in those thirteen years they lived together. Meanwhile Tamara had clicked her purse shut and placed a $600 bill on the table in front of him.

"Take it. You need it," she said with emphasis. (It was the truth.)

"Thanks. I'll pay you back," mumbled Krylov, embarrassed.

"The least you could do is not insult me that way, my friend," Tamara spoke gaily, fixing the pointed locks on her shoulders with her quick fingers. "You know very well I'm not going to the poor-house."

The $600 bill was very new and as maidenly crisp as new-fallen snow. Instead of the usual $100 Franklin, he was gazed upon by President Pamela Armstrong, an imperious woman with a rabbit nose who had held the world community in her fist for eight years and just four months ago had perished in Beirut, when the newly built American Center suddenly swelled up and distorted, like in a delirium, to the glory of Allah. The use of the vibration charge, as the respectable world media called it, was so unlike anything known that the newspapers started absolutely howling about an alien attack. Frames from the catastrophe, which looked exactly as if it had taken place in a giant blender, flashed by just a time or two on television. First four heavy drops fell into the heat-bathed hexagon, as if it were a reflection in the water, then the surface shuddered and stretched thin, and an insane whirlwind rose up, without hitting anything but the Center, but slicing the cypress standing at the entrance from top to bottom, like a cucumber. What remained of the Center looked like coarse instant coffee, and most terrifying of all was its perfect homogeneity—and perfect dryness. Afterward, though, all commentary disappeared with incredible speed (taken by someone professional to the point of the absurd), and in Pamela Armstrong's biography, which was published with lightning speed in every lan-guage, the main emphasis was put on the future president's difficult adolescence (she took care of lions and tigers at the New York zoo) and at her adoption of eighteen orphans of every existing skin color, from a Yakut as yellow as melted grease to a blue-black girl from Ghana.

This book in its iridescent holographic cover and the $600 bill were all people actually had left from the bewildering incident. Not only had Krylov never held a bill like this, he hadn't even seen one anywhere yet, other than on the posters pasted up at the currency exchanges. He noted with interest that, despite the global preservation of novelty, Tamara always had all the newest doodads, jewelry, and gadgets before anyone else. She must have felt the stuffiness in which, if he were to believe her, the world community lived, and so pressed up to the cracks to get a whiff of the fresh breeze of death— and maybe even the air of the future.

"Well, I have to go." Instead of a kiss, Tamara pressed her perfumed cheek to Krylov's hot stubble. "If you have far to go, my driver can be here in ten minutes."

"No, thanks. It's close."

"That's what I thought. Then good luck. Call me. Don't forget." Tamara's heels clattered on the wooden staircase to the first floor, where he heard the mosquito-y buzzing of two balalaikas and diffuse shouts.

Part five

★

1

★

INDEED, KRYLOV DID NOT HAVE FAR TO GO. HE SAUNTERED DOWN
Pushkarsky Lane, which was paved in rough stone. The stout little
cannons dating back to Peter the Great that stood here and there on
the porches of private homes and simply on granite pedestals
warmed themselves peacefully in the sun like large black cats. At the
World of Housecleaning store, Krylov bought a cheap but reliable
mixer. When he reached a mustard-yellow apartment house, Krylov
walked through the front door, which looked like an old kitchen cabinet, climbed to the fourth floor, and unlocked the door, behind
which the powerful infusion of a silence many days in the making
awaited him.

At that moment not a soul on earth knew exactly where he was.

Last year, in November, Krylov had had a windfall. His share
from the sale of the stones Anfilogov brought back from the first
expedition in his shirt pocket totaled an amount that wasn't bad at
all for everyday life but solved nothing in his basic prospects. Then
all of a sudden, on the god-forsaken, frozen trunk of a linden tree on
his way to the steaming puddles of the Metro, he saw tacked up a
note written in a lady's calligraphic handwriting. The fact that the
sheet of paper was coated in a reflective frost made the lines look as
though they'd been engraved on metal. It was a for-sale notice for a
one-room apartment practically downtown, at literally half the usual
price. Krylov dropped everything, called immediately, and when she
invited him over, he rushed there headlong—seeking out analogous
notices on his way in order to destroy them. Amazingly, though, he
didn't see a single one.

The owner of the property for sale was an almost incorporeal old woman with a face like a musty rose and wearing a maidenly dress of worn silk. The dress with its fading cuffs and her crimped hair gave off a powerful smell of camphor, which made it seem as if the old woman lived in her massive armoire, which took up nearly half the room. The old lady's beautiful manners could not conceal the fact that she was rather foolish. To Krylov's attempt to be honest with her about real estate prices, she responded, rounding her r's and croaking, that she found conversations about money traumatic. The old woman was flying off to France, where she had received an inheritance from her deceased sister. The deal was done in a flash. The shaggy young realtor whom Krylov invited to verify the legality of the contract looked at the apartment's seller with poorly concealed hatred—obviously calculating how much he could have pocketed had the old bag not written one notice on a piece of paper torn from a cookbook, in the unruffled confidence that it would do the trick.

For another month or thereabouts, Krylov helped his benefactress with customs clearance and shipping her furniture. Finally the old woman embarked, leaving behind a happy Krylov in his resonant space with the pink squares on the brown wallpaper and furniture marks on the reddish brown parquet. In those first few hours, Krylov dreamed of settling in here and inviting Anfilogov, Kolyan, Farid, and all the others to a housewarming party. Overexcited and tired from seeing people off and from the old lady's rickety suitcase, which might as well have been stuffed with stones and cotton wool, he fell asleep instantly on the short little mattress, his long leg in his half-removed sock hanging out. While he slept, mysterious processes went on around and inside him. Krylov woke up the next morning—not in someone else's apartment but in his own, as if he had been born here. Out the frosty window, thick gold smoke floated by like garlands of balloons, and the pock-marked parquet pieces burned like amber where the winter sun lay on them. Krylov glanced at the face of the antique marvel with the porcelain figurine fragment and figured out he'd slept for eighteen hours. In that time, no one had disturbed him. All his cares and worries were somewhere far away, and the walls of his empty inhabitation stood fast. Then Krylov decided he would never invite anyone here.

Before this, no walls had ever defended Krylov. He had lived within the confines of his own body, bearing up to the press of the surrounding world. Now the situation had changed, and it occurred to Krylov to create out of the apartment a dimension where not a single human being would enter until he died.

At first glance it was a wild idea, but at second there didn't seem to be anything impracticable about it. Fortunately, Krylov hadn't had a chance to brag to anyone about his lucky purchase. His mother, who was none too pleased with her son's return from his rich wife, thought he was spending the night with a woman and that he was gradually taking his razor, and sweater, and for some reason his old armchair there. Actually, she was almost impossible to shock. Very white and puffy, with feet like balloons and dyed black hairs on her little scalp, Krylov's mother was losing her mind before his very eyes. Unlike the usual insanity that concentrates on itself, as it grew, her insanity demanded an expansion of the space under its control. For a while now his mother had not thrown anything out that might prove useful for her waning life. She gathered up stray threads from the floor and tugged them from any clothes if they were dangling and fixedly rolled them up on slips of paper. These multicolored little skeins that lay about everywhere were like a picture of her damaged reason. In the kitchen, hall, and living room, entire fields of glass jars from pickled vegetables gathered dust under the table. Rattled by their close mates, they murmured in their glass throats. Naturally, Krylov's mother needed his room. While allowing the presence of this junk on his floor, the windowsill, and other free surfaces, he retained his right to the old couch, which had come from his very first homeland and occasionally would suddenly remind him of it.

No one knew his apartment's address or telephone number. No one guessed it even existed. After the expeditors from the consign-

ment store came in and took out the old-fashioned furniture (amusing constructions made of metal tubing, plastic shelves, and big and
small pillows as colorful as new watercolors), and after workmen
from Safe Partner had installed a mighty steel door, sending smoke
and rustling sparks flying in the vestibule, his territory's boundaries
were under lock and key.

At Krylov's disposal were fifty square meters of security. The first
thing he realized was that since no one was ever going to come in here,
the laws of the state did not apply here. If previously from time to time
vague thoughts about the illegality of his business and the possibility
of seizure (of a shipment of goods, of Anfilogov, of the workshop's
owner, of Krylov himself) came to mind, then now he knew that he
could stash a sack of diamonds or a crate of Kalashnikovs and no one
would ever be able to get to him personally. At the same time, Krylov
realized that even his steel door could easily be opened with a laser,
and there was also the window, through which the authorities could
fly in a SWAT team on ropes if they really wanted to. Simultaneously,
he knew that he and reality had reached—or rather, broken—a certain
agreement. Krylov had locked up fifty square meters forever and taken
them out of reality's jurisdiction.

When the steel door shut behind him and he flipped on the
heater, Krylov exited reality. He felt his bodily makeup thin in a split-
second, and having lost half his heat, he tried to come to grips with
how he felt. The chill of disappearance quickly passed after a cup of
hot cocoa, which Krylov made nearly as thick as cream of wheat.
Spending the night here stretched out on the orange and blue sofa
with some hefty, old fluff of a novel, Krylov was absent from the
outside world, not only by force of the law which says that one
body cannot be in two places at the same time, but *in general.* There,
on the outside, nearly every person, lugging his electronic devices,
received and emitted weak signals and himself was a kind of ampli-
fied electrical impulse, but Krylov followed a regime of silence so his
location could not be fixed. He never used the telephone, fearing

caller ID, although the antediluvian red plastic phone, which rattled in its cradle, like a piggy bank with coins, emitted a proper bass ring.

Soon after, it turned out that his castaway adventure in the center of the four-million Riphean capital was easier said than done. The city's roots stretched into the battened-down room of his apartment. Old electrical wiring came in, a very substantial water pipe went through it that looked like it had been assembled from the remains of Jules Verne's *Nautilus* and covered with a soggy crust of oil paint. Water, electricity, and gas were the municipality's business, naturally, but their representatives had no access to his closed territory. Therefore Krylov had to handle all emergencies himself. The week after he moved in a faucet burst and crumbling bits of iron and greasy dirt gushed into the cast iron tub and boiling water spurted through some crack. Krylov got good and coated with rust and his own blood before he was able to shut off the red hot valve wrapped with a well-steamed rag. Soon after, his upstairs neighbor created a leak: returning from his workshop, Krylov discovered that his kitchen ceiling looking like a blotter. That same evening, the honest man showed up to pay and tried to get into Krylov's apartment to assess the scale of the damage; it took quite a bit of doing to keep him from pushing through the cracked door, through which his neighbor tried to slip an opened bottle of vodka like a grenade.

In time, Krylov learned to use monkey wrenches, pliers, and other household tools whose crude grip confused the fine tuning of fingers he needed for the tip of his lapidary tool. Under no circumstances could he have repairmen in, so he had to live with the stains on the ceiling. The dangling wallpaper, which at times made the room look like a canvas stage set, and the scabs on the window frames also demanded repair, which Krylov would have to do himself.

* * *

Having left state power outside his door and shut himself off from the community of women, with their claims and local wars,

Krylov in fact had wished for something that had never been anywhere before. He decided to free his territory from the influence of the force that permeated the world. Only religion gave this force a name. It was a low trick, but for the individual citizen all other human creatures were representatives of that force and implementers of its incomprehensible decisions. Thus Krylov had so decisively divided humanity up into himself and everyone else; thus he had avenged any loss inflicted by anyone on someone else with perfect cold-bloodedness and could not stand being in debt.

Now, in his fifty square meters, he set himself the goal of not giving this force the slightest chance. Not a single object there could be moved without Krylov's wishing it. Krylov alone was the source here of all the cause-and-effect connections, which were of necessity maximally simplified. Each thing in the apartment existed simultaneously in Krylov's consciousness as a holographic copy. He could not imagine allowing himself to forget an object once he had put it on a far shelf. Therefore he ruthlessly rid himself of anything extra: he took out two boxes of his own and the old lady's junk to the garbage, including broken figurines of dead porcelain, a pot with an unidentified withered plant, and hundred-year-old dust-scattering books—the verbose works of forgotten mustached men. What was left standing on the wiped surfaces demonstrated to Krylov that his mind was limited. But now he could be fully conscious of everything that happened in his refuge. After a while, he noticed that the apartment's space had become *transparent*: nothing was concealed from the very first glance, but the possibility of penetrating from without was excluded. God, should he wish to get this human insect with his straw, would have to smash the refuge's transparency to white powder.

The sense of freedom Krylov experienced by shutting himself up here forever had no analogs in daily life and was like nothing other than getting rid of your clothes and their fastenings. In fact, Krylov acquired the habit of roaming about naked, thanks to the ancient radiators under the massive windowsills, which gave out a metallic heat that made water run down the glass, washing away the ice feathers. The absence of a mirror in the apartment allowed Krylov not to be shy; he threw a laundered towel over the kitchen stool, which felt clammy and cool on his cold-sensitive butt.

Now he realized with astonishing clarity that any person, no matter how insignificant, drunk, and senseless, could drag God into his refuge. Krylov literally saw His presence shining through the crumpled or simply everyday faces of his neighbors. Once, going down the stairs, he ran into the muzhik who lived on the other side of his wall: too drunk to make any sense, the muzhik was practically crawling, and on his shoulder sat a creature that Krylov first took for a snowy owl. After staring at the phenomenon he still couldn't get a proper look at the iridescent cocoon that the marvelous long-feathered wings stretched out each time the muzhik was about to ram his face into the sharp step and lifted its ward slightly into the air. Distraught, Krylov surprised himself by slipping the alcoholic a twenty-dollar bill. Goggling at the money squeezed in his blue (ink-stained?) fingers, he suddenly sobered up, and Krylov barely made it to the haven of his apartment safe from his gratitude, from the flashes from his agitated angel, and from the disgusting port splashing in the dirty bottle.

Lying on his back on his trusty couch, holding a novel on his naked, sweaty chest, with a hot breeze from the radiator on his free belly, Krylov tried to imagine a stranger appearing in the apartment for the first time in thirty or forty years. He thought that the space, once presented to the stranger, would differ markedly from the usual inhabitation. A secret would be revealed to whoever entered that every person has inside and carries with him (a sad, unneeded treasure which can't be spent on life or given to anyone), and in this way Krylov would unload this property inside his own walls—unwanted, perhaps, but not worthless either. He saw his objective after his death as spreading his soul in the air the way other people ask that their ashes be scattered in the air—and he felt an iron will inside to *leave empty*.

As if leaving the limits of his own body (evidently rejecting the usual boundaries along with his clothes), he attempted to pinpoint his incorporeal presence on the surrounding objects. A few times he thought the apartment did have a mirror after all. Probably too little time had passed, though, for any permanent effects. Krylov had no doubt, though, that a stranger walking into the apartment would see it first—not his body, which would also be lying here, more than likely, but his quite authentic and moving image: a naked man with anxious eyes. This Adam would likely not disperse in the very first moment; there might be enough of it for visits by a few outsiders— and then everything would be the same as everywhere else. On the other hand, Krylov was not going to go meekly to Him Whom he had not asked to produce himself in the world, Who had not reached an agreement with Krylov about anything.

Even before he met Tanya, who showed Krylov how one can suddenly, against one's will, put himself at the disposal of fate, though, unpredicted difficulties arose in making his refuge habitable in comparison with which the plumbing leaks and neighbors' sociability were as nothing. Due to the unusual freedom of Krylov's loins, an unshakable caprice began to overtake him. Nothing like it had ever happened to him even when he was a teen and locked himself away from his parents in the bathtub, which was hung with laundered underpants that looked like the torn banners of a vanquished army—and each time he feared that his overused friend, turning the color of an angry octopus, would spray at their especially stain-sensitive, freshly whitewashed ceiling. At the time he thought all the objects in his parents' apartment were allergic to his illicit sperm. Even now, locked in once again in the bathroom from he knew not whom, overcome by visions of women quivering like big fish on butchering boards, Krylov reached the same adolescent compromise.

Thus, by tormenting Adam, his refuge demanded an Eve. These torments ceased only with the appearance of Tanya, from whom

Krylov came home emptied and fell asleep with the sensation that his body was evaporating and that all that would be left on his pillow was his heavy brain, filled with color pictures, and two eyeballs, each of which had been screwed into a kaleidoscope. On the other hand, he understood something strange: because nothing could happen in the space without his conscious will, *nothing was happening*. In the outside world, where Krylov had experienced a feeling of unexpected power for a strange woman, had fallen under someone's higher tyranny, and had chased all over the city after God, like a crazy paparazzo, everything shone and breathed life, and each day could bring both happiness and dashed hopes—but on his sovereign territory, only the simplest physical and chemical processes seemed to occur. Everything else had to be done by hand. Putting out his own clothes, pouring himself cocoa from a crooked pot covered with burnt velvet, it was as if Krylov were purposely staging something, as if he were clumsily acting something out for someone.

The empty apartment itself became an undiminishing temptation for Krylov. More than once, running up against the lack of hotels in an outlying neighborhood, he had barely kept himself from simply bringing Tanya back to his place. Often, tasting illness on Tanya's cold, damp skin and observing the bandages covering her rubbed feet, he mentally cursed himself. Tanya, on the contrary, was unnaturally indifferent to her physical infirmities.

"You love like a woman," she said angrily when Krylov could not stop tears from welling up when she hacked into her caked handkerchief.

"I'm afraid you'll bust a gut," Ivan tried to vindicate himself. "If you get sick and don't come one day, what then?"

"Have no doubt, I'll come," Tanya replied morosely, breathing after her coughing jag as if she'd just run five kilometers. "If I couldn't come, I wouldn't have a long time ago."

"Why did we ever get started like this?" muttered Krylov regretfully, watching Tanya nimbly set out her travel vials of gel and shampoo, which she rubbed into her own flesh like overripe fruit, in the bare hotel bathroom. "We ought to have—"

"Just don't start!" she frowned anxiously as she perched on one of the two meagerly made up beds. "You know perfectly well it can't be any other way. Let's try to keep away from each other a little more and remember that the best is the enemy of the good."

He might have insisted had it not been for the bundle of mysterious keys Tanya had given him for some unknown purpose—scarcely just to tease him. Krylov always carried them with him, and the metal cluster at the bottom of the pocket of his canvas trousers slapped against his leg. Two of the four keys with complicated bits obviously belonged to expensive, high-precision locks; the other two—one looked like the letter "P" and the other like an ordinary nail—opened something uncomplicated. They may have been for different spaces, but more than likely the second pair went to the interior doors of the apartment, and the first opened the safe-door—which was tougher than the one Krylov had coughed up for. The magnetic button with the icy granules of chips spoke to the fact that a computer monitored the lobby. By all accounts, Tanya's apartment was fairly high-class housing—which did not in any way correspond to the poverty of her folkloric, practically vegetable-dyed clothing. At the same time, despite the presence of a husband, something told Krylov that if Tanya were to decide to end the experiment she could offer an option no worse than the refuge on Kungurskaya Street. And she had given Krylov the keys because sometimes, in a rush of optimism, she dreamed of this. On the other hand, in surges of pessimism, judging from the irritated looks Tanya cast at Krylov's removed or donned trousers, which were loaded with metal and clanked like a horse's harness, she thought about how most artfully to recover the dangerous souvenir. Krylov intended no matter what to hold on to the cluster, which kept getting heavier, as if it were ripening, which he had studied by touch down to the last notch, and which he apparently could read the information off, the way books for the blind are read by feel.

* * *

Tanya's appearance in Krylov's life did not lead to her appearance in his refuge. As a result, not a single soul knew exactly where he was when after his conversation with Tamara—tired and dumbfounded by the non-genuineness of the world he was accustomed to considering authentic—Krylov went up to the fourth floor of the old entryway, which was as broad as a street, and unlocked his nice new steel door, which responded with a brisk soldierly rumble to the entering man's push. In the hall, silence and a feeble band of light awaited him from the bathroom, where for some reason the electricity was on. Krylov gave the handle a jerk and was convinced that the bathroom was, of course, empty, and the leaky faucet, wrapped with dull tape so that it looked like a large insect crawling out of its chrysalis, was neatly aimed into the sink.

In the kitchen, Krylov found two unwashed dishes with picturesque traces of scrambled eggs; soaking in the dishpan, full of nasty water, was a cup from cocoa and another, with a fly at the bottom, was white on the windowsill. It was as if the apartment had taken Krylov for two people at minimum. This was not the first time he had had the distinct sensation that someone had been in his refuge in his absence. Either he found extra dishes, like today; or it seemed to him that someone had touched the books and put them on the shelf in an unusual order not characteristic of their owner.

Now, washing all the dishes, Krylov promised himself he'd be extremely tidy. Downstairs, in the shadow of the blinking monitor of an information kiosk, was a beggarly old man with a big, woolly beard who looked like a sloshed Father Frost left stranded in the summer in the big wide world. The time before last, a pale Tanya had been standing there next to him, waiting for Krylov. Actually, Krylov had long ago predicted that the fortune-telling on the city map would lead Tanya to his refuge; in enticing his woman away from his own windows and trying not to look up, he knew he was lying as he had never lied in words. Now, glancing down, he felt Tanya's absence there, next to the old man and the kiosks, and he realized that his uncurtained window, like a picture in a frame, preserved the most acute image of her absence.

Many women swathed in fashionable, wet-look dresses passed the old man. They were all as alien as Martians to Krylov. Across the way, on the other side of Kungurskaya, the district tax police's old-time façade was decorated, on the threshold of the city holiday, with long silk pennants that flowed down the flagpoles like honey or jam. A little farther off, projected on the tall butt-end of the academic institute, a gigantic slide with the mayor's portrait had started to smooth out but had gotten stuck and was jerking: all you could make out was his recognizable curly locks, which looked like a sheepskin, and his kind left eye, which the efforts of tiny workers had made wink joyously at the tiny passers-by.

This, then, was why everything was like this. This entire world, with its sufferings, poverty, and diseases, was simply *unreal*. A few wise guys who had taken up residence, especially, in the concrete institution decorated for the holiday with the ruddy-faced mayor and his sincere congratulations, had created a reality, that, rather than embody authenticity, robbed everything of it. If you thought about it, Tamara's message, which at first glance had seemed improbable, was confirmed by many facts—not even facts, really, but the quiet, hidden course of things. It had started about fifteen years before. The very air had come to seem used, which had made the richer folk rush to buy up containers of Alpine or Antarctic concentrate. Then it was the unrefreshed air of closed buildings, where unsealing windows was forbidden. There had been a format change, as the leading glossy magazines had written. Krylov recalled the avalanche of words on this topic, rivers of silky magazine pages where the multicolored portraits of lords and masters had floated and drowned like autumn leaves. The conservation of life served itself up as an unprecedented surge of novelty. Everyone suddenly felt like heroes in a novel, that is, like characters in a made-up reality; everyone wanted to speak without answering for a single word they said. Krylov had not forgotten how he and Tamara, young and happy, stylishly dressed (for the first time permitting himself, through Anfilogov's generosity, expensive trash from jeans stores decorated to look like saloons), had been part of the mob scenes at rallies and art shows—which were essentially one and the same. All the politicians presented themselves as art projects: the president of the Russian Federation looked so much more like the president of the Russian Federation than anyone else that afterward people kept electing the same kind of blond security-agency types. The mayor of the Riphean capital, who was curly-haired, even slightly negroid, like Pushkin gone to fat, was reelected soon after, and soon after that he was replaced by someone exactly like him, and then another—so that people talked as if the memorable politician, and his successor, and the present father of the Ripheans, who now adorned hundreds of buildings' butt-ends and facades on the threshold of the holiday, were one and the same person.

What next? In some way everyone must have felt the world's falseness; helping one's neighbor in his *inauthentic* sufferings made no sense. A new culture had taken shape that had an internal unity, a culture of copies without originals regulated by hundreds of restrictions prescribed in the Consumer Rights Protection Act. People gave willingly only to the poor because they knew it was a business and all the old men in moldy tatters, invalids with obscenely wagging red stumps, and dirty children with chocolate-smeared faces were in fact not poor people and earned more than some designers and advisers. The poor became actors in a truly popular theater, representatives of the sole living form of art—the art of presenting misfortune in conventional commercial forms. Other troupes reached the same heights in their demonstration of human infirmity as the circus achieves in its demonstration of human athleticism. Gutta-percha acrobats who knew how to hide their healthy limbs, bending impossibly and transforming themselves from harmonious people into knotty snags; illusionists in cleverly fitted wheelchairs that hid nearly half the person; clowns, jugglers, aerialists on long stilts—in other words, the elite of a profession from which Krylov particularly recalled a big-nosed gypsy who carried her own child's head in a pot in front of her—and very calmly let him run out from under her worn gathered skirts when there was no particular influx of an interested audience.

The original lied. The founding idea of the new art turned out to have deep roots. But these roots remained hidden. No one told a mother, for example, that her pitiful pension, which stretched far enough only if you bought the "charity" items in their dried gray packages, was nothing but a *convention,* a rule of the game. Her complaints about her swollen feet, her blood pressure, and the darkness in her eyes had long sounded like a lie—and she really was lying because she ailed *on purpose,* since objectively there were medicines that could refresh her inflamed kidneys in a few hours. How many times had Krylov been irritated not even at her complaining or her feeble voice from the next room but at the very sight of her slitted patent shoes, which looked like they had been coated on the inside with household soap. He was equally enraged by other manifestations of poverty, infirmity, and illness that couldn't be laughed off. Now he realized why all doctors, even very high-paid ones, had such bad personalities and why it had become acceptable for women to pile on makeup so that their faces looked like big-mouthed masks. What was the result? The theatricalization of life, the positioning of any bar or coffeehouse as a stage, the waiters as actors, the abundance of grandiloquent TV shows in the absence of intelligible news and the endless beauty contests without any actual beauty. *We are what we resemble.* Is it really so hard to pretend you're prosperous and healthy? It's much easier than actually earning money and actually recuperating—but nothing more was asked of the ordinary member of society. In some sense that's all he needed. What had Tamara been saying about half the Riphean population wishing they *didn't exist?* Evidently, rock hounds and extreme athletes still had good taste since they wouldn't participate in the casting.

This is what Krylov was thinking as he feverishly tried to formulate why he'd been caught. Apparently something *authentic* had happened to him, against his will, that is, by force. Something that had probably happened to lots of people before. From Krylov's point of view, getting attached to a woman who wasn't terribly pretty, and who was capricious and sullen, was absurd. His joy was just his memories of Tanya. For some reason he lagged behind himself and his own reality by several days. In order to be happy, he had to make all his days identical, that is, marry Tanya and lead an absolutely measured life, with today just like yesterday. Instead, he demanded (from an unknown, evidently heavenly office) that in his personal case the unverifiable be subjected to verification, and as a result he got a ghost for a wife.

Since nothing happened in the space freed from God's presence, the sole event of that evening was Krylov's dream. He dreamed of a dizzyingly deep mountain gorge with vertical cliff walls that looked like steel. Along its bottom, as detailed as a living map, a green stream rushed along with the rumble of an express train, raising clouds of water and smelling like wine. If he bent a little lower, literally ten centimeters, the distant noise of the water was instantly audible. His head was gripped by a sighing clatter, and the ravine's sweet smell rose up with the fine water-dust. The abyss beckoned more powerfully than the abyss that had opened up from the top of the wonderful Toadstool. The height gave him a chill, and butterflies flitted in his stomach.

People were standing and sitting next to him (from the side, it was like the blurry silhouette of a smashed bus); gradually, like beasts to a watering hole, they crept up to the very brink of the drop-off. In order not to throw themselves over, each one took things off and hurled them in to feed the deep, enticing air: attaché cases, boots, and cell phones flew into the abyss, somersaulting, and dark hats skimmed, as if greeting the right and left cliff walls in turn. But not one of the thrown items reached the bottom. Just when they were about to disappear, they blazed up in the sun and dove into the dark blue shadow and disappeared, as if the height itself had dissolved them, the impossibility of the fall, which you could never wrap your mind around.

Like the others, Krylov threw in his heavy bag, nearly swaying after it, and tore his steel watch off his wrist. Distressed that he had very few things compared to his companions (in his dream this was logical and accompanied by some croaking off-camera commentary), he wiggled out of his old, useless coat and jacket, which gave off the slight smell of novelty due to the emptiness of their pockets. Following the fall of his clothing, which swished in the rising and falling air streams, Krylov noticed that many people along the brink were following his example. Some had already stripped to their underpants and looked like swimmers ready to dive into this lake of wondrous air. Resisting the call of the abyss, they clutched each other or lay prone, literally clinging to the cliff, which was firm and reliable but did slant. Their untanned bodies, covered with gooseflesh and stuck-on pebbles, shook in the trembling of the sparse grass.

Here, pant legs swishing and coins scattering, someone's gray, badly creased pants flew off into the abyss. Looking more closely, Krylov saw that the same thing was happening on the opposite edge of the drop-off. People were lugging up their colorful clothing, hurling it away—even tossing it up a little—and then lying down naked on the stones, which shone moistly, as if they were greasy. Now both edges of the abyss looked like the beach; both here and there a broad-hipped female silhouette loomed, attempting to curl up into a ball. Suddenly, not far away, some stupid scuffle started that looked like beetles sparring: first a rounded piece of stone would roll and smash into the cliff wall, then one of the two fighting would wave his arms hard as if he were trying to backstroke away, break off, start getting smaller, shining white, and dissolve like a spoonful of sugar in water. Being omniscient in his dream, Krylov guessed what had happened: those who had nothing left to throw into the bewitching chasm had figured out that their yawning neighbors would do quite nicely for that purpose instead of themselves. Now Krylov's vague companions, having scattered, estranged, so that each could be alone with the enchantment of the abyss, began to regroup. Two, three, four ungainly dolls flew off, close to the sunny walls, some quite resigned, others with some remnant of jerking life. Those who hadn't had time to tear off their clothes were like flags.

Meanwhile, the gorge's enticing bottom remained *innocent*—unstained by a single one of the objects thrown from above. "The orchestra pit of the world theater," an off-camera voice said into Krylov's ear. Indeed, the calls of the abyss suddenly intensified, as if new instruments had harmoniously joined in on its soundless music. Barely able to contain himself, Krylov gazed into this eternity, where above the distant river an ominous mauve rainbow hung like a con trail. He didn't notice how they'd made their way to him. A half-naked fatman, cautiously bearing his nice little belly, as if it were sewn from silk, saw he'd been discovered and ran at Krylov with a desperate laugh, wounding his raw feet painfully on the sharp stones. He was as cold as a frog; his pale eyes dancing, he seemed to be trying to make Krylov sit on the ground. But just when Krylov thought he had almost wriggled out of his opponent's slippery embrace, his soles couldn't feel their support, and the void rushed up at him, like a grenade.

2

★

THE CORUNDUM RIVER GREETED THE EXPEDITION WITH A PIERCING chill. The stream, which squeezed their feet in their rubber boots, seized their very bones, and everything green on the banks seemed dark blue. Sweaterless, Anfilogov slowly caught cold; he strode mechanically over the grinding shingle and slippery roots, and his head in his sweat-soaked knit cap felt like it was floating along separately and a mighty power plant was rumbling inside it.

The professor had studied the corundum river's depiction and the map for months, and he knew it better than the crack in his own ceiling. Everything turned up exactly where it had been the previous year: the wind-blown cliffs covered in lichen that looked like copper turned green or like bright spots of bird poop set out along the banks; and the long pebbly shoals where in the mornings the whitened stones stuck together like ice cubes from the cold.

The expedition was moving along without stopping to wash ore or collect samples. However, the journey proved much longer and more exhausting than the professor had expected. The stream bed seemed tilted: having taken on water, the stream leapt more quickly over the stones, and the shallows had swollen. Making their way to the upper reaches, toward the particular fold where the horizon was fastened on the wrong button, the rock hounds, bent half over under the weight of their backpacks, kept ascending the mind-boggling steepness.

Now the expedition had more than enough food. But the mountain spirits were making their presence known. The rock hounds had not been able to eat a hot meal or dry their socks for a week. Each time, the diligent Kolyan gathered some good, crackling tinder and some dried-out fir branches, laid them according to the rules, and placed a live burning light there, like a bird into a cage. But as soon as the flame crumpled the kindling and started licking the smoky, sputtering branches, suddenly, a pale fire shot up from below like from a rocket nozzle—and the water in the pot, which had just come to a boil, was instantly transformed into a spongy ice that looked like a piece of the moon. A fierce chill came off the magnesium white campfire, where the burned branches stiffened like welded steel.

According to Anfilogov's calculations, the temperature inside the phenomenon was approximately seventy degrees below zero; at the bottom of the transparent white night, slightly crusted with soap-bubble clouds, the icy campfire eddied, like the flow at the bottom of a large, cooling bath. Extinguishing it, of course, was impossible. When Kolyan, out of stupidity, thinking to forestall the chilly flare, threw half a bucket of water on the steamed, still hot branches, it froze instantly, in flight, like an ice chip, and Kolyan's wet paws, the flesh adhering to the dull iron, started to be covered in granular little white beards. Fortunately, Anfilogov thought to throw in a rock, and the bared ice, which looked like a delusion, showered on the campfire with a marvelous ringing. Freeing the howling Kolyan, the professor urinated warm piss on his cramped paws, in which the blanched bucket was clanking ice convulsively, and then, unknotting the rotten rope around the victim's waist, forced him to do the same thing—moreover, despite the professor's squeamish assistance, a substantial amount of his body heat landed on his trousers.

They had to get away from the ice fire as quickly as possible because you never knew about buckets, and something even worse could happen. Rolling up camp, Anfilogov kept glancing stealthily to see whether the Dancing Pyralid would appear in the campfire, and indeed, a couple of times he did see a lightly dressed woman about a meter and a half tall, who was changing shape like clay on a potter's wheel, spinning in a snowy swirl; her narrow, browless little face, with eyes like drops of blood, was covered with transparent scales, or so it seemed to the professor. Remembering that the expedition could not allow itself to sacrifice its pot, Anfilogov, like a hockey player with his stick, knocked it out of the flame with a heatproof pole made for firewood; the pot stung for a long time and looked like a white fur hat. After dropping off to sleep in a kind of delirium in their Australian down sleeping bags (in anticipation of their profits, Anfilogov had not stinted on outfitting the expedition, although he did not allow himself to take any excess belongings), in the morning the rock hounds observed above the place of their former campfire a delicate luminescence: a colorful pancake, dribbling from the edges, was rising quite vertically toward the clouds.

The professor fought off his cold with the help of a powerful antibiotic; however, without hot food there was no way he could beat back the illness. Slaking his rough thirst with water from the stream was like trying to swallow a snake. The rock hounds did not deny themselves their fancy tinned goods or fatty "alpinist" chocolate. They applied themselves economically only to the professor's flask of Chivas Regal; if they had enough strength before going to bed, they rubbed themselves down with alcohol. In town, observing Anfilogov's food purchases, Kolyan looked forward to the expedition as to a picnic in the fresh air; now, when he was given something tasty he used to drool over at home, his appetite for some reason just didn't meet its planned capacity.

"That ham is making me sick to my stomach, Vasily Petrovich," he reported calmly, giving the professor back the can with barely a nibble taken out. "It's awfully pink. I can't."

"Have some cheese!" Anfilogov said angrily, himself experiencing strange flashes of revulsion for intense colors.

"I can't eat that either. It's awfully yellow." Kolyan made a face. "I'd like some hot tea, with sugar!"

"Don't be maudlin. You know very well the Pyralid is drawn to treasure."

"She'll just freeze us sooner, Vasily Petrovich," Kolyan responded indifferently, crawling into his sleeping bag. "I don't even care. Why does she have such an ugly face, like a mutant? I heard from Farid she was a pretty girl."

"All of Farid's are pretty," Anfilogov muttered under his breath, remembering how, a couple of years before, Habibullin, the old lynx, had suddenly introduced his friends to his absurdly youthful, unforgivably beautiful wife Gulbahor, who was unaware how rare her faintly drawn Eastern features, which looked like a coverlet of fine snow had been pulled over them, were. Of course, that had not ended well.

* * *

He himself had married this winter, too. The difference in their ages was also substantial, and inspecting his Ekaterina Sergeyevna without any concern for what she thought of it, Anfilogov did not find in her standard, somewhat papery appearance any specific signs of aging, but she did not at all match the subtle, milky, tear-stained image in which he dreamed of her by the corundum prospecting pits on the eve of his main find. Now when Ekaterina Sergeyevna slept in Anfilogov's bed—on her belly, hugging the pillow, her solid shovel-shaped ass outlined under the field blanket, the professor had a sense of untidiness, as if his coat were in the bed instead of hanging on its hook.

The professor was not terribly interested in why Ekaterina Sergeyevna had agreed to marriage. He assumed that any woman preferred the married to the unmarried state, and he conceded the phenomenon its natural nature. He did not think about whether Ekaterina Sergeyevna might have felt anything like love for him, for example; the professor did not encourage her skittish contact, as if she were a pickpocket trying to pull out his wallet. Ekaterina Sergeyevna's feelings and thoughts meant as much to Anfilogov as the feelings and thoughts of other people the professor dealt with, which is to say, nothing at all.

He had arranged his life so that every person from his so-called circle was a terminus, that is, a dead end. In the case of Ekaterina Sergeyevna, the professor had succeeded fully. There could be no question of informing the people around him of the joyous event, to say nothing of putting himself at the disposal of a wedding party. They had had the witnesses the law requires: Kolyan, who had decked himself out for the occasion in a turquoise blue silk suit with shoulder pads; and a meek woman with a fat face and a red crew cut whom Anfilogov had summoned by phone and about whom no one knew that she had once been the professor's first wife, the beauty of her school year, and the provincial figure-skating champion.

Anfilogov had absolutely no intention of altering the structure of his own life for the sake of Ekaterina Sergeyevna and so had not moved her in with him but had bought (for himself) her shadowy, oddly angular little apartment, where there was something of Siamese twins in the layout of the rooms and kitchen. Ekaterina Sergeyevna had rented it for a few years, also from some distant relatives. The professor added a little furniture (a bed on piano legs and a desk for his laptop) and started spending Saturday and Thursday nights at his wife's. He didn't give his spouse money for clothes and intentionally put up with her faded wardrobe. For some reason the professor found the notion of Ekaterina Sergeyevna in a mink coat highly distasteful. On the other hand, he quietly rewrote his will (without informing his two previous wives—the fat-faced one with whom the professor was in his own way friendly, and another, who had longed to run away from the professor and fate by achieving, through multistage plastic surgery, a resemblance to an unaging Madonna, any similarity to whom slipped right out from the plastic surgeons' hands). Now that all his personal property and real estate had been left to Ekaterina Sergeyevna (who knew nothing about it either), Anfilogov felt himself a complete beggar.

He found few joys in the unforeseen marriage. He got some satisfaction from feeding Ekaterina Sergeyevna some specifically male dish prepared with all the fine points: roast beef, shashlyk. For some reason he liked to watch his spouse cut the juicy meat—pink in the very middle and almost alive—reverently, crosswise, and her dry, fine-browed face grow warm from an expertly selected wine. Actually, Anfilogov had done this only four times, considering it unnecessary to give himself or others an excess of pleasure. Ekaterina Sergeyevna's presence conveyed nothing to his small heart, which was much like a beaker for chemical experiments—experiments that had entailed a couple of explosions, more like pops, but were naturally a thing of the past. On the other hand, her presence did remind Anfilogov that he would die one day. This unpleasant knowledge had never before occurred to the professor on lonely nights, as it does to other weak-nerved men who can't stand their own company if someone doesn't share this sad burden with them. The professor had always got on splendidly and had lived quite companionably with his library: his books, two colonies in the two apartments the professor personally inhabited (Ekaterina Sergeyevna's one-room apartment could not lay claims to being his third, especially since it was the sixth the professor had acquired), were night creatures and protected Anfilogov from delusions, gathering under his lamp in the dark time of the day. They spoke three languages with the professor, moreover some lay opened flat for weeks at a time, sprawling in leaning poses characteristic only of books printed in Russian. On Saturdays and Thursdays, which were set aside for his wife, the professor was first a little bored and then unbearably so. The small, tattered collection of cheap paper on Ekaterina Sergeyevna's shelf was as accidental as a collection of passengers on a Metro car, and Anfilogov, dispatching his spousal duties in fifteen minutes, preferred the despised Internet.

On Sundays, Mondays, Tuesdays, Wednesdays, and Fridays, though, he now experienced a completely new kind of sensation, as if the night before his execution had come, and the texts in his now alien books had become senselessly long, beyond the limits of understanding and life—and something important about the professor himself that had not found its way into a single one of the volumes that exist in the world had not been expressed. Ekaterina Sergeyevna must have had a long-distance effect on the professor. Approximately a week before the expedition's departure, Anfilogov, who had not contemplated anything like this the night before, suddenly told his wife the codes for all his credit cards and gave instructions for accessing nearly all his cached material valuables, including the contents of his aquarium. Her fright, her wet, wide-open eyes, which looked an overcast, moist grayish blue, suddenly softened the professor's heart. In the last few days, cautiously getting to know each other, they spoke in new voices, and when Ekaterina Sergeyevna, sniffing her pink nose, stroked his head, the professor did not get up angrily but sat patiently, as if he were at the barber's. They went to the opera, where in the crowded box they held hands to the aria of the fat toreador, who in his embroidered costume looked like a gold turtle. It was as if Ekaterina Sergeyevna were looking to the professor for protection from the dangers that threatened his expedition, and Anfilogov, inspecting her dried lips, which looked like air-dried orange slices, thought that he might, in principle, kiss her.

Now that Ekaterina Sergeyevna was back in the city, though, the sole heir and mistress of all his secrets, Anfilogov had the feeling he would never return.

★ ★ ★

They didn't reach the spot until the fourteenth day. That winter, after Anfilogov bought off the sector chief at the nearest (two hundred kilometers away) timbering operation and got him drunk, by some miracle he reached the river in a borrowed Buran, but he couldn't identify the small cliffs that concealed his first prospecting pits with confidence. Where the stream had been there was a white blank, as even and aimless as the empty sky with its small harsh sun, which completed its low arc in four hours. The steep bank stood over *nothing*, its snowy ledges, bitten away by the wind, hung utterly silently in the air. The beauty was terrifying. Everything was colorful and unreal except for the man—Anfilogov with his clumping white eyelashes, a mane of ice on the fur of his hood. The professor unloaded a gasoline can, which tore at the down mittens he was blowing on, into a cliff fissure covered with white webbing, and the can quietly drowned, leaving a round hole. This foray of the professor's might have ended badly but didn't. The cold of the sub-Arctic night weighed on him but the darkness didn't. In the light of the barbed stars the untrodden snow was like a television screen flickering on an empty channel; the northern lights flickered in the sky like a flame from burning alcohol. Following his own tracks, the professor reached the winter quarters—a half-ruined hut that looked like a small canvas airplane that had crashed—without incident. Now Anfilogov had in mind this route as well: to the southwest, via the winter quarters, where according to the unspoken law of the taiga there were always supplies and matches.

Indeed, Anfilogov had not missed the mark that winter. The gas can was discovered literally a hundred meters from the previous year's camp, firmly stuck between granite walls spotted with condensation. They freed the can and rolled it toward the tent. The stream, which had loosened up the dolomite, was still snarling, its water seething as if it were being poured from a boiling kettle; last year's tracks from the expedition stood out on the old biscuit-color grass the way the rectangles of removed pictures stand out on wallpaper. Only here, at last, the fire got hot and crackled; a much-cheered Kolyan blew the acrid, garbage-fed flame to the very skies, so that heat blew on their caps. The hot food lacked all flavor: the rock hounds absorbed only the warmth, sucking the liquid up with their baked lips and stuffing their bellies with steamed bread. They didn't have the energy to move away from the dying fire and hissing mounds of coals where the heat rustled, rang, and overflowed under a skin of gentle ash. They felt as if they were in front of the greatest possible treasure, for the sake of which they had traveled across wet windfallen trees and the Lenten stone porridge of the endless shoals.

While they were setting up camp, Kolyan plucked low-growing, mousy-wool mayflower bells. Half-reclining in his sleeping bag, he sorted and sniffed the faded plants and lounged in silence such as he had never before maintained for a single hour. Anfilogov noted for the umpteenth time that his sword bearer had undergone a powerful change. For some reason this change gave the professor a bad feeling. Last autumn, after reluctantly selling the incredible rubies to the most discreet of all the agents (a pale Pole with a very odd, layered, doubled shadow whose solid little core was always darker), the professor for some reason gave Kolyan an unfairly small share. Previously, Kolyan had invariably rejoiced at receiving money, any money, even a ruble, unaware of whether it was a lot or a little, whether he had come out ahead or behind—which is what had made him invaluable to Anfilogov, who calculated all too well. This time his sword bearer didn't even peek inside the shiny envelope, as if he had guessed at the insult. In depriving Kolyan, the professor had naturally not been seeking advantage; indeed, he had felt revulsion for the excess that remained in his pocket. It was just that Kolyan had somehow become superfluous. Ever since, last summer, Anfilogov had led his irreplaceable workmate over the glossy slide-rocks and cold, bile-filled swamps, to inhabitation; ever since he had taken him, whimpering in the upper berth, to the train station and his little house on the outskirts of town, where the traveler was met by his ninety-year-old granny, who looked like a bandaged finger in her kerchiefs; ever since these humiliating actions, Kolyan's presence had become a burden to the professor. In Anfilogov's eyes, he had become as good as dead, and giving him money now was like throwing it in the garbage. Kolyan sensed this, of course. The strangest part was that he seemed to agree.

He virtually never showed up idle now, and if he did have occasion, as before, to overstay his welcome at the professor's, he didn't start in about car prices or a book he'd just read but fell quietly silent, plunged in his own thoughts. In the interval between the two expeditions, Kolyan visited all his fairy-tale kin, which consisted primarily of women scattered throughout dreadful, inhumanly remote little towns and settlements. Each time, Kolyan returned from his sisters and aunts quieter and more subdued; he returned from Solikamsk, where he had once dreamed of driving in a foreign car, without his mustache for some reason, with a bare pink spot under his nose that looked like a bandaid. Somewhere during these winding wanderings, Kolyan had been baptized. Now he sometimes crossed himself modestly, as if he had buttoned his clothes on the woman's side. A dark, damp silver chain stuck in the gap in his shirt, with its equally dark sticking cross.

With mounting irritation Anfilogov observed his workmate prepare for death, quietly and systematically, without asking anyone's permission. It was stupid and just plain dangerous to drag someone like that along on an expedition. Kolyan seemed to have a presentiment of a fateful coincidence and was mentally preparing himself for it, which was just legitimizing it, asking it to happen. The likelihood that those circumstances would hook the professor, too, was virtually a hundred percent. Simultaneously, Anfilogov could do nothing against these moods of Kolyan's—and he couldn't replace him with another workmate because then he couldn't count on the deposit's secret being kept. Somehow there wasn't anyone suitable among the professor's painstakingly separated partners, who existed in strict isolation. Because no candidate was better than another, they all blurred and became a single face—infinitely alien and utterly uninteresting to Anfilogov. As it turned out, he and Kolyan were each other's only kindred beings.

Among other options, Anfilogov thought about the possibility of setting off north alone. But once informed, Kolyan viewed the upcoming expedition with such a pilgrim's awe that he couldn't refuse him the trip. Meanwhile, he knew how to wound Anfilogov by constantly reminding him of the ill-fated envelope. Instead of spending his miserly share on false teeth (as the professor insistently advised, with false cheer), Kolyan invested his last kopek in equipment. He bought a pump for pumping groundwater out of the corundum prospecting pits. Actually, by Kolyan's logic, there was no point in new teeth for him. Anfilogov had been trying without luck to drive away the vision of a skull smiling a metal, slightly rusty smile.

He dreamed of this skull the first night at the corundum vein. The skull was dry and looked like it was made out of cardboard, and it was hanging in a banner-crimson, sun-heated tent in the manner of a wasp's nest. Anfilogov's mouth was as hot as a sauna inside, and he realized he still had a cold. His fat tongue touched his teeth, and Anfilogov was convinced that they were falling out of their sockets quite painlessly.

Waking in a sweat, not yet opening his eyes, which were stuck with tears and the first soft swarm of midges, Anfilogov did not immediately realize that his American implants were just fine. A milky fog was covering the surrounding area with a skin, each stand of trees, transparent and curlicued, was in its own striated cloud, as if in its own atmosphere—and nothing around was moving except for the rapids-filled river, which seemed to have filled its stone jugs and be continuously and noisily overflowing.

Tendrils of acrid smoke were still rising from yesterday's huge fire, which looked like the remains of a burned hut. The rock hounds washed haphazardly from a gushing rock and breakfasted on the remains of yesterday's feast, which they had thrown for themselves to celebrate being rid of the Dancing Pyralid. Before going to the prospecting pits, Anfilogov checked Kolyan's injured paws: the burns from the frozen bucket had tightened the thin, bright pink skin and made his palms as hard and smooth as a baby's bottom.

The path trampled from the camp to the site of their slave labor was, strangely enough, intact and dark on the silvery slope, as if it had been drawn with a finger on a sweating glass. Anfilogov was extremely worried. Once again he felt that same attentive gaze on himself that last year had accompanied the expedition from this spot all the way to the train. In the distance he could see the rusty patches of fir twigs the rock hounds had used to camouflage their find from chance competitors. When they came up to it, the teensy needles turned out to have almost all dropped from the branches. Through the naked branches, which looked like a rust-eaten sewer drain, the water shone quite close by.

"Take a look, Vasily Petrovich! The spot's high, but it's full of water!" Kolyan was amazed as he threw the camouflaging aside. "I thought it would fill up less!"

Last year's pit with its walls of wounded stone exhaled a melting underground cold on the rock hounds' faces, and a puzzling odor added in—a very faint, bitterly synthetic smell that dissolved when you tried to sniff it. Kolyan leaned over the pit and flared his reddened nostrils.

"It's some kind of salt, Vasily Petrovich!" he reported, coming up on all fours. "Or maybe not . . ."

The still water in the prospecting pit looked like an inverted saucer. Lots of tiny trash had accumulated near the walls—frozen crumbs from the needles, some kind of wool, fir twigs that looked like little crosses. Risking falling in, Kolyan stretched his fingers to the still surface. The water cautiously took them with its black lips, the way a harmless goat takes a piece of sugar. Somewhere under the water, in one of the walls, there was an untouched underground treasure—plus a polyethylene package with the discards from last year's good fortune, which was also worth at least ten thousand dollars.

Sniffing his wet hand as red and dirty as a carrot, Kolyan did not come to any specific conclusion right away.

"Let's pump it out, Vasily Petrovich!" he exclaimed brightly, wiping his paw on his pants. "Did we bring the pump here for nothing? And we have the gas. Fill 'er up!"

The professor didn't like equipment and understood nothing about it as a matter of principle. On the other hand, Kolyan literally adored metal and happily spent an hour at it, after which it started banging, smacking, and splashing in good order in the mine workings. The pit, however, bared itself slowly. Several times Anfilogov went to see how matters were progressing. The damp walls, coated with half-liquid clay, as if they'd been plastered with rusty wet gauze, were dark and angular. Trembling water was seeping out of them here and there, water much brighter than what was pumping out through the clear annular hose and plopping out thickly, soaking the nice new grass. As the water level dropped, rather than dissipate, the strange smell got stronger. The pit smelled like the maw of some fatally ill stone animal.

Kolyan's reddened eyes were tearing, and his eyelids were like fat abscesses. Time and again there were small accidents at the outflow. The cloudy hose sucked and swelled. Then Kolyan, swearing lovingly, pulled the clogged bell out of the water, twisted out the mesh, and poked out some rotten feathers and something that looked like a clump of velvet scraps.

"A year's a long time, Vasily Petrovich!" Kolyan commented didactically, stirring the muck at the bottom with a pole. "All manner of beast drowned!"

Just in case, before starting the motor up again, Kolyan scraped the fattened bottom with a bucket attached to the pole. His catch consisted of two decomposing, by now unidentifiable birds, the scraggly felt frame of a small hare, the round little bodies of small rodents, and wet flocks of bats. Observing his workmate strain this black soup and bones, Anfilogov felt an unfamiliar tightening in his chest, as if air had stuck in his lungs at an angle.

Halfway back to camp, he again felt as if he were suffocating, and this time the spasm lasted much longer. "Mining gasses," thought Anfilogov when the wooden pincers that had grabbed his ribs eased up a little. "Or maybe it isn't gasses. It's more like industrial waste.

Even thought there isn't a plant around for hundreds of kilometers. The cleanest spot. It really is strange." The bitter synthetic stuffed his nostrils and glued over his mucous membrane, which made his nasal septum itch like crazy. "Could I still have a cold?" the professor asked himself, sensing that if he sneezed right now, his life would spill out. "I think I still have the capsules left. Did the gemcutter bring the sweater or not? Or was Ekaterina Sergeyevna supposed to get it? Probably she was, otherwise why come to the station? Yes, she was holding some kind of bag. She forgot to give it to me. Women are always forgetting things. And now, because of her . . ." At this the professor's mind cleared, as if a breeze had blown through it. "We'll gather up last year's stones and leave," he told himself firmly, standing in the camp on the edge of yesterday's big fire. "Enough's enough. But for what, actually? If you count. . . . That's nine hundred thousand. . . . There's a million and a half in euros. . . . Plus interest . . . I've already got more than seventy. Enough for Kolyan's Mercedes? It's idiotic. . . . Anyway, no more stone quarries. We're leaving as fast as we can."

Despite the decision taken, Anfilogov was busy until four setting up camp. There was absolutely nothing to do. Kolyan, soaked and dirty, kept fussing around the prospecting pit, sometimes running up in his sloshing boots, which were as full as buckets, to grab a sandwich with his unwashed hands. He didn't need help. The professor was presented with an unforeseen, utterly superfluous opportunity simply to be in a space that he remembered less from his waking hours than from his own dreams. A lot had changed, although to the outward, approximate gaze nothing had. Storing the food so that chipmunks and other voracious beasts wouldn't get at it, Anfilogov suddenly realized that the tiny thieves had vanished. Nothing was rustling, and nothing was busy in last year's stalks. Something was wrong with the grass, too. Here and there it was white at the roots, like the gray hairs in a grown-out head of dyed hair, and in places it had detached from the soil in felted scraps, in the shape of inhumanly large inner soles. Mountain spirits, concerned by the fate of the underground store, must have been watching, but they, of course, had nothing to do with the departure of the grass's inhabitants because they lived in a complex symbiosis with all creatures and in a sense consisted of their organic lives. The reason for the damage was, of course, man. Maybe some experiments with clouds, or radiation from the space stations that swarmed over this spot like metal ants.

At the same time none of this looked like an ecological disaster. If there had been certain effects, nature had resisted them. The thick midges, the beauty and scourge of the corundum river, continued to pound in columns in any space of air, splashing the skin like oil from a red-hot skillet. Unseen birds lifted their voices first here, then there. The sounds were mechanical and slightly husky, like an old clock chiming half-awake; and the small bird cherry bush kept ringing like a sack of silver coins. The sounds roamed, losing their original source; the pink sun didn't so much shine as pierce the cloudy air, and the granite cliffs looked like blobs on a porous blotter. The beauty which the professor, in setting out on the expedition, had hoped not to see anymore, was not going anywhere; it had merely levitated, making it seem as if the sky began literally a meter above the ground.

Looking around, Anfilogov felt as if he'd been poisoned. For the first time in many years of illegal expeditions, which had always brought the professor money and a sense of freedom, he wanted to be home with his legs wrapped in an old-man's blanket and treating himself to some new tea. At this it suddenly dawned on Anfilogov that his incredible corundum luck might be Kolyan's, not his. Not for nothing had his sickly sword bearer prepared so fervently for the expedition and kissed his sweaty cross, which looked like a fly, whispering to himself.

★ ★ ★

It was nearly four o'clock when Kolyan, blue with cold, presented Anfilogov with a clean pit that looked a lot like a scoured burned kettle. The professor lowered himself down the angular wall, and his sleeves soaked up the cold, slowly seeping water. The stone plug with which the rock hounds had sealed off their treasure the previous year had swollen and looked like a wounded knee. Smiling with his manganese-colored maw, Kolyan solemnly handed the professor last year's lucky ax. Anfilogov took a swing and struck: the damp dolomite marble fell apart, and Kolyan and the professor brought into the light a crunching, ice-shedding polyethylene package, which looked like a package of frozen meat.

Ripping off the frozen shreds with a crack, Anfilogov was amazed by its lumpy contents, as if he had not been the one to fold and fill this wealth into its stone womb spread wide.

"Let well enough alone," the professor spoke, after catching his breath. "If we don't drown the backpack this time, we can lie under a palm tree to the end of our days."

"I don't want to lie under a palm, Vasily Petrovich," muttered Kolyan, drooping and averting his tearing gaze from the ruby bits. "I've traveled around and seen things. It's a broom, not a tree. Nothing but hairs on a pole and a brush at the top. There's no life to it."

"Well, buy yourself a foreign car," the professor muttered through his teeth.

"Have we been on our way to left luggage or something, Vasily Petrovich?" Kolyan exclaimed, almost in tears, moving his short straw-yellow eyebrows in anguish. "Come on. Let's see what's farther on there!"

"You'd be better off squinting," Anfilogov spoke softly and terrifyingly.

But at that the fog suddenly dispersed, and the sun, striking the earth like a ringing ball, lit up the insides of the opened corundum vein. There, Anfilogov saw something that made his knees weak and made him clutch at his heart.

And so began the second spate of ruby fever. The magnetism of the corundum river returned, and once again the rock hounds felt in their hands and shoulders the familiar mechanical pull of the pick's blows. As if bewitched, insensitive to the bruises and little blue-gray wounds from the bits of stone, they destroyed the underground palaces.

They couldn't go back until they'd exhausted the grandeur that had revealed itself to the rock hounds in the light of their two head-lamps, whose rays in the quiet, almost rustling air of the cave were like gray shadows. In order to move on, they had to destroy what daily arose before the rock hounds in the cold dolomite, in the fan-tastic voids, one of which turned out to be the geode of a huge agate almond, which was almost but not quite unbelievable. Each succes-sive layer of underground beauty stripped any authenticity from the preceding one, the way, during a restoration, the painting of an ear-lier master, once revealed, strips the value from the removed layer of paint. Anfilogov envied the mountain spirits that moved freely in the underground stone environment, like fish in water or birds in air.

The professor was still trying to pretend he just had a cold. Meanwhile, his workmate wasn't looking so hot either. Time and again Kolyan gave a shudder and his maw turned unnaturally red and, when he yawned, looked like a hideous withered flower. When Kolyan rested, hanging his swollen wrists between his knees, his fin-gers twitched, as if they were playing scales. Once, right in the mine, a cruel cramp seized him. Rolled up in a ball, he got stuck between two fir struts, and Anfilogov had to chop through one, beating and crushing the wood, which was soaked through and sodden, like fish flesh. When the strut gave way and broke, streams of stone bits showered down, and the vault over the rock hounds shifted with a slow creak, as if it had dropped down like a dump truck discharging its load. Hurrying, Anfilogov strained and pulled Kolyan out of the pit and onto the grass, which was badly poisoned by the acrid under-ground water. The cramp was strong, like an armature. Anfilogov was barely able to loosen the seized muscles, while Kolyan was gasp-ing for breath and baring his bloody steel at the cross-shaped tops of the firs. Abandoning the sufferer at the first improvement, Anfilogov leaped for the mine: the vault had swollen, but the slabs, which had pushed out slanted, had somehow wedged each other. Bits of dolomite were still rising underfoot like clouds of dust, and among the bits was a wonderful sample with a ruby fire inside, which Anfilogov kicked.

The rock hounds lost count of the days. Déjà vu, which declared itself as soon as the camp was finally set up and things had been given a place, helped in this, and the men once again grew accustomed to the landscape's outlines. First they mixed up the twenty-first and twenty-fifth of the month, which were full of holes and had unexplained losses of time and a general tedious rain that wouldn't start or end but seemed to be roaming around in circles, dragging its tattered watery locks. Then the gap started expanding. They could no longer say with any accuracy whether it was yesterday or the day before that Anfilogov's medicine had run out. The most powerful déjà vu occurred whenever they set to any kind of work. At any attempt to take a step into the future, the rock hounds wound up in the past. Time stopped; the white nights passed over the camp like the shadows of light clouds.

They couldn't judge the time by the dwindling of supplies. The high-calorie delicacies lay there practically untouched in sturdy sacks of crude plastic. The rock hounds didn't eat any more than they had the previous year. Their stomachs were sensitive: the minute they were disturbed, bile gushed out with the same vile underground aftertaste. So open cans of pâté and ham lay scattered about the tent, their rusty lids flapping, until their contents were covered with a leathery mold.

Meanwhile, mysterious water discharged by the drops in underground pressure drowned the workings regularly. If they were lucky, the bottom of the corundum pit, which was half a meter lower than the small mine, accumulated just a round puddle overnight. More often, the wood stood in the mine like a long mirror tongue where the dark reflections of the vault were as motionless as the stones themselves. But sometimes the puddle would first get sucked into a curving crack and then suddenly return with a gurgling and sucking, and the water, like a ditch full of litter, would rise all the way to grass level in an hour. Something anomalous had happened in the system of geological faults, and they couldn't call the plumber in to fix the problem.

There was plenty of work for the pump and motor. The gas can was half empty. The water, heavy and swollen, was now aggressive, there was no doubt of that. Anfilogov could no longer pretend it was harmless. Kolyan's scarlet maw and his bright red nostrils, as if the hairs growing in them were burning, were sure signs of cyanide poisoning.

Nevertheless, as had happened the last time, Anfilogov was reluctant to leave. His will was paralyzed, and layers of colorless fog swam in his consciousness. Time and again the professor was doused with the minty horror of death, and his old knees got as weak as empty cardboard boxes. But the extreme cold, which warned the professor of danger, simultaneously promised him release from all earthly cares.

In point of fact, Anfilogov could not have found a better place to die had he lived another four hundred years. Here, in his corundum servitude, he recognized himself as both a prisoner and foe of that mysterious power he had so longed to reach. The terrible beauty that was dissolved in the thickest, bottom-most stratum of the undying sky, which here began right at the earth, an ineluctable beauty, cunning, diffused throughout, and painfully irritating to the professor's nerves, had finally become vulnerable. With perfect certainty, Anfilogov sensed that the improbable corundum vein was the *internal*, vitally important organ of this beauty. Now, each blow of the pick at the next underground wonder was a blow at the beauty that trembled on the surface and was becoming gradually scarcer. Here was the river, where each ray of sun had had the beautiful form of a smile and which had lost its gleam and was flowing sullenly, with black shadows near the bottom; a luxuriant bird cherry had shriveled and shaken off the fine trash from its brief flowering like cigarette ash. Beauty still clung in shreds to the sharp points of the birch branches, which had tried to smooth it out, stretch it out for the light, still clinging to the cliffs, which were polished here and there like slanted mirrors and here and there overgrown with fantastic moss. But the day began and the rock hands picked up their strong, worn picks.

The professor was more removed from people than ever before. One afternoon, he imagined human shouts coming from the river, like the chatter of birds. It was an illusion. Diving behind the small cliffs and pushing the apathetic Kolyan in there, too, Anfilogov leaned against a triangular beam of light formed by the wind-swept plates lying up against each other heavily. Four kayaks, jumping and banging their bellies on the foamy splashes, were racing down the small but deep stream, which tried to turn them crosswise and smash their small vessels against the wet granite. Driven by their powerful titanium paddles, the kayaks suddenly turned up directly under the cliffs. Anfilogov could discern the buckles on their huge life jackets, which looked like orange suitcases, and their dark blue helmets with splashed screens; one kayaker lacked a helmet and his face was twisted from the tension and shining from the water and sweat, like a piece of silver. Anfilogov's suppressed survival instincts cried out to him to wave, jump up, and call for help—but he kept squatting there, awash in horror at the thought that strangers would notice their tent and the fresh sauce stains from their workings, or that one of the kayaks would overturn and the blue-headed monsters would climb out on the shoal to dry off and be companionable.

Anfilogov knew that he couldn't withstand a simple human gaze now. He was numb, and he felt as if he had grown invisible wings beating on his back, or a large bird had perched on his shoulders to claw his cold spine. But Anfilogov's angel flapped in vain: the kayakers passed through the rift like needles through a sloppy seam, the last paddler's paddle flashed as it plunged into the tight dark jumble of water, and the kayakers were lost in the bubbling crevice, swallowed up by the solid, cave-stone shadow. Anfilogov straightened his tingling legs with difficulty and then helped the sleepy Kolyan, who hadn't even glanced at the river as he stood there on all fours, drooling into his beard, get up. Slipping around in his half-empty, mud-caked boots, Kolyan looked at Anfilogov with an apologetic smile, and the professor was suddenly struck at how little remained of his hardy sword bearer and how strangely his breathing kept breaking off, as if he were trying to climb higher and grab some other, heavenly oxygen. Nonetheless, the professor did not expect that the next morning Kolyan would actually die.

★ ★ ★

Especially because everything had been going as usual since morning. Kolyan had dug around among his greased blades and gone off like an automaton to pump out the underground water. His tottering figure subsequently appeared between the boulders as if were being born, like a torn banner, on a shaft of wood. Anfilogov was about to start cooking, but he spat and climbed into his still-warm sleeping bag, pulling the tight zipper right up to his nose. He woke up from the unusual, spacious silence. There were some sounds: a small bird was tinkling at the very top of a sunny birch tree, sounding like a spoon on a crystal glass, and the river was evenly noisy. But the space, to his perception, felt as if not a single radio or television station remained on air, as if the satellite network and the satellites themselves had vanished. The air was utterly empty, and the professor realized instantly that he was now alone.

Kolyan lay at the bottom of the corundum mine, face down in the remains of the groundwater, which the pump was still trying to suck out as it jammed with sand. Anfilogov gave something a jerk and the equipment stalled. Up top, Kolyan, in his crushed and rusty canvas overalls, looked like the remains of a mangled mechanism, and his darkened hair swirled around his head as if machine oil were dripping out. At first Anfilogov couldn't believe it. Lowering himself in three jumps, the professor tried to lift the heavy Kolyan up, but the body seemed to be glued to the puddle. Finally, Anfilogov pulled it away and dumped it on his knee. But no matter how much he struck Kolyan on the back, no matter how much he pressed, after turning the long-armed body over, on his recalcitrant ribs, he did not hear the saving cough or the cock's crow of life return. His attempts at artificial respiration into the stuck-together mustached mouth ended with tight red circles in Anfilogov's eyes. Finally, when his rib cage cracked like plywood, which made it look as if Kolyan were smiling, it became clear that there was no hope. Anfilogov sat there a little while, squeezing his pounding head in his hands to make it stay in one place. Then, leaning over and getting a better grip, he dragged his workmate up on the grass.

In the very center of the silence and emptiness the professor acted automatically. He undressed Kolyan on a sheet of canvas and washed him from a pot of heated water. The emaciated body with the sunken ribs reminded him of a squeezed-out tube of toothpaste. When the professor splashed Kolyan on the face, cautiously, holding his damp hair aside, he saw that his workmate had died with that apologetic smile, which had petrified quickly: first the dead man's violet mouth was covered with a gloss and started melting away inside, like a spring-time icicle, then the transparent became solid—and soon under his mustache a mayflower bell formed out of a fibrous charoite through which his steel teeth gleamed like cleavage fissures in a crystal matrix. Observing this well-known metamorphosis for the first time, Anfilogov couldn't help but stare at it. Spasms tugged at his weakened body, his flesh seemed to shrink, like fabric after it has been washed, and it became tight and uncomfortable for the lanky professor.

Overcoming the odd daytime twilight, Anfilogov searched among Kolyan's things for some clean linen, which smelled of cheap laundry powder. He could see that it had been put there beforehand precisely for such an eventuality. The package was carefully taped up, and inside a gilded paper icon of some saint that looked like a Christmas tree ornament was jostling around. Anfilogov was about to get angry at this kind of base precaution, at the ready-made invitation to death, but the feeling passed quickly. Somehow, by lifting the dead man's legs, he pulled the faded knit underpants over his body. Then came the turn for the relatively white T-shirt, which he had to put on by holding Kolyan in an embrace. The professors movements were as awkward and angular as the dead man's unwilling turns: one puppet dressing another. Anfilogov felt as if he had exactly the same kind of jutting bones as the dead Kolyan, bones that looked like rag-wrapped sticks, and he couldn't figure out just what the difference was between them now.

What for? The Stone Maiden, the Mistress of the Mountain, was probably displeased with the professor's behavior. But Anfilogov had stayed true to himself—the only person he had never, under any circumstances, not even an iota, betrayed. Wasn't this loyalty, this fidelity, worth something? You see, all his life Anfilogov had only done what rose in value! Even now, emaciated, poisoned, and frightening of face, like a bat, he clung to this unchanging, nearly undamaged "I," which could gather its forces and carry him to civilization.

Kolyan was lying on the canvas content, misbuttoned, and barefoot, because his boots, once they dried out by the fire, wouldn't go back on his wooden feet. Kolyan's eyes, clouded with a bluish milk, were still open; the professor brushed them with the palm of his hand and wiped the moisture off on himself. Then he went to the tent and dug around for a while, choosing the best stones and stuffing the rest willy-nilly into the unfastened sleeping bag. Returning, the professor stuffed all four pockets of Kolyan's weatherproof jacket with choice corundums, surrounded the dead man with the rest, like a goose with apples, and wrapping the canvas, made a long cocoon with the help of a rope. The sleeping bag, which was stuffed with stones and tied up, too, came out looking like a rasping mummy. The professor dragged it on the folded tent toward the poisoned pit, shoved it into the collecting groundwater, which was lightly touching the walls, and then dumped it into the sunken mine, where the last shoring groaned like an old man under the ceiling's slanted press. The motor and pump, most of the provisions, and the rest of the expedition's goods went in after the sleeping bag, which was seated in a human pose by the polluted wall. The professor left himself just a few cookies and jerky, which he intended to wrap up in the remaining sleeping bag and carry on his chest.

Finally came the straps' turn. Cutting them off the backpack, Anfilogov strapped Kolyan, who was supposed to serve as a container for the goods, under the knees and just below his heart. Lying across the swaddled corpse, the professor checked the straps, adjusted them, and moved his shoulders a little, feeling an elbow poking out uncomfortably under the canvas. Nonetheless, he could not bury Kolyan like a dog. He couldn't bring rescuers here to collect the body either. Anfilogov had no intention of sharing the secret and letting people come to the deposit, which he wanted to possess alone, from afar. That was his decision. The corundum pit—more fully and clearly than those special cupolaed structures—had proved to be a place for encountering nonexistent God, and the professor had no intention of making his personal catacombs accessible to all. Here he had earned the chance to leave God the loser—and to take his loot, dragging it out by deceit, taking a favor from a dead man. Alongside the winter hut, as best the professor remembered, grew a conspicuous reddish-brown birch with bark like oiled paper. Anfilogov intended to trouble his workmate a little and bury the choice corundums until better times, and then traveling light, make his way to the lumber mill and make his statement. There was no question of reaching an agreement with the local police, as represented by the hard-drinking, pot-bellied policeman.

Anfilogov spent the night under the open sky, across which

spread a single flat cloud that rippled all the way to the horizon. He rested his head on Kolyan, the same way he always arranged himself on the backpack he took hiking, but the bundle with the body had hardened awkwardly, and the professor's neck went numb. Anfilogov kept trying to drop off while simultaneously speaking to people. Kolyan wasn't among them, naturally, but his former wives appeared in turn, Ekaterina Sergeyevna, his business partners, and his son from his first marriage—a sparrow-like man he barely knew who wore a tie that was a little too big and was tucked into his trousers under his belt. Some of his colleagues appeared before Anfilogov as if alive; others in the form of familiar photographs. The latter were precise, whereas the former got blurry and tried to slip away.

Naturally, he couldn't get any better a night's sleep than you can in an overcrowded room. Nevertheless, with the first glassy rays of sunlight Anfilogov was ready to set off on his journey. After getting his sleeping bag and food well arranged on his chest, he lay down and threw himself into his main burden. He was able to get up after the first time. It was doable, only the ground kept rocking, like a raft piled high and floating off. Right then, Anfilogov saw the little wet, gold icon in the grass the corpse had crushed. He honestly tried to squat down for it with the crackling Kolyan on his neck, but he immediately realized he was never going to reach that icon in this life. Then the professor cast a stealthy parting glance at his bedewed corundum servitude and set off sideways with uneven, drunken steps and with a needle trembling in his heart like the arrow of a compass.

Part Six

★

1

★

HOLIDAYS ARE TIMES EVERYONE LIKES TO BE LIKE EVERYONE ELSE.
That's why Krylov didn't like holidays. For him the carousing and
partying were empty situations when he, sullenly pretending to be a
participant in the merrymaking, would goggle at the fireworks or
dance with yet another one of Tamara's "girlfriends"—on the thick
carpet, in boots that felt as if they were filled with sticky sand. He
didn't know how to celebrate privately either; he didn't understand
how it was done. But this time Krylov decided to give it a try.

With his arm around Tanya, he could hang out in a crowd without a care, and Tanya wanted this very much, too. She'd been excited the night before and laughed a lot, tossing salted nuts at her comically resigned spy. They'd parted content with each other, anticipating the fun—that is, essentially their first day off in the ten weeks of
their trying experiment. So that they could start having fun right away,
Tanya and Ivan altered their usual procedure. Rather than fortune-
telling with the atlas, they made a date to meet on Ascension Square,
where a big celebration was planned—a bazaar of folk arts, a parade
of military historical clubs, a flower show. Marking on his map of
the city center the next, not entirely legitimate spot, Krylov attempted
—unsuccessfully as always—to read some logic into the thickish
scattering of trysts. All he could see was that lots of streets looked
like the punctured veins of a drug addict. He was also struck
unpleasantly by how soiled and patched the atlas was. Krylov
thought it was long since time to buy himself and Tanya fresh sets of
municipal tarot cards.

But even this minor expenditure was a problem for Krylov. He
found he was almost entirely out of money. The six hundred dollar

bill Tamara had given him had not changed this state of affairs. It turned out to be a collector's item issued in a limited print run. Krylov was not up to finding a rich notaphilist, and it was insulting to change his "Pamela" at one of the regular currency exchanges that had displaced the cat-pissy entryways and free toilets. Tamara expressed herself entirely in this generous gift: the goods she showered on Krylov were breathtakingly excessive but not meant for real life. If the gifts found a utilitarian use, this unique excess, through which Tamara's feelings were manifested, was lost. The beauty of the silken candles melted, banally; a collector's wine in a stone bottle laid to rest in a wooden sarcophagus at the *right* angle was used like rotgut. Krylov never did understand its rich bouquet. The main thing wasn't the wine but this inviolable angle of storage and the precious dust, more precious than gilt, on the bottle, which Krylov could not bring himself to touch with his coarse fingers.

The whole point of the gift was that you couldn't use it. Rummaging for change in all his pockets, which were more threadbare than his summer and winter clothes themselves, which were still decent, Krylov was aware yet again that Tamara had absolutely no concept of his everyday reality. All he had was one thousand nine hundred eighteen rubles and twenty kopeks. Krylov realized that in a few days he would have to borrow from Farid—everyone borrowed from Farid—but he had enough for modest entertainments.

You could feel the holiday in the tense, chillier air. The many bands, which you couldn't really hear but could sense as the pressure increased on their diaphragms, seemed to inflate the day, like a huge balloon that was just about to sail away. On Ascension Square the crowd flooded out of the Metro, nearly dragging the turnstiles with them and carrying the nice young policemen along. Once out of the Metro the city dwellers found themselves among the canvas stalls, which fluttered and flapped like nomadic gypsy tents; inside, in the pink and yellow linen dusk, nesting dolls were heaped up like tropical fruits, and Madonna-and-child lights that worked either with a battery or a plug gave off electric light beams and flickered their golden halos. The jewelry stalls were doing a lively trade. Women with simple jug-faces pawed the round beads and berry-sized rings, sorted through the laminated boxes and the fat plunger-shaped candlesticks. The stones, as far as Krylov could tell, were milky and fibrous, with nasty, off-color inclusions, and he rejoiced, carefree, that he had not laid hands on that roguish assortment.

He still had more than an hour until their rendezvous, but Krylov preferred to take up the agreed-upon position immediately. He walked to the top of the ten broad, polished steps over which loomed the dais and a monument that seemed to soar into the sky with a canonical outstretched palm and a black head like a cannonball in makeup with a triangular Lenin beard. The holiday was swilling around in the enormous cold sunbath, the doves were storming, the flags clapping, and the advertising banners were swelling in the wind. Krylov had never seen so many people in his field of vision at one time; the awareness of this fact made him anxious. Time and again Krylov stood on tiptoe, his fists in his pockets and a chill in his fingers. People kept coming; excited children swayed on their fathers' shoulders like Bedouins on camels. Two priests strode past Krylov wearing thick beards that might have been ironed along with their cassocks; behind them hurried the artists in their folkloric sarafans, their eyes smeared like plums, and wearing worn red boots. Not far away, alongside a patrol car, which was calmly enduring the festive citizens, a fat police sergeant was chatting with a masked White officer who was sipping beer and working his jaws. The officer's saber was amusing, like a toy wooden horse. Maskers were mixing everywhere with the men on duty; puppets were wandering in the crowd, plush giants on skinny human legs that were hollow inside.

Tanya wasn't late yet, but from her mounting absence Krylov realized she certainly would be. Meanwhile, City Day was about to enter its final phase. On the dais, right above Krylov, the first of the city's leadership had already appeared; still not required, they looked like doves perched by chance, turning their heads distractedly, but clearly the mayor's appearance was expected at any moment. A White officer started running, holding his saber. The megaphones howled inarticulately, testing. And then he appeared: an old man with a dye job and a well-formed head on narrow shoulders, in front of his own portrait, which stretched halfway across the façade of City Hall, as if it were Judgment Day. Krylov could see his fastidious wrinkles, which were long, like sideburns spattered with a dark sauce. The mayor was a head shorter than any of his subordinates, but they had probably put a footstool there for him, and he suddenly rose, having placed his ostentatious little turtle-shaped hand on his granite-gray lapel.

Microphones immediately rose up in front of the mayor. His reverberating speech bounced back from the distance and echoed, rolling from the other side of the pond, so that it sounded like cannons answering. Meanwhile the police, stretched out in a chain, parted the crowd; the paving stones, littered here and there with colorful pieces of paper, were bared but also ominous, as if iron had been added to the humped stone. On the left, on a platform, a military band raised its burning copper muzzles in readiness and fell still. Suddenly the director made a desperate movement, as if he'd decided to leap from a skyscraper, and a march thundered out.

Krylov had no choice but to stand where he was. He had known that Tanya would not make it for the beginning of the parade of military historical clubs, and he craned his neck, trying to make out her familiar haircut and flat duck walk in the flowing jumble near the Metro. Meanwhile, a historical drama was unfolding on the square. First to march across the paving stones were mustachioed popeyes in green uniforms and tight white trousers, with chess caps of some kind on their heads. The eighteenth century was followed by Cossacks, who pranced nimbly on their glossy silken horses, to the playful music of their hooves, as splendid as if they were women in patent leather shoes dancing and clapping.

Then came an expectant pause. Something formidable was taking shape in the depths of Ascension Avenue, cock-crow commands rang out, and shadows were lining up. The director aimed his baton and gave his riveted musicians a fierce look, as if he intended to turn them into frogs and rats that very minute. Barely holding out until the director's sweep, the band struck up "Farewell, My Pretty Slav." On the dais the mayor assumed a dignified air, the buttons on his quasi-military coat flashing.

The gentlemen officers marched handsomely. Krylov was amazed at how foolish they looked individually and how imposing in formation. Their step in their sharp crease was smart, and the sun burned on each and every chest. Each White Guard was copied multiple times in the rank, which made it seem as if its power was mounting in a geometric progression. The march music, which at a certain height reached a doleful, desperate cry, could not drown out the synchronized boots striking the paving stones. Ahead of the officer rank, a black velvet banner fluttered in the wind, and from it smiled a narrow skull, and gold crossed bones sparkled like lightning in a cloud. Line after line, rank after rank, the White Guards took the shuddering square; one officer company marched across, and behind it, under the leadership of a stout, clean-shaven colonel who bore himself leaning nearly all the way back, came another, and behind it a third was implied. The drum cracked dryly.

Then, out of the depths of Cosmonaut Avenue, as if out of the very thick of the colorful crowd, other, jagged music rang out. "For the power of the Soviets . . . and we will die as one"—an old choral recording was carried by the wind, and somehow it became clear that everyone singing was now truly dead. The holiday crowd surged back from the pavement, and the linen trading tents shuddered, like sets during a scene change. In the gap that formed, they marched, their legs pushing open the long hems of their heavy, damp-looking overcoats. The Red soldiers were not so much marching as surging forward. Their high-cheekboned faces, which from far away looked like clenched fists, were white under their pointed cloth helmets. This whole sullen mass seemed to have come out on this sunny day from some never-ending cold rain. Red banners hung above the ranks, sticking together, and huge paper carnations bubbled. On the left, ahead of the formation, a short man dressed up like a commissar, who looked in his broad riding breeches like a swallowtail butterfly, punched out his military steps as best he could. Due to his short stride, he seemed to be hopping in place, lifting his legs in the air, driven from behind by the press of the revolutionary element. To his amazement, Krylov recognized the butterfly-man, despite his large service cap and lacy vertical beard. It was his old classmate, an earnest history major from a parallel course, who, like Krylov, had probably forgotten his university science, but who, like Krylov himself, like many, had held onto his ineradicable historical dream, which he was now attempting to bring to life in public.

However, the Red Army soldiers' appearance on the square was apparently not part of the holiday program. They probably represented a competing club or else had not submitted an application to the organizing committee. The police started getting worried, and their worried walkie-talkies started muttering, spitting red-hot ether. The patrol car beside which the cop and White officer had so recently been standing, peacefully drinking beer, switched on its flasher and, hooting, attempted to move from its spot—but the sluggish citizens just kept moving around in front of its bumper—each one absolutely had to be on the other side—and a fizzing soda can flew out of someone's hand and spilled sweet bubbles all over the hood of the car. Krylov's nerves were already stretched to their limit. He hated Tanya's absence with every fiber of his being—and suddenly he saw her coming up the Metro steps, digging in her shoulder purse and reminding him of a hen that had decided to peck itself under its wing. Krylov's first impulse was to run toward her—but the thick of humanity between him and Tanya was rocking, and it would be the simplest thing to miss each other, so Krylov could only wait for

Tanya herself to make her way to the agreed-upon spot. Now he was irritated at her, at the crowd, the wind, the plum-colored plush monster that was blocking his view of Tanya, and the self-appointed speaker who had climbed on the roof of a van and brought with him a good-sized banner of an insolent red, on a pole that looked like it had been yanked from the nearest fence. An alarmed saleswoman stuck her head in its plastic cap out of the van and shouted something; the speaker paid her not the least mind; he stamped his army-booted feet and shouted poetry in a hoarse voice.

Because he was tensely following Tanya, who kept disappearing and reappearing, Krylov did not see the Red Army soldiers turn onto Ascension Avenue. One quick glance, though, and he was struck numb with terror. The military maskers were about to clash head on. The area of free paving stones between them, marked in the middle by an airy ice cream cup that was trembling in the wind, was closing quickly. On both sides of the parade the crowd was literally hanging on the chain of policemen; the cops, crucified by this inordinate weight, held onto each others' tensed arms, as if they were tied in fast, blood-soaked knots. People's bright holiday caps were knocked off at the least pressure. Glancing quickly upward, Krylov saw that the fathers of the Riphean capital had hastily quit the dais, shielded by their bodyguards' rectangular backs.

Meanwhile, the Red Army soldiers had changed their pace—and now the first wave of greatcoats split up and, boots thumping, broke into a heavy run. The back rows, lagging behind by a few seconds, reached uncontrollably after the first, as if the square under the Red Army soldiers were tilting, sending them forward, against their class enemy. The ranks of White Guards stumbled and their black banner swished. The Red Cavalry in front were already galloping like horses, overtaking their masker commissar, who looked like he was hobbling on needles. The orchestra gasped; someone's fire-breathing loudspeaker drowned out the orchestra and started thundering either threats or panicked and muddled commands.

Meanwhile the ranks of White Guards straightened out and shifted to a civilian quick-step. Some officers made a strange movement, as if they were checking their watches as they went. One, fair-haired, with a pelican sack of a second chin, held back, digging around. Then, as if doing something purely personal that had nothing to do with anyone else, took aim.

A dry and powerful shot rang out as if a limb had cracked at a bend; the masker commissar took a little leap and fell writhing on the paving stones. In that first moment his men surged away from him, letting people see his short legs kicking in their wrinkled boots. Then isolated shots began hopping like fleas. Another Red Army soldier lowered himself heavily to the ground, like an old woman, and turned his tear-stained face to the sky. Another leaped over him, whipping a whistling, cooing chain in the air. Many shed their heavy greatcoats as they ran, taking out iron rods and homemade nunchuks. One little policeman leapt out in front of the running men, turned his head, firing his government-issue gun into the air, and was immediately knocked down and a smacking noise was heard, like the sound of a horrible kiss, and the little policeman started crawling, all twisted up, unnaturally, pressing the black spot under his heart with his red hand.

Krylov watched the slaughter completely removed, as if his brain's translator from his outer to his inner language had been turned off. Working her elbows and turning this way and that, Tanya was making her way crosswise through the human mass, which was still calm, lazy even. From time to time she threw her arm up in its torn green sleeve, and Krylov threw up his own in response. The sunny scene on the far shore of the blue-striped pond was surreally distinct. There, evidently, no one knew anything yet, and the folklore artists were dancing in a circle near the bright pond, shaking their triangular kerchiefs. Krylov's glance latched on briefly to one other familiar face. The spy, naturally. He was sitting literally ten meters away from Krylov, having hoisted himself onto one of the granite spheres that adorned the porch of the old mining college; like a caricature of Munchausen on a cannonball, the spy set his spurs into the stone sphere, meanwhile not letting go of his heavy plastic bag, which threatened to tip him over. The spy's view was superb; his face reflected horror. Suddenly the spy leaned back, fixing his gaze on the unnaturally clear and festive sky: an ominous scream was mounting there, accompanied by a smooth, almost soundless whistle that made Krylov's lips numb, swept by a shudder.

That same moment, from behind City Hall, from behind the statues of kolkhoz women and steelworkers poking up on the roof, like Apollos and Artemises wrapped in old newspapers, massive federal helicopters emerged, dark and glittering in the sun. With flickering propellers in three places, propellers that seemed to be turning in different directions, the massive machines looked like sledgehammers with dragonfly wings and were clumsy in the air, like a terrible waking dream. Spreading a low wind that choked the holiday flags, the helicopters hovered over the square, where the battle between White Guards and Red Cavalry had turned into a champing, cursing jumble. Krylov, who had seen all kinds of fights, was sickened by the bloody heaps and the slippery stirrings of the wounded, crushed by the dead. You couldn't fully believe in the reality of the carnage. You could barely hear the women's cries in the rows pressed up to the police cordon, and many spectators' eyes could have been looking at a wall. From his accursed spot, which Tanya, borne off to the side by the tossing that had started, still couldn't reach, Krylov could see what was left of the commissar: he seemed to have been smashed to pieces inside his clothes, and there was what looked like a dead fly on his forehead. Krylov realized that the minute he descended to the paving stones he would cease to see Tanya and everything would probably be nearly over. The word "over" reverberated inside him like a simultaneous striking of all the keys on some monstrous black piano. He tried to send Tanya strength with his look, and she, in her twisted top, with a vivid scratch from her wrist to her elbow, was making a new leap in the hard human waves. About half an hour had passed since the moment she had appeared on the Metro stairs, and in this time dozens of people on the square had managed to die.

Meanwhile they had thrown coils of tackle from the helicopters, and broad-shouldered figures packaged in something resembling a brownish-red chitin, were sliding down them. Simultaneously, from the side-streets, a double chain of riot police wedged into the motley crowd, their helmets catching the light. Now, for the first time, Krylov sensed a tectonic shift in the swaying crowd. Everyone standing nearby started falling the way people do when a Metro car brakes to sharply. They were crushed and knocked about, and the steps underfoot turned into pits of treacherous depth into which rows of people dropped like loose earth. Tanya's green shirt flashed in Krylov's eyes, and there was a flash and a gasp nearby, as if they had torn a piece of air and stone flesh out of the world with wooden tongs. Above Krylov, the layered branches of a now pink maple tree shook, and some kind of black berry suddenly started falling from there, lashing Krylov's shoulder.

* * *

The two and a half hours Krylov spent on the cordoned square seemed like an eternity, as the saying goes. The crowd was stormed. Squeezed in on all sides by frightened people close to fainting, Krylov was dragged first to one side and then back, all the while trying not to step into invisible traps, of which the most dangerous were the treacherously round and nimble bottles.

At first he tried to go in the direction of where the green patch had last flashed, but he soon realized there weren't any directions. The whirlwind from the chirring federal machines would let up and then swoop down again, not letting him breathe; the clutches of balloons beat madly, vibrating like colored turbulence. The trading tents drowned like sailboats; the speaker on the food van had lost his balance and fallen to his knees, and his white leaflets dropped out of his roomy jacket with a soft thud and immediately rocketed upwards, covering the square.

For a while, Krylov stood on one leg, his face hidden in a woman's fine hair that had stuck over his face like the barest cobweb; then, having attempted to move where it was freer, he nearly stepped on a child—a little girl of about four, tear-stained, with little eyes so wet each seemed to have shed a lake of water. The weakened child was trying to sit up on a paving stone, looking around and tucking in her checkered skirt. Praying to he did not know who that he wouldn't lose his balance, Krylov picked the child up under his arm, grunted, and sat her on his shoulders, following the example of other men on the square who were holding their children up high, away from the jumble of feet. The child's body was a little heavy and drooped; suddenly Krylov's neck was wet and warm and smelled like chicken broth, and the little girl, sobbing in a whisper, covered Krylov's eyes with her cold little hands. Grabbing the child by her soft little wrists wrapped in little bead bracelets, Krylov gave his passenger a ride, pretending to be a pony, and simultaneously tried to relax, obediently yielding this way and that along with all the other crushed bodies.

He wasn't thinking about anything anymore and only set his sights on anything green, catching sight of a shirt with mud streaks and then a giant carnival frog with a man poking his head out of it, pale, like white bread soaked in water. The poplar in front of the college was flooded and choking on the whitened greenery, the maple's leaves were swimming in their own sap. At times it seemed to Krylov that nothing bad had happened yet. The main thing was not to fall. Instinctively, Krylov shied away from a package caught in the crush in which the humped pieces of crushed crockery were rubbing huskily and scratching the plastic. The crowd, pressed into a briquette, bore numerous inorganic admixtures: the most innocent objects— holiday purchases, umbrellas, even pens—which could cause injuries just as bad as small bombs exploding on the field of class warfare and which sprinkled Krylov with some kind of acrid, crumbly filth. Krylov was amazed he was still capable of thought. There was a doughy daze on most of the faces turned up and swaying around him and the languid child. Others, revealing their rush-hour habits on public transportation, pragmatically straightened their slipping eyeglasses on a neighbor's shoulder.

After a while, the swaying stopped. The crush rose and then began quietly thinning out. Krylov found himself in front of a chain of riot police who had evidently divided the human mass up into small, nonthreatening segments. "Respected residents and guests of the Riphean capital!" a pleasant woman's voice that had some honey added thickly to its officialness, rang out, reverberating multiple times. "In connection with the terrorist act that has occurred, we ask everyone to pass through a document checkpoint. Please, show your passport as you leave the police cordon. Ambulance brigades are awaiting the injured. Please, remain calm. Our mayor, Sergei Ignatievich Krupsky, expresses his profound indignation at the acts of the mob that disrupted Ripheans' long-waited holiday."

Meanwhile, the artificially cloudless holiday stretched on as before, and the wind died down, and there was so much sun that it spread like a layer of golden fat on the smooth surface of the pond, heated the broken glass, and sprinkled the anguished faces with a shiny white powder. The nearest riot policeman had some kind of dark, cooked blob on his shield, like spilled soup on a burner. Not far away, a lanky teenager with purple hair that looked like the result of electroshock, was pissing, having unfastened his Teflon trousers, against one of the interlocked shields. But the guardians of law and order were imperturbable and paid no attention to the wobbling stream of popular protest. The announcement about the document check was repeated every five minutes, like in the Metro. Someone in the crowd decided to light up, and streams of tasty smoke wafted by. Farther away, beyond the cordon, someone's green Panama flashed by and then was lost.

Suddenly a grinning guy was doing a kind of desperate Australian crawl in Krylov's direction; his eyes looked like they were laughing, though in fact that was the bluish bags under his eyes twitching.

"Papa! Papa! The nice man put me up high!" the child shouted and blissfully tumbled into the trembling arms, freeing Krylov from her moist, velvet yoke.

Immediately Krylov felt as if he'd landed on the moon. The man fell to his knees and kept feeling and pulling, hugging and hugging again his little one, trying to wipe her face with his wet finger wrapped in a handkerchief.

"You're fine, just fine. I found you, Mashka," the man murmured. "Mama, we'll call Mama right now. Oh!" He discovered her wet tights and turned his helpless round face with its short, feathery eyebrows toward Krylov.

"That's all right," Krylov said in a voice that stuck. "You wouldn't have a cigarette would you?"

"Of course, of course." The man jumped up and held out a crushed pack of Parliaments. His last cigarettes rattled around like limp noodles. His lighter flicked. Krylov's head spun from the deep drag, and his brain unclenched like a fist, releasing quick images that immediately whisked over the legionaries' shields.

"I can't thank you enough. I don't even know how to express it," the man kept talking, greedily champing his cigarette and exhaling smoke through his tiny nose. "Anything you need from me—help, money—I have it. Not a lot, but some. I'm a programmer. I work at Riphvideoplus. I write games for computers, cell phones, children's laptops. . . . Dronov! Pavel Alexandrovich Dronov." The man stretched his still trembling hand out to Krylov, though his handshake was unexpectedly warm and a little much for Krylov, like a sheepskin mitt. "Here, let me give you my card!" His new acquaintance opened his wallet and took out several cards with the Riphvideoplus logo. He gave one to Krylov and dropped the other, just to make sure, like a letter into a mailbox, into the pocket of Krylov's jacket, which had been scorched by vitrified chemical grit. "And by the way! Your clothes are ruined!" The card in his pocket was followed by a green hundred, silky from being carried around in his wallet, doubtless his deep reserve. "No, don't refuse!" The man's eyes implored him. "Put yourself in my place. A fine one I'd be if I didn't clean up after Mashka!"

"You talked me into it. I won't," Krylov laughed. "Krylov, Venyamin Yurievich Krylov, historian. I teach. Actually, your clothing isn't looking its best either!"

With comic despair, the man spread the lapels of his velour jacket: its shredded lining was hanging like bast, and a hole trembled under his arm. Only now was it obvious that his new acquaintance was a whole head taller than Krylov. Despite his button nose, one sensed serious goodness, *normalcy,* in Pavel Alexandrovich Dronov's appearance, and Krylov, who suddenly found himself without Tanya in a now alien, mercilessly sunny world, felt a little better at his massive presence. The little girl, who had already forgotten Krylov's existence, was hanging on her father's leg like a kitten on a tree and eating a huge messy apple, burying her wet rubbery nose into his leg.

"I was really shaken when Mashka suddenly vanished from my arms!" the programmer told him in a happy voice, offering to share the last two cigarettes from his crushed pack with Krylov. "Actually, you were lucky. A homemade bomb blew up, like a school chemistry experiment, but dangerous. If it splashed your skin it would have eaten through to the bone. People say there was one other explosion, more serious, on Cosmonaut, close to Actor's House. While I was searching for Mashka, there were all kinds of rumors going around. It was as if a group from Ural Heavy Machinery had been strongarmed by Red Army soldiers into sorting things out with the cops, who were protecting the historical clubs. Those bandits better change clothes because they're giving themselves negative advertising. They order the fanciest style from the designers, paint designs on their SUVs, and drive all over town like a circus on wheels. No, these weren't from UHM. But who were they? If they were music fans, then they're a little old. And they're not Islamic terrorists, or they would at least have been dressed up like the Basmach. You're a historian. What do you think?"

"It's 2017. That's the whole point." Krylov, who really thought that he had caught something, some logic of this secondary world that existed in place of the real one, spoke slowly. "Hallucinations just like this are happening all over the country right now. Red Cavalry helmets and White Guard epaulets are going to be firing on each other everywhere, because of the anniversary, and it's going to end in excess everywhere. Right at the most important public events. The form of clothing demands it. Understand?"

"No," the programmer answered honestly, raising his eyebrows on his prominent forehead. "I don't know whether you saw it or not, but the blood there is in pools. But people were just going to a holiday parade. Does there have to be a real reason for this kind of outrage?"

"The reason is the same as in the Great October Socialist Revolution," Krylov said, mechanically looking around in search of Tanya. "The rulers are unable and the ruled ones are unwilling. Only in our day and age we don't have formal forces capable of expressing the situation. Therefore they're going to use hundred-year-old forms, because they're the best we have. Even if they're unreal, false. But history has a reflex to them. The conflict itself recognizes the maskers as the conflict's participants. The conflict has always existed, since the 1990s. We just haven't had these rags yet—the revolutionary greatcoats, riding breeches, and leather jackets. The conflict didn't have anything to wear to go public. It's been slipping. And now, in connection with the centenary, we've got all the rags you want. So we can look forward to some happy holidays."

"That's more like mysticism than science." Dronov laughed

shakily, covering his child's head with his capacious palm, like a cap. "People aren't marionettes. I don't care how you dress me up, I'm not going to shoot or get into a fight."

"But you wouldn't dress up like that, either," Krylov objected. "And those who would, well, revolutionary clothing inspires them. They don't have anything else, right? No banner or leader. How else are you going to get them to fight?"

The programmer shrugged his stooped shoulders, perplexed. Krylov, his eyes watery with exhaustion, looked at the line of riot police, which had not budged but seemed to have settled a little. Here were troops not fated to go down in history because history had stopped. Even at first glance, the legionaries' uniforms looked contrived and upon closer examination were a jumble of details, including the "dog-ear" collars fashionable five years ago and yellow aiguillettes that might have been torn off the suits of movie extras. As a result, the riot police looked like identically dressed deserters. There ought to be a real world in place of our false one, Krylov thought, a world genuine in its every manifestation. Now he would have to distinguish intuitively the organic from the artificial and ask himself whether the sufferings of the injured and the coldness of the dead were genuine. Actually, the latter, as Tamara asserted, had crossed a line that was more genuine than anything in all human reality.

Right then the programmer's cell phone started playing a polyphonic ring tone at his waist. "Lelya! Yes! Everything's all right! Mashka's with me and we're fine! No, don't go anywhere. They're just about to let us leave. What did they show? Oh, that's nonsense! No! Don't even think of it! We'll be there very soon! Wait for us, put dinner on the table!" The programmer turned off his phone and turned a guilty red face toward Krylov. "Here, my wife's worrying at home, and before you know it she's going to rush out to the square for us. We must be just about to move. Over there they say they're letting people with children out first."

"Naturally." Krylov smiled. His despair, which had been quelled briefly by his conversation with this chance acquaintance, crept up and licked at his heart. Looking in the direction where the exhausted citizens were dragging along, Krylov saw that there, near the exit from the enclosure, they really were presenting children, who looked like they'd been put to sleep with a horse-pill of reality. All of them, even the big ones, looked like the doomed infants the beggars dragged around the Metro wrapped up in rags.

"Be sure not to throw out my card," Dronov spoke hurriedly. "I realize, in instances like this people usually don't call, but you keep it and call! I'm not asking you for your phone number because no one gives that to strangers, but you're not a stranger to me now. Come over for pie. My wife and I would be very pleased. Everything in life happens for a reason, not arbitrarily. What if we end up being good friends? You can't rule it out! Especially with this prehistory. Mashka's still small, and she doesn't even understand anything, but I, it's true . . ." At this the programmer's eyes squinted and a tear glistened. He grabbed Krylov's hand in both his hot paws, held it, and let go.

"I'll call," Krylov promised. "Good luck getting out of here."

Looking at the programmer's powerful shoulders, which Mashka, who had been picked up, was peeking out from behind, making energetic faces, Krylov took a while to realize that he could pass through the police cordon with them, at the front of the line. He decided he was never going to call them. Mentally he sent signals to Tanya, who might still be somewhere very nearby. If such a thing as telepathy existed, he would have heard her dolphin reply in his tense brain. But his brain had scanned the general background, the crackling, the muttering of stormily climbing bubbles of emptiness and the faint murmur of someone's inarticulate thoughts, and over all this, this capacious void, relief from pain, and light, transparent and indestructible, triumphant and unreachable. Simultaneously, Krylov observed two men in rubberized suits, oblivious to the otherworldly light on their shoulders or their shiny clasps, were dragging the empty sleeves of fire hoses across the terrible paving stones. They let 'er rip, the hoses stiffened, they turned the rings over from side to side—and the foam that washed over the square was like what you see in a pot where meat is cooking. The streams rumbled, eating away the blood from the sticky stones and squirming over the cracks, but the pink was apparently ineradicable. A bright cameraman attempted to get in on the act by looking over a fireman's shoulder, but he got water in his camera and face and passed out. Overtaking an overfull cloud that was slowly crawling into the unwatched holiday sky, the wind lashed the crowd with bursts of rain. Here and there, umbrellas popped open.

★ ★ ★

At the exit, Krylov was vetted by the same police sergeant who people had kept from quietly drinking his beer during and after his shift. The sergeant's face was gray; the stubble that had popped up looked like iron shavings. Several times he passed his uncomprehending glance from Krylov to the passport photograph and back; apparently he could open his puffy eyes only halfway. Then Krylov was led through a metal detector where the gentle lilac slush had been trampled. A bell tinkled. Someone's weary fat hands took Krylov aside and backed him up against a brown wall. The magnetic wand searched him crudely. The stuck cluster of Tanya's keys chirped. Without any metal at all, like an angel, Krylov soundlessly, behind a narrow maidenly back with anxiously squeezed shoulder blades, sailed through the detector freely, like driftwood with the river's current, and evening shadows spread. They returned his confiscated property to him without the slightest civility. Krylov felt as if he'd been freed from prison after a ten-year sentence—and had landed in a completely unknown, unfamiliar world where no one was waiting for him.

He set off on shaky legs toward where the Mercedes ambulances' flashers were spinning energetically and white coats were moving incorporeally. From the stretchers being loaded into the vehicles hung arms in woolen uniform sleeves, dark, as if they'd recently been digging in the earth; here, not far away, on the shaggy grass, which was already splattered with dead green, prematurely fallen leaves, lay a row of closed black bags. There were ten of them, if not twelve. Krylov caught a heavy bear of a woman doctor by the elbow, and her angry eyes stared at him under the fallen tuft of her pink hairdo.

"The woman's name?" she snapped, interrupting Krylov, who had attempted through frozen trembling and cracked lips to tell her Tanya's distinguishing features. "The lists are there!" the doctor, through talking, twisted her elbow away and rushed off, her white butt shaking, toward the emergency station awning.

Not knowing what that could do for him, Krylov wandered off in the opposite direction. There, on the same long brown wall to which the mustachioed cop had pinned him and where right now spread-eagled men were standing in a row with helpless napes, long lists of paper covered every which way by different markers were fluttering. Alongside each one craned the necks of squinting people; from time to time someone from the medical service pushed his way through to the lists, skewering a piece of paper, and added one or two sweeping lines at which several tear-stained women rushed at once. The released citizens quickly left the square through the wet, puddle-dotted side streets, and their tense backs shrank faster than the small amount of perspective allowed. Each one left behind a little emptiness for Krylov, and Krylov slowly turned around in this emptiness, not feeling the humped asphalt underfoot where the beer-colored spots of the streetlamps shone gold.

Suddenly he saw at the checkpoint next to the one he'd gone through a familiar rounded figure: the spy, frowning, was distributing the things that had been taken from him during the search in the various pockets of his hideous elastic-waist trousers. He looked like someone Krylov had for some reason just dreamed up without advance warning. Actually, there was only one option—to grab the scoundrel at last by his collar, where some soiled scrap poked out, as usual.

Krylov had absolutely nothing to lose. To cut him off, he climbed onto a slippery, soapy-feeling lawn; simultaneously his memory tensed and shuddered. There was something about this combination—the police and ambulance flashers, the black body bags, and the white figures of medics squatting—that reminded him of the very first time the spy had appeared in Krylov's life. Holding his breath, Krylov stopped—and the memory immediately dimmed. He took a step—and once again something started working in his subcortex. A vague image began to shine in comparison with which the spy, who had pulled out of the heap of examined bags his own slippery bag made of ripping, lacily disintegrating plastic, was nastily material and excessively heavy.

At the sight of Krylov, the spy's capricious face expressed a total absence of personal interest. The next second, the spy's eyes rounded and he jumped up and seemed to click his heels. Abandoning his stuck property—something he had never once done before—the spy quick-stepped diagonally across the side street, where labyrinths of damp structures and sheds descended toward the river. Krylov limped after him, skipping, also reluctant to break into a run in front of the police. The spy, still simpering, ran down a small iron staircase the size of a sled and into a curved gateway and attempted to accomplish his usual sleight-of-hand: to slip behind a fold of air. But something jammed in the mechanism, and the spy, clipping his shoulder on a battered column, ran off with unexpected pep, flashing his black, flipper-flat boots. Krylov gave a threatening wheeze and rushed after him.

The spy wound his charge through passageways. He bolted with the enthusiasm of a cartoon character, tromping through puddles that looked as though the spy had drowned there running through. Evidently, though, he really knew these crazy labyrinths. He led Krylov in circles. A couple of time they raced after each other past a bleached wall of old bricks that looked like packages of farmer's cheese covered with sour cream—first one way, then back. Deep arches, crumbly like anginal throats, led them into irregular tight spaces with dilapidated yellow windows, piles of boards, and dangerous holes deep inside of which burst pipes leaked. Scraggly cats that looked like caterpillars were darting in and out everywhere. The rare people they encountered were rather disturbing, like soft toys thrown in the garbage, and they made shamanistic gestures at the chase.

Looping around, the spy seemed to double right before Krylov's eyes. Suddenly, after making some clever maneuver between the black sheds that Krylov, picking up speed, could not repeat, he jumped out and ran straight at his pursuer. Ahead was a bricked-in dead end without a single gap. Burning up, unable to catch his breath, Krylov started slowly for the spy, inviting him to pass with his shaky hands. The spy started backing up. For a minute they exchanged silly crooked smiles, and the fatman looked like he was trying to wink at Krylov with his watering left eye, which glittered like a pearl in its shell.

"I'm going to rip your head off, you bastard," Krylov rasped, his hands on his spread legs and bodily blocking off the narrow path to the spy's home labyrinth of human henhouses. "I'm going to ask you an interesting question, and you're going to sing me an interesting answer."

"You can kiss my ass, you little shit," the spy whispered.

Right then, just as if he were giving his opponent the chance to make good on his offer, he turned and started climbing the brick wall. What through the salty blur had looked like the shadows of mighty rust-colored weeds suddenly turned out to be latticed boxes that might have been readied on purpose for extreme flight. With the caricaturish sport of despair, the spy clambered up this inauthentic, spectral construction, which fell apart as he climbed and stretched to the top of the wall, where tufts of hairy grass were growing. The restless no-good had his support moving out from under him, but nonetheless he managed to grab hold of the top of the crumbling layer. He squeaked and gasped for a minute, his legs dancing like a marionette, and then caught the tip of his shoe in a brick blister and scrambled up, grabbing at the dark branches with the dropping leaves that reached over from the other side. He tumbled over, flashing the sagging fold between his trousers and his hiked-up jacket. You could hear a tree crack, a curse of complaint, and a crunch.

Only then did Krylov come to his senses. Picking up a broken box in each hand, he stood in front of the wall, baffled as to how he could stack these flimsy, jerking things with the tin ribbons poking out to the sides. Close by, on the right, he heard hacking sounds, as if someone were trying to blow his nose: the scoundrel, who had survived, was starting his faithful Jap. Finally the motor caught and started running, and two nonidentical light beams—one a little stronger, the other as if sprinkled with dust—waved over the limp mass of leaves and the ulcerated plaster, which was as frightening as the plague. The scoundrel got off safely. Once again it was dark and quiet, and Krylov could hear the river water, as if it were slapping literally underfoot.

Krylov didn't know why, but he smashed the boxes hanging in his hands against each other, like bird skeletons with dislocated wings. As he stood there he felt as if he were drowning, as the water of despair rose higher and higher, like a tight cold ring, touching his belly, his stomach, and his heart, and the cold dark slipped over him like a sock. Even in this dead darkness, though, you couldn't really die: your body was still alive and felt like smoking, and your appetite was whetted by the evening air's freshness and the smells wafting over from something searing in a skillet, and Krylov's stomach twisted into an empty seashell. If he could have sat down on something and not budged, Krylov probably would have stayed right there and frozen. But the hummocky grass was damp and nasty, and an unfriendly creature of the cat species seemed to have put on mirrored sunglasses for the night and was following the outsider out of the brush, as if having taken over for the spy, who had driven off to have his dinner. Calming the echo of his heartache, Krylov quietly dragged himself uphill, and uphill some more, to the distant Metro.

2

★

KRYLOV'S SLEEP WAS DISTURBED, AND EACH TIME HE SURFACED FROM the watery fog of dreams, he remembered the catastrophe. Telling himself the expedition would return, maybe even the day after tomorrow, he felt that if he and Tanya found each other through Anfilogov everything would be different than they had arranged at the start, than the way they had taught each other. Everything would be in full view, entirely above board and monitored, added to the row of phenomena of the inauthentic world—and thereby destroyed.

However, hope remained—a lonely rock amid the seething black water that Krylov was holding onto so he wouldn't slip off or surrender to the enormity of the disaster, which was immeasurably bigger than his point of support and so somehow truer. His hope consisted in the following, actually: Krylov did not believe that Tamara had actually refrained from keeping track of him, especially in this nonstandard situation; that would be utterly unlike her. Consequently, given how systematic she was, she already had the real full name, address, and other coordinates of the woman with whom Krylov had he didn't know what kind of relationship. The invisible beings she hired may well have dug up more than a husband of ten years would know about his own wife. But Krylov had no need of any informational delicacies, fishy or not. All he needed was the address of the apartment the keys on the ring he had fit. Tamara could keep everything else for her own contemplation.

By the time the cold, sleepy abysses released Krylov, it was almost four in the afternoon. He spent two more hours rattling in the half-empty, sun-filled commuter train, hiding behind the folds of his silky raincoat, which was hanging on the hook. Today he had tried to look his best. He had pulled out of the solid press of his long unworn suits a bright ginger jacket from Kenzo that had stuck its sleeve out, found some coffee-colored trousers that went with it, and ironed his limp silk shirt, which smelled like baked peaches under the steam of the iron. Krylov realized that at Tamara's party he would look like he had dressed from a secondhand store; but he hadn't made the effort for the party. He'd made it for the moment he rang at that unknown door and heard her familiar, uneven steps. He believed that was going to happen today.

Every year, on the day after the city's patriotic holiday, Tamara had a party at her private home for a mismatched elite rather the worse for wear, having overdone it the night before either at the governor's ball with its warm parquet and strong vodka, or at the mayor's reception in the cleverly lit park that looked like it had been mined by Tatishchev, or at the palace of the president's viceroy, where they celebrated standing, in the middle of a military structure with white columns and state symbols on the walls that was capable of withstanding a direct attack by serious bombardment. Relaxed, mingling, the elite had a good time at Tamara's without their ties. They ate and drank, hugged and kissed, teased the crocodile, lounged on the inviting velvet couches, blew in each other's ears about their affairs—and left behind, along with their picturesque swinishness, a thin layer of gold dust that lent Tamara's manse the status of perhaps the fourth residence in the Riphean capital.

Usually the house was shining by about seven. Today, however, there were no extra lights on the gloomily bright façade, and the tall windows of the first floor shone identically and looked empty. The half-lit sand of the driveway was pale and even, like untrodden snow. These changes could scarcely be explained by the black crape on the lowered flags: the state flag and the city flag with its heraldic, ratlike bear and stylized furnace. Lately hostility had been thickening around Tamara and her funeral business. When Krylov walked past the fluttering banners, an additional alarm went off inside him.

Despite his worst fears, a certain number of guests were nonetheless hanging around the reception hall. True, on closer examination, he discovered that it was mainly the second-tier people who had gathered: mid-level officials in gaudy tweeds, elderly lady advisors decked with cascades of beads, a few young public relations assistants—twenty in all, no more. The guests were floating through the hall with a vacant look, holding their almost untouched glasses in front of them, sometimes cautiously sniffing their aperitifs like tiny bouquets. All this reminded Krylov of a scene by a monument or fountain where tens of dressed-up people had made dates and dawdled, each unto himself, because no one had come for them.

Krylov found Tamara in the smoking room next door. She jumped up to meet him, dropping her unlit cigarette, which had long since wilted in her fingers.

"You were there, on that square!" she exclaimed, looking into Krylov's eyes up close. "Thank God you're all right! Do you have any idea how your outing might have ended?"

Krylov thought Tamara was about to cry, but she merely sniffed her abundantly powdered nose. Sluiced with a black lamé evening gown from her pierced ears to her ankles, with bare white arms and an artificial, luxuriantly bearded flower on her shoulder, today she looked weary, having dressed reluctantly, at the last minute, when she would have preferred lounging in her robe with a mug of milk. She took Krylov by the arm and led him over to the sofas, where, under the shelter of fluted tropical leaves and Chinese lanterns, the better society had arrayed itself—better, that is, than the society lingering in the reception hall on the bare mirror-bright parquet. True, even this society was palpably thin, which made the very air in the smoking room, where the cosmos seemed to shine through the blueness of the cigarette gas, seem thin.

To his surprise, the first person Krylov saw was golden-haired Mitya Dymov. Up close, the delightful child didn't look so delightful. Rejuvenating nano-technologies were no match for the idol's

244 ★ OLGA SLAVNIKOVA

new raging masculinity, and the translucent skin on his cunning face was getting sugary. Dressed like a prince in a waisted dove-gray outfit and a silk jabot of pristine whiteness, Mitya, lounging, had sat Tamara's favorite stuffed bear—which had always lived upstairs but for some reason had wound up here, among the drunken guests—on his knee. Krylov remembered that Mitya had liked to fondle this same bear with the snub-nosed face and rubbed belly back during his brief residence in Tamara's bedroom.

"How did that get here?" he asked Tamara in a whisper, indicating the hideous phenomenon with his eyes.

"He came to apologize for the disruption on-air," Tamara answered in a low voice. "He's inviting me back to his studio. Over there's the bouquet he brought. It's so big I barely found something to put it in."

Indeed, preening in one of the horrible tubs of Zairian malachite that had always offended Krylov's professional taste was Mitya's deluxe present: a bouquet the size of Australia, each rose like a head of cabbage.

"I hope you turned him down," Krylov said through his teeth, trying not to think about the bedrooms, green and blue, where the orphan bear whiled away his days with no place to go, lolling over his parallel paws on the blue or green designer rug.

"Of course, not. You know very well I'll go. That's all I need, being afraid of journalists!" Tamara exclaimed louder than necessary, for which Dymov, who was eavesdropping, thanked her with an innocent smile and a fluttering of his lacy, painstakingly mascaraed eyelashes.

Infuriated, Krylov was about to inform everyone within hearing range that Dymov wasn't a journalist, he was a small-time prig being kept by an old idiot, but just then his attention was distracted by an even more radical phenomenon. A live, neat, ordinary-size pig walked into the smoking room, delicately tossing aside the mother-of-pearl beaded curtain. Those sitting on the sofas had a good laugh and reached for the alcohol. The pig was gray-haired and had intelligent little eyes that looked like tiny, fuzzy, half-open flowers. Stepping on its clean hooves, like a stout lady on high heels, the pig approached a platter of canapés amidst the bottles and began sampling them with pleasure, wiggling its wet button-nose in search of the tastiest morsels.

"That was a present for me for the holiday from Mrs. Adelaida Semyannikova," Tamara informed with a false laugh, forestalling the stunned Krylov's question. "She literally planted the pig on me out of the goodness of her heart. This morning they brought it in a special veterinary van with a note and best wishes."

"Is she afraid you're going to bury her spouse?" Krylov inquired, not taking his eyes off the blissful beast, which had left its greasy diggings on the platter and was grunting and rubbing up against a quaking little antique table.

"The spouse is alive and well!" Tamara announced optimistically and added under her breath, "Imagine, our classic suddenly decided to chase after me, which is pretty funny. He turned out to be such an enterprising gentleman that half the city already knows about his lofty passion. He says he's started writing poetry again, like he did in his youth."

"I think you've revealed your talent for getting into trouble," Krylov said, wiping his cold forehead where the pain had condensed like moisture on glass. "Adelaida's going to smear you all over the wall, write a slogan above it, and call a rally. Don't you have enough problems with your funeral business? Now you've decided to contend with a pack of females in khaki?"

"I'm not interested in female politicos," Tamara parried haughtily, her eyes, sunken from exhaustion, flashing. "What would you have me do, drive the old man from my door? The day before yesterday he spent three hours sitting in my waiting room, and then they called in cardiologists from the American Center for him."

"Well, I don't know. You used to know how to get rid of

unwanted admirers," said Krylov biliously. "That means you need this now for some reason, all these Mityadymovs, Semyannikovs, and all the other freaks whirling around you."

He instantly regretted what he'd said. Shrugging listlessly, Tamara dropped into the first chair she came to and seemingly lost all interest in the surrounding reality. All these imposing types lounging here and there in anticipation of dinner were not supposed to see Tamara's weakness, to say nothing of her inadvertent tear. Sitting down next to her, Krylov poured a little cognac into an empty goblet whose glass stem was garishly adorned with the remains of someone else's alcohol. He needed a drink before he could move on to his reason for coming. He couldn't put it off any longer.

"Let's get out of here," he whispered to Tamara, taking her cold, heavy arm. "We have to talk. Right now."

"Fine," Tamara replied quietly without raising her head. "Take care of this," she addressed the panting maid who had run in at the noise raised by the pig.

"Shoo! Shoo!" The maid waved a towel at the confused pig, which was staring angrily with its rusty little enameled eyes. This simple Afro-Russian woman—first name Zina, last name Krasilnikova—had been working for Tamara for more than three years and took everything very much to heart, her heart being about the size of a bucket. Zina, who weighed a good centner and had a powerful lion's nose and a curly mane, looked a lot like a maid from the old Hollywood films, which was why she'd been hired. But she behaved like an ordinary Russian woman, that is, she always expressed her opinion, wasn't afraid of anyone but a crocodile, and pitied her mistress her feminine foolishness, but loved Krylov because even though he suffered, he didn't drink.

With the concerned and gracious look of a hostess hurrying to solve a small problem, Tamara slipped between her guests and through a solid door, into a large, dimly lit hall where a transparent spiral staircase wound straight up in the air, like a dinosaur skeleton asleep in a museum. On the stairs, tiny lamps lit up in response to the weight of her steps, lighting Tamara's pointy-toed shoes with their faceted silver heels, and Krylov's dust-covered boots.

★ ★ ★

Upstairs, both bedroom doors were open. The rooms held a nearly identical gloom. To the right it was greener and thicker; to the left a little lighter, with a hint of blue. The night did not recognize the difference between green and blue, picking out only a few bright objects; both beds were tightly made up in silk, and not a single wrinkle spoke of Dymov's recent presence. Krylov heaved a sigh of relief; he touched a trembling Tamara's elbow ingratiatingly; it was soft, like a shriveled apricot. Tamara stopped short and turned around, and Krylov was pierced by the awareness of her homelessness. No matter how many bedrooms you own, a woman has to have a room of her own, as she does a man.

The confusion lasted literally a second, and then Tamara laughed unpleasantly, as if she were spitting a fine needle from the corner of her painted mouth, and started quickly down the hall, past the broad-hipped floor vases and oil paintings that were mute in the semi-gloom. She led Krylov toward her two home offices, which were arranged identically and changed strictly simultaneously. Right now the change was obvious from the threshold. Instead of her old PC, which had been very elegant but still looked like expensive kitchen equipment, on her desk was something fundamentally new. At first glance it looked as though a broad transparent monitor had been fused to a gigantic flash of golden amber, in the depths of which one guessed at large, honey-infused insects, specks of dust, and rainbow bubbles. He didn't understand how this machine from outer space, which appeared to have no ports, turned on. But iridescent Tamara dropped into a taut armchair with a rustle of her abundant sequins, plunged her index finger into the first rush of substance, and her purple fingerprint slowly filled with red, like a tiny iron.

Instantly, a sensory keyboard popped up in front of the mistress, and her screen saver beamed on the monitor: a bird's-eye view of her house patrolled by a line of smooth, two-headed eagles with glossy necks.

"Just the design is new; the hardware and software are nothing special," Tamara commented offhandedly, her manicured nails clicking on the keys and quickly paging through the menu. "Remember, I told you, they don't let our gentlemen scholars have any fun now. Still, this machine is good enough to hijack a military satellite if you wanted."

"That's so cool!" Krylov cautiously touched the "amber," which turned out to be soft and a little sticky, like marmalade. Tamara gave the keyboard a quick click, his finger turned cold, and the machine informed him in a dead, silvery voice, "Fingerprint accepted."

"Not bad." Sucking his finger, which felt like it had been injected with icy champagne, Krylov watched dumbfounded as his hologram quickly coalesced on the monitor out of vague cubes, with the twisted collar of his reddish brown jacket and a crooked smile somewhere on his cheek. "I could never figure out this equipment!"

"It's worth it," Tamara remarked in a strained voice, rummaging in the crunchy contents of a drawer she'd pulled out. "This is actually your machine and your office, if you ever want to come back. Now where's that cassette? I'll never find it."

Krylov said nothing, feeling a biting heat rise up over his face and turn into moisture in his eyes. Horrified that all this could be taken for pathetic male tears over their wonderful past, he hastened to grab the first knick-knack he came across on the desk: the same two-headed eagle, silver, with dragon heads and an intricate little key between its polished wings. When you turned it, an empty, mirrored hiding place opened.

"All right, let's stop beating around the bush." Tamara shut the drawer, which made a sucking sound, placed her cold hands on the icy black desktop, and looked Krylov in the face. "Tell me what kind of jam you're in this time."

"It's the same one we were talking about at the Plow," Krylov replied gloomily. "Only now it's much worse, you see. I'm sorry, but I don't believe that, how shall I put it, that you haven't wondered just a little. Naturally, I didn't see your professionals, but I'm sure they were hovering somewhere nearby. Basically, I need the information you gathered."

The look he aimed at the calm Tamara must have intimidated her. After a pause, she answered Krylov with a good-natured, triumphant smile.

"Fine, I'm not going to be coy. I did know you'd come running for this," she said, tapping out sharp commands on the keyboard. "Only I don't like that word, 'wondered.' I'm no scandalmonger gathering gossip for lack of anything better to do. As I already said, though, your beloved rock hounds are, from many points of view, a club of suicides. Leaving you to your own devices would be careless on my part to say the very least. I did ask people at one very civilized agency to watch after you. I don't think they disturbed you in any way."

"They were like the air," Krylov confirmed sullenly.

"Let's start with the fact that the agency where my friends work had an interest of their own in the case," Tamara continued, swinging a shoe. "They told me that rumors have been lingering in your club for about a year about some spectacular find. I mean, that kind of home brew is always sloshing around in your shaggy heads, but this time it was something more specific. Your friend Anfilogov and some other Pole who Interpol is crying over have settled out. From my friends' point of view, those two wreckers are set to spoil the gem corundum market. No one's going to let them do that, naturally. There are other interests involved, not even Russian ones, actually. The agency never was able to find out exactly where your professor gentleman dug up his underground riches, but they're waiting for him to come out and they'll never allow him to sell what he's found."

"So that's it," muttered Krylov, hiding his eyes. He felt as if his very blood had suddenly faded. The hope he'd lived and breathed all this time left him suddenly and simply, and all the pictures of future prosperity he had secretly, ecstatically drawn for himself became alien, like ads about the beautiful life that the country's entire population had learned by heart.

"Why so sad?" Tamara looked at Krylov with stern and gentle amusement. "I realized you were counting on cashing in big time. I also knew they couldn't do it without you. But you have to understand: this world already has everything it actually holds, and it has someone who owns it. New valuables, be they unique stones or, for instances, paintings, however brilliant, simply don't count. It makes sense to produce only what I consume and drop into the toilet. Food, TV series, cheap housing that will be razed in thirty years. You can get rich now, of course, but only gradually and with the permission of those who control the processes."

"What about you? I wonder who gave you permission?"

Never before had Krylov asked his wife this craven question, and now he regretted the words coming off his tongue. It was like belated jealousy at the rotund young men of apparently Komsomol origin, with ribbed gold watches on white wrists and full-length cashmere costs splattered in back with stony Riphean dirt, in whose company Tamara had made her first money while she was still practically in the university classroom. Krylov had stoically believed Tamara when she returned after midnight, feeling the walls, from restaurants he didn't know, when she flew away and didn't call, condemning Krylov to insomnia. He had all kinds of claims against Tamara, but in his heart of hearts Krylov understood that the truth was in blind, calm faith, nothing else. Together they had rejoiced at their first serious purchases, especially their first car—a white BMW sports car, as elegant as the porcelain in a nobleman's dinner service, a 1970-something, which Tamara drove clumsily, so that the BMW jerked forward, like a toy car on a string, amid the angry honking Zhigulis. Tamara never hid the details of her business from her husband, but he didn't like listening to her narration about the war between the Black and White accountancies, and Krylov didn't delve too deeply into the dubious processes of making money out of thin air. The only thing he was prepared for was to lay himself down for Tamara at any minute in the event of an attack, after first laying low as many as he could with the tough old revolver Krylov kept in the entry on the upper doorjamb. Somehow, though, they got by, and the husband's participation in his wife's affairs was never required. All Krylov could do was love his strong woman, nothing more. Now, especially, there was no call to ask her about the past.

Not that Tamara had any intention of reporting to him.

"I just jumped on the last car of a departing train," she told him irritably. "Today you can't even see the caboose. Still, I don't understand why you can't be content. If you need money, take it from me. Believe me, I won't be any the poorer. Instead, you're caught up in that amateur act of yours. You're all involved with Anfilogov—and who is this Anfilogov? A mineral with an awl up his ass. You could live comfortably for a year on the money I paid the agency. I should have given it to you. What do you think?"

"Stop!" Krylov squinted, trying not to lose sight of an important point. "That means the place the professor went to hasn't been found. But how can that be if you can see through the earth from satellites, according to your reports? And the professor himself isn't exactly a needle. He's going to be bigger than any corundum."

"Something came up," Tamara admitted reluctantly. "Supposedly there are anomalous zones in the north. Naturally, no particular deposits have been discovered there. But we've been receiving snapshots from satellites dating from two years ago and more, moreover the dates go backward from the present. You get the impression of someone transmitting old tapes to the satellite, on rewind. Look"—Tamara gave Krylov a quick sideways glance, as if apologizing for the absurdity of the message—"you know, there are some strange rivers there, in those parts. They look like someone was pulling threads and unraveling a sweater. I saw it myself. They broadcast it on all the news: that helicopter fell into the Kavatuisky swamps—remember?—and shot up as if it had been fired from a cannon. That's where your old fogy's dived in, and the edges of the zone are nasty, all wet, kind of. Judge for yourself whether what he drags back from there does you any good."

Not knowing what to answer, Krylov said nothing. The information Tamara had reported was incredible. All this affected his future badly, but this evening it was utterly beside the point. Right now he was much more worried about whether he'd be able to find Tanya and whether he could show up at her place late at night. Correctly interpreting his feverish abstraction, Tamara sighed and rested her hand, crowned with a black pearl the size of a grape, on her lit up mouse.

"Fine, let's get down to business. I'm not sorry, you know. I only did it for you."

On the translucent monitor, which Krylov could view from the back, a familiar face suddenly leaped out of the cascade of snapshots. The spy had probably been holographed a few years ago; he looked younger than now and at the same time more disheveled. His tight green jersey, saggy from too many washings, looked as if it had been put on backwards, a square black hole gaped in his month instead of one front tooth, and his hair, amazingly, was long and gathered up in a messy tail, like spaghetti twirled on a fork. The hologram was immediately covered in tiny text turned inside out for Krylov. He leaned forward, trying to make out the creeping symbols.

"Viktor Matveyevich Zavalikhin," Tamara introduced Krylov to his accursed acquaintance. "Born 1983, Russian, less than a high school education, married common-law to a tenement rat just like himself, has a daughter Varvara eight months old. Lives at sixteen Svarshchikov, apartment three. In his younger days he boxed for money. He was the kind who agreed to hold off until the third round for the knockout. Twice convicted. The first time he got two years' probation because he was a minor, for robbing a bookstore where only money was taken. The second time he did hard time for robbery, three years, maximum security. He just got out, in 2015. He picks up occasional work for a close relative; the rest the relative gives him out of the goodness of his heart. And you know who that good man is? Your employer, who, in turn, is working for Anfilogov and robbing the professor of everything that's not tied down."

Tamara leaned back contentedly in her chair, admiring the spy, who also seemed to be looking around the office trying to figure out how to lift something that would never be missed. The information did not surprise Krylov. Whenever his mind played hide-and-seek with him, it invariably got "warmer" whenever Krylov combined the spy's present-day image with his old cellar workshop. However, Krylov could have sworn that among his boss's buddies who stopped by for a beer and in appearance, for some reason, always coincided with the plump spy—the spy wasn't there. His memory set up a kind of police lineup for Krylov and slipped him an approximate likeness, suggesting he agree to it and be content with that—but Krylov wouldn't agree because he knew his torments wouldn't end. Right now he thought that maybe the mnemonic itch could be explained by the family resemblance between the spy and the workshop owner. He attempted to picture his employer's face as clearly as possible, mentally removing his lowered glasses, his characteristic checkmark eyebrows, and his second chin. And suddenly his roving memory did a pirouette and gave him the snapshot: the owner, his fat little back shaking, freezing in a birdlike pose next to the hooks where Krylov's jacket was for some reason pulled out above the heap of other clothing, spread as if his employer, out of kindness, had decided to brush it clean; here was his boss, looking disinterested, for some reason standing by Krylov's side and floating away from his desk in tiny steps. His city map with the previously entered points was usually rattling around his desk or in his jacket pocket. Krylov nearly burst out laughing at how simply it was all explained: the vulgar soiledness of his cherished atlas and the ubiquity of the spy, who arrived at the spot nearly before his charges. There was nothing mystical left in the actions of Viktor Matveyevich Zavalikhin, petty criminal. Just then Krylov felt a chill of the supernatural return. The hologram was looking at him with nasty eyes that looked like spoons of soup gone cold, as if to say, "Here I am again. It's me, whether you like it or not."

Frowning, Tamara observed the changes in Krylov's face, and she could tell some secret thought was setting a strict limit to his candor.

"Basically, you did a good thing running over here so disheveled. You really should be worried about this guy," she informed him, removing the spy from the screen. "It's hard to believe he's working for a big-time client. Guys like him usually don't get past face control. Most likely the two relatives have decided to rob you and the professor in the most ordinary way and are waiting for Anfilogov to emerge from the forest, too. But they're foolish and greedy enough that they could just as easily stick a knife in you. I doubt you could deal with that, but in any case I'll put it all on a disk for you right now. Although you refused the laptop I tried to give you. Fine, I'll do a printout."

Tamara gave the mouse a spin and several pages fell out of the printer, turning in the air. Krylov leaned over to collect them, and in the tight space of the desk, armrest, and small shredder full of curly dust, he clumsily brushed Tamara's hip, which trembled under the muslin and scales. Hastily returning with the tousled, messy goods to the visitor's chair, he saw Tamara's eyes fill with tears.

"Wait. That's not all!" he exclaimed, forestalling her attempt to stand abruptly and head for the exit. "I'm interested in a second person. That woman, the skinny blonde in glasses. You know who I'm talking about."

"What?" Tamara's eyes dried up instantly and became two nonidentical spots. "Yes, I know who you're talking about! The tape they brought me left no doubt as to the nature of your relationship! And you're asking me who she is?"

"I'll swear on anything you want," Krylov spoke in a frozen voice, "I don't know her first name, her last name, her phone number, or her address. And she doesn't know anything about me. We lost each other on the square and now we can't find each other."

Tamara looked at Krylov the way people look at a disaster. From downstairs, through a half-open window panel, came the blurry hubbub of voices and—suddenly—a lush, hissing explosion and light. A crimson rocket drew a phosphorescent trail, its fiery core flickering low over the scalded garden, and was extinguished in the darkness, like a coal in water. The guests, having forgotten the official mourning, must have got to the supplies of fireworks. Broken dishes crashed ringingly.

"I don't know what to tell you." Ignoring the disarray, Tamara sat very straight, in a pharaonic pose, so her high feminine breast was utterly superfluous. "Krylov, you're insane. It's true. This is unnatural. This is worse than anything you've done before. I can't even imagine what vileness this holds, but you're not just mocking me. It's as if you've hardly lived. Look what you've come to!"

"Fine, I'm vile. I'm a scoundrel," Krylov agreed irritably. "Only I know one thing. You collected information on that woman. I realize how much you hate all this. I'm sorry. But you can't deny me, you can't hide her address from me. At least the address."

Tamara sighed with restraint and looked down at her lap. Another rocket burst, quivered, and spat, and below they shouted chaotically, opening the tall windows, to judge from the close ringing. Tamara frowned.

"Yes, you've studied me pretty well," she said finally. "It's true, I couldn't have hidden that kind of information. Only here's the problem: I don't have anything on that spectacled blonde of yours."

"You're lying," whispered Krylov, feeling as if something heavy and viscous had grabbed him by the back of his neck. "You are," he said, studying Tamara, her empty face, which seemed to hold nothing but red lipstick. "But why? Huh? Why this time in particular? After all, you've always spied on me. You've always taken a keen interest in my women. You've relished and envied each one, foisted young ladies on me yourself, just so you could participate and not feel left out. So why the sudden scruples? Have you decided to play the lady? Put me in my place? Or have you thought up something else?"

"Did you think I was going to wait for you forever?" Tamara spoke in her iciest voice. "Did you think I was going to watch over you, protect you, be jealous of every skirt you latched onto? Have you counted how many you've had for my own Dymov? Eighteen, and the blonde is the nineteenth! Damn you and them, too!" She suddenly whacked the desk with her fist, and the silver eagle fell clumsily on Krylov's boot, striking some sensitive bony protuberance.

"Take it easy!" Krylov jumped up, stumbled, and reached for the bird from his chair, rummaging in the very thick carpet as if it were plowed soil.

"Oh, it does hurt? You'll survive." Tamara, unattractive, swollen with anger, glowered at Krylov. "Yes, I was jealous of them, the blondes and brunettes, and I dreamed of becoming one of them so I could start over with you as if you were someone else. I was afraid you'd screw some bitch and bring me some nasty infection from her. I trembled over you like a mama. But I'm sick of it, do you hear? I absolutely do not care about this origami heron of yours that no man with taste would even look at. And you know what that means? That means I don't care about you anymore, either!"

"Well and thank God! Finally! I never thought I'd live to see it!" Krylov struggled to stand, grabbing the strewn printouts in both fists. "I'm tired of being on your leash, too. You've got a terrific choice. You can have Semyannikov or Dymov. Just let me go!"

Tamara stood, too, trembling, and stepped back, trying to hold her ideally placed head as high as possible, as if the water were rising around her.

"Excellent, Krylov," she spoke calmly, looking Krylov in the face as if over this high water and not seeing all of him. "If it weren't for today, it would have been a long time before I noticed how much you've changed. Now I can see how indifferent and vulgar you've become. You toy with things that every sane person ought to respect. You despise the simple gift of life and search for depraved forms of relationships. That's why you're not with me but with that woman, who agreed to share your mockery of both your mutual feelings. But that's the last thing you'll get from me. Get out of my house and out of my life. I've already forgotten your name."

"The best thing I can do for you is disenchant you," Krylov cut her off.

Seemingly, it was all over with Tamara. This wasn't how he'd imagine this parting, but how had he? As a very private, very vague dream, in which Tamara, tear-stained and beaming, quickly told him something sincere and then left without looking back, with each long, divine step expanding the space for Krylov's future life. Now Krylov understood the utter impossibility of that happy process. In fact, if people have loved each other that long and hard, the only way they can part is by figuring out a way to turn each other into enemies—so that they can bear the insane spasms of memory and the buckets of blood that fill their heart.

The door from the office to the hall was ajar. Krylov stumbled into it, producing a series of clumsy shufflings with the wobbly door, and found himself on the dark side. To make sure he didn't end up unintentionally in the middle of a badly heated-up holiday, he headed for the uneven and very narrow staircase that led to the back yard. Coming up toward him was big Zina holding an empty plastic container that was sticky inside. She let him get around her and proved to be bright pink under her blackness, like a petroleum-smeared lozenge. She seemed to want to tell Krylov something but just opened her mouth twice and stared goggle-eyed.

Part Seven

★

1

★

THE SPY'S HOME, WHICH KRYLOV FOUND ON THE DEFILED MAP, WAS A reddish-brown, three-story sick man built for some reason in a damp pit filled with mud and stormy vegetation and sat much lower than the asphalt canvas over which the trucks raced at a rollicking gallop. The building's plaster was covered with winding cracks that divided the damp façade into different states, sort of, with three or four windows apiece. Multigenerational life filled the twisty little apartments. Here and there dilapidated windows were flung open, and a flat-chested teen with an antediluvian Walkman would fill the opening, or a large materfamilias, cooling off from the kitchen heat, would gaze tenderly at nature as represented by woolly asters and tiny speckled sparrows. The windows to apartment number six were deader than the rest. No matter how much Krylov peered, he couldn't see any movement behind the blue-gray windows; there was just damp muslin billowing and subsiding in the open window pane.

Before, the spy had so often lingered near similar structures awaiting his two charges in the most visible spot that even now Krylov expected him to materialize out of thin air at any moment. But he didn't. For a week, Krylov had been patiently loitering around the corner, standing a little ways from the transformer booth, in the company of his own wet cigarette butts, which had populated the old thready grass. From here he had an excellent view of the right entryway with the prisonlike metal door, which clanked against the concrete side of the settled porch whenever it opened.

Meanwhile, the gemcutting workshop's owner had vanished. His shaggy jacket was hanging on a chair in the smoking room, and embittered clients would come in to see this by no means blameless soul, but the boss did not show up or answer telephone calls. The craftsmen were getting gloomier and gloomier and would chip in for cheap beer, digging deep in their pockets. Everyone realized that the workshop faced a speedy and inglorious end. But the problem of money somehow never bothered Krylov. Having mentally gained and lost a fortune, he didn't worry about the crumbs still rattling around in his purse. He was much more worried about the information the elusive spy had to possess. Krylov was being eaten alive by the hope of finding the real Tanya in the city's catacombs, the Tanya who, like he himself, was directly linked to the lost expedition.

Now Krylov spent his nights mostly at his old apartment, where the dusty television still worked. Getting the better of his mother's dissatisfaction—she lived according to the popular soaps' schedule—Krylov was glued to the news. The national channels gave scant coverage, with scarcely recognizable panoramas of the Riphean capital and the same disheveled Red Cavalryman raising his mighty red banner with the fresh wet spot in the middle to the blue sky and the carnage on the square. Local television channels showed the consequences of the explosion on Cosmonaut Avenue in more detail: the widened corner of the arcade, the policeman's bloodied, sticky buzz cut, and the strange, tattered foliage where granules of unknown chemistry had spilled, just barely missing the demonstrators, fortunately.

The commentaries weren't much use, except that according to some reports (not all), criminal charges had been brought. Only Riphean Channel One gave viewers intelligent reports about the victims, including those whose identity had not been established. Krylov, whose heart sometimes plunged into the abyss, stared at the distressing photographs that scrolled down the screen. No one who looked like Tanya was among the eleven dead women, to whom, at week's end, a twelfth was added: a petite upperclasswoman with little round eyes in square glasses who died from internal bleeding at the Fourth Municipal. Nearly diving into the electrified screen, Krylov thought that maybe Tanya was watching the same program right now, horrified, searching for her Ivan among the shaven and unshaven male shadows dropping smoothly into oblivion.

Very soon, however, the otherworldly encounters came to an end. The television was flooded with more astonishing news for which the Riphean events served merely as a pale prologue. Krylov had not anticipated that his idea about a maskers' revolution in Russia, mentioned in passing to a chance acquaintance, would start happening so quickly and ubiquitously. At first, confirming Tamara's idea that the world consists of things, the changes were expressed in things. The popularity of Red Cavalry and White Guard uniforms emptied out the theatrical costume shops. Clothing factories, rushing to satisfy the mad market demand, were put on a military footing: the sewing machines stitched away and were buried in waves of crudely embellished fabric, drowned along with their single-minded seamstresses. Quick-thinking traders brought greatcoats and riding breeches in from a roused China, but the goods often turned out to have been lined with cotton wool or crunchy, nasty-smelling feathers. Separate workshops manufactured epaulets, cockades, and chevrons. All the market stalls were piled with pointy Red Cavalry helmets and new, acrid-smelling felt boots.

Hundreds of thousands of Russian citizens wanted to dress up and join one of the participating sides. At first, municipal celebrations served as the occasion for the carnage, as well as other entertainments that crowded the August calendar. In Perm, the Reds, firing on an entire crowd with a single grenade-launcher, managed to sink an entirely innocent, decked-out motorboat on which the local White Cossacks had intended to sail to Astrakhan for their sweet watermelons. In Astrakhan, in a wooden and flammable part of the city, other White Cossacks, on a day of public merrymaking, torched fish warehouses belonging to the Communists. In response, high cheek-boned Young Communists, throwing their thick leather commissar jackets right over their soaked T-shirts, smeared the Cossacks against the white walls of the Astrakhan citadel. In Krasnoyarsk, costumed Kolchak soldiers who had decided to take the Siberian stronghold, which had once been so unhappily lost by Verkhovny, stormed the enormous opera house, which looked like an American gas station magnified many times over and where the troupe had taken up their post after changing into khakis and service caps with red stars. Simultaneously, in spotless old Irkutsk, where the wooden and brick architecture was all white, having been refreshed for the start of the new year with canticles and lace, other Kolchak men drowned by the hundreds in the Angara—because the Ushakovka, which a century before had taken the executed Kolchak under its Siberian ice, white like frozen milk, had silted up and barely stirred.

In Petersburg, revolutionary sailors had seized a branch of the naval museum—the cruiser *Aurora*—and attempted to fire a tank gun at the damp Winter Palace; but everything on the cruiser had been welded shut and thickly painted, therefore the matter ended with just a large iron crash and the hooligans being brought in to the nearest police station. Meanwhile, faxes started coming in to Petersburg's largest newspapers as the Separate Pskov Volunteer Corps of the Northern Army, under the command of Major General Van Damme, announced its existence. Intrigued reporters besieged the elderly Hollywood star, trying to clarify why an actor was taking part in Russian riots. To this, Jean-Claude Van Damme, who after the plastic surgeon looks like himself playing the flash-frozen Universal Soldier, distinctly reported that all his contacts with Russians were limited to a long-ago fight with a Russian congressman in some restaurant, and that had been the end of it.

What they showed on the television news was not a Hollywood action movie. The victims of the costumed clashes numbered in the hundreds—and that was only what the official reports said. The most blood was shed in super-quiet Tobolsk. The town seemed to have fallen asleep long ago on the flat Irtysh, which looked as if it had been spilled on a table and flooded the rotting wooden towers that had once been the pride of Siberia's historical capital; the walls of its citadel soared over this wooden swamp as peacefully as wet linen hung on clotheslines. Having its name appear in the media in every language in the world is never a good thing for a town like this. In Tobolsk, romantically inclined students declared the city the new Gallipoli and, dressed up like good Whites under Drozdov's command, got into the habit of gathering afterward alongside the ancient, Riphean-made, cast iron cannons whose ominous black row entertained tourists in the citadel. In the last warmth of summer, the cannon muzzles were stuffed with sweet ice cream wrappers, and boys in service caps that were too big for them and sported raspberry bands were rehearsing a play. Reds appeared in a rank, all with tickets for the museum. Discovering the enemy between themselves and the start of the exhibit, some of the Red soldiers rushed to the attack, waving their model rifles, which were curved like goat's legs, and the rest quietly ran off somewhere. The students dropped their soda bottles and scripts and were pushed toward the Swedish slope—a wide, paved conduit leading from the upper town to the lower, into an escape labyrinth of spreading vegetation and lopsided ruins. Right at the exit from the trap, though, the Whites were met by fast-thinking Reds, who had not left the fight and gone home at all but had taken up this strategic position.

Before the forces of law and order, summoned by the museum workers, could arrive, the Swedish slope was turned into a bloodbath. The raspberry service caps were crushed and reduced in number as if they'd been eaten by the worker-peasant mass pressing in from above and below. Those who attempted to scramble over the smooth sides onto the grassy shoulder were met by trained and concentrated gunfire, shot point blank out of homemade guns that looked like prostheses with mechanical pointers jutting out in front. They also fired at their own, at the terrified faces of those who had had second thoughts and who blinked at the fat, freshly forged bullet coming for them.

The slaughter was stopped only when tear gas was released into the formless jumble. When the heavy clutches of brawlers fell apart and dropped and the garishly colorful smoke dispersed, no one could tell the dead from the living at first. The boys (among the Reds there some were quite young) lay side by side, with scarlet bullet holes and thick bruises on their faces, as if they'd been kissed all over by greedy old lovers wearing greasy lipstick. The number of victims in the incident totaled two thousand one hundred thirty-two. The mayor of Tobolsk, a round-headed good soul known for his hospitality and well-repaired roads, at first stood firm, but the morning after the battle he suddenly resigned and, wiping away tears with both hands, suddenly started handing out scandalously large sums of money left and right—as a result of which the prosecutor's office, yielding to pressure and dragging its feet, was forced to bring criminal charges against the former mayor under the economics article. Also arrested were several zealous participants in the slaughter. The cells were filled primarily with Red soldiers, but they also arrested the commander of the Whites, in real life a geography teacher who strangely, as if in a dream, resembled the Whites' Major General Mikhail Drozdov with his solid gristle, his cleft chin that turned up at the bottom, and the artful fit of his steel pince-nez. Some of the Reds went down the Irtysh in a rusty barge that melted in the fog—a barge that, in the opinion of the port's specialists, was definitely not seaworthy. Several other miracles occurred in super-quiet Tobolsk—just short of resurrection. Far-flung, unopened sections of the cemeteries accepted the additions at a stroke and came to look like military bivouacs; sticky, nasty winds flowed down the Swedish slope, which had been washed with shampoo and bordered in crape.

Naturally, there could be no victors in the maskers' revolution because, strictly speaking, the warring sides themselves didn't exist. The general impression that the Reds were winning was probably explained by them being more organic in the inorganic world, because their expressive and emblematic uniform had originally been created as a costume. Krylov could not remember exactly (the remnants of his historical education had drifted off into the gaps of destiny) for which event the last Russian sovereign had had the "bogatyrki" (the pointed helmets later called "budyonnovki") and the greatcoats with the flaps created, whether it was the three hundredth anniversary of the House of Romanov or else the Russian victory parade in Berlin slated for the summer of 1917. In some sense, this transparent parade that never took place also demanded consummation and drove the young men with the five-pointed stars on their brow to their bloody rehearsals.

One way or another, the "Russian style" developed by the ingenious Vasnetsov under the influence of his dream of folk hero pickets and handsome tsarist riflemen couldn't help but give birth to this kind of historical dreaminess in their weak, impressionable heirs. "An insufferable dream," whispered Krylov with his prickly unshaven lips, peering into the television's flickering window. Now he was struck by the sweep with which the masquerade scene had been readied a century ago: the Bolsheviks who robbed the tsar's military warehouses had had enough funny uniforms to dress the real army that crushed Russia and its entire colorful and gilded history. He thought it would be interesting to follow the role of theft as a factor in the development of design. Krylov now saw theft as a metaphysical act. Thanks to theft, some objects of the genuine world became toys because the thief didn't understand their purpose, but something make-believe, like these masquerade uniforms, suddenly acquired authenticity and turned the world upside down.

As if responding to Krylov's thoughts, a report went out over several channels at once that in Gatchina, near the train station, searchers had found well-hidden storehouses with the same tsarist hats and caked greatcoats that had edible mushrooms as soft as cheese growing on them. These riches had emerged from underground at the very moment they had become important and meaningful. Young businessmen had made good money off those storehouses. On the news they showed the lucky ones from Moscow and Petersburg who'd managed to grab an antique uniform. As far as you could tell from the television picture, the fabric had faded over the hundred years and was the color of yellow and white grass like you find under rocks. The greatcoats' sleeves, which wouldn't unbend, hung on the Young Communists' shoulders in long pieces of dried-up felt, and their caps fell apart. These rosy-cheeked boys seemed to be putting on the clothes of dead men taken from their graves. He had to remind himself that no one had died yet in those uniforms.

Actually, Krylov realized that the antique clothing would not be virgin for long. Highly solvent Moscow, which was sucking up more of the uniforms than anywhere else—and weapons, too, probably—was still quiet. Helicopters were patrolling above quieted Tverskaya Street and above befuddled Pushkin's malachite head. Frivolous tents vanished from the hot streets, and you couldn't buy any of the colorful, cheerful summer drinks. The All-Russia Exhibition Center, built like the ideal Stalinist collective farm, a palace of a collective farm, suddenly became a small military base, and the display models in several of the pavilions turned out to be real. There were now an unusually large number of sullen policemen and pregnant rats as big as porcupines in the Moscow Metro.

No matter how hard the authorities tried to pretend that nothing was going on, the maskers' revolution took its toll on that most sensitive Russian substance: money. Prices in the bargain supermarkets climbed cautiously upward. Private banks, which had always played twenty-one with the state, suddenly went drastically over count. After banks attempted to freeze the deposits of frightened citizens, the state gave them a huge injection of tranquilizer in the form of loans, after which they quietly changed owners. The banking crisis was suppressed in forty-eight hours. The citizens who had run from ATM to ATM, from line to line, ripping out their cash earnings, suddenly were left holding these packets, like the remains of their own life, which could be spent in a few days. Almost to a man they brought the cash back, like last year's snow to a big industrial refrigerator where at least it didn't melt too fast in the overheated inflation.

As always happens in instances like this, the population swept the store shelves clean of cheap nonperishables: noodles, canned food, even gray past-date barley and clumpy flour. But the state acted amazingly intelligently. Literally immediately, on those same shelves, there appeared analogous goods—true, with an unfamiliar look and taste. Large crude packages, gray paper that looked greased, tin cans smeared in thick, almost weapons-grade grease with extruded rows of numbers on their impregnable lids—evidently the reserves from Soviet military storehouses had been put into circulation. The civilian population was offered spongy gray cookies that you could eat only after steaming them over boiling water until they were like putty; sugar that looked like granite; dry, clayey household soap in pieces that looked like they'd been chopped up with an ax. In an age of triumphant lighters, matches were a strange good; they were sold in blocks of twenty crude boxes, moreover the boxes lacked labels and were broken off from the blocks together with a plywood chip. Most of the canned meat was tender venison in a bloody bouillon with a greasy bay leaf in each greased can. Krylov vaguely recalled the history of the nuclear tests in Taimyr, which he thought had been conducted in the 1950s. At the time, the deer, which had cropped the radioactive moss, were killed off by the herd and frozen, like mammoths, in the permafrost, so that they could be taken out when the strontium and other dangerous filth degraded. In all likelihood, this was that meat. Its exoticness created the illusion of a rich array and even luxury, which combined paradoxically with the thick tin and the bare cardboard cartons.

Krylov thought it was odd to use food that was more than fifty years old. There was something biologically wrong about it, something that violated the natural cycles. But citizens, under the influence of their genetic memory of famine and wars (sparked as well by the stern look of the reserves), rushed to snatch up the army provisions, which cost mere kopeks. Actually, this didn't last long. No matter how the stores emptied out in a day, in the morning the shelves were full again and loomed before the buyers like military fortifications. Eventually, after exhausting the possibilities of their home basements and meager purses, the civilians surrendered and retreated from the food fortresses that they had failed to seize or destroy. His mother, having brought in, over Krylov's protests, a whole corner of kilo cans of venison, which even at home looked more like antipersonnel mines, now stumbled over them and couldn't bring herself to eat them—not because she was afraid of radiation but because the very look of them gave her a feeling of a safe future guaranteed by the Homeland. Each tin can seemed to contain, in the event of war, life—or maybe death, which were practically the same thing in the stylistics of the Soviet state, which had suddenly emerged from underground storehouses to the light of day.

★ ★ ★

As a result of the strange and terrible events of the maskers' revolution (which had already been palpably squelched in the media by the standard domestic and foreign policy news), people who hadn't seen each other for years started calling each other and getting together again. Once again there were topics for discussion; once again people crowded into sleepless nighttime kitchens and confused thoughts puffed in cigarette smoke. Old friends gathered and drew close. They discovered that many were gone and the rest were tired of life, especially the women, who sat with destroyed faces over cold coffee grounds. Worry hung in the air and mixed with an impotent agitation; public passions didn't flare but rather decayed and emitted fumes in the universal spiritual gloom that the glassy August sun barely penetrated.

Krylov kept planning to call Farid for a loan and ask about work and just to talk, but he never did. Farid himself sought Krylov out, rousing him with a phone call at eleven thirty one night and telling him about a gathering that coming Sunday. Leaving his sentry duty by the television and his post by the spy's home (where four balconies there now bristled with nice new raspberry cotton flags), Krylov rushed across town to the familiar tenement, where a gnarled old lilac bush had become badly overgrown and its broad leaves had faded to gray.

The general impression that all was always well with Farid was maintained only because Farid would not have it otherwise. In fact, his days passed in measured, deeply concealed grief; Farid seemed to be taking this grief on an hourly basis, like homeopathic pills, and that was what was keeping him alive. The year before last he had married a young beauty, Gulbahor, who had just finished high school and had loved him very much then. After a brief while, Gulbahor meekly and guiltily gave back all of Farid's presents and left him for young Gumar, a golden youth with hair thick as a stallion's, a distant relative of Farid on his mother's side. The catastrophe corresponded to the course of events and restored the natural order violated by the marriage between the semitransparent girl and the weathered-brick fifty-five-year-old. So the event was not a catastrophe in the strict sense, which deepened Farid's loneliness. He put up no protest, to say nothing of complaint. Only he would suddenly frown as if he were now constantly looking at the bright sun. Farid's friends were indignant, and Roman Gusev, ruddy from the port, raged especially, reminding him that the girl had herself hung on Farid's neck, set up a watch around his building, and begged to mop his floors. Scoutmaster Seryoga Gaganov, a connoisseur of how high school girls tick, was the far side of forty, and had hair as smooth and black as a raven's feathers and not a single scratch on his conscience, explained authoritatively that a woman at such an early age is a talking organism and has no understanding of her own words. To this, Farid fell silent. Gulbahor's hologram still stood on Farid's computer desk. The young woman, as bright as the first snow, was wearing a fancy pink blouse with faceted buttons and holding a velvet doll.

By the time Krylov arrived, the main group had been sitting at the table for a long time. Gaganov was in fine fettle; leaning back in his chair, he was grinning dreamily at the ceiling, where a few flies were hovering, buzzing as if singing to each other. On the table was the same pink venison dumped onto a plate from several cans; in a deep porcelain bowl shreds of cold pelmeni were now stuck together in a mound. The men had probably been sitting there for a few hours —and drinking more than eating. They welcomed Krylov with raucous cries, fetched him friendly blows to his bones, and scrunched him over, shaking hands, onto a free stool. Instantly it felt good to be in this perfect, force-filled crowdedness, shoulder to shoulder with all his old comrades—who really had aged tremendously. Their rough tan and black apish paws and broken nails told you that most of the main guys had just returned from the forests. Always at August's close, rock hounds back from expeditions looked as if they'd aged drastically. But now they seemed more rusty than tanned; their drawn sinews and piebald napes with defenseless red bald spots—all this was for old men.

Happily spreading mustard on a slice of jellied fish, Krylov looked around the familiar and dear apartment, which bore the spotty traces of bachelor cleaning. Nothing had changed on his glassed bookshelves; in front of the death-gripped volumes were washed druses of citrine, smoky quartz, and rose crystal. At the sight of these magnificent nesting places filled with beings whose firm mirrored or ribbed hides preserved marvelous mute zones of transparency, Krylov felt his craft sing out in his heart and the tips of his fingers. He wanted and could lay these eternal souls bare, give them a new faceted armor, force them to speak in the harsh, imperious language of refracted light, so that you couldn't turn away. In combination with his thoughts about Tanya's existence, this was like anticipating the Christmas holiday. Krylov thought he was happier than many at this table, though he did know for a fact that his comrades, on the contrary, felt sorry for him for having sat the summer out in the city heat, pale as street dust.

The conversation droned on, passing from the alarming and incomprehensible social changes to fresh forest stories and back. Two of them, Gaganov in Lyalinskoye and little Vitya Shukletsov not far from Lake Utkul, had seen the ancient silver-hoofed deer, the oldest of the mountain spirits, which had appeared the last time in the early 1950s to show the "tails" of gold sand to some poor devil by the name of Makeikin—who had gone to prison for fifteen years for his good luck. According to Seryoga and the blinking Vitya, the paleontological specter was tall and barely hidden by the stormy birch forest, and his rack, four meters wide, looked like eagle wings of bone and frightened the birds. The Pleistocene beast smiled with its black suede mouth, showing its scimitar-teeth, and the silver hooves on its powerful forelegs splattered with swamp mud were badly oxidized. Judging from Seryoga and Vitya's contented and mysterious faces, Silver Hoof had not left them without a rich treasure.

The other prospectors weren't complaining either. There had been many precious pangolins: the narrow, beaded-like creations were quite unafraid of man and romped, describing figure eights, on the grainy boulders. In the hot, silky grass, grass snakes had slithered like streaks of oil, which was also a favorable sign. A few times the prospectors removed from branches and rough cliff ledges a vibrant, sharp thread—a hair from Goldenhair, the Great Snake's daughter, a woman three meters tall with an eyeless head wreathed in liquid gold who was capable of turning into a powerfully magnetized underwater snake. According to unreliable witnesses, occasionally glassy, crackled little eyes did gape on the creature's flat face—and then the overzealous prospector, bathed in sweat and deadly trembling light, was instantly transformed into a gold mummy-like statue. Like any mountain spirit, the Riphean Gorgon was capricious; however, her hair placed in an ordinary bottle would live without taking in anything for several years and bring its owner fantastic good luck, if he wasn't greedy. Reckless Roma Gusev had brought his fabulous sample to show off: the blue medicine vial closed with sealing wax looked like a flashing police light, and the blinding thread in it danced, imprinting a mad white spiral on your retina.

In general the season had been a success for the rock hounds. As usual among the main figures at the table, they kept mum about their own finds but talked a lot about the changes in the landscape, and their faces became distraught and emotional. They talked about how even the bright swamps covered with armfuls of vegetation and lustrous yellow globeflowers this year looked like paradise. Once again the forests springs had gushed, the fine sand in them swirled as if sugar were being stirred and stirred into the sweet cold water. The stream channels were so clean that the cornelian and quartz pebbles spread there made them like the window of a jeweler's shop. The mountains smelled insanely of berries and pitch. The countless bird voices heard nearby and far away let you sense with your ears the forest depths—the damp, smoky chasms permeated with cigarette rays of sun and the equally incorporeal dark trunks out of which, here and there, wove more complicated, flexible, and bizarre specters. The mountain glades, forest edges, and even slopes of worn, rock-sprinkled routes looked just like the Red Books that listed endangered species, but opened up. Curly wild lilies filled with powder and spectral violet irises bloomed in abundance, as did fat-lipped lady's slippers with their stitched leaves—to say nothing of the plain sweet William, abundant clover, and tiny rumpled poppies on slender yarn-like stems. The small black lakes had mysterious white patches of damp star lilies; the large, sturdy flowers surrounded an enchanted boat, and their stems, underlit by the sun, faded into the golden gloom, dancing with vivid flecks. It was hard to resist the temptation; your hands reached of their own accord to pluck the beauty—and the boat was pulled dizzyingly on its line until somewhere far away, deep down on one side, the tight umbilical cord broke and the trophy and its rubber hose ended up in the lap of the ecstatic poacher. As for the Ilim preserve, it was a functioning temple. The monolith of cliffs and the mass of transparent blue air were identically stone and identically air; round

Lake Ilim was so transparent that it magnified, like a loupe, a small barge that had stunk there two hundred years before and that looked like an uneaten chicken. The rare white-tailed bald eagles released from the Central Riphean Zoo without any particular hope of success were raising fledglings.

Krylov might have told his ecstatic comrades a thing or two about these unusual phenomena. He imagined with terrible clarity the anomalous spots visible from the sputnik, their wet edges consuming reality. Everyone who described the unprecedented luxury of this refreshed nature had been there under the mantle of transparent, flickering Medusas—but had returned alive and well, perfectly real, although Krylov kept wanting to touch them.

★ ★ ★

"By the way, isn't Petrovich back from the north?" A morose Menshikov inquired into space, having sat the entire evening over a full glass like a fisherman over his float.

Everyone gave Krylov a questioning look. to which he shrugged in silence. Now, in the last days of August, Anfilogov's absence had become not simply tiresome but alarming. He alone was missing among the elders of the Riphean rock hounds, and this absence was suffered by everyone to some degree.

"I heard it's practically heaven on earth in the north—and hell simultaneously," muttered Roma Gusev, rubbing his chest under his wrinkled checked shirt. "Supposedly the Kama is brimming with fish, and even sturgeon are coming up from somewhere. But they say people have seen all kinds of small stuff floating belly up. It's bad."

"Maybe it's algae?" little Vitya suggested hopefully. "It happens when the water heats up drastically."

"Or maybe they're deafened by explosions," Vadya Soldatenkov, who was large and gray, as if he had collected the cobwebs and dust from many ceilings on his head, said softly. "It's not just poachers doing business there. They say it's like a war."

Unlike most rock hounds, who went on foot on principle, Vadya preferred traveling by boat. He had an inflatable polyplast Shark with a compact motor that fit in the bottom of Vadya's huge backpack. This summer, Vadya had fumbled over tributaries of the Kama and seen horrible things. First off, he ran into a submerged chain stretched across the mouth of the Chusovaya and barely visible on the surface of the water, like a perforation on silky paper. The polyplast screeched, and the nose chamber expelled lots of yellow bubbles, and Vadya had to row forward onto a low bank. In the morning he was awakened by the damp, heavy smell of burning; the fog around him was oddly earthy. Hiding his possessions in the wet bushes, Valya traveled quickly upstream for about ten kilometers. First he ran across fat gray logs poking out of the river, sometimes so numerous they looked like outlandish canes and the formless remains of a ship's steel. The water where these submerged things were was darkened by gelatinous patches that looked like scorch marks. Here and there along the river fiery tufts floated past, falling apart, hissing, an inflamed pink in the fog; quietly, an empty angular specter, a burned-out barge, slipped by.

Farther on, Vadya thought he saw two badly crumpled motor boats that had slammed into each other. But as they came closer, lashed by branches full of water, it became clear that there were many more vessels in the warped heap. Every ten meters another one turned up—crumpled, gulping water through its pipe, or the outlines of the stern barely glimmering, like a fishing line drawn low over the waves. Terrified, his heart pounding in his chest, Vadya halted. He had the impression that if he went straight up to it, the heap of distended, chewed, and lacerated metal would rise to the height of an apartment building. Slinking away, he turned back—especially since behind him mountain rifles were pounding tautly and almost silently, and his peripheral vision caught here and there, under the grassy and cliff banks, solid patches that could well have been wet human clothing.

"In 1919, as they retreated, the Whites destroyed the Kama fleet just like that," the erudite Menshikov informed them, raising his tearing eyes in their bright pink, unstuck-looking eyelids, at Vadya. "Maybe you didn't see it. Maybe you read it in some magazine, hm?"

Insulted, Vadya sniffed and turned on his kitchen stool, which was small for him, like a stump under a bear. Stretching each leg in turn, he pulled two worn envelopes out of his tight jeans pockets.

"Anything's possible," he said wheezing. "Maybe my brain's turned to mush in my old age. But what do you say to this, sirs? What do you think this is?"

From the envelopes Vadya shook out what first appeared to be serrated scraps of leather and dried paper. Upon closer examination, they turned out to be birch leaves—tiny, sub-Arctic, early yellowing. The strange part, actually, was not their premature autumn fading but the nature of it, the distribution of the color. There was none of the usual birch freckledness and northern rustiness. The leaves' patterned, almost scaly surface looked like reptile skin. It was as if the swarthy, twiggy little trees they'd grown on had sucked up something unusual from the soil and the leaves had been given a mysterious injection.

"I think it's some kind of industrial chemical," Gaganov said without confidence, examining the amazingly sturdy leaf flesh, which did not tear, in the light. "Or even radiation. It's obviously poisoning. There you have it, gentlemen. What nature restores, man must defile."

"You can't be certain it's man," Farid objected dispassionately, collecting the dirty dishes and passing out to his comrades clean ones with shining crackled cornflowers, serving up his bachelor cleanliness as the best fare, which the rock hounds had grown unaccustomed to in the forest next to their acrid campfires.

The table fell silent. Once again they poured vodka, drank it down, and wiped their mouths on their sleeves. Then they started talking, lowering their muffled voices, about the strange disappearance of time. Virtually everyone who had been on expeditions this summer had encountered this phenomenon. At first, time moved normally, but then suddenly it vanished, like a river going underground, leaving the shining world in blissful stillness, in the distinctness of each and every being, in the childlike immortality of everything, from the black glacial boulders, like stones from a giant's hearth, to the tiniest water skaters, which ran like a cursor over a liquid screen, moved by the wireless device of an invisible user. All the expeditions had a moment when the participants lost track of the days. Then both the days and the nights became amazingly transparent: the ordinary mechanisms of oblivion ceased to function and everything that happened happened today. The reason for this may have been the beauty dissolved in the air that had expressively renewed every stone and every beast; no matter where you cast your eye, beauty dispatched man into eternity. A sojourn in eternity—that was what the expeditions of the summer of 2017 were for the rock hounds. They didn't know the date or the time and were unaware of being alive or dead. And then, due to a concatenation of events that seemed quite accidental, they left for the rail and bus stations, man after man, and woke up with a start in an unfamiliar land. Either the revolution of a hundred years ago was playing itself out in the form of sanguinary mysteries, or else, unfortunately, there had been an outburst of crime, or secret political strategists were playing games with the population in order to cook up some new leader in their cauldrons—maybe one hiding horny goat's hooves in his elegant shoes.

"What's so characteristic is, it feels like nothing's happening," little Vitya Shukletsov reasoned, scratching his little beard. "No one I know has lost his job, the ruble hasn't fallen, everything's still in place. If you don't turn on the television, you can live without a care in the world."

"It's been an awfully long time since anything's happened,"

Farid responded from his seat at the head of the table. "Nothing has any consequences. There haven't been any changes. They're asking nervous people not to watch."

To this, Menshikov, who had taken the least part in the discussion, responded with a new shrug not characteristic of him before, as if he were checking for his head with this unconscious movement.

"Do you want to see what happened to us?" he offered, addressing no one in particular. "I'll show you right now."

Frowning, Menshikov reached under the table where he had lying by his leg, like a dog, a shapeless sack, and he pulled out a plump book. Its glossy cover, sticky it was so new, looked like it was filled with fruit gelatin.

"What's this?" Roma Gusev reached for it, curious. "Is this yours again? Aren't you the writer! Good going! Let me take a look!"

The book went from hand to hand to an approving rumble of voices. Everyone showed everyone else the photograph of a smug Menshikov where he looked like a canned apricot. The author, much paler than on the cover, even more faded than his own worn-out shirt, which was disintegrating at the folds like an old newspaper, shook the outstretched hands and made his way through the handshakes to the dark bookshelf.

"Farid, can I rummage through your stuff?" he asked over his shoulder.

"What's mine is yours," replied Farid with oriental ceremony, although in his personal case this formula of civility very often turned out to be the pure truth.

Menshikov ran his fingers over the bindings and pulled out a small, naïvely blue book that evidently had something to do with the legendary times when the book's price was on the back cover. He smiled at it tenderly for a minute, like at an old friend, or rather at his own photograph as a child. Then he put both books in the middle of the table, which had been cleared of dishes and crumbs.

"Here they are," he pointed to the blue one, "my first stories. Nothing special, really. I had a glimmer of an idea, but at the time I could do so little and I didn't understand my own nature at all. But here it is, gentlemen, my best, I promise you." As if giving an oath on a Bible, Menshikov rested his hand, covered in pale hair, on the fruity cover. "Compare them and draw your own conclusions."

Not everyone, but many at the table really did see what Menshikov was trying to show them. The blue book had solidity and weight and held something apart from the book itself—it was a valuable ingot you could feel with your hand, which couldn't help but weigh and caress the object. The new one was as empty as a husked kernel, and this *emptiness* was not a function of the text but existed independently. The book was bookless. The large font for the illiterate took up nearly half its yellowish flecked pages. The novel seemed to have been spread on the paper in too thin a layer, the way an economical housewife makes one tin of caviar cover fifty pieces of bread—and because of this the novel lost certain properties, at least its taste.

"Yeah," a grumpy Vadya Soldatenkov, who, by the way, had an advanced degree in Roman-Germanic philology, began slowly. "For some reason I haven't been able to read anything lately. You open it up and see that the point of the text is not to forget my letters. But I think I remember them. By the way, I wonder what weirdo drew your cover."

The cover's stunning beauty would catch your eye a kilometer away, but somehow it was immediately obvious that the blonde with the hairdo like an éclair and the good-looking gay guy in the modest country lace had no connection at all to the novel's heroes. The cover was like someone else's clothing. In comparison with this edition, the little blue volume looked like a pure-bred object of culture and really did immortalize every printed word. The little book gave off the venerable, old-man smell of a library, whereas the new one was obviously not intended for long-term preservation. Somewhere in its publication data you should have found a use-by date, "Best before . . ."

"My new novel could have as much in it as a Bulgakov or Olesha," the imperturbable Menshikov announced, ignoring the disbelieving grins. "Only no one cares anymore. Nothing's happening—and it's not supposed to. Even the news on TV and in the newspapers—the point is to make sure there isn't any news. The flow of information washes away everything that might have any meaning. They published my book just so there wouldn't be an unpublished manuscript. So it wasn't left lying around. And didn't get into that flow. Oh, you know what I'm talking about."

"Stop it, Volodin," Gaganov smiled conciliatorily, topping off his untouched glass. "You writers have to have your insults. Life's fine, basically. If people don't appreciate your novel, you think it's a catastrophe."

"All right," Menshikov downed the very wet vodka in one swallow, jerking his Adam's apple. "I have one copy. Who should I inscribe it to?" he asked, catching his breath in the sleeve of his gray jacket, which looked like it had been sprinkled with baking soda.

"Me!" A joyous Gusev jumped up, forestalling his comrades who had stirred. "You know I love books," he defended himself with a maidenly blush in anticipation of a gift.

Smiling crookedly, Menshikov opened his luckless progeny until it cracked and scrawled a few lines for Roma in tiny script, attaching his long-tailed writer's signature. Roma took the book carefully, as if he were afraid the fresh words would spill off the page. While he was beaming and grinning, trying to sort out the loops of the small spliced handwriting, Menshikov bent over his bag again. What he pulled out was an officer's service cap with a St. George's ribbon instead of an insignia.

"Have you turned stupid or something?" Gaganov gawked after accidentally knocking off the table the pharmaceutical vial in which the relic hair, which had stuck to its sides, trembled like a little bolt of lightning.

With both hands, as if he were doing this for the first time in his life, Menshikov put the cap on his bony, crudely coiffed head. Instantly, his rather loose and long civilian jacket seemed to disappear, his tautly stretched temples stood out, and in the cap's predatory shadow his eyes became transparent, as if his brain were shining through an old cracked window.

"Oh well, I'm off to war," the transformed Menshikov spoke, looking from somewhere far away at this circle of comrades, at their large rounded shoulders and gray pates. "I want the Lord to say a few words to me personally."

"Who doesn't?" the bulky Soldatenkov muttered as he rose, knocking the table from below and making the dishes jump.

★ ★ ★

The party of men had grown cold and was starting to break up. The other guests followed Menshikov into the cramped vestibule. There, on a rather empty rack, in the vicinity of Farid's rumpled jacket, was a homemade greatcoat, reddish-brown, a horse color, sort of. Despite the warm evening, Menshikov put it on. Its crooked seams showed through, and when you buttoned it up he looked nothing like his former self. Nudging each other, the rock hounds sorted out their heavy footwear, gnawed away by Riphean stones, slapped each other on the back, and lit up on the staircase. Written on many of their faces was a new interest in what was happening in the city. The night was quiet, like the rattle a mother takes away from her sleeping baby, sprinkled only lightly with the faint sounds of distant gunfire.

Lingering, Krylov gave Farid a questioning look, and Farid indicated with his eyes that he should stay. Leaning his shoulder against the doorjamb, Krylov watched those leaving sadly, acutely aware of how vulnerable they all were because they always wanted to be in contact with their own destiny, to tug at its spy to make him turn around. Right now three or even four of them were holding themselves slightly apart in the crush, with minute fires in their squinting eyes—which spoke to the infectious example of the writer Menshikov, who obviously was planning to go straight from Farid's building to the shooting. Krylov realized with unusual clarity that they would never gather in today's particular configuration again.

A little later, the light went out in a small, thoroughly smoke-filled apartment. Gusev, tipsy, covered in his shaggy worn checked blanket, was snoring on his sofa, his cheek pressed against his gift book. The August night came through the opened window pane in the form of black, grapey air, and the tobacco curtain was slowly washed out of the rooms.

With an ache in his bones, Krylov was sitting in the tiny square kitchen under the bright white ceiling where little bats were flickering like stars on an old, breaking, black and white film. The money —a loan of a thousand dollars—had already been given, naturally, and put away in his rather fatter and firmer wallet. Now Krylov was telling his story—not hurrying, returning several times to the most difficult episodes, especially those where Tanya stubbornly repeated the fact of her nonexistent husband.

Farid listened closely, and his long oriental wrinkles, which had been his real facial features for some time, softened a little. His yellow lynx eyes watched calmly.

"This means you've had a visit from the Stone Maiden," he said at last, pouring himself and Krylov some thick tea brewed to a brick red. "If you want to live, you'd better not go looking for her."

"I'm sorry, but when you have a relationship with a real person, it's pretty hard to believe in fairy tales," Krylov challenged—and then remembered something. The strange transparency of Tanya's whole makeup, her fadedness, had always raised doubts about her reality that Krylov had hidden from himself. In fact, Tanya had always seemed like a figure showing through a page depicting the real world—and because of that she was filled with a light Krylov could not now exist without.

"What fairy tales?" Farid chuckled, not answering Krylov's

quick-tempered retort immediately and looking as if he were listening closely to something. "Why couldn't you do it the usual way? You could have rented an apartment."

"The usual way would have been . . . inauthentic, sort of." In his embarrassment Krylov scraped the spoon in the sugar bowl, which was lined with sweet coarse clumps. "You see—"

"Yes, I see everything!" Farid interrupted him, tearing open a solid cube-shaped packet and sending a silky loose stream into the sugar bowl. "By the way, about her spouse. They say that the women the Stone Maiden takes up residence in aren't just plucked out of thin air. They have their own biographies, too, sometimes even children. This kind of woman will destroy a man, lead him into the mountains, and then, as if nothing had happened, go back to her job and family. Oh, she may scratch her pretty face with branches and then lie that she doesn't remember anything. As for the husband, I don't think you need to look for complicated options when in fact it's all very simple. It's Anfilogov."

"No way!" Krylov gave an unnatural laugh. "The ages don't even work out," he said, and he immediately recalled the impression Tanya had made at dusk and sometimes in her sleep when rather than warm up or flush, as happens with all young creatures, she cooled, oddly enough, and her mouth became fine, with soft pouches in the corners. She was ageless. Her few conventional wrinkles looked like they'd been penciled on wax paper that wouldn't take lead. She could easily have been past fifty.

"And by the way, I once had a peek at Vasily Petrovich's wife," Krylov hastened to add. "She's old, and fat, and red-headed, and she was wearing a pink skirt."

"And I saw a blonde about forty, wearing a waisted outfit with a bow on her butt," Farid informed him caustically. "Did Petrovich tell you in so many words that the fat one was his wife?"

"No, you know very well he never says anything like that and never introduces anyone," Krylov mumbled, distraught.

"There you go," Farid spoke hortatorily. "Petrovich could have four wives, and not because he's a Muslim. He doesn't care about Allah or Christ. He's a law unto himself. That's Petrovich's principle: no one and nothing can be unique for him. Not a wife, or a friend, or a passport, or a home."

Krylov gulped down his oversweetened tea as if it were vodka, feeling the hot gulp immediately appear as sweat on his forehead. That was it. Anfilogov. No wonder vague rumors went around about the professor being a bigamist, if not a trigamist—and not out of any love for the fairer sex but, as Krylov had guessed, exactly the opposite. In any case, this was just like Anfilogov the conspirator: to avoid being pinned down, to clone himself and his destiny, literally every hour of his own time, at the expense of other people, their lives, and their destinies.

"And by the way, about his home." Farid, hunched over, was looking out the brightening window where the remains of the pale moon looked like an aspirin. "Our Petrovich is rich, as you know. I've heard he bought himself a special apartment that he decided no one would enter until his death. Like he was cultivating his own ghost, the way people grow tomatoes in a hothouse. As if when he died this duplicate of his would stand sentry over Petrovich's treasures."

Fighting a wobbly drowsiness, Krylov shuddered. Now he knew for certain exactly what door Tanya's "souvenir" keys opened—the keys were on him now, on him like a node on a tree, like a cunning steel parasite.

"There, you do believe in ghosts!" Farid exclaimed. "Fine, it's morning. The cock's crowed and the ghosts have melted away. It's time we got some sleep. I'll make up the chair for you now. Only here's one last question." Farid suddenly looked Krylov closely in the eyes, breathing warm alcohol fumes on him. "I'm only asking so that I can understand how bad things are for you. Tell me, the ruby mines people are yakking about, that Petrovich supposedly found in the north—do they exist?"

Krylov smiled helplessly. He well remembered the rock hound's rules, which said you weren't supposed to talk or ask about big finds. But Farid was staring hard at him, hovering over the sugar-scattered oilcloth. Then Krylov nodded sharply a few times, swaying with the stool over a sleepy abyss. His heart beat strangely. He would have given a lot right now for maximum simplicity in his life. But he had absolutely nothing to give in return.

"Here's the deal," the darkened Farid spoke gloomily. "Now you have to do what I tell you. Don't look for anyone anymore. Don't try to track anyone down. Sit tight and wait for Vasily Petrovich. Speak only to him and sort this out. And if anything happens—hightail it over to your uncle Farid and don't look back."

2

★

NATURALLY, KRYLOV DIDN'T LISTEN TO FARID.

He made an honest effort to free himself of the woman who had taken possession of him, illegally, without any right. Mentally he searched for and found in Tanya many shortcomings. But the moment that infernal work (which reminded him in some way of efforts to mend hopelessly torn clothing while you're wearing it) stopped, her image was immediately restored. Apparently, this image could not be done the slightest harm.

Krylov alone suffered the loss. On the one hand, Tanya's betrayal flattered him no end. Only Krylov understood what it was to give a lover the keys to her husband's refuge, even if she didn't tell him the address. On the other hand, the feeling that someone spent time in his apartment in his absence strengthened manifold. For some reason, he collected too much trash when he cleaned up. That much couldn't collect from one person in a half-empty space. Sweeping into the dustpan the transparent dust, which held nothing of the earth and was engendered by this space, Krylov discovered in it scraps of cellophane and tiny pieces of metal whose origin he couldn't explain. Just in case, he inspected his spare keys, which he always kept inside the apartment and were never removed from it. Two spares round wound with waxed thread were rattling around the hollow drawer of the light orange cupboard. Together with the set Krylov carried around, that made three. But for some reason he imagined there had been four initially.

Wrapped up in all these worries, for a while he forgot all about Tamara, as if she'd never existed.

He barely watched television, where they were showing old

movies now instead of news. From time to time when he stayed at
his mother's he channel-surfed mechanically and would come across
the croaking of a Hollywood comedy, or the peacock howl of the latest girl singer dressed in fishnets and sequins. Once, hearing the
bravura theme song of "Decedent of the Year" and seeing on the full
screen the flashing face of Dymov framed in frosted logs, Krylov was
just about to hit the remote when Dymov floated off and he saw the
clapping studio with the mirror floor onto which stepped a magnificent Tamara, boldly placing her shoe on her dancing reflection.

Evidently the very broadcast they'd been negotiating over for so
long was happening. Feeling a strange abandonment because what
was going on no longer concerned him, Krylov prepared to watch.
Tamara was ushered with all due respect into the chair for the main
guest—a ponderous configuration of dark wood without armrests
and with a Gothic back whose angle of incline, as Krylov knew, was
invisible to the eye and did not permit the sitter to sit up straight.
Tamara managed to seat herself handsomely, however, crossing her
bright legs and holding her straight back an imperceptible millimeter
away from the concave board. She was wearing a fiery dress that was
unfamiliar to Krylov, and something was sparkling friably in her
pinned-up hair. Through the screen's dusty glass he couldn't make
out the details.

The camera passed through the studio, and Krylov was
extremely unhappy with the guests. There wasn't a single important
face in the front rows, that is, not a single worthy opponent whose
presence could guarantee the show a respectable level. The faces
were all ordinary and common, and they all bore the deep stamp of
dissatisfaction. Decorative coffins were floating through the air with
their carved sterns forward, put in motion by a complex system of
silvery blocks and tackles. The long-legged ladies who performed the
program's dance numbers were parading around this time in silk Red
Cavalry caps, teensy jackets seeded with big red medals, and breath-
taking fishnet stockings.

"Now let's meet our experts!" the angelic Dymov announced in a festive voice. "Andrei Andreich Goremyko, doctor of engineering!"

The gentleman summoned shyly parted the bead curtain where the guests appeared, poked out halfway, and then all the way. His body, which was narrow in the shoulders and expanded evenly from his armpits, made him look like a large rodent; a gray stripe of vegetation did what it could to mask the absence of a chin, instead of which hung a sack. Mr. Goremyko's looked like a trained animal. Cautiously, taking little robotic steps, the expert crossed the treacherous mirror and sat down, both hands clutching the edge of the square table on which lay folders of some kind.

"And Riphean Women's Committee chair and City Councilwoman Adelaida Valentinovna Semyannikova!" Dymov exclaimed over the applause that burst up like a ponderous flock of pigeons.

Mrs. Semyannikova was undoubtedly in excellent form. You could have cut yourself on the lapels of her superbly ironed field jacket, and her head, driven firmly into her shoulders, sat there too firmly to be ripped off. If Krylov had for some reason created his own personal image of an enemy, he could not have come up with anything better than these gleeful bulging eyes and pickerel smile. Seated at a little table symmetrical to Goremyko's, Adelaida gulped down a glass of mineral water, wiped her mouth with her handkerchief, and immediately drank down another.

"Today we have a very special broadcast," Mitya began ingratiatingly and unusually literarily for him. "We have with us a guest whom we have been looking forward to ever since our program began. Mrs. Tamara Krylova is well known in this city as a brilliant lioness of society and a generous philanthropist. This dazzling woman, however, has a business that's anything but feminine. Granite offers funeral services. Services, moreover, that are quite original, shall we say. Tamara"—he warmly addressed his guest, who was standing at attention and could be seen by all from the top of her head to the tips of her shoes—"tell us what awaits us when we die and find ourselves coming to see you."

"After you die you won't be coming to see me," Tamara protested with a gentle smile, holding at arm's length a furry microphone, which looked like a blue carnation. "Each of us is rendered to where we are according to our faith. Granite operates here, on this side of that line. We do our utmost for the living: the near and dear of the newly departed. We are by their side to ease their loss and make the job of a funeral easier."

"Tell us! Tell us in more detail!" Mitya exclaimed impatiently, gazing greedily at his victim, who still had not displayed the least sign of confusion. Many in the studio leaned forward; here and there women's eyes grew moist, and some scrawny activist who was so wrinkled he looked as though a pencil had been dragged up and down his angry face dropped his written pages from his lap.

"I'll attempt to explain as clearly as I can," Tamara began, gazing benevolently at those who had gathered. "We all want to live well, on a modern level. We're interested in furniture, appliances, and clothing. But our farewell to those close to us is also a part of our life. Each of us must do this at some time. Isn't it important for this ritual to be done with dignity? Doesn't it ease one's grief if the deceased leaves us surrounded by beauty? But look: everything around is getting better except funerals. Styles and technologies are changing. But we still have those vulgar paper flowers and lace on our coffins. All this makes us think of disability and prison. Who usually operates in our difficult field? Workshops for the disabled and convicts. This alone casts a shadow over a funeral. Relatives seeing off the deceased are given a feeling of doom, and many afterward suffer from depression."

"You mean you want to turn funerals into celebrations?" the activist shouted from his seat in a squeaky voice.

"Friends, you will ask Mrs. Krylova your questions afterward," Dymov, flushed, reined in the activist. He was noticeably pleased, though, that the audience was heating up, elbowing each other and fidgeting in their chairs.

"But why? Let me answer," Tamara responded, sending the scrawny viper one of her most shimmering and precious smiles, the likes of which many high and mighty people dreamed of earning. "Not a celebration, of course, but a dignified, emotional pageant, like in a good theater. For this we want to do away with the traditional sordid environment and offer our clients completely different concepts for funerals."

"But have you thought about people's feelings?" a scandalized shout rang out suddenly in the studio. The camera quickly groped for the shouter: a tear-stained woman with yellow hair the color of a banana skin wearing a black gauze kerchief and a black T-shirt with an Adidas logo across her loose bra.

The audience began murmuring sympathetically. Dymov surrendered picturesquely, spreading his hands in their white lace gloves. One of the young ladies holding a Red Cavalry hat ran up to the woman with the microphone. Other young women from the corps de ballet, who had obviously been left without assignments today, were crowding around the decorative tombstones and whispering excitably, making idle dance movements with their identically fishnetted legs in their patent leather shoes.

"Hey, I already asked. Let her answer," said the lady into the microphone in a surprising raw bass voice. "I'd like to know how she fired the disabled people from that Granite of hers."

"Yes, I'd like to know that," a confident woman in a light-colored business suit that was a little tight on her, grabbed the microphone away. "What happened to the workers from the Society for the Blind, who, as we know, are protected by law?"

"Not one disabled person was fired. We simply have the workshop making something different now," Tamara replied with that particular, distinct grace that made it clear she had already dealt with the confident lady and had not formed a very high opinion of her. "Right now the blind are gluing together Christmas ornaments and garlands, and we're buying all of this for children's homes. I assure you, work that is full of celebration is much more suitable for the disabled. You see, they're as naïve and sensitive as children."

"I have different information," the lady continued to insist, holding the microphone tight while several hands reached for it at once. "We have a complaint from Gennady Petrovich Serebryakov, whom you let go—"

"We did let Serebryakov go and sent him to a drug clinic for treatment," Tamara interrupted, frowning quickly and unattractively, after which she returned her face to its icy graciousness. "If we hadn't done that, Gennady Petrovich would have very quickly found himself among Granite's special clients. I'm surprised that you were able to incite that poor man, who understands nothing, to write a complaint."

Tamara's last words drowned in a frothy surge of music, to which the young ladies who had not managed to disperse to their places automatically made several synchronized movements.

"We'll return after these ads!" doll-like Dymov exclaimed, making an emergency appearance in the frame.

The coffins went round and round like a carousel. Evidently, Mitya had chickened out after all, in spite of his sanction to set up a kangaroo court, a sanction issued, presumably, by the media service of the governor himself. An A-Studio ad started across the screen: the sun, visible through a column of water, looked like blue scrambled eggs; and a cheerful rubberized dolphin with a head like a rubber boot. Then a long-haired fairy languid with pleasure put a mug under a smooth stream of a nonalcoholic ladies' beer—and Krylov, fleeing the fateful beauty of the slick advertising creatures, headed for the kitchen, where the plastic, roach-infected radio was muttering. His mother, angry and sleepy, was sitting on a stool in front of a cup of yellow tea, and her mongrel kitty, spread out like a thick speckled pancake, was purring in her lap.

"That means they're showing your ex on television," his mother said listlessly, scratching the bristly hair on the cat's little furrowed brow with her finger. "She's still sending me presents every holiday. She won't show her face, though, she's afraid. She sends her driver. But I send it all back. Don't even look at it. If she'd show up herself, I'd talk to her. As it is, sending drivers, and not even the same one, and all of them so young. . . . She has no conscience."

Krylov's face turned red but he managed to restrain himself. Tamara had always been a good and patient daughter-in-law, and if his mother had not held on with a death grip to these rotting walls covered in old wallpaper that was like a fur coat, she would have lived in a decent apartment long ago. For her deference and generosity Tamara had received from her mother-in-law only animosity— organic, with pursed purple lips, without rhyme or reason. Presents from her were accepted only in the form of heavy gold jewelry. Even now, a jumbled gold lump with large earring-flies and massive pretzel -bracelets was kept somewhere in the depths of the moldy furniture where even his mother had not looked in years.

"Go on, then. Run back to her. Admire her. She forgot all about you long ago." His mother tipped the melancholy kitten, which had short torn scraps for ears, from her lap and turned up the radio, which was talking about unidentified flying objects.

★ ★ ★

There was no getting past his mother's insanity. Today it seemed like everyone was denying Tamara justice. Equipping himself with a slapdash sandwich made out of a fluffy roll and stale slices of ham, as red as abrasions, Krylov went back to the television. The ads were over, and Mrs. Semyannikova was standing conspicuously so that she filled the screen and playing with her necklace of large, flaking pearls.

". . . Krylova has good lawyers," she said in a chesty, slightly gurgling voice that for some reason always mesmerized listeners. "We aren't going to find minor violations at Granite. But that's not the point. That's not the point! Spirituality and morality! Spirituality and morality! That's what's upsetting people. And I tell you, you can't trick people. No, you can't!" Semyannikova took in the attentive studio with her light protruding eyes, her gaze brushing over the young ladies who reflexively squeezed their gorgeous knees together. "Mrs. Krylova thought that this program would be free advertising for her flourishing company. But you and I are not idiots." Semyannikova chuckled sinisterly, as if a boiling liquid had bubbled up. "We know very well that they are experimenting with people's feelings at Granite. People who have just lost their loved ones receive offers to play the lottery! What is this if not sacrilege?"

"She's already been thrashed for that!" a gristly fellow in bottle-glass wire rims that flashed slantwise, jumped up and shouted from his seat.

"That's nothing positive," Mrs. Semyannikova said didactically, and the fellow, confused, felt around behind him and lowered himself into his chair. "We, the Riphean Women's Committee, are opposed on principle to such excesses, but if Mrs. Krylova comes to us for assistance with this, we will render her all necessary aid."

The studio audience began to applaud. Tiny bouquets flew in the direction of the now languid Semyannikova. Goremyko sat in a disciplined pose at his symmetrical little table; he had a water bath on his forehead. Goremyko probably didn't understand what was going on very well and was extremely nervous before his own appearance. If Krylov could have destroyed this awful spectacle by smashing the dusty TV and everything in it on the floor, he definitely would have. But he continued to sit there and tear at the tenacious sandwich with his teeth, swallowing tough pieces, and bellowing powerless curses.

For some reason they didn't show Tamara for a very long time. But now here she was in the frame sitting at the very edge of her medieval armchair.

"You talk about people's feelings, but when you talk like that what moves you isn't anything humanitarian. It's cowardice." Tamara's voice was remote, and her wide-open eyes were looking past the studio, with its coffins, girls, and quiet Dymov, who looked like a chocolate rabbit in silver foil. "When we see our loved ones off, we're crushed by fear. We think that on this day we and all our feelings have to belong to death. We make a symbolic sacrificial offering, not letting ourselves even think about the fact that life goes on and that life has its rights, too. We don't let ourselves be alive. So even our grief rings false."

"How dare you!" the gristly four eyes exclaimed, wrinkling his spotted forehead.

"Here's how," Tamara cut him off without even turning to face her spiteful critic, who had nervously straightened his silk tie, which looked like a firebird's feather. "I have those seeing off their loved one let them go. I break the cabalistic agreement allegedly reached between us and the old man with the scythe. Since everyone has been hypnotized, abrupt action is required, a trick, if you like. Our lottery suits this purpose very well."

The camera held the confident lady, who had gathered her lips into a twisted thread at the ready, in close-up.

"Allow me if you would," she interrupted Tamara, glancing over quickly at someone's directorial signal outside the frame. "Three years ago the main prize in your lottery, a Caribbean tour, was won by Nina Sergeyevna Kucherova. Do you know what happened to that elderly woman who succumbed to your temptations?"

"Naturally." Tamara shrugged her splendidly large shoulders, which flashed under the light fabric. "At the time, many Russian tourists in the Caribbean perished in a natural disaster—one hundred eighteen people altogether."

"Don't you think this was nature's answer to your lottery?" Mrs. Semyannikova's stealthily broke in, pointing to the screen that had come up in front of the studio's viewers.

A newsreel came up and took up the whole screen. The sea, an unbelievable minty green, with zones of smoky, very gentle mirages, suddenly swelled up and lashed out, carrying the wicker furniture out of the nice little bungalows. The next frames were familiar from the news from three years before: the dead gray beaches that looked like they'd been poured from liquid lead; the boundary between the boiling sea and the land heaped with debris, like a barricade the sea simply could not destroy and carry away and the land could not withstand. The hurricane's apotheosis was a furious mist and shadows turning, waving, angular in the mist, palm trees swinging as if they were stripping a raggedy wet shirt over their head. And there it was, the shadow itself, which looked neither human nor bovine, with a clumsily smashed head, a head of Russian origin, as was confirmed, soaring slantwise into the heavens.

"Stop there and zoom in, please," Tamara's calm voice was heard outside the frame.

The newsreel shuddered, rewound a little, and the silhouette of the man-cow froze and started enlarging in jerks, coming closer to the viewer. But instead of getting more detailed and precise, it got more and more incorporeal, more and more transparent, until it seemed that the viewers could walk right through it, as through darkened air.

"It's a computer graphic," Tamara commented with a satisfied smile. "It's a forgery, and not a very high quality one at that."

"That doesn't change anything!" people shouted at her from the studio audience.

Actually, some of those invited, in spite of their class hatred for the gorgeous undertaker and the strict instructions they'd been given before going on air, were obviously starting to have their doubts that they were on the right side. Coarse faces softened. The yellow-haired woman in the clumsy mourning, her mouth half-open, gazed perplexedly at the gray screen, where only emptiness remained.

"That isn't you shouting, it's your fear. But I'm telling you that you don't have to be afraid of death." Tamara, pale now, with a wet patch on the bridge of her nose, and rocking slightly on her chair, holding the wrist of her hand, which was holding the fuzzy microphone close to her face. "Did you know that many pathologists secretly write poetry? I discovered this when I began working with Granite. This is one of the mysteries of the borderline between life and death. I'm not very fond of poetry. But individual lines have a strong effect on people like me who don't use poems. When I was just starting my funeral business and setting up my first office, a coverless notebook came my way along with some old furniture. It had been left by a doctor who at that time had also passed on. I don't remember the author's name right now, but here is what he wrote, "I want the trace of my gloves left on the face of death." I realized that this was about me. I don't want death to dare take more than it's due. And since we're living in a material world, I'm trying to achieve this by material means. That's all."

Krylov relaxed and took a deep breath on his complaining couch, only now realizing that he had not had a lungful of air in quite a while. He didn't want to watch Tamara, who had obviously triumphed again, anymore. Even less did he want to admire Dymov, who was raffishly leaning an elbow on a gilded tombstone decorated with the oval portrait of some red-mouthed blonde.

Something in the rascal's expression stung Krylov again, though, and he stayed on the channel, at the disposal of the studio cameramen's generous zoom. It was good he did because on the screen, as if the director had overlooked it, a completely different newsreel suddenly began. Judging from the mountain outlines and the predominance of right angles, this was the Riphean north, fairly close to Pripolyarye. They showed a large territory of perfectly bare land—land that looked more like petrified scum than land, without a trace of the variegated Riphean figuredness or a single blade of grass on its sloping humps. Along the territory's perimeter was a low forest as boring as a fence. The camera took a closer look and the reason for this boredom became clear: the forest was half-dead. The scabrous remains of small pines looked like rusty iron rods; bare, dead branches poked out on the deciduous species, and their sparse crowns were the color of bile.

"Dear Andrei Andreich. Now we need your help." Dymov turned graciously to Goremyko, who had jumped up. "Sit down, please. Sit down!" The expert plumped down awkwardly, looking fearfully at Dymov with the cloudy gray eyes of a two-week-old kitten. "Tell me, do you know this place?" Dymov gestured discreetly at the screen.

"Uh huh. I do. Of course. Yes." Goremyko cast a quick glance at the frozen scene and shuddered. "It's one of the cyanide heap leaching sectors for the Severzoloto gold-processing plant. Former plant, so to speak."

"And what position did you hold at Severzoloto between 1998 and 2004?" the moderator asked insinuatingly.

At this Goremyko turned pale, like a sweating window.

"Chief engineer," he managed to say, mopping his forehead with a gray wad.

"Now tell us what cyanide leaching is." Dymov measured out the perimeter around the expert in resilient steps, and the cameras devotedly followed first this and then that advantageous angle on his face, which had been powdered to a moonlike glow.

"Cyanide leaching is one of the ways of processing gold ore," Goremyko began muttering obediently, rustling his prepared documents with trembling fingers. "The method is based on cyanide's characteristic of dissolving noble metals in the presence of oxygen. The solution uses sodium cyanide."

"Is this substance toxic?" Dymov, who had never understood anything about chemistry or any of the other subjects he took at school, interrupted the expert. Now he was apparently quite happy with his role of slick prosecutor questioning the trembling witness in court.

"The problem is that the cyanide ion forms compounds with many elements," Goremyko was still mumbling, his eyes darting, so he wouldn't have to look at anyone specifically. "Some are toxic and some are relatively safe. The most toxic form is molecular hydrogen cyanide. But this is a short-lived toxin. Therefore, at Severzoloto, as all over the world, they used passive detoxification of cyanide heap leaching areas."

"You mean, the ore left over from the cyanide is just left to lie there and detoxify?" the quick-witted Dymov clarified, ignoring his opponent's scientific explanations.

"A reinforced screen is laid under the ore piles!" the expert exclaimed in a whining voice.

"Fine, then." Dymov locked his arms behind his back and stopped in front of Goremyko who tried to make himself smaller and sat as compactly in his chair as he could. "If this screen of yours cracks and substances end up in the groundwater, could they become poisonous again?"

"Under certain circumstances," Goremyko whispered, screwing up his eyes.

"So what is this?" Dymov exclaimed with pathos, pointing to the screen, where under the dead branches it showed some dead animal that had only its dirty hide and tiny bony grin left.

"Certain circumstances . . . or rather, uncertain . . ." Goremyko's voice rustled even more softly. There, on the grass, they could see inexplicable patches, as if someone had run green oil paint over the dried feathers and stubble. The camera showed a panorama of two or three sectors of overboiled land divided up by eyelash-sparse zones of birch grove and a small UFO that looked like a child's balloon and was hovering low over these barren fields, testing the soil with a lowered thread.

"What happened to your plant in 1994?" Dymov asked another leading question.

"The plant was shut down in 1994," reported Goremyko, gasping a little. "The Zayachye deposit played out and was judged unpromising. It was considered safest to pour the solutions into specially constructed reservoirs with antifiltration protection. The remains of the cyanide salts from the chemical storehouse were also preserved."

"You mean they shut down the plant and abandoned the poison without supervision?" Dymov commented caustically, looking the pale expert over from head to toe.

"You have to understand!" Goremyko shouted, raising his face, twisted from grief, to his elegant tormentor. "Taking cyanides out over those bumpy dirt roads—there was just a major accident in China. And we don't have the transportation, and the treatment facilities aren't operating anymore. Everything's ass backward! If the proper technologies had been used in constructing the reservoirs, there would have been exactly no danger! Guaranteed!"

"If!" Mitya raised his slender index finger significantly. "What an interesting subjunctive. But we'll return to this later. Right now let's watch a little more of the newsreel."

What looked like the inside of a huge concrete egg appeared on the screen. The light, first skewed and pale, then rounded out to the full vividness of a summer's day, penetrated through an upper hatchway into a damp cave. The dampness thickened the stagnant air and ran down the walls like the last of the jam. There, on the walls, you could distinctly see dark strips—some thinner, some fatter, some closer, some farther apart, as if the cave were a vase that a hideous bouquet was drinking blossoming water from. Through the hatch hung a slender rope ladder that kept trying to twist, and down it, slowly, lowering their fat legs in formless shoe covers one at a time, climbed two clumsy figures completely upholstered in crumpled silver fabric.

Something about these figures reminded him of the chalk outlines left on the floor when dead bodies are taken away for further investigation, as if these outlines had stood up and started moving around. The filming wasn't professional; the camera bounced around, and obviously some third person was shooting, and sometimes his fat-fingered ribbed gloves ended up in the frame. To the side, on the wall, a small equipment balconette of eaten-away steel popped up. There, the first two, reflecting each other in their face shields, set about assembling the apparatus, which consisted of spiral cables and mirrored cylinders, and the camera, together with the flashlight's beam, looked down nearly from the root of the scattered gray gloom. Down there lay the bottom: cracked, it looked like a hardened dead cobweb in an abandoned corner. You could tell the concrete of the underground space had originally been a sand pie. The cyanide solutions poured in here fifteen years before without any purification, leaving something like a dark jelly—the sediment of an evil whose sticky moistness was maintained not by the remains of the solvent but by the groundwater that breathed heavily and noisily around the destroyed reservoir in which the silvery crumpled cosmonauts seemed to be swimming.

"Looks like your solvents have all gone into the ground," Dymov said.

"They cut so many corners," Goremyko spoke wearily and bitingly. "No hydraulic seal for you, no drainage layer, and the cheapest possible brands of concrete. With a little extra sand." Leaning on his elbows, he covered his pale face with his dark hand with a raised pinky that looked like a swollen gray caterpillar.

"Andrei Andreich, don't fall apart, please," Dymov began to fret, stepping closer to the expert. "We have one question left, the most important one. Who exactly cut the corners? Who stole the money allocated by the provincial government to bury the cyanides?"

"The general contractor stole it," the expert woke up, wiped his face, and glanced behind his back. "Stroyinvest. Its director and owner is Mrs. Tamara Krylova. She's sitting over there."

But Tamara wasn't sitting there anymore. She was standing alongside her unshakable throne, in her twisted skirt, trembling on her high heels.

"What's the date of that film?" she shouted in a little girl's voice, brushing the hair off her forehead. "I saw numbers in the corner, the date of the filming, please!"

"Mrs. Krylova, right now we're not talking to you. Right now the experts are having their say!" Dymov signaled to someone from the studio staff. "Turn off microphone one! Adelaida Valentinovna, please!"

At that, Tamara's suddenly young voice disappeared from the acoustic system of the light-filled studio. Her own barely audible shout was drowned out by the cooing of Semyannikova, who was holding her microphone like a delicacy and touching her kinky curls with her tapered fingers.

"Look at how simple human truths are revealed to us," Semyannikova said, smiling maternally at everyone, even the now somber Goremyko. "Look at where the money comes from that Mrs. Krylova is using to build her suburban mansion and to found Granite. But it isn't money she stole. No, not money! She stole life from nature and maybe even people. Yes, people! There are four settlements in the area of the ecological disaster! One of them has a high school! And after this, Mrs. Krylova is going to say she's an opponent of death? Why, she *is* Mrs. Death! Look at her!"

Everyone was already looking at Tamara, who had suddenly thrown the useless microphone away, behind her carved chair. Striding tall and shakily, as if she were trying to disengage herself from her own reflection in the mirrored flower, she headed for Dymov, who had suddenly started to smile a human, pathetic, trembling smile. The slap from Mrs. Krylova's hand, which was as heavy as a gold ingot, was crushing. Losing his balance, Mitya hung from the carousel with the rocking coffins, and a crimson calamus blossomed on his cheek. Mitya's eyes were weepy and completely senseless. The whole studio jumped to their feet, and so did Krylov. He managed to see Mitya being picked up and disengaged from the warped carousel tacking and the coffins collide in mid-air, scattering the tenacious heaps of artificial flowers. Then, without any caption, an animated insert, "Decedent of the Year," ran across the screen: paperclip-shaped skeletons danced the can-can.

Part Eight

★

1

★

KRYLOV'S FIRST IMPULSE WAS TO CALL TAMARA'S CELL IMMEDIATELY. He screwed up his courage several times and picked up the phone— but at the third or fourth number his agitation became unbearable, and cursing himself, he slammed the receiver down. He had this crazy idea that Tamara could grab his hand over the telephone. Finally he punched out the eight-digit number that was as kin to him as his own birthday, only to hear a polite message that the subscriber was unavailable.

The next day and the day after that all the numbers Krylov knew were either turned off or else answered with endlessly long signals. Suddenly, a wall of telephone muteness had arisen between him and Tamara, a wall that seemed made of impregnable, resilient glass. At every attempt to break through, Krylov felt its taut power, the responding vibration of a hostile dimension. Only once did her office cell phone, which was usually with Tamara's driver, answer in the expectorating voice of Kuzmich, Granite's former owner. Krylov rejoiced even at him, as if he were dear to him. Only Kuzmich wasn't in any mood for long chats. He was at his wits' end, shouting over the snip-snap of some highway, and from time to time he dropped out, as if cut off by a chain saw.

"You saw it. They want to shut our girl up! They brought charges! Why don't you quit calling here. This isn't any of your business, ex!" With these words, Kuzmich hung up and plunged into wherever all of Tamara's colleagues and staff had vanished, her entire business machine, which had been working so superbly so recently and now had disintegrated into tiny pieces.

In the mornings, Krylov bought up all the newspapers and rum-

maged through the colorful stacks with one single goal: to find information about Tamara, to read something between the lines. Finally
the wild *Young Communist of the Ripheans,* which consisted of
nothing but pictures, devoted a whole column to relations between
Tamara and Dymov; moreover, the faces of all the characters were
the color of sausage. The more respectable *Provincial Gazette* ran
commentaries by a lawyer and an ecologist. Tamara's prosperity
apparently rested literally on the misfortune of the entire Riphean
region, and some of her actions constituted various crimes, including
minor assault, inasmuch as TV commentator Dymov had received a
concussion on a live broadcast. A lot of the rest was sinister, vague,
and alarming. Glib pens wrote about a "cyanide autumn," mummi-
fied trees, and a mass die-off of fish. They wrote about game wardens
allegedly seeing the corpses of tourists whose mucus membranes were
like rotten tomatoes, obvious testimony to cyanide poisoning. All this
was directly linked to Tamara Krylova, "Mrs. Death." The journalists didn't worry about lawsuits and pushed on, stopping at nothing,
from which Krylov concluded that they had been given the go-ahead
from very high, almost inaccessible spheres.

Everyone who could piled on to the bandwagon of harassment
sanctioned from on high. The *Riphean Observer,* a contentious
tabloid scattered with the grain of misprints, came out, by the way,
with a column-long interview with Granite's former owner. There, the
kind-hearted Kuzmich, shown in a photo with spread hands and an
open mouth that looked like the hollow of a tree, amiably shared the
details about how he had had his cherished, thoroughly traditional,
and highly law-abiding funeral business taken away from him.

The mystical feeling of any Riphean that everything involving
the forest, woods, and beasts has something to do with him personally had somehow dulled in Krylov. To be truthful, right now he
couldn't care less about the ecological catastrophe or the dubious
origin of Tamara's business. He wanted one thing: to talk to Tamara
for half an hour and make sure she wasn't miserable and knew what

to do. Her irritating absence was especially painful in the context of thoughts about the missing Tanya, as if the women had plotted to create for Krylov a personal hell.

Dragging himself out of the house, breathing in the cold delicate smell of the early autumn, Krylov sensed around him a strange unresponsiveness, which made him realize that Tamara's professionals had continued to look over Krylov until the very last moment—and now were gone. The city's population seemed to have halved. Maybe there were more police dressed up in new gray uniforms criss-crossed with white straps on the occasion of the universal military masquerade. The more guardians of law and order there were, the smaller and punier they became, as if they had created two policemen out of one. Nonetheless, these boys were omnipresent and were fiercely checking the documents of anyone wearing a counterfeit uniform or carrying large bags.

Abandoned, forgotten by everyone, needed by no one but old Farid, Krylov now had only one worthwhile occupation: standing sentry at the spy's lair, which is what he did, adapting himself to sitting on an enormous old stump that looked like a turntable with a record on it and occasionally shaking the brazen ants from his jeans. He could not believe his eyes when Viktor Matveyevich Zavalikhin in person stepped out on the cement-patched ruins of his porch. The spy had filled out and was as pale and gray as a mushroom. He was wearing a boy's jacket with little buttons and shoulder straps that was way too short for him, and on his round head was a flat leather cap. From his paleness Krylov guessed that the spy had been sitting inside all this time, behind those gray windows and faded, clay-colored curtains, without stirring once. Now the criminal squinted matter-of-factly at the pale sun as if it were a light bulb he personally had screwed in and that had meticulously turned on.

By an effort of will, Krylov stayed where he was. He couldn't let Viktor Matveyevich whisk back into his den. At the same time, he couldn't let the spy leave in his Jap car, whose flat rusty butt Krylov saw nearby, in a protected parking lot ringed with torn chain link. Fortunately, the spy displayed no intention of getting behind the wheel. In no hurry, slapping his fat knees, he started walking up to the highway along the gravel-crunching path, to the bus stop. Whistling through his nose, he passed literally a meter from the frozen Krylov, who was sure the bird cherry leaves hiding him, which were already a little papery and not firmly attached, would rustle treacherously from his constrained breathing. On the spy's round back, on the jacket's nap, which looked like boar bristle, Krylov saw the traces of something dried—maybe bright oil paint. He waited a little, letting a slow-moving old lady with a torn plastic bag who was noisily scuffling the gravel with her thick boots go ahead of him, and then he cautiously started after his tormenter, trying to figure out the best way to approach him.

He barely slipped through the hissing doors of the bus, which immediately left the stop with its crushed, many-headed load. The spy skillfully passed from handle to handle, like a spider across a web he personally had woven. On his paw, which stuck way out of his hairy sleeve, was a ring with a cornelian cabochon that looked like a wart. The bus began to gallop downtown, shaking its passengers, and Krylov, afraid of missing his foe, who was looming closer to the front platform, kept near the exit. When at the seventh or possibly the eighth stop the bus doors were burst open by the incoming crush, the spy suddenly wriggled his whole short body and literally plopped out onto the sidewalk. With a moment's delay, Krylov made the same maneuver, forcing his way through the dense jam of people, dragging with him a large woman who looked like she'd been inflated and was wearing a plastic Panama hat and who obviously had been planning to get on, and he inhaled the cold sharp air of freedom. Meanwhile the scoundrel's cap was already flickering in the distance, a brown spot. Overcoming his dizziness, Krylov rushed after him.

Now the city seemed overpopulated to Krylov, as if all the residents who had vanished had returned with another million and a half on top of them. At every step he ran into pedestrians, as if he were pounding into oncoming waves of some impersonal element, trying not to lose sight of the quick-moving brown fleck. Sometimes the oncoming blows were so powerful they nearly snapped off Krylov's head, inside of which a heavy fledgling was stirring, as if in an egg. In his wake came indignant cries and unflattering words, and once scattered apples rolled underfoot and seemed to multiply among the pointed shoes and fish-pale summer boots.

All of a sudden the spy vanished, as if he had fallen through the earth. Krylov ran forward a hundred meters and turned back, distraught, stepping in circles as if he were performing a tango without a partner. He was plunged into the deep glass shadow of the mirrored towers of the Economics Center, on which the reflections of multistory clouds passed like a film on a giant plasma screen. Ladies dresses burned in the transparent infinity of the shop windows like tropical butterflies. Suddenly the steps of a noiseless escalator spread out smoothly at his feet; glass elevators entwined with green cascades of water slipped by. You couldn't tell whether you were standing in a shop window, in an arcade, or under the open sky. Only the puddles on the pink paving stone and the damp strip of washed grass let Krylov feel that he had not yet been drawn into the transparent aquariums where people seemed to be passing through walls. For the first time in his life, *transparency* seemed like his enemy. The spy could not have found a better place to disappear.

★ ★ ★

Nearby the lightweight tables of the summer café were white in the glass twilight. Krylov crashed behind the far one, which tottered under his elbow. The fledgling in his heavy head was pecking away, getting ready to peck through back of his skull. Instantly Krylov was faced with a waitress wearing an ironed tennis skirt with a high cutaway view of her long bronzed hips and carrying a racquet under her arm. The prices on the menu, which was decorated with pictures of

Wimbledon and the Kremlin Cup, seemed excessive to Krylov; he had never encountered anything like it in his outings with Tanya.

"You can get food and alcohol at the bar. It's cheaper there," the young woman said sympathetically when she saw her customer's confusion.

She was attractive, with a peeling little snub nose and dark freckles that looked like melted flecks of chocolate. Krylov guessed that she liked him, despite his worn clothing and droopy pockets, which were obviously empty. This kind of thing had happened pretty often before he'd met Tanya, and sometimes these kinds of random girls with the mournful eyes gave Krylov a few festive weeks. Now, though, the muscular beauty of the tanned athlete was as alien to him as the beauty of a thoroughbred horse. Automatically obeying the wave of her golden arm, he turned toward the bar and immediately jumped from his chair, which had toppled over.

The spy was taking tiny steps away from the bar, as if all was well, holding in front of him a disposable cup of red wine, soft from the weight, and whispering to get the liquid not to spill. As if crossing tightly stretched fabric, Krylov approached the scoundrel from behind and grabbed his fat forearm with pleasure. The half-portion splashed the scoundrel's reddish-brown boots. The spy spun around and through some internal effort made himself twice as heavy, driving his legs into the whole shaken earth.

"What's wrong? I don't understand." His bloodshot eyes glanced over his shoulder, over the fold of fat between his color and his cap. "Oh, Mr. Krylov! You're still alive. What pleasant news!"

"The topic here is you, creep," Krylov spoke softly into the spy's dirty ear, which was as hot as a jelly doughnut. Because he was out of breath, it came out too softly, and Krylov added more loudly, with hatred, "If you so much as budge, I'll kill you."

"All right already! Why so harsh today!" the spy protested in a reedy voice. "Let's sit down. Let's sit down and hash this out. Isn't that what you used to say when you were shoplifting at the Oriental?

Now they say 'let's lash this out.' And 'point,' not 'topic.' You've got to stay closer to the common people!"

"Stay right where you are, Linguist." Once again, Krylov saw the dried yuck on the spy's shoulder, as if someone had tried to draw in shit on an angel's wing. The spot was so irritating, Krylov started scratching it off voluptuously. The scoundrel groaned and grimaced, and the jacket on his back turned into wool and smoke. People were looked at them. The snub-nosed waitress was gesturing her frightened objections to the ruddy young security guard, who was anxiously smoothing his sleek hair with both hands, getting ready to act.

"Care to clean my boots, too, my dear man?" the spy asked innocently, putting one short foot forward after another. On his cracked, reddish-brown, down-at-the-heel shoes the wine spots looked like wet liver. One wrinkled pants leg also had a spill starting at the knee. Clucking with regret, the spy lifted his pants a pinch, and this feminine gesture revealed disgraceful socks that looked more like kitchen rags. The spy's ability to make Krylov's hands itch was irresistible. Krylov delivered a light chop to his yellowish neck, which proved rather insensitive, like a sofa bolster.

The young security guard, flushed to the roots of his hair, which was glued with gel into flat dry ribbons, moved forward indecisively.

"Everything's fine, just fine!" the spy exclaimed, halting the guard halfway. "This is my friend! Him threatening to kill me, that's just his way of joking! He makes jokes like that! By the way, his name is Krylov," the scoundrel added boastingly, putting his arm around Krylov's waist. "His wife is the famous Mrs. Tamara Krylova they're writing about in the newspapers!"

The scoundrel's announcement aroused excitement at the little white tables. Well-dressed customers began turning around to look at the odd couple, abandoning their wine and holographic toys, which flickered like flocks of moths. Although newspaper reading had long been considered something the common people did, these people were clearly caught up, evidently foraging for information from more high-tech and respectable sources. One curly head whose hair was like a bouquet of tiny yellow roses and whose nose was the shape of a pencil, quickly changed the attachment on his professional camera. A gentle rustle and a white glaze washed over Krylov, like cold water from a hose. Satisfied, the spy belatedly assumed a dignified air, raising his spattered glass to the health of those present.

"The on-line magazine *Ripheans Illustrated!* One more picture, please!" Curly was now aiming at Krylov from below, shifting from knee to knee, completely swathed by his narrow suit into a silvery strip.

"Stop it! Get out!" Krylov edged him away with his elbow, and the security guard, nodding respectfully, began to advance on the reporter with widespread arms, as if he were trying to catch a chicken.

"Were you aware of your wife's crimes? What do you think of her affair with Mitya Dymov? Is it true that Mrs. Krylova preserved the dead for future resurrection?" the pressed reporter shouted, jumping on the guard and raising the camera aloft, where it clicked and flashed in his hands like a madman.

"Interesting questions, by the way," the spy noted, taking a sideways view of the poor relative, as he sat down on a free chair. "I read an article like that! How about it? Are you going to sit down, too, or are you going to start beating him up right away? Why don't we finish our drink and then you can beat him up!"

Krylov shifted from foot to foot and then sat down opposite him. He saw that the reporter finally saw the good in hopping into his humped little car, slipped out of his parking space, and took his Promethean fire to his own dear editorial office. The scoundrel, sipping his wine, which made his wide mouth the color of sealing wax, looked at Krylov with feigned horror. Something told Krylov that this fake clownish fear concealed genuine fear. That was what he wanted to bring to light.

"What do you want from me, poor man?" the spy spoke, sighing sadly. "My God you're good-looking!" This was to the athletic waitress, who had silently put a clean wet ashtray, certainly wet from her tears, in front of Krylov.

On the waitress's splendid little face chagrin was battling burning curiosity, which really had moved her light, jeans-gray eyes to tears. Krylov guessed that as she was gazing at him through her clumping eyelashes she was thinking of Tamara, Tamara's dresses, and Tamara's intriguing fame. This young woman was like that homeless girl painting her sagging little face in front of the mirror of Tamara's Porsche. For the umpteenth time, Krylov thought what a magnetic effect Tamara had on women, as if she were playing some invisible instrument for them.

"Oh ho! She likes you!" the scoundrel chuckled, resting his chest on the tottering table. "Some people have all the luck: a rich wife like a favorite cat and plenty of girls! What on earth do they see in unwashed, unshaven you? If only I had that kind of satisfaction."

The spy blinked sweetly, and Krylov noticed that before leaving the house his foe had carefully shaved—probably shaved off an overgrown beard. Not only that, but the scoundrel stank of some noxious cologne, like a freshly crushed insect.

"And how is your dear uncle's health?" Krylov inquired politely.

Unexpectedly, his question hit a sore spot. The spy's ugly face went through several instantaneous changes from one unhealthy pallor to another, and fear, the real thing, not feigned, danced on the tips of his hard square fingers, which trembled finely on the table.

"My dear uncle is temporarily on vacation!" the spy nervously informed him. "That's right! He's talked a lot about you. A genius, he says! One of a kind! A master! Everyone respects you so much! And for me it's a great honor—"

"Shut up," Krylov interrupted the scoundrel's word stream, and he immediately shut up, nervously drumming the little table. For some reason the mention of his uncle had made him hysterical, Krylov realized. It was odd. Why had this ugly face seemed so familiar to him before, as if Krylov himself had sculpted it once?

"Basically, this is the deal. I don't really care why you've been dragging around after me and the woman I love. What I need from you is her address and telephone number. Tell me and you're free. I won't do anything to you no matter how much I want to."

"Aha!" The spy's short eyebrows crept up under his cap. "Why is it she's so afraid of you? You mean she didn't even give you her address? If I were you, dear boy, I'd spit on that lab mouse," the scoundrel said suddenly in an intimate little voice, shifting over toward Krylov along with his hopping chair. "My God, our waitress is a lot prettier! As your good friend, I'm telling you! And what about Mrs. Tamara Krylova! I can't even imagine what a man could do with that lady except admire her beauty!"

"Give me the address," Krylov said wearily. Once again he had the feeling the spy contained some part of himself so that he was dealing with himself, and that made his overtaxed brain even wearier.

At Krylov's words the spy took offense, turned sideways, and crossed his legs, displaying his disgraceful sole.

"Yeah, sure," he muttered, grimacing. "I wanted to do the right thing by you. Okay, write this down: 18-16 Radishchev Lane."

Everything inside Krylov sped up or possibly down, from a tremendous height. And hid in a dark impasse.

"You're lying," he said in a cheerless voice.

"Now you're the detective!" the spy said in admiration and even slapped himself on his tight linen knee. "Yes, I'm lying. You know, I'm an honest man. If I happen to tell a lie, then I answer for it. Yes, I say, I lied! Fine, for your quick wits here's the real address: 130 Prikolnaya Street, block 8, apartment 208."

"We don't have a Prikolnaya Street in this town," Krylov grinned.

"Oh, right, you're the specialist here," the spy checked himself. "You've always got that atlas in your pocket. Evening falls and you're off on some excursion. Only here's what I'm going to tell you, dear specialist, if you're in such a pinch. If that four-eyed lady got her hooks in you and threw you—"

At this the scoundrel shot an inquiring glance at Krylov, but Krylov restrained himself. Lord, he thought, if You exist, make her be looking for me, too. It felt like he was singing and rasping without making a sound, like a bronze horn aimed at the sky.

"In short, dear man, let's talk as one serious man to another," the scoundrel went on, his bulk sprawled on the little blue chair. "Sometimes very major valuables fall into people's hands. Then those people start behaving restlessly, which is very easy to spot. At home they hide the valuables with their underwear, or in jars of rice, in the freezer and other clever spots. When I was a kid I had a hamster named Rex and he lived in an aquarium. I called him Rex because I wanted a dog," the spy clarified, heaving a sentimental sigh. "Basically, the animal hid reserves, because it was smart. It stuffed seeds into its cheeks, dropped them in the corners, and covered them with straw. It thought it was burying things the right way, but I could see his whole treasure through the glass. That's how people are, my dear. They never suspect that their little hiding places for grain are easily seen by an outside observer. That's why taking extra valuables away from people for whom they're too much doesn't take any particular effort."

Krylov understood what kind of grain the scoundrel was talking about. Tamara had been right. Uncle and nephew, two cowardly fatmen, had their sights on the loot from the expedition. It had been a mistake on Anfilogov's part to sell last year's stones. Although large finds themselves set bells to booming even if no one pulls the cord. He wondered whether the evil Anfilogov corundums were too much for the fatmen themselves.

"Now let's move on to the topic at hand." The spy held his index finger with its wavy yellow, cockleshell-like nail up significantly. "All of a sudden two participants in our story about the grain, he and she, start to behave improperly. A mutual sympathy develops between them, so to speak, and certain shared plans. This was unforeseen! Is there any chance they're conspiring to take the grain for themselves and build a happy new life? Yes, and quite a substantial one! They need a lot now, and that has to be taken into account. This is why a third person who is already involved and is, let us note, family, has to keep an eye on them. Drag himself all over town without any time for himself! Raising the suspicions of his lawful wife! It's hard, unpleasant, and troublesome for everyone. But you see we could also reach a civilized agreement! For instance, one of the two, who will certainly get the grain for finishing, makes a quick phone call. They knock very lightly at his entryway. And then he gets not only the lady's address but an attractive small percentage."

"How about a punch in the face for that suggestion?" Krylov interrupted. To him, calling thieves up the way he would a taxi or pizza delivery seemed so crazy he nearly burst out laughing.

"You all get a real kick out of my face! I know I'm no beauty!" The spy tugged the bill of his stiff cap right over his eyes. "You think I'll double-cross you? No way. I'm an honest man! You can believe it. They shut me up for four years, and I was more honest than all the people who knocked the confession out of me, tried me, and kept me in the zone put together. Maybe not what I do, but my essence, my human core. You know what I mean? No matter what I had to do, by my nature I'm a good person. Nature is the most important thing! Should I make you another offer?" Without asking, the spy plucked a couple of cigarettes out of Krylov's pack and bit down on one of them casually with his big yellow incisors, which looked like wood chips, flavoring it with the tall tongue of flame from a fake gold lighter the size of a small flask.

"I understand. Talent and creative plans! A major professional opportunity!" he went on with enthusiasm. "After all, you can collect the stones after they're cut, too. You can trust me—I'd agree! After all, those Israelis and Amsterdammers don't have anyone better than you. You're a master. You can be the author of unique stones. Unique! People will give them names! And they'll pay you more for them than that weirdo professor of yours!"

Stunned, Krylov looked at the spy as if he were looking at himself in some live convex mirror. This fat clown had somehow managed to guess Krylov's deepest desires.

"You oaf, the stones aren't mine. Don't you get it?" he asked with savage amazement, irritated that he'd let him suggest a dirty trick like that.

"Whose are they?" the spy flew up. "The state's maybe? Or the Stone Maiden's? Are you a total idiot? Your professor—you know he stiffs everyone. He's been smothering my uncle for twenty years! He and my uncle were partners first, with equal capital, they went in together. Then Anfilogov took his money back and my uncle was left empty-handed! Even though my uncle could have got in touch with his cops and wouldn't have been any the worse off. But for the professor, you see, every little person is separate, like a collection. That's his principle!"

Krylov thought the spy, who'd suddenly turned as purple as grapes in a press, was about to bust a gut. But the spy recovered his breath. Pulling off his cap, he wiped his sleeve across his sweaty forehead, which was crossed by a nasty pink dent that looked like a bite cast, and slapped his head gear back on, leaving a wet semi-circle on the table, the way a glass would.

"I don't rat out my friends," Krylov said distinctly.

"Glory be, how very noble we are," the spy puffed up at the insult. "And how convenient for you. I end up wasting my precious time with you again. You know, you hero-lover, while I was shepherding you and your lady friend, I had a deal, a profitable deal, go south. And I got such a toothache I thought my skull would crack! You think they're going to let your professor make his hideous profit? Go stick a nuclear warhead up your ass! You'll remember my generosity and it'll be too late. Hey, garçon!" the spy shouted for the guard, who immediately jumped up, his striped acetate tie hanging like a cat's tail when he made a little bow. "Tell me, good man, where's the toilet here?"

"The café doesn't haven't one. It's in the arcade. Take a right and down the escalator," security informed him concisely, casting nervous glances at Mr. Krylov, who had gotten into their ordinary establishment he had no idea how.

"Hey, where are you going?" Krylov tried to hold the spy back by the hem of his short jacket, where he could feel his heavily loaded pockets.

"What, I can't take a leak?" the spy grumbled dully. "I'll be back in five minutes. If you want to you can come along." He waddled toward the glass doors, which parted in front of his concentrated weight with a roguish whistle.

★ ★ ★

Krylov sat there a moment gazing dully at the arcade's tropical depths, which were full of artificial sunlight. He was ashamed to say it, but he was held back by the thought of the ten or even thirty they charged in places like this to use the toilet. All of a sudden he jumped up, slapping his forehead.

Krylov took the sloping escalator in three bounds, fed the coin slot, which giggled as if the coins he dropped in were tickling its insides, and burst into the men's room, which here was the size of a Metro station. The few men standing with tensed necks along the green urinals or washing their pale hands in front of the mercury mirrors did not include the spy. From the stalls came the sounds of toilets flushing, as if they were starting the ignition on a shuttle, but the emerging gentlemen, who were zipping up their trousers not without some satisfaction, did not include the spy. It took Krylov a minute to realize that the scoundrel had had no intention of coming here. Without partaking of the blessings of this elite sanitation, which looked like it had been washed in bubbling champagne, he made a dash upstairs, wild-eyed.

He was surrounded by the spacious, ballroom flashiness of glassed and mirrored retail shops. Amazingly few items of clothing were on display in the boutiques that shone along the cool gallery fanned with a minty breeze; the bioplastic mannequins with their little bilberry mouths, wearing silks caught up low at the hips, seemed to be waiting for an invitation to dance the husky foxtrot coming through the hidden speakers. The shoe departments looked like bird cages where the narrow men's models looked like geese and ducks and the women's like hummingbirds. Real birds were flitting high up under the green glass arches filled with blind sunlight, like happy bathers in a huge upside-down pool. And everywhere there were changing rooms—invitingly open or with the curtain pulled and feet stamping around that you couldn't quite see. After running the length of two or three stories and discovering new commercial infinities in the depths of which hundreds of plasma televisions were on simultaneously and glaring with intricate worlds more like planetariums, Krylov stopped to catch his breath on a blue bridge that hung over an elegant presentation of umbrellas shooting their colorful cupolas as if they were firing a salute in their own honor.

It was unlikely the spy had gone down to shop. More likely he'd simply made himself scarce. Each of Krylov's feet felt as heavy as a hundred pounds of lead. There was absolutely nothing to do in this retail paradise, so once he'd made his way out of the arcade from the quite unfamiliar back side—into a narrow almost car-free alley that looked like it had slumped on its side—Krylov dragged himself away from his failure. Rewinding his conversation with the scoundrel in his head, he thought he ought to have agreed and sweet-talked him because now the spy was going to hole up, of course, and there wasn't the slightest chance left of catching him again and entering into negotiations.

That day, though, fate evidently was firmly moving people toward their intended denouement. It was *present* and getting ready to come to pass. A ferocious chill stirred in Krylov's hair when he saw the spy in a niche between some disemboweled old buildings covered in flapping plastic where he was happily pissing on the graffitied wall like the punk he was—much more his style than the perfumed paid toilet. There was an inscrutable mysticism in him materializing yet again, appearing on the backdrop of these must- and decay-filled architectural frames, as if he really were a figment of Krylov's mind, Krylov's projection onto *suitable* landscapes and circumstances. Krylov suddenly fancied that he couldn't lose the spy because he kept him close all the time. Thus a man takes a walk with himself but sees his own reflection, which he doesn't recognize at first, if he happens across a mirror on the street.

Meanwhile the spy was attending to business, tightening his crude belt in its loops. Pleased with himself, he headed for the exit and immediately noticed Krylov, his jaw dropped, on the other side of the alley.

"My bosom buddy! Why is my life like this?" The spy slapped his sides and, nearly crying, spread his short little arms to either side. "I just can't shake you! Tom and Jerry! Fuck! You mean you still don't recognize me? It's me. Me! Look! Look at me!"

Krylov staggered back. Viktor Matveyevich Zavalikhin's apoplectic face seemed to be vibrating bizarrely and swarming into his eyes. The plastic sheeting on the ruins was being sucked into the gaping cavities with a rustle and then billowing out with a light slap. Some obscure obstacle was billowing and collapsing in exactly the same way in Krylov's brain.

"Come on you stupid jerk!" the fat scoundrel mocked him and suffered, taking a few discreet steps back. "One time I thought you'd figured it out. I followed you like a grenade up your ass! Why are you sniffing me out then? What are you trying to do to me? Get me in trouble again? I don't want to! Hear me? I'd rather scram than get tempted again! I believe in God now!"

With these bizarre words, the spy pulled off his comic cap and crossed himself with emotion. Then, tossing his head gear aside, which flew off, wobbling, into a pile of dead construction trash that had turned to cement after the rains, the spy bent his strong crimson head and ran straight ahead. Krylov instinctively shied, freeing the path to freedom for the spy. Looking around wildly, the spy dashed down the curving alley, as if he were following flashing blips to where everything was just about to happen.

Starting from that moment (maybe even earlier), events unfolded with the incredible precision that stuns you on a videotape run in reverse: wet shards pull together across the floor, collecting the puddle into the unharmed delicate vase, which kisses the spot where it fell and magically rockets onto the shelf; a suicide who has thrown himself into the sea jumps out as if he'd been spat out by the water gathered and turned inside out around him, and drying off instantly, stands up on the cliff with the grace of a circus gymnast. All the participants in what followed acted synchronously and deftly, like a team of professionals. Krylov felt the feedback from this inhuman agility when he was running after his absconding foe over slippery pipes, over the flimsy gloating little board thrown across a repair dig. Simultaneously, two sober and formidable plumbers, happy at the warm weather, were sitting on some rough scrubby grass over a scowling cliff at the bottom of which stretched railroad tracks that looked like they'd been spilled on by bright water. The men were taking their time nibbling the ripe flesh of an Astrakhan watermelon hanging out of its leather rind in cock's combs and discussing wages. Simultaneously, a long freight train was setting out from the marshalling yard; moreover, a handsome segment of it consisted of flatbeds on which new Ladas were stacked two stories high and secured in latticework. One car, a modest beige, seemed to be signaling to someone with sharp flashes of sun in the corner of its windshield.

The exact same kind of car, only good and ragged, almost ran Krylov over when he and the spy jumped into the stream of cars, which were spinning like herring from a seine. This was not according to today's rules, though, so Krylov wasn't even frightened, and the driver of the car, whose hands, turning the wheel, seemed to Krylov as if they were swathed in white gloves, was also nonchalant. From time to time, Krylov tried to attract the spy's attention with challenging shouts. The spy stepped it up without looking around. It was like a movie. They were crashing across the slate roof of some warehouse that crackled with stiff fried trash, like the drip pan of a stove that hadn't been cleaned in a long time—even though above the roof was only sky. Then they dashed nimbly, like lovely ladies table-dancing, across the top of a long van in which booming load-ers were dragging something around, and leapt off, one after the other, right in front of the angry expeditor flipping through the flimsy bills of consignment.

Meanwhile, the earnest plumbers suddenly experienced a wave of enthusiasm and decided to return immediately to their interrupt-ed work. Neatly, so as not to spoil the landscape, they camouflaged their watermelon rinds right at the brink of the precipice and head-ed amicably toward the co-op tower going up nearby where they were installing complicated whirlpools that looked like Martian devices from a book by H. G. Wells. Enough invigorated dexterity had been communicated to the plumbers by their nicely fitting par-ticipation in the moment-to-moment realization of fate to fill their quota threefold and really earn some decent money. As they walked away from the railroad, they saw a freight train crawling out around the bend, as endless as the Great Wall of China, and they cleared out just in time for the spy, who had forced his way through a thorny thicket of wild raspberries, to find the way along the precipice com-pletely free.

Charging in his wake, Krylov was now shouting nonstop. His voice was instantly drowned out by the rumble of the freight train. The path above the precipice, trod ceramic-hard, first ascended and then descended. Krylov felt as if he were chasing his enemy inside the train, from car to car and vestibule to vestibule, in the opposite direction of the train, and so was standing in place. Below, closing in on his clumsy run, open cars of silvery coal and smudgy cisterns were crawling, then picking up speed; the greasy bushes, which felt as if they'd had cabbage soup poured over them, trembled at the weight passing over the rails. The spy scrambled up a steep slope; he'd already climbed to the peak, after which he would be hidden at the bend in the path. Tears came to Krylov's eyes, and colored dots lit up: the cars on the flatbeds.

"Stop! Wait! I agree!" he shouted, but not very loudly, trying not to break the thread stretched taut inside him.

At that, the freight train jerked and a rumble passed from its head to its tail, as if the train were an artillery gun firing a ceremonial volley. Destiny must have been a few seconds shy, although it was beyond human understanding why that beige Lada caught its fancy so. This time, despite the steel din, Krylov's words reached the spy. Finally he'd heard what he'd wanted to hear. Hands on hips, he stood in the sun, whose sharp rays pierced his clothing. But all of a sudden he gave a quick wiggle and, like a video on rewind, seemed to dance a quadrille ass backward. This awkward dance allowed him to push off the clumpy edge of the precipice in a way he never could have even if he'd undergone long training. The next second his body flashed in the air and plopped onto the windshield of the beige Lada, which had just rushed up; the movement of the train threw him forward, head cocked, into the angrily gasping rush, and the Lada, with a frost of cracks instead of a sunburst, passed smoothly by Krylov, who was standing on half-bent legs.

Instead of descending to the track bed, Krylov for some reason started scrambling uphill, where the spy had just danced his last dance. There, on the flaccid grassy crest that hung over the precipice, he saw the squished pink watermelon rinds and the dark, spat-out seeds on the damp piece of newspaper. All of a sudden the freight train came to an end, as if it had been chopped off, and there was a silence into which the dry dragonflies rushed with their cellophane rustle. Krylov had a hard time straightening up from the water-melon mess. From here, from this crest, he had an excellent view of the perfectly still body. The spy was sprawled out in the wrecked vegetation, like a reveler on a slipped mattress. His head, scratched bloody, was oddly twisted, as if the spy had tried to take it under his arm.

Suddenly the height gave Krylov a chill, as if someone had passed a bow over the strings stretched taught across his legs, groin, and cold belly. The height wasn't that great, but the distance from the squished watermelon to the lacy acacia bush that held the dead body in its arms seemed impossible to traverse—and live. The boundary poor Tamara had always sensed must have passed. The railroad ravine with its empty rails below now seemed as if it were half filled with transparent *death*—and you couldn't plunge into it. Now Krylov remembered—not even remembered but was beset by a huge specter through the rough reality—a recent dream: a fantastically deep mountain gorge and the enchantment of the abyss. Immediately he wanted to hug the earth and latch on hard to something.

Nevertheless, he had to climb down to the victim and find the thready pulse. Formally, there was still hope, although even from here, up top, he knew that spy didn't have a pulse. Krylov couldn't see where his twisty feet were stepping, he just grabbed onto every-thing, letting the burning branches with their shredded leaves pass through his fist. Suddenly he dove into the shallow pit full of leafy mold and gaping tin cans—and bumped into a damp foot in a stained reddish-brown boot.

★ ★ ★

Why did it take him so long to identify him? His facial features were like a fly killed on a white wall. Probably the identification that sounded in Krylov's soul like a mute thundering chord was waiting for that expression to come out—as if someone had played a trick on the spy and done something unimaginable to him. Here he was: Leonidich's murderer. Greatly aged, although just twelve years had passed. At the time he'd looked like an undernourished teen. At the time, death had passed through him like an electrical current, but he had jumped back and saved himself. In the place of his white crest, in all likelihood dyed, was emptiness and fuzz and the dulled luster of a bald spot covered with swollen scratches.

Dead. No question. Moaning, Krylov tried to find a heartbeat on his fat neck, but all his fingers felt was the faded warmth of heated paraffin. The motionless body seemed unnaturally warm and puffy —warmer than Krylov's bony wet hands, which were green now from grabbing at leaves. The dead man's head wasn't lying there, it was lolling—quite independently—and flopped from side to side like an empty beer bottle. Now Krylov could easily have been convinced that he was the man who had murdered citizen Zavalikhin—pushed him off the precipice, for instance, after first cracking the base of his neck. He'd have believed that more willingly than the loaders and expeditor who'd observed the wild chase. More willingly than the security guard and waitress who with their own ears had heard Zavalikhin say, "Him threatening to kill me, that's just his way of joking! He makes jokes like that! By the way, his name is Krylov."

So that's how it was. It hadn't been some stranger hanging around the workshop then. This man knew that the gemcutters had been given their pay and would come out with money after a little drink. That's probably what the nephew fetched up from his uncle for shitting on the place where he ate. Zavalikhin had been locked up for burglary and theft, but he hadn't gone down for the hit. Leonidich's murder, committed that spectral June evening, may well have been Zavalikhin's only experience. He must have lived under the impression of it for a year. The paint never dried on that painting for him—especially the red paint. And now his kind uncle had sent him to keep an eye on that same bad kid who'd been walking a little ahead of the gemcutters in their drunken haze and the only one to see the criminal straight on. It would be interesting to know, by the way, what kind of image, what kind of instant picture of Krylov had been retained all these years in Zavalikhin's memory. Probably a vague smear, a glass vessel filled with smoke. Or, on the contrary, a distinct mask of frightening firmness that couldn't fit a living face or express anything but a threat. Nonetheless, when he set out spying, Zavalikhin knew who he was dealing with. The constant danger of being recognized baked his face hotter than the summer sun that tanned him so deeply during their wanderings. Now, after a month shut in his damp tenement, the traces of his tan were like the gray film you see on pale toadstools. Still, you had to respect him for his restraint. What had he said then about temptations? Panic had shouted into his hairy ears to spit on his uncle's plans and get rid of the dangerous witness. He'd frozen in fear but hadn't tried anything. He and Krylov had been tossing a grenade with a pulled pin back and forth—and Krylov hadn't even realized.

Krylov's damp hair stirred in the wind; the Siberian express was creeping by, its hot wheels screeching. In the windows, like frames on old-time film, stood passengers, singly and in groups, their bags already packed and ready to get out at the station. What did they see in the dark bushes at the bottom of the slope? One alcoholic still standing on all fours trying to rouse another, who was conked out. But here you had at least another hundred witnesses. The quick-witted reporter in the nice striped suit who'd taken a photo of Mr. Krylov and his unfortunate victim, who reeked of wine, did not yet guess his own good luck. Does the accused say he didn't want the flying conclusion? No, the accused doesn't say that. He had returned Leonidich's death to his environment, that is, he was back to the zero to which he had always aspired.

For any citizen who finds himself next to a corpse, that's the time to think about his own neck. He should have called Farid and consulted with him about what to tell the cops and reporters who would pick up the scent and not delay in showing up. How should he draw his relationship with the dead Zavalikhin while avoiding the topic of the corundum deposit? How should he keep Tamara and himself from falling under the wheels of a protracted and frenzied trial against her? Not because he would immediately sort this all out but because only Farid would find this interesting. In this proletarian district that crowded around the railroad, he now had to find a payphone that happened to be working.

Suddenly, a quick glance, and Krylov noted the beating of life on the weak-willed body. Not his pulse or his heart but, what was astonishing, his liver. It had literally poked out from under the dead man's ribs and was shaking was if prepared to burst under his pulled-up jacket. In a superstitious and horrible hope, Krylov touched the tensely vibrating protuberance and immediately realized his own mistake: the dead man's antediluvian cell phone was vibrating in his pocket.

The jacket's pockets were small and stiff, which spoke to its provenance from his uncle's secondhand store. Krylov was barely able to free the cell phone, bringing with it a hail of rustling, almost sugary coins. It was clunky in its crude black case with its worn buttons—nonetheless the display was plasma and 3-D, and on it a nimble icon was rolling up, confirming the call. Incredibly shocked, Krylov mechanically hit "talk" and saw the hologram of his employer taken at some holiday table taking a big bite out of a luxurious, caviar-spilling, open-faced sandwich.

The workshop's owner immediately shouted out.

"Vitek! Vitek! It's me," the employer announced ironically, as if the very fact of his existence were a joke. "We have bad news. Very bad news. They found our professor gentleman in the north, near a winter hut, dead. He was sprawled out under a birch all bent over, like he'd been digging himself a hole, like a dog, and died like that. His assistant was with him, all wrapped up. According to the reports, looks like he passed away a week or so before. And no corundums. Nothing. Zip. Vitek, listen to me carefully now," his employer's voice came closer, and Krylov thought he could feel his hot, wetly whispering mouth with his ear. "You know very well our partners are serious men. We pathetic creatures are no match for them. We promised them mountains of goods and took an advance. It was a sure thing! Now we're coming to them empty-handed, too. Our partners could take offense. Gather up your people fast and take them to your favorite uncle. You know where. We'll get this sorted out before you know it. We'll explain ourselves and settle with them. Your uncle won't fail you!" the workshop's owner chuckled nervously, as if shaking his ever-present sadness before consuming it, a sadness he consumed steadily, the way a quiet alcoholic does homebrew. "Come on, Vitek, don't dilly dally! If you're really afraid, take some Pampers from your daughter and put them on!"

With this mordant wish his employer hung up; his holographic portrait, which depicted complete happiness, immediately faded.

If the professor really had died, then only Krylov was left. . . . He had nothing left. The unique rubies were going up in red smoke, and his lost woman was vanishing for good. Could he survive this?

Moving farther away down the thoroughly fried, greasy, black track bed, as if the dead spy might eavesdrop on the conversation, Krylov dialed Farid's home number on the fat buttons. A huge shudder went through him when he heard the baleful voice of its lawful owner coming from the telephone.

"To use this phone, enter your password," suggested the spy, whose spread-eagled legs were poking out of the bushes. "If you're wrong three times, all the information in my phone will be destroyed. Fuck you to kingdom come, you lousy creeps!" he added with a kind of childish pleasure, and Krylov, taking the soaking wet receiver away from his ear, saw on the screen the implied organ, looking terribly like an angry turkey.

Hastily disconnecting, Krylov bent double from sudden laughter. He literally vomited thick masses of laughter into the harsh grass—and simultaneously relaxed a little. No, no matter what Farid said, Krylov wasn't going to surrender to the cops right away. Let his running away from the dead body be an argument for the prosecution. He himself was so weak and felt so guilty, he would give the investigation even more fatal arguments. Right now they could easily convince him a crime had been committed—and convince him in such a way that afterward he wouldn't remember what had actually happened. Casting a final glance at the comfortably stretched out spy, who looked like he was enjoying his new oblivion—his body would probably be taken for a while longer for an unpicky drunk who'd had himself a solitary picnic in the bushes. Krylov dropped the cell phone with the unharvested information into his pocket and kept moving, stumbling, over the greasy reddish-brown ties and between the thundering, frenzied walls of the oncoming trains.

2

★

This was why he'd purchased and equipped his refuge. Entering it, Krylov experienced his accustomed transformation into a cloud of free molecules and a momentary stiffening—with the possible loss of some particles. It was like the steep drop in an express mirror elevator—but only for one floor. The air in his refuge was just as he'd left it: the fumes from the sausage he'd burned the week before was bluish, and in the low sunbeam the same furry dust motes danced, some the size of tiny seahorses.

Here Krylov really was safe—safer than ever. No one was going to come in here as long as he was alive, and if cops did get in, or neighbors, or, say, his former employer's mysterious partners, that would mean Krylov himself was no longer among the living. All this could be described with the simplest mathematical model, by an elementary equation: Krylov = humanity. Today he had finally reached what he'd been striving for his whole conscious life: his equation, with its horrifyingly cumbersome right side and its uncountable unknowns, had acquired validity. Moving any element of one half of the equation to the other would mean a change of sign. This meant that any visitor who got into his refuge would immediately become a negative value; or, if he did succeed in destroying the territory's sovereignty he would get only a minus-Krylov.

Since there was no God on this territory, all cause-and-effect connections were launched manually. There was a mountain of dirty dishes in the sink, which was full of water, like an abandoned, multitiered fountain with food scraps and blackened parsley leaves floating in it. Since he had to eat and drink out of something, Krylov started the washing up, squirting in a good dollop of liquid detergent and swishing it around cautiously. Any work here had to be done by Krylov himself, adding to the physical effort much more effort of will than in any ordinary place. In the old refrigerator, which dated from the old lady and kept products wet more than cold, lay three steel tins of preserved venison, and a piece of rubbery cheese covered with puffy white dots was shriveling up. Krylov decided he could hold out for a few days with these supplies. After a meager supper, which consisted of grated cheese and warped gray crackers, Krylov got under the shower, hoping to wash away the experiences and sweat of the day with the harsh water served up from the outside world. The showerhead, with its rusted little holes, looked like a pepper shaker, and the streams flailed his reddened skin, giving him the chills. Krylov mopped himself off haphazardly with a faded, threadbare rag with an occasional ivory button, flung himself on the couch, and stared at the ceiling with its yellow stains from old leaks. The time had come to assess everything calmly and work out a plan.

Right then, though, the vacant, long turned off bell rang and right after there was a distinct rap with a hard little bone.

This soon? How did they manage it? Krylov scrambled up without making a sound, as if he were rising into the air. His plans had changed drastically. What should he do if they started breaking the door down? Put up or shut up, as Krylov used to say when he was a teen. People don't joke about things like this. Since the absence of God forced Krylov to keep each and every thing in his mind, he couldn't keep a weapon on this territory. His loyal friend, his lovingly greased revolver, here was too heavy for his consciousness and had been left with his mother, in the bottom drawer of her heat-cracked sideboard. Now Krylov regretted this madly. What else was there? The kitchen knife with the wobbly blade was too short to reach the heart. That was the nitty-gritty, ridiculous though it was.

The knock, exactly the same in tone, was repeated. This was too fast for the police. It hadn't been even four hours. But what if . . . ? What if Tanya had searched for and found him? After all, it could happen, he did ask. . . . And although Krylov had had no intention of getting any closer to the safe door, he suddenly discovered that he was standing in the vestibule, in the darkness, staring at the shining peephole, which looked as though it was filled with a drop of hot oil.

"Open up. It's me." A horrifyingly familiar female voice rang out very close by, a step away. The voice was silken from agitation, and in the peephole a white hat, pulled low, with a brim as wide as a skirt, swayed.

"Hold on, wait a minute," Krylov replied huskily. For some reason he ran on tip-toe back to the room and in a panic grabbed his only jeans, grass-stained, from the only table. He gave a hop getting into the too-long pant's legs, which kept flapping in opposite directions, then pulled on a not very fresh T-shirt, and then, now almost calm, went back to the doorway, took the keys from the table, and carefully unsealed the door.

He hadn't been expecting Tamara, but it was she, like no one else, who was fit and destined to bring nonexistent God to his refuge. He who had created her had not begrudged her anything. She literally shone in the reverberating cave of the doorway. She was paler than her flax-colored coat, and her unpainted mouth reminded him of a shabby, wind-frayed poppy. At her feet, which had accumulated a deadly exhaustion visible to the naked eye, was an oval suitcase with a glossy scrap on the handle—a United Airlines baggage tag.

"Hi. Can I come in?" Tamara asked without crossing the threshold, bringing her shoes right up to the invisible line, like in the airport in front of the passport control zone.

"You don't have to ask. Come in!" Krylov hastily dragged her into the vestibule and grabbed her suitcase, which had obviously been packed in haste and looked like a plump pancake with hard, uncooked lumps. "You can't imagine how glad I am to see you," he said, smiling foolishly and not knowing where to put his awkward arms, which were trying to hug his unexpected guest.

"You know, I'm not about to be bursting into tears," Tamara announced gaily, taking a black speck out of her blinking eye with a fingernail.

Krylov helped her off with her coat, which was crumpled in back and held the strong smell of her familiar warm perfume, and once down to her smooth dress of the same linen, in which her body looked like an asexual tailor's mannequin, she removed her wavy hat with both hands. Under her hat, her hair was felted, like a chignon made of someone else's caked curls, and there was a chunk of coal under each of her marvelous, tired eyes.

"Listen, are you alone?" Tamara asked suddenly, craning her neck.

"Yes. Why?" Krylov wondered.

"No, it's nothing. I just thought," Tamara mumbled, still looking over Krylov's shoulder into the open room.

Then and there Krylov knew the specter he had fantasized about here all these lonely, hollow evenings, had materialized. He immediately took fright that the phenomenon, in all likelihood, would wander around naked—and do who knew what, considering Krylov's past need for female companionship. Tamara's presence let him feel that his essence, his soul, was more like an ape at the zoo. He himself, however, quickly turning around, saw only the plastic rack with colorful shelves that looked like playground equipment and a blue pillow on the floor.

"Well, show me how you live," Tamara spoke briskly, and following Krylov's gesture of invitation went into the empty room, from which the smeared shadow slipped into the kitchen with a shine of its milky butt. Paying no more attention to the specter, now declared nonexistent, she sat down on the edge of the crumpled sofa, and, rubbing her legs together like a fly, kicked off her shoes, which fell heavily, as if thousands of kilometers of trekking had clung to them.

"Are you just coming from Koltsovo?" Krylov asked, picking up the pillow, a half-strewn book, and a dusty cocoon-like sock and holding all that in his arms.

"No, I flew as far as Orenburg," Tamara responded, casting a dreamy gaze over the nursery-like atmosphere. "And from there by taxi. The driver was no fool. He got a thousand euros off me!" She burst out laughing, swinging her legs like a schoolgirl. "I pretended I didn't understand Russian very well. My good driver kept explaining all the way that people shoot people in Russia ànd it was very, very dangerous. Bang bang, Bolshevik!" She made a hilarious face, pretending to shoot from her finger.

"What can I feed you after your trip?" Krylov said, dismayed. "Let me run out to the corner and I'll bring some salads!"

"No, don't go anywhere!" Tamara turned even paler, as if a grainy rime were coming out on her lips. "Do you have any vodka?"

"A little." Krylov extracted from his memory an opened bottle standing on a bare shelf.

"Bring it!"

Krylov took a look around and once again dropped everything he was holding and with a shaky step headed for the kitchen. There, as he had expected, he saw himself sitting on the stool, which shown through the singed towel draped over it. Krylov imagined himself more muscular, without these gnawed bones and jutting spine. The ghost was so unstable it could have been taken for an unsuccessful, low-quality hologram. First to melt were his tucked-under toes, then the hand holding the glare of a china mug disappeared—and the whole vision elongated, made a deep crease, and dissolved, glancing at Krylov afterward with its long hazy eyes from the peeling ceiling.

Smiling, Krylov wiped the cold sweat from his forehead. Then he took the bottle of Stolichnaya out of the half-empty cupboard, ripped open the venison, which was coated in fat, like seventy-year-old northern snow, and grabbed freshly washed mugs, two of the three.

When he got back to the room, Tamara had opened a pack of salty French crackers, probably taken out of her suitcase. In front of her, on the little plastic chair, was some pretty pink pâté, a tin of fat beads of glossy caviar, and next to her, on the couch, a white folder with some papers in it. Krylov added his venison, which smelled distinctly of blood, to the delicacies and gurgled the vodka into the fat mugs, where it looked like water.

Their linked glasses clattered like stones knocking together. Tamara drank it down, frowned, covering her face, and suddenly bit her arm, leaving a wet violet trace on her wrist.

"There's no way I can go back to Koltsovo now," she announced, taking a deep breath. "They've brought criminal charges and they're looking for me. This is all complete nonsense, a spectacle to scare people. The governor's team is going to fuck me over good. They're going all out searching-and-smashing, arresting me, and jail. I don't want to go to jail. A week there and your health is ruined for years. These guys are going to get what they want, you know."

"It's that serious?" After all the day's adventures, the warm foul vodka was delivering a jolt to Krylov's brain, and he gave Tamara's shoulder, with its touching silky bra strap slipped out from her dress, a good squeeze.

"Yes and no." Without moving away, Tamara kept looking straight ahead with burning dark eyes, terrible eyes, like a silent film star's. "I've already got good lawyers working for me. They'll overturn the case. There's not even anything to overturn. Right now they're in talks about suppressing it. They'll probably arrest me formally and free me on bail. But I have to hide out for a few more days. That's why I came to you. You see"—she shuddered with a smile—"it would never occur to anyone that you might own any real estate. You aren't registered at this address. Until they figure it out . . . Not only that, but everyone who needs to know knows that you and I are mortal enemies. Remember how we shouted at each other? Downstairs everyone was all ears."

"Of course, stay here, live here as long as you like!" Krylov exclaimed heatedly. "I'll be sleeping by the door in any case. I'm just going to pop out to my mother's for my revolver."

"Nonsense!" Tamara jerked her shoulder away. "No, really, don't be angry. That's all we need now, shooting. Preferably at the police. Everyone around us really is firing, but in the foreseeable future they're not going to let anything pass. When are you ever going to grow up?"

Krylov frowned.

"Maybe it is nonsense," he said sullenly. "But that's all I can do. Objectively. And those guys fighting on the streets for the Whites and Reds, that's all they can do, too. They're sinking into childhood. But it's as if nothing were happening. Just think, a couple of hundred corpses have been created somewhere."

"Remember how we used to say that humanism was over?" Tamara replied wearily. "You're the historian. How much was a human life worth back in ancient Egypt or the Middle Ages? Well, right now it's worth about as much. The Communist model failed thirty years ago, and now the Western model of democracy and its liberal values is blowing away little by little. All this may well be horrible. At the same time it's all happening in the best way. The best possible way. With the fewest losses. Only not many people are capable of appreciating that."

"But it's also true that there's a kind of person who can't sit around and do nothing. Naturally they're superfluous and there's no role set aside for them. So they wave their arms, get all puffed up, and pretend to be brave. That's what I'm like. As a result I come out looking like a total jerk." Krylov slapped the couch in search of cigarettes and found a crumpled pack under Tamara's heavy hip. "But the sick, the cripples, and the disabled look even more ridiculous than I do. The ones who don't have enough money to pay for an apartment or send their children to a decent school where they might get taught something. What's their problem? What are they complaining about? You see, this is all on purpose. In fact, a marvelous new world is being kept somewhere in the central scientific flask, a world where everyone is healthy, educated, and secure. True, no one told them that. So here they are playacting and looking awful."

Krylov frowned and took a puff on the bent cigarette. It tasted shitty. After all of the day's adventures, his eyes teared up, and his mouth kept filling up with a burning, viperish poison.

"I don't remember the reason for your sarcasm." A thick velvety flush crept up Tamara's face like a cloud. "I'll admit something to you. I hate the so-called common people. The moment they start talking about society's shortcomings, they start cursing the corrupt officials and the stupid politicians. No one has the nerve to say that the main reason for this world's idiocy is them, this mass of social idiots. This terrible, global passivity. You can't give them themselves. They can't stand themselves. The main secret of this marvelous new world isn't the frozen scientific discoveries but the irrelevance of most of the population to the economy and progress. The minute that gets out, no matter in what form, we're going to find ourselves a meter away from fascism." Tamara caught her breath and continued, crumbling the cracker onto her tightly squeezed knees. "The common people have the sullen suspicion they're being tricked in order to make the world worse. But here's the paradox: if anyone wanted to make the world better, they really would have to trick them. All of them! Because they need a holiday, as *they* imagine it. They have to be told only what *they* want to hear."

Krylov shrugged, sensing how bizarre all this was. Here he and Tamara had come together. They'd missed each other. Each had gotten into a bad scrape. And now they were talking about world problems. In the open window, the hulking poplar was as black as a mountain of coal; the patch of moon was burning faintly. Meanwhile, in the room, the air pressure seemed to have changed. Bubbles were stirring tensely in Krylov's ears and also in sensitive intracranial pockets.

"I feel as if I'm still on the plane," Tamara complained, plunging her sharp fingers into her matted hair. "It really is strange being at your place. You live like a teenager left behind by his parents. The furniture is children's future, and the canned meat. . . . Eat." She gave Krylov a cracker on which gleamed a moist mound of cellophane-like caviar, and at that he recalled his employer, up to his ears in happiness. His heart contracted as if the workshop owner had died as well.

"You know, I've changed a lot lately," Tamara admitted, digging the pâté out with a big black-toothed fork from the remains of the old lady's silver. "I feel sorry for everyone. Take these common people. In the old days, they respected artists, writers, and scholars and so on as their superiors. Now they don't need anything beyond the limits of their understanding. They think everything's boring and tedious and they aren't buying that. I met this Russian in New York, where he teaches, a pathetic hopsack coat and eyes with pupils as sharp as two pencil sharpeners. He says that all the awful terrorist acts and disasters of the last few decades, starting with the Twin Towers and ending with the Rome bombings, are happening because people have stopped perceiving great art. They're simple, crude, bloody substitutes for Shakespeare and Dostoyevsky. So that every soul can experience an upheaval at least once in his life. A repulsive guy, I'm telling you, fuzz all over his cuffs, stiff threads that looked blood-stained, although he wouldn't have harmed a fly. But he may have been right. After all, what, in fact, is the worst horror? Every day of their lives so-called common people feel immortal. Therefore they think their mundane truth is immortal. Remember that pensioner, Parshukov, he had a red Zhiguli, and you promised to buy me one just like it to drive to the market? He was always telling me that in the old days they put people like me in front of a firing squad. That Comrade Stalin purged enemies of the people, but now, he said, we'd multiplied. At the time I was still in school, and I have no idea how I annoyed him so badly."

"Parshukov died a long time ago," Krylov spoke in a muffled voice. Before his eyes there suddenly arose the angry old man, as if he were alive, with a galosh drawn on his prosthetic leg.

"He died, but he didn't *understand* that," Tamara objected

heatedly. "You probably wonder why I didn't spend another week or so abroad. Here's why: that's what everyone expects of me, for me to get the hell out and live as far away from here as possible, in some nice comfortable European spot. For me to eat through the money I have left there—if anything is left. Riphean Industrial and Investrosbank closed my lines of credit. All my structures have had their accounts frozen. They're looking for somewhere where we didn't pay taxes. They're really tightening the screws on Granite. Plainly they can't take away a controlling or even a blocking package of shares. On the other hand, they aren't letting us work, and they've sealed our warehouses and workshops. Clinics are refusing to lease to us. Issues involving earth removal that were all decided are now hanging. But people are dying every day, and someone has to see them off. Look, no matter where you look, another company, Final Journey, has popped up everywhere we used to be. Who do you think its owner is? You won't believe this. Evgenia Krugel! The one who starts shaking and flashing all her jewels at the mere mention of a cemetery. Papa Krugel himself must have gone into the business. His Excellency the governor is going to be our main gravedigger now."

"Suits him," Krylov couldn't help himself, remembering the television broadcast from the governor's residence. His Excellency's study had been finished in formal oak in the style of the most pompous funerals, and Papa Krugel himself looked like nothing so much as the seller of all this carved and polished luxury. Even his face, mournful on the occasion of civic incidents, fit.

"Only what they don't know is that I'm not going anywhere," Tamara declared, and picking up the bottle the wrong way poured what was left of the vodka into their mugs as if she were watering flowers.

"I don't think you're any more mature than I am." Krylov grinned, taking most of the nasty stuff and leaving Tamara what was on the bottom. "You keep equipping a boathouse at the passage across the Lethe, and it has to be here instead of somewhere else.

You keep trying to teach people a new way to die. And you want them to understand the right way. That's what they can't forgive you for. They'd stone you if they could."

"They're trying, but not everyone can. Unfortunately, I'm going to have to intervene until they ruin me to the point of no return. It's a matter of days." Tamara shook her head decisively. "I didn't take that flight for nothing. I found support and credit. Now I need to meet with someone here. Suggest cooperation. Give a nice personal bribe. No one here can replace me, you know that yourself."

"Just don't get caught, please," Krylov begged, full of impotent vexation at Tamara's obstinacy and the impossibility of intervening in her grand affairs. "If they catch you red-handed giving a bribe, you might as well get shot. Are you sure your supposed friend isn't just going to hand you over to jail?"

"It's not in his interests," Tamara said sternly. "It doesn't happen any other way, believe me. I'll come back anyway. Right now let's drink to everything working out for me. Then I'll answer the question you want to ask me but can't bring yourself to."

★ ★ ★

Sucking down the last drop of vodka, Tamara gave a childish noisy exhale and smack into her mug. She attacked the fragile little sandwiches, not forgetting to take the soapy shreds of venison. Krylov, who couldn't get the food down his clenched throat, had tried to determine whether it was worth listening to Tamara's justifications or it was better not to know about the Severzoloto factory or the activities of Stroyinvest.

When had it happened? Somewhere around 1994 or 1996. The financial pyramids had collapsed. People were selling flat leather jackets and bootleg liquor in old entryways, perestroika public toilets, telephone booths practically. Rubles were mutating monthly, like generations of drosophila flies. Punks were driving around town in rusty foreign cars, drowning out everything with loud rock and roll as if they were music kiosks. That was when Tamara had bought her first BMW sports car. Fancy cars were few and far between in the Riphean capital, and passersby watched Tamara go by, leaning back in the driver's seat, driving her white beauty onward over the Riphean dirt, which was puffy from the snow.

That was also the time of those strange business trips and the telephone silence, and trips for someone's birthday to the first stone dachas, where mighty fireplaces fitted with malachite smoked like Vesuvius and the barbaric furniture upholstered in brocade was stunning. Some of today's faces were already popping up then, faces that didn't stand out particularly among the other faces, maybe even less than those who were later wiped out. At the time, Pavel Petrovich Bessmertny, a middle manager and permanent deputy to some boss, was wearing a part-wool brown suit that suited his pointed mustache's color and texture. The graduate student Volodya Grechikhin looked blurry and downtrodden, and the young women obviously didn't like his long, too-translucent ears, which stuck out of his fine, shoulder-length hair. The hosts of those celebrations patronized Tamara and listened to her intelligent speeches with tender emotion, the way adults listen to a child recite verse. What exactly she told the chubby old men in gold glasses and what exams she took Krylov didn't know. He was always distracted by something uninteresting, an exhibit of dried-out stuffed birds or the polished jasper tile they were thinking of installing around the toilets. At the time he was still the family's breadwinner, and he felt uncomfortable that business was being done in his presence but not with him.

"You just wouldn't have signed onto it," Tamara told him, reading Krylov's thoughts, as often happened with her. "You were still untrusting and hardened, and you kept giving us wolf looks. You would definitely have asked yourself whether they weren't trying to take advantage of you and get you to take the rap. Well, I wanted to stand out. I wanted praise and for everybody to say I was perfection itself. Just imagine, I worked out a scheme all by myself to respond to their precise wishes. I felt like their favorite assistant. And I loved them because these advanced, mature men let me join their game. Though the constellations taking shape at the time had room for everything under the sun except emotions."

"You mean the idea was to grind you into dust," Krylov clarified suddenly.

"That's why I didn't initiate you into anything," Tamara replied in a cheerless voice. "I thought you were too spiteful. That you'd interfere and embarrass me in front of my friends, who hadn't done anything bad to me yet. Just the opposite, they'd only helped."

"Gee!" Krylov was indignant. "Fine discoveries I'm making in my old age! So as long as they weren't putting you in jail or shooting you, as long as they weren't saddling you with debts with interest, they're holy men and it's a sin not to believe them. Even though they're the ones who created all these opportunities for themselves and others."

"I created them myself," Tamara reminded him quietly. "I took part in this, too, and very enthusiastically."

"How did you manage to extricate yourself?" Krylov inquired sarcastically.

"Not in bed!" Tamara blazed up.

"That's not what we're talking about. Get to the point."

Tamara hunched over, slipping her hands between her knees and rubbing her palms and knees together like a hobbled grasshopper. This was a habit from her teenage, high school years, which manifested itself only in moments of confusion, which were very rare in the adult, successful Tamara. She sat like that if she knew no stranger was looking at her.

"I realized it two weeks ago," she finally spoke. "The truth came to me on the air, when they produced Mr. Goremyko and he started talking. You know, the thing is that they built those reservoirs for the cyanide solution. They really did! And for more than twenty years I've been certain there never was any such thing as the Severzoloto plant!"

"What do you mean?" Krylov was stunned.

"Think back to the early 1990s. Think back to what those times were like," Tamara continued patiently. "It was as if everyone was drunk. It felt as though the new economic geniuses were just about to build capitalism here. They promoted every kind of project you can think of! Traditional bake houses, a fast food chain called Russian Blini. As if to say, let's take the shine off all their McDonald's! People got loans to do this, and they sold share certificates to the public. Note: not the shares! But the public didn't see the difference. They just brought their nice money to these crafty firms. They stood in line."

"But afterward no one ever saw any Russian fast food or bake houses," Krylov recalled. "And for some reason they forgot very quickly, even what those companies were called."

"That's exactly it!" Tamara chimed in. "This was fraud in the purest form. No one had any intention of building anything. All those conjurors were shot or put in prison, especially after the MMM crash. Remember that Vasilisa trial? That traditional baker, Vasilisa Churkina, that huge woman, with a hairdo like a boyar's hat and eyes like chicken eggs. She gave an interview from jail saying she'd just been getting ready to build her first bake house when the state swooped down and took away the money that belonged to her depositors. They didn't let her off unscathed, meanwhile, but they let her go pretty fast. Then she became a folk healer and lifted curses on television, and she had people signed up for her to tell their fortunes six months down the line. Five years ago I saw her brochure in a shop: Vasilisa Churkina, hereditary folk psychic, charms for love and money. Two hundred thousand copies printed!"

"I still don't get the connection," Krylov interrupted.

"I'll explain again. I thought Severzoloto a phantom like Russian Blini. When they started imprisoning the illusionists— though not all of them—I was sure my friends would cover for me. But there really was construction going on at Severzoloto, it didn't matter what quality. That's why there was never an investigation against Stroyinvest at the time." Tamara took a few quick gulps of air and suddenly yawned tenaciously, without unclenching her jaw, and her eyes watered. "Stroyinvest was a fly-by-night operation," she went on with a lump of yawning in her mouth. "The money landed in my account, the same loan, and spent a little over a week there. I'm not going to go into the details. I paid myself supposedly for a project that didn't exist. That's where it all ended. Even I'm amazed now at how strong the financial virtualities were then. After all, I'm over forty, and I never once got around even to searching for Severzoloto on the Internet."

"In the studio you were shouting something about the date of the photo," Krylov recalled sternly.

"So! You did watch!" Tamara livened up. "Just don't say you warned me. At least Dymov got what was coming to him. A concussion to that pea-brain plus damage to his pretty face. His loving Bessmertny took him overseas on dragonfly wings to consult American doctors. Do you think I haven't wanted to do something like that all these years? And how!" Tamara gave an unkind belly laugh, which made it clear that without her diet and exercise she had grown a little belly. "Now as for the film. They took it on an old digital, and in the corner of the studio screen a date sometimes popped up. August 2010! That is, they knew about the cyanide leak seven years ago. They knew and they did absolutely nothing! Now they're trying to saddle me with everything. We'll just see about that! If we really dig, then Mr. Bessmertny, for instance, won't be collecting his own dice. I have my lawyers negotiating right now. Damn, if only they'd unblock my accounts!"

Scowling, Krylov looked at the agitated Tamara from the far corner of the couch. He didn't like her like this—as if she were pregnant with revenge. He suddenly thought that Madame Death had come to see him in his refuge after all and kissed him on the cheek, but leaving him alive for some unknown purpose.

"Don't look at me like that!" Tamara began fidgeting angrily, pulling at the tight, crumb-strewn linen on her knees. "Do you want to know whether I'm tormented by pangs of conscience at night? No, I'm not. I'm sorry. When all this happened I was a little girl, and I would have been horrified at the death of the creatures and the poisoning of the forests. I would have sobbed into my pillow. Nothing would have made me take part in that. Even now I wouldn't, but for other reasons. Too much water has passed under the bridge in twenty-plus years, and most of all what's changed is me. If I can scramble out of this and afterward do something for the polluted area, I will. But don't expect anything more from me."

"Fine, then." Krylov jerked to his numb feet, and the parquet seemed to flow under him like a wave of wood. "You know, I never did get a chance to tell you that I'm on your side no matter what. I don't care whether you're guilty or not. You're dearer to me than the forests and the little beasts. And now, if you really don't need me, I'm going."

"Wait." Tamara stood up, too, and grabbed Krylov's hand, which was already holding his jacket. "Wait. That's not all yet."

★ ★ ★

Krylov turned to see stars shining in Tamara's eyes, which were half-covered by wet eyelashes. This was a familiar sign. He must have slipped and said something he shouldn't. Was this really that insane hope of hers that Tamara had tortured him with for four years? No, apparently not. Tamara really had changed; something about her was different. Enchanted by this change, Krylov allowed himself to be pulled back to the couch, which looked like it had been crushed by passionate lovers.

Still not letting go of Krylov's wrist, Tamara took the wrecked folder out from behind her back and scratched off the magnetic seal. The zipper hiccupped as it opened, and Krylov saw two pieces of white paper stapled crookedly in the folder.

"I have something for you." Tamara put her barely trembling hand on the file softly and mysteriously. "But before I give it to you, I have to tell you . . ." At this Tamara squinted so that there was no gleam left at all between her Assyrian eyelashes. "I have to tell you that Professor Anfilogov and his friend Kolyan are no longer among the living."

Krylov felt his insides heave hot and terribly. Maybe the second time it had finally hit him. Watching him stealthily, Tamara probably could not have guessed for the world that what she had to say was not news for Krylov. Still, it was too sudden a blow, moreover at his fresh pain, which Krylov now felt like a flashing emergency light inside him, complete with sirens and droning. He felt as though his hands were blazing red through his skin.

"Go on!" Krylov threw back at Tamara, who was looking at him with suspicion and had already risen to look for medicine.

Tamara was smart and didn't start to argue. Sitting very straight on the couch, she continued in a precise voice, as if she were reporting to her board of directors.

"Anfilogov's and Kolyan's bodies were found in the north of the province, ten kilometers to the east of Balakayevsk logging. According to the preliminary conclusion, death came as a result of cyanide poisoning." At this Tamara seemed to choke on something, and Krylov guessed that the feeling of guilt she reflected so clearly was simply very well sealed up. "Actually, that is in fact what happened. Apparently, your friends were just swimming in the cyanide solution. Their mucous membranes had turned to mush. And there were other obvious symptoms, too."

"That's all right." Krylov reached to touch Tamara's silky knee. "I already told you you're more precious to me than the forests and beasts. You and I have enough life lived together to withstand the professor and Kolyan, too. So tell me more."

"It just so happened I was able to buy the conclusion from the local native healer who went out for the bodies," Tamara continued in an even voice. "Unfortunately, right now I can't allow corpses to be added to my 'cyanide autumn.' Therefore my trusted staff has moved the dead bodies to one of Granite's last remaining morgues. The official death certificates were written out there. The cause of death was listed as acute cardiovascular insufficiency. Naturally, my employees immediately got in touch with the dead men's relatives. And got official agreement for rapid cremation. The cremation and placement of the urns in the necropolis took place this morning."

Krylov turned around. For some reason he recalled the professor's collection, which was kept in dilapidated cardboard boxes under his sagging iron cot—and how the very first night he and Tanya had felt the collection with their moist bodies, as if their magic boat had brushed the rocky bottom.

"I realize all this is highly regrettable. Believe me, if I'd been in the country this morning, I would have thought of a way to bring you there to say goodbye. But at that time I was flying across the ocean." Tamara held her pause for a few seconds. "What I'm leading up to is the main thing. The dead men's relatives."

"What of it?" Krylov asked aloofly, trying with all his might to call to life his image of the professor's niece who had come for the session and nearly seduced him. But the evasive young woman, her watery little eyes playing, her luminescent nails flitting, stubbornly refused to be embodied.

"There turned out to be only a few," Tamara spoke with restraint. "All that was found at Kolyan's registered address was his one great-grandmother. And I mean found: in this crooked hut, like a potato rolling around in a box. The old woman is ninety-two and can barely scrawl her name. She was very grateful for our money and thought it was her great-grandson's pension. Well, and the professor, if you can imagine, turned out to have a young widow. Ekaterina Sergeyevna Anfilogova. Your blonde."

That was it! Although even that was not really news. Krylov had been wrong so long about Tanya and the professor because he'd seen the kind of identicalness of their palms at the station that happens only with close blood relatives, a brother and sister, for instance. Those precise Latin letters that coincided perfectly through the thick train car window, as if a copy had been taken of the gray glass. There they were, the Stone Maiden's things, the Stone Maiden who so thirsted for all of a man's love, his entire being, that she couldn't help but acquire him physically: she stole his ears, his nails, and his lifelines, and she wore his hair like a cap.

"I get it. So, Ekaterina Sergeyevna," Krylov spoke, randomly touching his stubbly face. "So that's her name. But tell me, did you pay the professor's widow, too? Did she take the kickback from you?"

To this Tamara replied with an impenetrable silence. She sat with her eyes lowered to her folded hands, where her two randomly crossed index fingers displayed a slight tremor, like short-circuited wires. It was obvious she was going to remain silent as long as it took but she would not stoop to confirming the unseemly fact. But she wasn't going to shield Ekaterina Sergeyevna either—she simply wasn't going to deign to give her rival the slightest comment or a hint of her attention. Only now did Krylov really see how terribly the denunciation and harassment had hardened Tamara. Her silence was monolithic. This silence stripped Ekaterina Sergeyevna of any qualities whatsoever and made her something it was indecent to discuss.

"That means the widow took the kickback," the grimly smiling Krylov confirmed for himself.

And so Tanya had revealed the first signs of her *real* life. Krylov was choked by waves of mounting shame, as if he had been heated up and sprinkled with sugar, as if he had benefited from the professor's death by taking the shameful bribe from Tamara. Along with the shame a nausea rose up inside him, possibly an acute presentiment or poisoning by some future time.

Tamara meanwhile was not coming to Krylov's aid but was simply maintaining the proper pause.

"Relations between Granite and its clients are regulated by a standard contract," she spoke finally, almost officially. "When I found out who the professor's spouse was, I asked her to fax me the contract in New York. There's no doubt as to Mrs. Anfilogova's identity: the professor and his partner were being watched by the same people as you for purposes of your safety. I brought you the contract. I think it will come in handy."

With these words, Tamara handed Krylov the crookedly stapled pages. The fumes from his shame made it a little hard for him to see. The narrow, pointy handwriting, which was strangely even, as if the words had been written not with a pen but with the tines of a fork, all four at once, was completely unfamiliar to Krylov. Actually, he didn't know Tanya's hand; he'd never received a letter or a note from her. "Ekaterina Sergeyevna" just didn't stick to her; and "Tanya" had been obliterated. The nameless woman referred to as "Client" in the contract confirmed in writing that in such and such instances she would have no claims whatsoever against the "Principal."

"Her address and phone are on the second page," Tamara prompted him, having suddenly brightened with a weak but genuine smile.

Trying not to hurry, Krylov turned the page. Tanya's signature was a brush with a strand of hair. Indeed, an address: 28 Eremenko Street, apartment 17. Krylov bent lower, pretending he couldn't make it out. Evidently it was not Tamara's fate. No matter what she did, no matter what presents she gave him, no matter how sincerely she tried to help, it was all to Krylov's advantage. Right now he didn't even remember where he had hidden his collector's Pamela Anderson: maybe in one of his Alexandre Dumas volumes, maybe in the box under his cot. Nonetheless, it was all a little too much: the third false address in this long day. He and Tanya had gone to Eremenko Street, to the professor's apartment, in a crazily beat-up taxi. That day she hadn't let on that she knew the place. That day she'd had that ridiculous bra, two tussocks of ratty lace on tight straps. That day she hadn't been able to find the switch in the bathroom and for a long time ran her hand over the wall, which looked like a white mosquito in the semi-gloom, until it finally flicked on. Evidently, all this had to be put down to the caprice of the deceased professor. She may have had no idea whose apartment she was in unless she recognized the old shirt hanging on the back of the chair or some of the books.

Tamara was waiting, shining with a quiet, moist light, her forehead gathered into small velvety wrinkles.

"Thank you very much." Krylov's sentiment was heartfelt. He was delighted that the spasms of laughter in his clenched voice resembled suppressed tears. "I'm very touched, really. I appreciate it greatly."

"That's just fine. You see, I carried out your request, albeit with some delay." Tamara smiled with restraint, and her eyes loomed and tossed like night fires on a dark autumn river. "So now, really, you should go. I'm tired. Tomorrow—or rather, today—I have a very hard day."

They rose from the sofa simultaneously, like people who had sat briefly before a long journey, as custom would have them, and were now ready, tickets in their pockets, to set out. Here now was the parting Krylov had thought about for so long and had always hoped to see. It had truly come. Right now he loved Tamara as much as he had in the days just after their wedding, but he knew this would soon pass.

Then Krylov laid out before Tamara a set of steel keys, pulled out the drawer of the empty end table, and showed her the spare sets pushed into the corner. He didn't leave himself a single one. He took out sheets that smelled of flowery soap and had been crammed into the cupboard. His refuge's space changed markedly. Evidently a dehermetization had occurred, and outside air flowed through the window cracks in layers, like jam from a pie. What was left of the lacy tulle rustled, and the cornice mounts creaked. For the last time,

Krylov cast a sentimental eye over his former holdings—with the distinct feeling he was seeing all this for the last time. The old lady's century plant was vigorous and green. The faceted glass ornaments on the chandelier shook, casting blurry stars on the ceiling. Tamara, her arms wrapped around her shoulders, saw Krylov out as far as the hall. There he quickly kissed her palm, where slightly bitter moisture gleamed like golden sand along her strong life lines promising a long life and happy marriage.

Dashing out onto dim Kungurskaya, which sent its runny electricity rolling downhill, Krylov looked around and saw that his former window, which he had always kept only partly drawn, was now firmly curtained. He thought about Tamara there, inside: if God hadn't been in his refuge before, that meant no one was looking out for her. Next to the information kiosks and phone booths, where so recently Tanya had stood in her flat, worn sandals, two large poplar leaves, which looked like wet soles, trembled at the gusts of moist wind, as if hesitating to take a step. In the phone booth Krylov stuck the card into a tight crack, dialed Farid, and briefly laid out for him the latest circumstances and received instructions to get over there right away.

Part Nine

★

1

★

GOODNESS WAS FARID'S OLD SECRET, WHICH HE TRIED TO HIDE, literally running away from the scene of the crime and not showing his face for a while. But now that Krylov had moved in with him, he had nowhere to hide his goodness, nowhere to put it out of sight. Since Krylov came without extra clothes, Farid immediately gave him his brand-new leather jeans and good sweater. Farid's refrigerator, which was always almost empty, was now well stocked with food. Farid, a kitchen towel tied at his hip over his crumpled checked boxers, threw together dinners and suppers, working the burners of skillets and kettles like a jazz drummer working his drum kit. Krylov was moved into the narrow back room with every possible convenience. An ancient television that its owner, he assured him, almost never watched, was moved there. When the rains kept up, a lined raincoat bought on sale appeared as well as sturdy army boots on thick tractor-tread soles. Those soles remained virgin for a while, though, because Farid thought it was too dangerous for Krylov to be walking the streets.

The night Krylov showed up at Farid's place, shivering from an attack of nerves, they sat up until morning again. They recalled Kolyan and the professor, without clinking glasses, each staring into his own faceted drinking glass. The story about the death of the spy, who had turned out to be Leonidich's killer, was paid great attention; the flight from the body, which was probably still lying there damp in the bushes, was, contrary to expectation, deemed the correct action.

"No one would have taken the time to get to the bottom of this with you. There's a big soap opera being created about your Tamara. You'd suit them just fine, and that would be that," Farid told him, crumbling the pillow-soft, tasteless round loaf on his plate.

They recalled Leonidich and Viktor Matveyevich Zavalikhin, who may now have met somewhere in the heavenly sphere and discussed all this. Farid poured Riph Special into their glasses with such amazing accuracy that the cloudy glasses seemed like communicating vessels; the levels of liquid in them evened out of their own accord. The vodka, much more decent than what had been drunk in his refuge, didn't claim Krylov at all, it just glassed over his consciousness, which made it feel as though he and Farid were also communicating through some little pipe, and when Farid stood up to add something to eat to the table, Krylov felt palpably heavier on his wobbly stool.

Farid asked him to repeat every detail of his conversation with Tamara, who had suddenly arisen out of the night. Naturally, Krylov concealed a few things. Farid listened, drinking and scratching his lynx nails over the jagged oilcloth.

"Valuable information," he summed up when Krylov fell despondently silent. "This isn't the address or phone of Mrs. Ekaterina Anfilogova, who I never heard of before. Ten kilometers east of Balakayevsk logging! That is a royal present from your Tamara!"

"Not a bad present," Krylov muttered.

"Don't forget, I'm the only professional geologist in the whole rock-hound community," Farid spoke didactically, nodding to himself. His head resembled nothing so much as a dried-out head of garlic and was covered with dry gray hair. "Just look. The cyanide catastrophe occurred in the Neivinsk District, not far from the village of Kedrovoye, in about 1999. Hydrogeology isn't my exact specialty, of course. But I can assume that this district has a confined aquifer defined by the synclines there, that is, by the downwarping of the rock. The cyanide infiltrated the groundwater. For eighteen years it's been moving through the water-bearing stratum to where the aquifer discharge coincides with the dolomite outcrops. This could be an interface between aquiferous and impermeable strata stretching a thousand kilometers. But your Tamara gave us our hint of the second point. Are you following me?"

"No," Krylov answered stupidly, looking into Farid's squinting eyes, which burned with nonidentical sparks.

"Listen up one more time," Farid spoke patiently. "Everyone knows the infiltration spot, they even showed maps on television. Lots of people already know about Kolyan and Petrovich dying. Every last one of our people knows, naturally, and the information about where the bodies were found is spreading. But only the two of us have the information about the reason the expedition perished. Therein lies our advantage, even if it is only temporary."

"What are you planning to do?" asked Krylov with a sudden chill in the pit of his stomach.

"Find the corundum deposit," Farid answered angrily.

* * *

The next evening he dragged in a roll of Whatman paper interleafed with something slippery. He dropped the roll, which was as heavy as a rug, in the hall with a deafening crash. Out of his backpack he took folders made of antediluvian cardboard with yellowed labels. Right after dinner, he dumped the dishes in the sink and spread the papers, which had been mended along the folds and edges with wrinkly plastic, on the table. These were strange maps consisting primarily of concentric lines, fragile in spots; the plastic made them look like mica. Concentrating, Farid brought up the same images on his computer screen, which labored to boot up—but even to the dilettante's eye it didn't all match. The holographic editor, which the underpowered machine didn't really support, kept locking up. Muttering through his teeth, Farid tried to transfer certain clarifications from the pages into the files, which made the picture on the screen break up into black and white squares. After making a mess of the petrified forty-year-old knots, he pulled out of the folders yellow stacks of frayed documents and rusty staples, and transparent roaches that looked like flat flowers dried for an herbarium came spilling out. Spreading out over the chairs and the balding rug, this documentation consisted of old typed pages and a few manuscript scraps that had faded not from light but time and looked like they'd been written in brown blood. Often they came across hand-drawn diagrams of deposit positions and photographs attached to the documents. The photographs barely showed the quarries and mug-faced trucks with small drilling rigs that looked like stepladders.

"It's not all that simple," muttered Farid, digging through the stale archival bounty. "It's not all that simple, my dear fellows."

So as not to disturb the apartment's owner, Krylov installed himself at a slight distance, in a shabby armchair, and for lack of anything better to do started examining the spy's cell phone. The standard keyboard was as worn and gray as a seed hull. But when he tried to turn the phone on, ten boxes came up, not the usual four, and the quality of the video display, which this time depicted a sleek reddish-brown cat that looked like a chocolate roll, was so fabulous that Krylov could even see the wet fur going the wrong way because the beast had been licking itself before the shot was taken.

"What's that you've got there?" Farid inquired during a smoking break.

"It's that trophy cell phone." Krylov handed Farid the clever toy with the video-cat clawing some furniture ruin. "The owner's dead, but the cat remains."

"Yes, interesting." Farid turned the nonstandard electronic device in his hands. "From its looks, it's like the ones flopping around in women's purses. No one would ever want to steal it. But in fact it's got a processor like a souped-up laptop. My old piece of junk doesn't even compare. If only we had a hacker!" Farid squinted dreamily at his cigarette smoke. "To unlock the codes in this fucking thing. You never know. We might find something useful. To tell you the truth, I can't tell you how badly I need a techie! The district was badly reconnoitered and there are more contradictions than you can count on your fingers. Those meteorologists have dynamic models, very effective. I wish I had one!"

"Couldn't we find someone we know?" Krylov asked hopefully. "Together you and I know half the town."

"No, you and I can do without someone we know." Farid heaved a sigh, propping his head on his hand. "An information leak won't do us any good at all. Now, if we could just find someone who was completely out of the loop. But who had reasons to help us. Only where are we going to get him, our benefactor? Unless he falls out of a clear blue sky."

At this, Krylov choked on the smoke and slapped his icy forehead. Apparently he had to be grateful to himself for having so few pieces of clothing in circulation. Paying no attention to Farid, who had half risen, Krylov headed for the wardrobe. Inside the bare hangers, yellow as bone, with women's sashes in different colors hanging on them, he got a sharp and ragged whiff of camphor. There it was. The jacket Krylov had been wearing that day on the square. He hadn't even taken it to the drycleaner but had simply washed the shoulders and back off by hand. It had turned into a loose sack speckled with moth holes and eaten into by the explosion's filling, which looked like bits of halvah. However, Krylov had continued to wear it, humbly, keeping all his pocket contents. Now the bent business card was right where it had been, where his chance acquaintance who had implored him so to call him had stuck it.

"We have our man," Krylov told Farid, placing in front of him the business card of Pavel Alexandrovich Dronov, creative systems designer at Riphvideoplus.

★ ★ ★

Dronov could not bear to wait a minute. He came at that late hour, huge, wearing a fresh white shirt and tie, with a Browning High Power, as precise as a drafting instrument, tucked into his belt.

"I'm very very glad to see you!" He gave Krylov a big smile, shaking and warming his cold hand for a long time with both of his large, warm, goldenly wooly paws. "Lelya and Mashka send a big hello! I've thought of you often, you know. You and your words about future excesses. You predicted it all so accurately! Even I've already taken part a little, and you know I so didn't want to! The day before yesterday, it wasn't even dark yet, I had to shoot at these scarecrows in overcoats. Over their heads, of course, and they're shouting at me, 'Gold, dollars, chase him, a bourgeois!' "

Collected and kind, Dronov looked like a doctor on a house call where the whole family was ill. Leaving Krylov, he formally introduced himself to Farid. The specialist kept running into lamps and seemed to shake the cramped apartment with his steps as he was led into the kitchen, which immediately became tiny and poorly lit. Farid heated what was left of the Ceylon tea until it was red hot, and in honor of their guest put out a Tatar honey treat, chak-chak, that was obviously not from the pastry shop but homemade and brought to Farid on a handsome blue patterned dish as a present.

Dronov listened without interrupting to the brief exposition of the extraordinary circumstances. This took quite a long time. When he learned who the famous Tamara Krylova was to his friend, he looked at the younger man with new respectful interest.

"She's an amazing woman!" he spoke with enthusiasm. "Such a rarity. My God! Such beauty! You wouldn't think, no one would believe, she alone was to blame for this contamination in the north. The newspapers are blowing this out of proportion, that's all! In fact, officials are mixed up in this story. It's great you helped her!"

After this Dronov wiped the honey off his big white fingers and asked them to show him the mysterious cell phone. For only a minute he fingered and examined the device, which looked like a little black larva in his hand.

"But I was the one who made this," he reported in amazement, testing the case's fastener with his index finger. "That's the way it goes! This earned me a Volkswagen for my Lelya, who really wanted one. I was doing all kinds of moonlighting, and this sad guy comes to see me, about fifty-five, and he asks me to make him a super-phone, only without any flashy design, so it would look like something old. His business required confidentiality, he said, so no one could get to the data. He paid well! So I did my best."

"You mean you can get the information out?" Krylov, who suddenly imagined his search for Tanya had come to a happy conclusion and he had only to live until the morning, rejoiced.

"That's hard to say right off. I'm saying I did my very best," Dronov replied guiltily, looking first at Krylov and then at Farid with childishly bright eyes. "Well, it was interesting for me. I used a few sweet innovations in this phone. You're not going to capture the information here that easily. Inside, it's almost like it's alive. That is, it's not recorded in a specific place; it's constantly flowing around, stirring, moving back and forth. Like a lizard or a centipede. It has lots of room. I got it to be very sensitive. The instant you touch it it slips away. And you just can't hurt it. It's got a small but nasty terminator sitting in a dark corner. The moment it determines the lizard's had its tail torn off, for instance, it instantly pounces and gobbles it down. It's not even a matter of codes. We can pick up the codes."

"I guess we're out of luck again, then." Krylov waved his hand, accidentally knocking over his glass straw and releasing a heavy white stream onto the floor. There didn't seem any point in living 'til the morning. Now all Krylov wanted to do was sleep—sleep for a year or four, so no mornings bothered him.

"You mustn't get so upset," Dronov was concerned. "At least I can try! I do know its habits, this lizard-centipede. I'll find a way to grab it from behind. I'll synchronize with my laptop and try something through a network. If the terminator crawls out, we'll take him to pieces right away!"

"He needs to sleep. The man is completely exhausted," said Farid, whose wrinkles had turned to putty in the dreamy haze.

"Then let's put him to bed," Dronov began to whisper, putting down his cup.

Together they picked up Krylov, who shuffled his legs awkwardly over the spilled salt as if he were drunk. Their faces blurred in the middle from the spot where their voices were coming from.

The bed seemed as deep as a pit full of water, and he practically floated out of the clothes concerned hands freed him from.

"Now let's go take a look at your computer," said the invisible Dronov, covering Krylov with a quilt.

2

★

FROM THAT MOMENT ON, KRYLOV LAPSED INTO A HEAVY TORPOR. The same state of sleep went on and on, with breaks for wakefulness to which sleep was a dark alcoholic admixture. In turn, his wakeful state persisted in his sleep. Immobilized and breathing heavily through his nose, Krylov continued to sense the dark, narrow room around him where he actually lay on his left side. He had lost all sense of time. He might wake up in the afternoon to an empty apartment pierced by the pale autumn sun, an apartment he had now studied much better than his parents' junk-filled tenement and even his own refuge—better, probably, than neat and thoughtful Farid knew his own residence. He could wake up in the middle of the night, make his way to the middle room, and see Dronov, concentrating, rustling the keyboard of his transparent notebook, and Farid taking a bite out of a sandwich distractedly, his elbows resting on the heavy hydrological maps, which looked like they were covered in ice.

Dronov was now coming over nearly every evening, bringing with him the cold smell of his will, and hauling in fruit-colored— rosy apple and ripe pear yellow—pages. He and Farid had found common ground very quickly and genuinely so. During breaks they sipped smoky tea and chatted, nodding at each other, amiably tapping their hot cigarettes, smoked right down to the filter, on the ashtray. Farid's old computer was deemed a pensioner, wiped of dust, copied onto disk, and banished to the balcony. In its place, Dronov brought a new machine that consisted of not only a laptop but also a pair of holographic monitors and lots of electronic innards that looked like beadwork on fine steel. All this he spread out on the computer desk and mainly on the floor, spending a long time installing the parts so that they were oriented toward each other properly for Dronov. Now half the room was taken up by something resembling an electric train set, where each ribbed block held in its field of vision several others, exchanging arachnoid signals and winking drops of green and gold electricity. Placed in the middle of this spiderweb was the spy's phone—or rather, what it had become after Dronov removed its case and added boards, glassy displays, and colored cables. It was as if an insect had hatched from the larva, a very stubborn insect that would not surrender the spider and from time to time emitted a delicate chirring that made you cover your ears.

Dronov walked through this whole setup with high cautious steps, managing not only not to graze a single piece of metal but also not to touch a single one of the invisible threads woven above the dusty floor into an information cocoon. His main craft of toymaker suited Dronov very well because in his big hands everything became trusting and toylike. He managed to type very quickly on the tiny keyboard, flitting all ten of his blunt fingers in a way that seemed to make his subject even prettier and inherently fancy, like a box of candies. He zipped onto corporate networks and downloaded for Farid incredible gigabytes, after which he wrote his own program using analogs: the concentric lines on the monitor went into motion, like the waves drawn by stones thrown at random. Meanwhile, with Dronov's appearance, the bachelor shut-ins started eating very well. No matter where you went there were homemade meat patties oozing warm juice and varnished pies with all kinds of fillings. Often, waking in the afternoon, Krylov would find on the kitchen table a basket of fresh, sunflower-gold curd tarts complete with a friendly note and covered with a clean dish towel.

For Dronov, Krylov was evidently an inexhaustible source of a special kind of satisfaction. Looking at him, the huge programmer experienced over and over again Mashka's miraculous rescue, the happy fact of Mashka's very existence. Dronov probably saw Krylov, who had unhappiness written all over his face, as a distressingly black spot. Krylov noticed that the new friends who had unexpectedly found each other through the bent business card with the cataract of a sodden hologram treated him as if he were gravely ill and did not summon him to their quiet war councils.

He had no objections or aspirations. His mental process, which resembled a book with agonizingly familiar and marvelous illustrations and a worn, vanished text, kept developing steadily. Out of the blue the Asian city of his early childhood started surfacing in his memory, piece by piece. The dark claret peaches that looked wrapped in gray cotton wool were always hot, the grapes cool. In winter the trees' bare branches gleamed in the sun, as if they had a metal armature growing out of their knotty trunks. Did all that really exist somewhere now? The elephant legs of the minarets, the stork nests at their tops, which looked like old sheepskin caps. The echoing narrow streets, the tiny carts made of two boards and covered with insanely complicated and worn-away carving on their tops and sides, and the rusty gas lines. The perfectly still pond with water like buttermilk, men on a platform laid with rugs bowing their bald brown heads in black skullcaps tightly to their drinking bowls. What was that place called? The Hotel Lyabi. I could get a plane ticket and be there in a few hours. Go there and find myself a job. Do something totally ordinary, plunge into the street life of my childhood, tan until I'm black, drink green tea in the evenings, gape at the scalded European tourists, and sell them lousy trinkets for a few dollars. Find some five-story building with faded roses by the entrance and under the windows an irrigation ditch lined with blue bathroom tiles. There are people today living there, on the third floor, in apartment 12, who have no idea of Krylov's existence. A beautiful unmarried aunt there twirled barefoot in front of a trifold mirror and fastened something around her neck, under a smooth electric wave of hair—laughed, put lipstick on, and fixed her braid, which, with its red ribbon, looked like a long fat, gladiolus; she let young

Krylov pluck the rainbow stones out of her darkened brooch—magical pieces of glass that called up the first impulse of this ineffable knowledge that Professor Anfilogov later defined as a "feel for stone."

His beautiful aunt—how many years had it been since Krylov had thought about her? And how old had she been when the family left and she stayed behind for some reason? Twenty-seven? Twenty-eight? No, of course not! Nineteen! That impossible figure was suddenly swapped for the adult Krylov's seniority, and the light maidenly specter suddenly lit up the depths of his memory with a strange, non-living, flickering light, as if a flare gun had been fired into a dark mine. What in fact had happened then? What could have been done to the beautiful Russian girl by sweaty, compact, shrill men or jeering teenagers with clutching fingers? In the daytime they all still looked almost like ordinary people, although they refused to understand Russian and wouldn't sell anything; but in the night they did something together around the campfires, and the nights smelled of meat, and after those nights sometimes strange corpses were found stuffed into very narrow cracks. Two representatives of the police surfaced in Krylov's memory—identical, nasty, with faces like whiskery butter, who had for some reason come to the house, where his aunt had been absent for several days. For some reason his father first spoke with them in a demanding and angry voice and protested when the mustaches shook out on the floor the contents of their suitcases, which were packed for departure, and rummaged through the clothing and linens with their feet. Then something happened (or was that the next time?) and his father, with a trace of sweat on his left temple, humiliated, handed the mustaches a packet of money for some "respected man," and the policemen ate something from a plate, licking their fingers, and casually counted out the reddish-brown tens, bossily frowning and capriciously exclaiming. To cap off their pillaging, they rolled up his aunt's colorful, defenselessly elegant dresses in a ball and took them away, and that evening his father hissed at his weeping mother, repeating, "She had no call. Because of her it all nearly fell through."

Was his mama's younger sister still alive when the rickety, wheel-whining train hauled Krylov and his parents across the steppe and into the unknown? Where do people go who are neither dead nor alive but simply went missing one day? Just as the spy and Leonidich's little murderer suddenly converged into a single person lying dead for all to see in the bushes, so, out of the strange inertia of this convergence, Krylov began to imagine some mysterious similarity between his aunt and the missing Tanya. There was something similar in the drawing of their eyebrows, the set of the head, and most of all, the perfection of the inner foundation, the architecture of the delicate skeleton. In the absence of both originals, the similarity took on increasing power. This third had no name or face and he could not love it any more than he could live on the moon.

Nonetheless, Krylov could not stop wanting to see Tanya, to live with Tanya, and he had no interest in knowing any Ekaterina Sergeyevna who had suddenly taken her place. Their meetings had been a succession of losses—and now Krylov had lost more than he could imagine. Tanya seemed to have taken away everything that had been in Krylov's life up to the time he met her. What had been taken away was nothing more than his soul's childhood property, which lay at its very bottom: those hot pears in the bowl, the warm cake in his school bag, the blue, almost armored-looking domes on the old clay city, the dirty worn street, and in a gap, like the cover of a book of Oriental fairy tales, a marvelous Islamic arch leading through the golden darkness straight to the adventures of Sinbad and Aladdin. Apparently, evil Asia had once again become Krylov's one true homeland. If people who found themselves in the same position as he was asked him to share his experience, he would say, yes, only your childhood remains unpillaged, absolutely nothing else.

He also discovered that time does not heal pain; rather than possess any healing properties, it has the ways of a vampire. Living through an hour, let alone a day, was grueling work. No one had ever taken the trouble to tell Krylov—starting with the cold autumn sky, increasingly free of leaves, birds, and other flying objects—how long this would go on.

★ ★ ★

Silently, his illness's perpetuity made Krylov and Farid closer. Sometimes, in Dronov's absence, thinking Krylov was asleep, Farid spoke with the hologram of Gulbahor—not as if it were a living person, but as if it were a cat or a canary. Such was one of the forms of existence for the missing, a lesson Krylov learned standing quietly in the doorway.

One day, squinting at the sunny window while outside the wind bore radiant golden rubbish, Farid said as if by the way, "I think I need to make a quick trip to the deposit before winter."

"Are things going well?" asked Krylov, sitting down to the sugary buns and the ashtray, which was full of tightly screwed butts.

"They're going fine," Farid confirmed. "Pavel just has a few steps left. Only I don't think we're the only clever people around. If you and I sit here until the spring thaw, we'll get there and find barbed wire around the perimeter and guards with submachine guns. We don't even know what turn things will take in the spring. Yesterday Menshikov was wounded on Green Hill. General Dobronravov was pensioned off, and there are new tanks at the marshalling yard, supposedly brought for an arms expo. So we'd be better off taking care of this before the November seventh national holiday."

His announcement brought Krylov back to reality. From time to time he had turned on the television, which seemed to swell with the crackling from the plugged-in electricity. Almost nothing remained there of news, and the news announcers, drawing the viewers' attention to amusing items like the regional housewives' contest or a zoo birth—back in June—of a pair of bear cubs, spoke with the intonations of the "Sweet Dreams, Baby" show. Odious signs kept

slipping by everywhere, dark spots of reticence. Life was overflowing its banks, but not because it itself was overfull; rather, it was as
if a huge, muffled, alien body had plunged into it, and life had
splashed over the edge, leaving half a bucket's worth.

"I probably should tell you something," Farid spoke looking at
him stealthily. "You don't really have to go. Whether we come back
alive or not—it's fifty-fifty. Petrovich and Kolyan didn't, for instance.
For most people, life's more precious."

Krylov grinned. Fifty-fifty was the exact ratio a Riphean could-
n't pass up on principle. A maximally uncertain outcome opened up
the broadest possible channel for communication with the force the
Riphean spends his whole life trying to get to turn around and look.
He couldn't imagine what those eyes would be like, but after the
demise of the first expedition, the corundum deposit really had
become akin to a launch pad into outer space.

"You know I can't not go," Krylov replied calmly to the perfectly still Farid, who at that moment became a very old man completely detached from everything. "And you can't for the same reason
as me. What's to discuss?"

"Right, that wouldn't be in the cards," Farid agreed with
restraint and ceremoniously poured a strong, nearly taiga-quality
drink from the stained teapot full of hot, plump, tea-leaf kasha.

The corundum deposit was now something like his life's crown-
ing moment, a cleared spot in the usual order of things. There is a
precise time and place where a man meets his own destiny. Not
showing up for that rendezvous would be insanity for any Riphean.
The friends didn't discuss it, but Krylov might be wanted for
Zavalikhin's murder. Krylov simply wasn't where his old life was—
if, in the light of revolutionary events, that place even existed. But if
he was going to be going wherever his feet took him—among the
multitude of directions, he would find the true one.

Krylov simply could not turn down the expedition. In spite of
the emptiness Tanya had left him, in spite of the vibrating, blaring

Asiatic summons, inside he kept hearing the Riphean's chief demand, "God! It's me! Talk to me!" Actually, only now did the extreme literalness of this demand become clear to Krylov: "Talk to me, God! Or else I'll do something that won't let you sit this one out anyway!" Long ago, Krylov hadn't been able to turn away from his gemcutting tools and the infinite world in the crystal's depth. Now he had been presented with a ready-made platform for an experiment to make God manifest—plus the understanding that you only conduct this kind of experiment on yourself.

"We'll give Pavel his share," Farid proposed, enjoying the tea and sugary buns. "He's been working with us, and he has Mashka. Twenty percent, what do you think?"

"Suits me," Krylov replied, knowing perfectly well that if the expedition did return and bring in the stones, the income would be divided into three exactly equal parts.

★ ★ ★

Now Farid did not object to Krylov leaving the apartment once in a while for fresh air. Weakened, holding one hand over his heart and the other on the wall, he was hardly fit for their arduous prewinter dash. In the afternoon, Krylov sat like a pensioner on the damp courtyard bench, wrapped up tight in a warm coat, and looked at the frowning wet asters and the bedewed spiderwebs that sparkled everywhere and reminded him of cracks in cold glass. At night, when only three or four oily-dim windows in the whole courtyard were lit, Krylov went out in Farid's woolen athletic wear and did pull-ups on the chinning bar, from which abundant streams of cold water flowed up his sleeves. Then, radiating heat and fanned by the air's chill, he would run the paths of the half-wild park, where, in the darkness, among the trunks, fallen leaves rustled over the earth and rotten wooden gazebos with vaguely Chinese contours were occasionally illuminated by mellow lights from marijuana cigarettes. At first he had no luck with the running or the pull-ups;

but suddenly it was as if something freed up inside him and he now he could pound out kilometers of damp asphalt for hours in his running shoes.

Meanwhile Farid prepared systematically and stubbornly for the expedition. Somewhere he got a hold of a not very new but sturdy winter tent with inflatable insulation and down army sleeping bags with sleeves like the ones used to fit out mountain game wardens. A corner of the kitchen was taken up by a tower of canned fish and meat that slid apart like heavy little pucks if Dronov happened to tramp too hard. Farid's pride and joy were the polymer balloons for water that did not lose their elasticity down to forty below; demonstrating to Krylov the tautly coiled, sticky pods, he explained for safety purposes they would have to carry their water from a settlement as well.

Finally, the apotheosis of Farid's scavenging abilities: the very same silvery biohazard suits Krylov had seen on television. Their seams were like tractor treads, and you could feel flexible pipes through the layers of fabric. After dinner, the delighted Farid demanded a fitting. Krylov was by no means able to get into the opened sack on which the boots hung immediately. He got all bollixed up, wagging their corrugated metal soles. Finally, the dressing was complete and Krylov found himself inside a kind of fabric bathtub with a stiff load tied to his soles; something like the cap of the armature rose up behind him and had a transparent face-guard that clicked into a hermetic slit. Immediately, breathing became work. From the outside, Farid waved his huge white glove with its ribbed fingers at Krylov. The mirror in the crowded hallway reflected two whitish figures who looked like hares from a child's New Year's party, only without the ears. Because the silvery cocoon isolated him from the world, and because the glass-reinforced plastic shield emitted a scratchy turbidity; the mirror with the two formless creatures looked to Krylov like a television screen seen from a distance running a broadcast from the future. But a future that was right around the corner. For a minute a chill ran through him, like in the oncologist's waiting room.

"You realize, you and I are going to be working in diapers!" Farid's voice, which was little, like a rattling pea, boomed in Krylov's ear. "How do I sound? How's the reception?"

Farid believed that Krylov did not leave the safety of their courtyard during his afternoon outings. However, his feet in their donated army boots sometimes took him fairly far away. A couple of times he was on Kungurskaya. For a long time he stood in front of the safe door decorated with a dead little bell that had dried up on its wire. No one answered his knock. Due to the steel plate on his feet, an emptiness tugged at his heart. His refuge doubtless had worked just as Krylov had intended. When Tamara went inside, she stepped out of reality, and not because when she hid there she could not simultaneously be with her officials and lawyers; she disappeared *altogether*. This was as impossible to comprehend as it was to imagine eternity. From the outside his refuge's windows now looked fake, and the balcony hung on his promise, as if it had been tied to the house with the old lady's rope.

Krylov also made a trip to Eremenko Street, getting there with three transfers on the Metro, which was lit at half-power and had strange drafts blowing through it and where the human masses flowed over the escalator, which was on the blink, in a slow, muffled rumble, as if they were crushing ore at an enrichment plant. In any case, Krylov had prepared a note for Mrs. Ekaterina Anfilogova; in it he indicated Farid's telephone number and asked her to contact Ivan, who had made her the bracelet, as soon as possible. But he saw that the deceased professor's aged door was already planted with many notes stuck into the tattered leatherette; and the mailbox, its stuffed slit grinning, was also overflowing. Apparently, news of Anfilogov's death had only now begun to spread. People who Krylov had previously taken for the professor's entry neighbors were crowded on the stairs. None of them was talking to anyone, but they were all looking at each other with a question in their eyes, which seemed to be searching for someone who was missing. It was as if they were expecting some administrator to come out of the professor's apartment at any moment and tell everyone what they should do, collect their notes, and send them on to their proper destination.

It took Krylov a moment to realize that these definitely weren't neighbors. These were the same people who Professor Anfilogov had kept strictly separate, and now they didn't know how to communicate or span the void that had formed between them. This meant the professor had succeeded. Without him, the void proved even stronger than his separating presence. Nonetheless, Krylov stuck his note behind some upholstery that had come away from the door, poking other people's crowded pieces of paper inadvertently inside with the scraps of insulation, which looked like old caked-on scrambled eggs. Feeling as though he were turning around at the halfway mark, and whispering apologies, he started pushing his way downstairs. Now people looked up at him, briefly thought they might have recognized him, and immediately turned away, disappointed. It wasn't hard to guess that they were waiting for the professor himself, not some administrator. They were waiting, despite the dull dark news, because they couldn't get along without him.

Downstairs, in the courtyard, a tall woman wearing a narrow black suit that revealed her bony knees and a huge black hat that looked like a slipcovered typewriter was walking around in circles over the bright yellow scattering of leaves. From far away, through the fine veil, he could see her thick pale curls, her long chin, and the vivid line of her delicate mouth, which was so still it might have been drawn on with a ruler in red pencil permanently. There were people hanging around here, too, and on the bench by the entryway a bottle of vodka that didn't seem to belong to anyone.

"When'll they bury 'im?" a decrepit old woman wrapped up in an alpaca shawl over a synthetic purple quilted jacket asked Krylov, who had lit up.

"Not yet," Krylov answered into the open space, wondering whether he should ask someone about Ekaterina Anfilogova and realizing there was no point.

"D'they put Vasily Petrovich upstairs t'lie?" the old woman was indignant. "Yest'day people were standing, and the day before, and t'day, there's a whole stairs full of people. Startin' t'stink. Shoulda brought the coffin out long ago!" And the old woman, shaking her little head, as if saying no to everything that had happened, dragged herself to the entry, on her way deftly dropping the unclaimed vodka into her scruffy denim bag.

3

★

WHEN KRYLOV RETURNED, WORN OUT, HAVING BREATHED HIS FILL of wind, Farid and Dronov greeted him with a meaningful silence. They had obviously been waiting a long time for the second member of the expedition, killing time over a small chess board with pin-pieces, over which they often sat now, as if they were tatting lace together. Krylov thought that now they had a right to lay into him for his long and unsafe absence. No one said a word until he had taken off his leaden raincoat and sat down at the table.

"Well now." Farid rose to his feet ceremoniously, stood there blinking, and then got a topographic map out of the refrigerator. "The lower bounded aquifer gave us a very hard time, it was so atyp-ical, but we found it!" Dronov commented, carefully putting the board with its miniature black-white group away in the corner. In the free space lay a tattered map, clearly military, with the coordinate markings restored by these clever do-it-yourselfers.

"Here it is, that little river. It's called the Pelma." Farid pointed with a quarter of a pencil to a winding blue vein. "The deposit is either here, or else here." The pencil airily touched two nearly symmetrical ends between which was probably about a hundred kilometers.

Krylov looked like a man bewitched. The Pelma River, whose small channel's movements reminded him of a lizard, seemed like the perfect image of happiness. All of a sudden Krylov had an acute desire to go there. He felt as if he had discovered a mysterious new way of seeing the reddish brown autumn water shrouding the stones on the shallows, swaddling them like infants in a taut blanket. He saw the tiny yellow sprays of birch leaves against the spruce dark-ness and the boulder with the large brow on the long pebbly bank, which looked like it had frozen into its own shadow. It was as if he were going upstream on aerial stilts. The windswept cliffs revealed themselves—outcrops of powerful stacks of stone pressed together by some terrible shift, friable karst holes, high terraces edged with beaten slabs, lichen, green and coppery, slanted slabs with darkness beneath, retreating into the wave. The shadows beneath the cliffs were deep and vibrant; the stone masses were reflected in bright patches on the racing river. Here and there, its breadth sufficed to reflect the sky as well, and the river stuck to the sky from below, like a body to a blue cotton shirt. Above, the sky's blue was almost unbearable; the mountain summits, with their folds of snow like bird feathers, hung in it without any buttress. Insane beauty permeated everything, and where the sun's cold ray with its dusting of metal did not reach, a birch leaf rushed over the water like a carved, capsized little boat.

"Well, do you like it?" Farid asked, returning Krylov to reality. "We head out in less than four days. I still have things to do at work. And I have to choose some comfortable footwear and buy some more rope, tea, and groats. But basically you and I are pretty well fitted out. Just look at what Pavel's put together for us!"

With these words, Farid handed Krylov the spy's phone. which was back in its case but equipped now with some new jacks— slender funnels where liquid metal seemed to be circulating.

"This is a three hundred-hour battery," noted Dronov, beaming modestly. "And you'll have five extras with you. You aren't going to have to pay B-Line or anything; the phone itself will pick up any network and it can't be blocked from outside. It picks up in a cellar or a cave. Just in case, it has an external antenna. It charges itself if there's wireless electricity anywhere nearby. It picks up all TV channels and decodes everything, and the screen has holographic expansion up to fifteen inches. You can watch movies at night!"

"And, what's most useful for us—satellite navigation!" Farid added with pride. "A GPS module with thirty channels! Over our

Pelma, of course, you can only get four satellites. But Pavel plugged into the American master station in Iraq, so we'll know our position's location with an accuracy of less than a meter!"

"Awesome," Krylov mumbled. "You mean you couldn't get the old information off it?" he asked, trying to sound casual.

The friends exchanged glances.

"Not quite," a distraught Dronov said, with his glance imploring Farid for restraint. "I lay in wait for a long time, and last night I tried to catch it. It turned out to be pretty cunning. It learned a lot on its own. Only seventeen files didn't die. The biggest ones, because they're videos. The rest just scattered like beads off a thread."

"But there is something you'll find interesting," Farid weighed in. "I think you lucked out. Pavel downloaded the film onto his own computer so you could see it. Only eat first or yours will get cold."

Although he hadn't eaten anything yet, Krylov's throat felt as though an unswallowed morsel had stuck there like a tight knot. He threw down his fork and silently rose.

In the room Krylov saw that the electronic device that only this morning had covered the worn crimson rug had been wrapped up and packed away in cardboard boxes, leaving angular marks, velvet marks, like the snaky traces of wires, on the graying rug. Like a concerned doctor, Dronov sat a subdued Krylov in the old computer chair. Squatting, staying half a head higher than his patient, he awkwardly slapped the keyboard, letting his large, soft pinkies stick up.

"The camera in the phone is excellent and the sound card is the best there is," Dronov went on, launching his homemade program by unleashing strings of symbols. "Only the microphone was directional, and the user was unskilled. He should have held the directory arrow down, but he just moved it by hand. So there isn't any scale at all; it's mush. Here, now look"—and with his index finger he clicked "Enter."

A soundless, sunny mix of sun and leaves, light-filled and honey-sated. Now it blurred and jumped to the side as if it had been wiped with a rag. Tanya was sitting on a bench in her spreading peasant skirt; a couple of swallows were hopping near her dusty sandals like windup toys. She was smiling and frowning into her open compact, as if she were holding herself, reflected in the mirror, in her own lap, like a child. Here she was at a table, under a striped awning advertising German beer. Someone's hands were serving her a parfait glass of ice cream that had already started to melt, as if the sun had licked the treat with its hot tongue. The person sat down and turned out to be Krylov. He didn't look much like him. Tanya had light in her hair. They were talking and laughing. So young. As if years had passed, not months. The camera followed Tanya's pale hands, which looked covered in hoarfrost, get something out of her purse (the same compact again, banded for safety with a pharmacy rubber band), and then dropped under the table, where Krylov's dilapidated briefcase stood like a ruin and two pairs of knees touched and rubbed, as if the man and woman were sitting at oars.

"He didn't have to go shooting that," Farid commented, embarrassed and angry. "There's zip operative information. It's probably for his report to his client, so he can say, We're working and here they are, the lovebirds."

"Download that for me onto my phone," Krylov whispered, riveted to the screen.

"Okay," Dronov replied, softly running his index finger over the velvety sensor as if it were a kiddie slide.

Next file: Tanya and Krylov roaming, craning their necks, amid five-story brick apartment buildings compacted like briquettes. Tanya's limping much more than Krylov realized at the time they really were walking around in circles, in search of number 13 maybe. A shot at a bus stop, somewhere on the outskirts: the view from the highway onto a damp green field that looks like a scrap of velvet with a half-torn-off pocket—a crooked little house with a flowery vegetable garden. Tanya's wearing Krylov's jacket; all you can see of Krylov is his elbow; Tanya is telling him something, looking up—as if she were speaking a foreign language. Through the silence and light Krylov can hear Tanya's voice: a little doll-like, a little bird-like. The impression of a foreign language probably comes from the fact that her lipstick is all smeared and her lips are blurry. And here's the reason for the blurriness: a criss-cross kiss, noses red from the cold, and all this being shot unconscionably from behind intervening bush branches. Another outdoor café, little tables, more little tables, nearly all of them taken, in the corner, by the railing, sunspots like a flock of large butterflies, and when they land on Tanya's pale skin, the tips of their wings turn pink. The camera is constantly jerking and capturing something extraneous, green, and living. Time and again someone walks between the cameraman and nature, dark and enigmatic, like the Snow Man.

"Show file fourteen," Farid's stern voice comes from behind Krylov's back.

A hotel's front steps, apparently. Morning, apparently. Tanya's arm is raised and she's stepping off the sidewalk in front of trucks that are flying across a huge pink puddle, like swans on broad watery wings. Tanya jumps back but her bright skirt is splattered with gray. Now an old Volga covered in suede-like dirt stops. The front door opens, Tanya says something in a foreign language and climbs inside, and the Volga pushes off and is lost in the stream of wet transport moving away under the hazy monorail where trains flash by as if someone were running a finger over a comb.

"Stop! Do you realize what she's doing?" Farid exclaimed, grabbing Krylov by the shoulder. "She's giving the driver an address!"

*　*　*

"Just don't go fainting. Listen to me," he continued in the kitchen, shaking Krylov, who was limp and kept dropping his ash-dangling cigarette. "There's no mystery here. Everyone knows you're a little deaf. Everyone's noticed that when you talk to someone you look at their mouth, not their eyes. That means you read lips! You don't realize it because you're used to it. But other people can tell that half of you listens and half of you finishes reading visually. That means the lack of sound is no obstacle for us! I've watched it a few times; the face is photographed clearly, and the words are literally sculpted in the air. Come on, concentrate!"

"Yeah, it's as if I can hear a voice. Only it's like a doll's, not a person's," Krylov mumbled.

"That's just great! If we have to we'll enlarge it and run it slower!" Dronov rejoiced.

"So, let's get to work. The smoke break's over," Farid ordered, lifting Krylov by the elbow from the sunken stool.

From time to time, Krylov felt like he was sleeping and seeing something absurd. "Quiet!" Farid commanded each time before Dronov, squatting, replayed over and over on the screen the little piece of that soundless wet morning. Bigger. Slower. Tanya's face swells up, hisses, and whispers like soap bubbles. Silence stuffs his brain like cotton wool. From the top again: the pink pond slimy from the light and the hood of the filthy Volga, which looks like a battered spade. The image grows again, occupying the screen in jolts; Tanya gets closer and closer, more and more detailed, and more and more inaccessible on the screen; it was as if they were choosing stronger and stronger glasses for Krylov. Through the harsh optical fog, through the black, now nighttime silence, he couldn't hear anything at all. The computer chair creaked and tilted to the side; sitting on it was like riding a camel. "Show it to me normal size," Krylov asked almost without a voice, and once again Tanya, chilled in her thin cotton, is leaping into the street and pulling hard on the car door.

Everything was in the present tense, as happens when you're incredibly tired in the middle of the night. In the kitchen, all the leftover steak had been eaten, and so had the slightly soured cheese fritters, and yesterday's dried-out pirozhki. They'd emptied the ashtray twice into the scorched trash pan, which was full of powdery peelings. A hinged window pane had been opened onto the cold autumnal darkness where web-footed creatures were flying around, like in a cave. The dregs of black coffee in the cups were cold, almost icy.

"That's probably enough for today. We have to let the man get some rest," Dronov proposed, embarrassed, himself barely stifling a yawn that was trying, like Samson, to pry open the programmer's leonine jaws.

"I read lips best at the workshop. It's always noisy in gemcutting," Krylov muttered, propping his head, which seemed to be emitting an intense drone, on both hands. "There's some kind of sleight-of-hand going on. I need to plug up my ears a little."

"The workshop, you say?" Farid perked up. "That means we need knocking and whining and whirring. We'll sleep later." With these words he opened the doors of his flimsy kitchen cupboard with both hands, and out of it tumbled black-toothed graters, sieves with plugged up holes, and pot lids, which meshed into a little bit of chaos.

Soon he had a whole mishmash of steel in the room. Additionally, Farid and Dronov dragged in a rattling toolbox plus a good-sized old basin that was beaten like armor. They wasted no time in turning on the washing machine, which had been manufactured at one of the converted defense plants. This heavy metal object with the thrashing centrifuge inside skipped over the tiny bathroom, threatening to smash the tacky old tile. Blowing the hair from his forehead, Farid drilled holes in the basin; surprising even himself, well-behaved Dronov ran a file over the grinding grater and simultaneously kicked a tin can filled with nails. The wakened neighbors upstairs and downstairs banged on their radiators, filling the pipes with an outrageous din. Not a bad resemblance. Krylov even imagined he saw the cheerful Leonidich for a second holding a blinding stone spark in front of a loupe, like a beauty in front of a mirror. Nonetheless, the noise lacked a certain pneumatics, air pressure. Suddenly outside, somewhere past the tenements and park, there was a clap of explosions: the dishes clattered and the window shutter opened of its own accord. And in that very second Tanya said in her ordinary voice, "18 Dachnaya. Near the Zavokzalnaya Metro. Will you take me for two hundred rubles?"

Part Ten

★

1

★

THEY'D BEEN HERE TOGETHER, TOO. THEY MET NEAR NUMBER 36, which turned out to be a low-slung clinic with a tiny park and flannel patients, even some on crutches. At the time a brief but considerable downpour had been passing through, barely wetting the asphalt, as if you could catch up to it and lead it downhill, toward the river. That was where Krylov was heading now, holding the hot cluster of keys in his pocket tight. He flew around the clinic park. Lightweight black plastic bags were dragging down the sidewalk with the leaves. Their dry twigs gently scratched the asphalt, rustling in the lee like torn cigarette wrappers.

Before Krylov could determine which of the two five-story buildings, the brown or the dirty green, was number 18, he saw Tanya jaywalking. A separate, artificial light perpendicular to the ordinary daylight was falling on her. An exultant patch seemed to be playing on her face. "Tanya!" Krylov shouted, jumping up with an outstretched arm, but she didn't hear him.

She was heading almost straight for Krylov, bearing left, toward the bare square with the scrawny birches and the vague monument. She was better dressed than everyone around her. Something shiny and leopard-printed clung to her, the wind was blowing her opened pink fur jacket, and rhinestones sparkled on her legs, which wobbled in pink boots with mirror heels. Tanya was flying like a blind woman, her face was a spot, but on it shone such happiness that Krylov wanted to sit down on the asphalt and cry. A woman rushing to a rendezvous—that's what she looked like. Tanya had exchanged her old haircut for serpentine locks. It was all so flamboyant and vulgar that it betokened Tanya a broken heart.

At least they could talk. Grinning, Krylov rushed to intersect her straight across the wet grass, tangled like a mop—but Tanya turned abruptly. Now she was rushing ahead of him, and Krylov, his heart sinking, prayed she wouldn't trip. Her life, entrusted to her alone, was like a spark in the lee; Krylov imagined that the energy of the chase itself might suddenly lead her out to the grassy crest over the abyss covered in slippery watermelon rinds.

But Tanya was racing, not hearing Krylov's shouts, oblivious to everything. Her life was flitting like a butterfly on a minefield, and these flittings made Krylov gasp. He thought he was just about to catch up to Tanya and grab her puffy sleeve.

Suddenly, though, she ran up steep front steps, working her elbows, and vanished behind a heavy door sheathed in sugary fiberglass. Krylov threw back his bare head, which had been plastered down by the cold and wind, and even took a step back. The sugary door led to the lobby of one of those fanciful buildings built about four years before that stood half empty due to the high price per square meter. Glassed-in loggias loomed like stacked crystal glasses, and pointy little towers, also covered with tiles the color of fly agaric, rose symmetrically from the red brick roof. If Tanya had a rendezvous there, inside, with a man, then there was absolutely nothing Krylov could do by being nearby. On the other hand, this building was just the kind the set of keys that had tormented Krylov might fit.

He had tormented himself because he himself had been like a lock the toothed metal had been left in, crackling and rattling the workings. He felt a physical need for a light turn and an easy click. In fact, he only hesitated a few seconds. Behind the sugary door there was another, a dull, stainless steel mirror. The button key with sparkles of chips evoked a welcoming clang in the outside sensor, and the door came unstuck with a sigh of relief, or so it seemed. Suddenly shy, Krylov stepped into the lobby, so polished it might have been sheathed in ice. If right now anyone had approached him, he would have slipped outside in embarrassment. But the concierge's faceted booth was curtained and the way to the glassily tinkling elevators, which sounded like they were carrying a fine porcelain service to heaven, was perfectly free. Above the elevator doors a scrolling green light stopped at "22."

Under the call buttons there was a discreet triangular opening. In a flash of intuition, Krylov stuck in the object that had seemed like a crude nail. Nothing happened. But when he abruptly pulled the key out in fright, something suddenly opened behind his back with an otherworldly ringing. The mirrored cabin of the tiny elevator waited, gazing curiously from the ceiling with the magpie eye of a TV camera. "Twenty-two," Krylov prompted himself, pushing the button. The ascent was swift. Krylov felt as if he'd been sucked in, held, and gently released by a glassy ocean wave. The metal doors parted, delivering him to a landing decorated with an artificial rosebush that gave off the strong smell of attar of roses.

The next door had a small rug laid out in front of it in the form of a rainbow heart and blocked the hall to several apartments. In all, Krylov counted eight identical bells with numbers from 169 to 176. He could put an end to this trespassing and just press the buttons from top to bottom, offering profuse apologies to strangers and waiting for Tanya's dear voice—from the acoustic mesh where a nasty darkness crackled. But the five-pointed bundle itself led Krylov on, as if his own fingers were wearing the serrated metal and eager to plunge up to their webbing in the ravishingly yielding mechanisms. The key that looked like the letter "p" came to mind with the simple and crude firmness so essential in a shaky moment. Krylov moved it forward.

There were plump leather armchairs in the hall around a magazine table heaped with flyers. Someone seemed to be sitting in the nearest one, which had its glossy back turned to him: a checked sleeve hung down nearly to the floor. Even after he'd convinced himself, by walking around it on tip-toe, that it was just a checked throw left lying across the arms, his agitation did not abate in the least. Polished numbers shone on the identical doors, also upholstered in leather, and in the four corners of the ceiling gray TV cameras rotated like mechanical birds. The last two keys, the most intricate of all, suddenly seemed as fragile as icicles in spring.

Trying not to make any noise, he began clockwise. The first fine-toothed keyholes wouldn't take the keys, and there was no sound inside the apartment. The next latched on so firmly to the foreign object that a mere trembling wiggle, as if tapping out Morse code, succeeded in freeing it. Scarcely had Krylov touched the locks of apartment 171 with his scratched housebreaking tool than a storm of excitement broke right by the door, as if a New Year's tree had been dropped there and was being shaken: it was a big dog dancing and whizzing his nails over the floor. Another attempt, a desperate chattering, and a crunch. "I'm coming, I'm coming." An old woman's cotton-wool voice rang out from what seemed like a very long hallway. "Zhenechka, I can't be quick." He heard shuffling, as if behind the door people were skiing ten kilometers over a thin crust of ice. Breathing through clenched teeth, Krylov cautiously pulled the key out of the gleaming lock, as if he were taking it out of a sleeping man's hand. Apartment no. 173. Another failure. The shuffling was getting closer as if it were a champion athlete hurrying, not an old woman. The next to the last door. "Zhenechka, I'm home," a crone a few meters away from Krylov said coquettishly and she started throwing bolts. And all of a sudden the long-suffering key, which looked like a crystalline dendrite, turned with magical ease in the upper keyhole. Then the second went right into the ring and gave a sweet click. The neighboring doors opened simultaneously, and Krylov, slipping away, caught a glimpse of the old woman's blue curls and gilded glasses sparkling with curiosity.

★ ★ ★

His instantaneous dissolution into free atoms and instantaneous coalescence into a stinging, formless lump told Krylov what kind of place had opened up to him behind the door, which from the inside was an armored plate. It was a *refuge*. There the pink boots were, on the wood floor, their unbuckled tops leaning against each other. He heard Tanya singing, off-key and sweet, and he imagined Tanya flying around the room like a magical bird.

The long hallway ended in an archway filled with cold dancing light. Afraid of falling apart, afraid of breaking down in tears, Krylov leaned over to take off his boots. When he had pulled the wet weights off his cold feet and straightened up again, he saw a strangely narrow male silhouette, like the eye of a needle.

"Hello, professor," a shaken Krylov whispered with just his lips.

This is exactly what he had expected, but he still wasn't prepared. Professor Anfilogov, wearing a stretched out house shirt that looked like it was made of tissue paper, was standing in an iced-over puddle of sunlight but was not reflected in the hallway mirror. The observer's imagination always had a hand in creating Anfilogov's image, and now Krylov was certain that his imagination was working at full throttle. He tried but could not look into his green eyes, which were oddly blurry, as if a whole vial of medicine had been dropped into them.

The professor nodded slowly—maybe to Krylov, maybe to himself—and went off into the depths of the apartment, getting his dark feet stuck in the puddle of cold sun. Before he reached the turn he got very thin and then vanished, like a needle sleeping under the skin, as if his entire liquid content had been injected into the empty bright space. Tanya's singing instantly became audible. In just his socks, dragging them like flippers over dry land, he wandered toward the sound.

He obviously had poked his head in the wrong place. A long built-in cupboard, as empty as a train car. The apartment had a lot of room but very few things. Two identical chairs with unforgiving straight backs between the two tall bare windows. New eggshell-color parquet that had never known the pressure of furniture legs or the material weight of life. All this could be held in one's consciousness without the slightest trouble. Krylov now saw all this through the diagram of the deceased professor's mind: lots of unoccupied rooms, lots of compartments and shelves covered with untouched, moon-cast dust. And once again Krylov imagined the professor's eyes, like two big spoonfuls of water, looking straight at the back of his head.

Tanya struck him in the eyes like light. She was alone in the conditional bedroom, which was marked, as if on a computer mockup, by an equally conditional bed in which no one had ever slept. The pink fur coat had struck a playful pose on the bedspread, which was as white as a piece of the ceiling. Tanya was standing with her back to him, for some reason plunging her hand into the round, roiled aquarium, where among the torn algae and clumps of rotten fish food pink fish as fat as pigs rushed about. Swelling, the aquarium splashed water on the glass table and from there dripped onto the wood floor.

All of a sudden, sensing someone's silent presence nearby, Tanya shuddered and pulled out her hand as if the water were hot, splashing the bedspread badly.

"Who are you and what do you want?" she cried out, blocking the aquarium and the puddle on the table with her body. "You?" Her glasses, the same ones, the old ones, the awkward ones, slipped down her nose, revealing her radiant, utterly insane eyes.

"Aren't you pleased?" Krylov asked in an over-dry voice, as if he hadn't used it since he'd lost Tanya on the square.

Suddenly Tanya yelped, her whole lanky self leaped in place, and she rushed to Krylov like a cat to a tree. He grabbed her—she was surprisingly long but familiar down to the smallest hollow, the last vertebra of her long spine. Tanya was mumbling and laughing, and her wet hand was ruffling Krylov's hair. In a few seconds she had torn him to pieces. All of a sudden she pushed him away and took a step back without letting go of Krylov's tightly held hands.

"Now this is great, this is great," she muttered, gasping. "But how? How did you get here?"

"You were the one who gave me the keys," Krylov reminded her quietly, becoming very still in front of this stranger, this elegant stranger in the leopard dress that looked like it had been pasted over with spots of warm chocolate.

"Why, that's right!" Tanya exclaimed, giving Krylov a jerk. "And I kept wondering where they'd got to!"

Deep down inside Krylov it got dark for a second. All of a sudden he felt how defenseless he was, like a patient on an operating table. The slightest cruelty could kill him. But Tanya was laughing again and her fragile tresses were bouncing amusingly.

"Listen, listen, there's nowhere decent to sit here," she kept talking, drawing Krylov over to the smooth bed. "Come over here. Let me take a look at you!"

But they couldn't see each other anymore. Light and gloom flickered in their half-shut eyes, as sometimes happen in a madly racing car. Both kept turning their heads so that they couldn't kiss the right way. Krylov couldn't really get his arms around Tanya and get close to her because there was some unfamiliar energy dancing around inside her that had absolutely nothing to do with what was happening between them now. There were no fasteners whatsoever on Tanya, as if she were a reptile, and her clothing shifted around like a slippery skin. Krylov kept trying to catch a whiff of the old Tanya smell—a bitter pharmaceutical smell from her paper-thin, intoxicated skin—through her heavy new perfume. But he kept picking up the thick and heavy sweetness—behind her large, inflexible ear and her sprayed hair—and it just wouldn't quit, filling Krylov's nostrils and head with a stupefying haze. Tanya seemed to have been embalmed alive with this perfume, as if her very blood now smelled of it.

"Oof! Let me catch my breath!" Tanya turned away and, beaming, fluffed her hairdo with her fingers. Then she ceremoniously folded over the edge of her tousled pink fur coat, as if covering something up there. One, two, several compact dollar bundles cleverly criss-crossed with different-colored rubber bands slipped out over its silk caramel lining.

Embarrassed, Krylov looked away. That was when he saw the sodden piece of paper on the water-swollen glass table and on it a mound of glittering wet grains. Unable to restrain himself he stood up to look. Diamonds, approximately one and a half to five carats, cast a slight northern glow onto the paper's damp whiteness; the water, rather than soaking the stones, trembled on them like dew. Judging from the dispersal of light and the quality of the cut, several of them were so good that they were more like theoretical concepts than material objects; without a doubt, this was the fortune and legacy of Professor Anfilogov, who had seen the theoretical part of things above all. At this, from the faceting of the girdle and a few other fantastic elements, Krylov recognized among the professor's theorems stones of his own work. Once again he imagined that Anfilogov was somewhere nearby, literally in the room.

"You see, Vasily Petrovich didn't say exactly how many diamonds he hid in the aquarium," Tanya spoke, puzzled, smoothing her leopard hem on her knees. "I think I've already sieved everything there three times. But I keep thinking, What if there are still some left? Pouring the aquarium out entirely—well, I feel sorry for the fish. They've survived here on fish food from the dispenser and could live another year at least. On the other hand, you can see how much it might be worth. And then I would always be thinking and imagining it lying here without me."

★ ★ ★

The sediment in the aquarium gradually settled. The torn algae was silver on the water's surface, which had gone down a third, and the big fish, with faces like metal masks, weren't swimming but floundering there, wagging their torn tails.

Tanya's hand, which Krylov was pressing, too hard probably, was still damp and cold.

"Tell me, did you love him?" This was one of those questions that should never be asked under any circumstance.

"Well, here we are again, talking about my husband," Tanya smiled slyly, thumping Krylov's shoulder. "Just like old times. All right, if you got here that means you've already figured about Vasily Petrovich and me. We were married a year. Did I love him? I don't know. But now, now . . ." Her face, touched with the latest kind of rouge, became pious. "Now I'm going to love him my whole life, as if he were my own father. Imagine, he left me everything. Everything! The apartments, the house in Zurich, the jewels, and the money! What a good man he turned out to be!"

"You're going to take all that? You really are?" Krylov was stunned, still not understanding anything. "What about you and me?"

"Oh, it was all wonderful with you and me. But now I just can't think about that." Tanya pulled her hand away from Krylov and started fiddling very quickly with the heavy gold pendant on her chest. "When he was leaving on the expedition, Vasily Petrovich gave me the codes for his credit cards and the passwords for his bank accounts, and he told me where he had different hiding places. But of course I didn't dare touch a drop and lived on my salary. Remember how you and I never had any money? I was actually afraid I knew too much and that something might go missing before Vasily Petrovich arrived. I had no idea how much of it there was. I didn't even take a kopek for the funeral!"

Krylov was badly stung. He had guessed, in a general way, that Tanya had had money at the time of the funeral. It was better never to talk to anyone about the origin of that sum.

"Then last Thursday a lawyer called me in," Tanya kept telling her story, gazing enthusiastically into space. "He read the will. And then I realized that it was all mine now! I can't tell you what I felt. I think I broke something there. They all smiled when they saw me out of the office. You can't believe how much money there was in Vasily Petrovich's accounts! Can you guess how much?"

Krylov shrugged mechanically.

"All right, then hold onto something." Tanya gave him a merry and terrifying look over her glasses but then suddenly frowned hard and fell face down on the pink coat that was about to slip off the bed. "No, I won't tell you! I want it to be just mine! Believe me, I can't sleep more than three hours at night. All of a sudden I wake up as if I've been shocked and right away I remember how much! And I completely lose it! I wander around my old apartment and wonder how I could have lived there so long."

Now the happy patch that had flashed in front of Krylov on the street turned into a full and intolerable glow of happiness. Tanya was looking at the ceiling as if it was a starry sky and a star was burning in her heart. What had recently been Krylov's—her tiny breast flattened by spotted silk, her long-toed foot with the bone that jutted out encased in a black orphan stocking that didn't match her expensive new acquisitions—was here, but as if it had been sent into storage.

"Let's talk about us." Krylov took Tanya's elbow and sat her down sharply beside him. 'I love you. Remember that well. I'm sorry, but I won't let you make a joke of that. We spent a long time experimenting, and now I want to start a normal life with you. Like all normal, regular people."

Tanya looked at Krylov with a stranger's over-bright eyes. She seemed to have gone quite blind. Krylov squeezed her slippery elbow, which she tried to raise in order to protect her unbearable star, which was piercing her through and through, even harder.

"You and I don't need that money. You alone could accept the inheritance, but if we're going to be together, then no way." Stubbornly, Krylov would not turn his tearing gaze away from the happy fire that seemed to be burning Tanya up from inside. "We can't handle that kind of money. I don't know how, but that money would crush us. Is it worth that? The professor had other wives, too, and they're not young now. He left a son. Let them inherit."

"Did you just drop down from the moon or something? What are you talking about?" Tanya interrupted him, and a familiar expression of dissatisfaction came through the rather tight facelift that had obviously been done very recently. "Don't make such a big deal of it. Yes, we dated. So what? If you want to know, I had another lover before you while I was married. For a week, but even so. How else could I have stood all this?"

"Wait, wait up. Either speak well of the dead or not at all."

"To hell with that!" Tanya broke away abruptly, jumped up, and looked nearly as tall as the ceiling. "It wasn't you and me, it was Vasily Petrovich who set up the experiment! Do you think I left a good life to marry him? No, and he knew that perfectly well! I was hoping he would make me happy in some way. But Vasily Petrovich was apparently keeping me in everything old and in an old apartment on purpose. He saw visitors there! He said he'd wait an eternity for me to love him. An eternity. Just imagine! How he used to look at my torn stockings and my disintegrating boots! As if he were expecting his displeasure to make them grow back together themselves. You can't believe how awful it was for me. As if all my things were rotting on me, like on a corpse in a grave. People don't live an eternity!"

Saying all this, Tanya feverishly rummaged in the pockets of her fur coat, ejecting new packets of money on the floor. She got out her cigarettes in a flat embossed case and a gold lighter dusted with a fine diamond sprinkling. She flicked a trembling flame and inhaled it all through her cigarette-straw, as if it were a cocktail.

"Now you want me to refuse the money. Well, here's what I'll tell you. The failure isn't the one who never had a chance but the one who had a chance and didn't take it. Damn, damn!" Tanya gave her hand holding the cigarette a shake; it had burned all the way down in a few drags, like a sparkler. "I just can't get used to these fancy slims, and now there's no ashtray. There isn't anything in this apartment. You could count everything here on your fingers!"

Taking a look around, Tanya drowned the butt in the puddle on the glass table, where it immediately swelled up and popped, like popcorn. The whole amber wood floor was covered in Tanya's long tracks, like a hare weaving in and out to escape the hunt.

"Fine then." Krylov was dying for a cigarette, too, but he couldn't do anything here, in this conditional space, where every object looked like it had been drawn on a bare plane. "I may have money in a couple of months. I can't promise, but the likelihood's great. Why can't you take my money over this ill-starred inheritance?"

"Do you think I'm greedy?" Tanya shook her head with a sarcastic smile. "What's money to me? I'll tell you. Just a matter of life and death. And I'm not talking about my health. Poisoning would have been pretty easy for me; Vasily Petrovich wasn't really paying attention. A couple of shots at five thousand euros apiece would have taken care of everything. But you have to understand, a woman has only one illness: old age. Up until age thirty we're all equal, we all have our rights. After that, some keep living and some start dying. Before, the law of nature functioned identically for everything. So old age wasn't so repugnant. But now? We have everything now: serums, plastic surgery, nanotechnologies. A woman over fifty has to spend a few thousand euros a month on herself. And the longer she lasts, the more she spends. But even if she's a top manager, an irreplaceable employee—her powers tap out. And they send the horse that was ridden too hard to its deserved respite! If you're pension's good enough, you can eat and pay for your apartment. But health insurance? Don't make me laugh! Even dentistry now is for separate money. And where am I going to get that? Who's going to tell me that? No one stays eternally young, of course. But have you seen rich old women? They're like dolls! And all the rest are like dirt. Do you realize we're talking about my life? Are you aware that I was born and I'm going to die?"

★ ★ ★

Blinking his hot eyes, Krylov listened to this monologue and felt Tanya having a *direct* influence on him, striking with all the strength of her being at some vulnerable spot and drilling a hole in him. Even now he couldn't have said how old she was. The congealed haze that had concealed her age had vanished only to be replaced by hydrocosmetics, probably like what Tamara used, which covered her face with a thick, perfectly clear liquid that came out of fat vials of dark blue sunblocking glass. Tamara and Tanya now would probably have quite a lot in common—for instance, the gold jewelry from Tiffany that Tanya kept twisting mechanically, looked like it had come out of one of Tamara's safes. The radical rejuvenation would soon make Tanya rubberized, with a body temperature a degree lower than the human norm. Her sagging tummy would be flat, the sweet scar that looked like a thin thread of noodle would disappear. And what would be left then?

"I did think of you from time to time," Tanya spoke feverishly, hugging herself back to her shoulder blades with her long arms. "Do you know what I used to dream about when you and I were wandering around? I used to think, What if we found some treasure? Or a platinum credit card with a million dollars on it! It's stupid, I realize. You can't imagine all the stupid things that built up in my mind. I used to put our bus tickets into a separate box and imagine getting as much money as the numbers on them. I started spending it in my mind, allocating it. And there was never, never enough! Do you remember that jerk who photographed us on his telephone? I stole two thousand rubles from him! You see what I'm confessing?" Tanya began laughing huskily. "And still I'll tell you one more time: it's not money I love. After all, you didn't just ask me to give up the inheritance but those minutes I had in the attorney's office when they told me . . . and the nights I have now, when you lie there on your back and try to catch your breath . . . and the number I'm never going to tell anyone, that's in my head, like a fat diamond in a safe. If I write rejecting the inheritance now, all that will have been in vain. Just think. How can you take away someone's happiness, whatever it's made of?"

Krylov dropped his head, examining his white socks, which had sagged badly from Farid laundering them in boiling water. Oddly enough, right now he felt almost nothing.

"This inheritance came to me like an act of grace," Tanya, dark and narrow in front of the watery window, spoke in a muffled voice. "Almost everyone is doomed to a miserable, prehistoric life, when we have *everything* right here. Almost everyone dies when there are ways to save the patient—except that the patient doesn't have the money. Almost everyone's life is inauthentic."

A huge shudder went through Krylov at the last sentence. Tanya's talking about that, too! Man must have a secret organ that sends him signals about the world's inauthenticity. Tanya had nearly hissed the word "inauthentic," and her movements were like the dance of a snake when it winds its scaly rings with a thick congealed strength.

"Let's say you're right," Krylov spoke dolefully. "Let's suppose you start living at the level of medical and every other kind of modern progress. But a woman can't be alone, can she? Will you be happy alone? And if not, won't you think back to us after all? Open your eyes!"

"You don't have to scare me!" Tanya cut him off, pale. "A woman's fear of loneliness also stems from poverty. And from the briefness of her time, because youth passes so quickly. But now everything's going to be fine for me. I'm in heaven. Heaven! Understand? The place where no one wants for anything. I don't have to worry about anything anymore. And this is going to last for a long, long time."

Tanya wrung her intertwined hands over her head, took a little dance step, and then another, testing the parquet with her flexible dark foot; there was something didactic in this attempt of hers at ballet, like a teacher running her pointer over the blackboard. It had finally hit Krylov that only now had Tanya landed wholly beyond the looking glass. A place where nothing could touch her anymore. Unless she really did live for a very long time and at age ninety-eight her money suddenly ran out. What would it be like for her to awaken from her heavenly dream?

"Why are you looking at me like that?" Tanya asked angrily, turning on her toes and rocking the small crystal chandelier with the top of her shining head.

"You look taller," Krylov marveled. "How could that be?"

"Because of my heels," Tanya said casually, dancing in her stocking feet.

Krylov shook his head. All of a sudden he remembered how a

long, long time ago, at the train station, he had stolen a glance at the stranger and tried to guess whether he was taller than her or not after all. If she had been taller than him, he probably wouldn't have started talking to her. Now that she didn't need Krylov anymore, Tanya had grown like a teenager in the last couple of months. People say that the Mistress of the Mountain, the richest woman in the world, is nearly four meters tall. So this is how all this happens. What Krylov had taken for a facelift done at a beauty spa may have been the onset of mineralization. Tanya's skin looked like it had been seized from the inside by cold quartz ice.

Nonetheless, she was still alive and real. Krylov had one more fairly strong argument for her. He might get rich in a month or he might die (at this every vein of his body was struck, like strings). He knew mortal danger threatening a man had an irresistible effect on a woman. "No, I want it to be just mine!" a voice rang out in Krylov's mind, a voice very much like Krylov's own. Immediately he felt protected, as if a hand lay on his head, softly clouding his consciousness and shielding him from Tanya's cruel stars, which were still burning in the relentlessly white ceiling.

Meanwhile, blissed out, Tanya was still worried about something. Krylov even thought she might be seeing the professor popping up occasionally in the doorway, like the watermark of this space. But Tanya wasn't looking in that direction and didn't notice the dim thickening of the air in which one inferred more than saw the triangular eye sockets, the cheeks, and the grooved jacket buttons, which were so much more distinct than everything else that they looked like they were just about to spill on the floor. Tanya apparently had no inkling of her dead husband's presence. Her attention was directed inward, where clockwork seemed to be ticking away, eating up the seconds.

"You seem so tense all the time," Krylov noted without feeling the slightest sting of jealousy. "Are you expecting someone?"

"No, no one." Tanya looked down. "But at eight this evening I have a plane to Geneva. Tomorrow my attorneys and interpreters are expecting me. You have to excuse me." She stumbled and her glance flickered, as if she were trying not to look at some point known only to her. "I need to get something here. And pack my suitcase. Don't wait to see me off, really, otherwise I won't get anything done."

"Fine, then. I'm leaving in a couple of days, too, for Novosibirsk, on business." In order to keep his gaze from stumbling indiscreetly on the hiding place Tanya was dreaming of opening up as soon as she was alone, Krylov looked only at her. "I'll be back in a month or so. When will you be coming back?"

"Oh, in six months or thereabouts. When I officially inherit. Unless there's a revolution here, of course." Tanya spoke quickly, choking a little. "It's terrible what's happening here! Officially they're going to operate on the President, but in fact it's house arrest, not an operation. A few days ago I saw a man dragging a machine-gun right down the street with my own eyes, just like that, as if it were a vacuum. No, for now I want to get as far away from here as I can. The accounts in the Geneva canton bank were opened in both our names, mine and Vasily Petrovich's, plus I'll take a few things with me, and that will be enough for a while. Then, if everything's good, I'll move into this apartment! I never imagined I'd have one like this!"

"Well, bon voyage. I won't be bothering you. Maybe we'll get together in six months," Krylov said, standing. He was gripped by an infusion of unhappiness, as if a few thousand people were standing up in the room with him.

Jammed into a corner, Tanya was biting her bent finger. Krylov calmly headed for the doorway. Suddenly he understood what a man feels as he's led to his execution. He's horrified by every patch of earth his feet touch. What's left of life in him tears him to pieces. A few meters before the spot he dreams of suicide. This whole realization suddenly came over Krylov halfway to being rid of the woman who was biting her bone, nearly dislodging tears. Krylov himself was perfectly fine.

"Wait!" The woman suddenly rushed after him and nearly fell, slipping on the wet floor.

"What do you want?" Krylov turned around woodenly. Once again he smelled that sweet, heavy smell he used to sniff. The smell stretched from the woman in sticky threads, blindly seeking someone's breathing, catching it the way a predatory plant catches a butterfly's flutter.

"Wait, hold on." Shrinking, Tanya leaned up against him, and it was immediately obvious that she really was about five centimeters taller than Krylov. "All of a sudden it hurt so much. I really don't understand what's happening to me now. I'm not myself probably. Let's not lose track of each other again. So it doesn't turn out the way it did then, on the square, again."

Krylov took a deep breath as an ocean surged into his soul.

"Why don't I call you," he whispered, his lips touching her firm cheek down which a salty drop was winding without wetting the surface.

"There's nowhere to call," Tanya said piteously, snuffling. "I won't go back to my apartment. I'm just abandoning my things—and getting the hell out of there. All the walls there are papered in my unhappiness. And I never bought a cell phone here. I decided I'd buy one in Geneva. I saw a platinum Super-Com in a catalog. I've had my eye on it. I'm such a fool!"

"Never mind. Never mind." Krylov stroked her narrow back and slender shoulder blades which had the marvelous perfection of crescent moons, or maybe heavenly grape leaves. "Let's agree that you'll call me. As soon as you land and get settled, so straight from the hotel."

"I have to write down your number," Tanya said through her nose, breaking away from Krylov. Her eyes were leaking under her glasses, and she had a wet mustache gleaming under her nose.

"How about here." Moving aside the swollen jewels on the wet piece of paper, Krylov tore off a fibrous scrap, as if it were boiled beef.

"Only I left my pen at home," Tanya mumbled, rubbing her swollen eyes.

They looked around for a while in search of something to write with or at least scratch his telephone number on the disintegrated paper. They circled as if each were dancing solo. Their transparent circling bore them into the other rooms. Nothing had been *forgotten* anywhere, absolutely nothing ordinary, just dust, mysteriously laid down by the emptiness, silver on the bare surfaces, suggesting that she write on them with her finger. Like astronauts in weightlessness, they floated from wall to wall, pushing off, spinning, finding themselves somewhere other than where they'd been looking, thinking they were looking ahead.

At last they met up again, shaken by the sterility of the rooms and the total absence in them of any human trace. Tanya was twirling her sole find in her fingers: a grooved, dusty man's button.

"Fine, then you'll just have to remember it," Krylov said sternly, and Tanya nodded obediently. "Six hundred fourteen. Eighteen. Forty-one. Come on, it's simple. One more time."

Krylov declaimed Farid's number slowly and distinctly, staring into Tanya's face, where he was impeded by her glasses and the salty blobs drying on the lenses. It was as if he were trying to impress himself on her with his number and voice. He felt a limit in her, a block. She was so tense trying to remember the numbers that they leaped from her ringing consciousness.

"Enough, now," she whispered, at last. "Enough, enough, enough."

Never had Krylov kissed anyone so roughly. He held her, binding her in his arms, and standing on tiptoe, ate her vibrant, salty mouth, not allowing her to jerk away or take a breath. She seethed in his arms and stamped her soft black foot powerlessly. Finally he pushed her away, flying back toward the wall. Her features had blurred, and on her upper lip, which was swollen like a duckbill, there was a black drop of blood.

"Six hundred fourteen! Eighteen! Forty-one!" Krylov shouted in that plaintive and pathetic voice, and he ran down the hall, nearly knocking over the pink boots. He thought Tanya shouted something, too, but the armored doors had already shut, quietly clicking their stainless locks.

It was darker in the hall now than it had been half an hour ago. The blue-curled old lady who had been there before was sitting in the leather armchair, her very soft hands folded on the knob of her cane. "Six hundred fourteen, eighteen, forty-one," thought Krylov, looking stealthily at the aging Malvina, who had raised her rejuvenated silicon face to him. The express mirror elevator bathed Krylov in bands of flickering life from below, as if it were taking a few Xeroxes of him. He felt no better in the fresh air. The low gray sky was slightly silvery, and there was a rustling coming from everywhere: the early Riphean snow, fine and stinging, was scratching the golden leaves, still in all their glory, and salting the drab grass. The patch of Tanya's tears on Krylov's cheek froze. He bore it and kept repeating, learning the telephone number for Tanya, repeating it to the rhythm of his broad, pointless steps. The strange lightness of his gait was explained by the fact that Krylov no longer had Tanya's keys in his pocket. For months, the five keys on the wire ring had not cooled to the usual metal temperature, fed constantly by Krylov's body heat, like a radiator with electricity. They were somewhere in the apartment and their fate was unknown. None of this mattered. Krylov was worried that something might happen in the snowstorm-filled air to the plane to Geneva, that the takeoff strip would ice over. If he had any prayer he could offer up for Tanya to the nonexistent God, it was only this, "Six hundred fourteen, Eighteen. Forty-one."

2

★

WHEN KRYLOV TURNED UP AT HOME, WEARING HIS RAINCOAT LIKE a frozen elephant hide, permeated with a syrupy perfume sweetness, and utterly out of his mind, Farid didn't ask any questions.

"A little early for snow," he commented, brushing the icy grains off Krylov. "But the forecast has it all melting in five days or so."

That whole evening and the following day Krylov and Farid packed their backpacks, which rose like columns amid the instruments, clothing, and supplies set out around the room. A lot of what Farid had set aside for future use he rejected, sending it to the reserve pile. Krylov wondered whether this pile was going to outlive them. His hands worked intelligently, but his emotions and hearing were riveted to the old Panasonic. For Krylov, the telephone became like an artificial respirator; if it didn't ring for too long, his chest tightened up as if someone were gathering Krylov into his fist. When the phone, buried under piles of expedition goods, did twitter, Krylov started flinging junk aside like a dog, but then, embarrassed, he let Farid take it. Arching one eyebrow, Farid would connect with the caller and start talking, and Krylov would realize that, once again, it wasn't for him. Not wanting to listen in enviously to someone else's communication, he would go out on the balcony. There, lighting up a damp cigarette that gave off an autumnal bitterness, he took a parting look at the piebald yard with the iced-over chinning bar, at the big trees and the last few reddish-brown leaves that had frozen in pinches, and at the human tracks in the petrifying clay, airy white from the fine snow, as if it wasn't people who'd tramped through but angels dancing.

The day Tanya was supposed to have been settled and called

from Geneva came and went. Krylov lived through those twenty-four hours as if he were on a planet with fivefold gravity. If the telephone hadn't rung at all, he probably would have died. But the Panasonic did twitter frequently. Roma Gusev, Seryoga Gaganov, and Vadya Menshikov called; Vladimir Menshikov, who'd been shot in his left lung, called from the district hospital. The date of the October coup was fast approaching, and something was afoot in the country. Reluctantly, through their teeth, the media were confirming the rumor of the President's illness. His ear crushed, the receiver in his hand damp from his breathing, Farid would drag Krylov in off the balcony and make him watch the television. There, instead of the ill but live head of state they showed the clinic where he was being kept: a compact building that resembled an old-fashioned Russian stove, where above the rectangular tower the gilded and eagled presidential standard listlessly licked its pole.

At three in the afternoon Moscow time, the presidential press secretary, an energetic functionary with an apple-pie Boy Scout smile, announced that the government had stepped down. The press release was shaking in his hands, as if the press secretary were afraid of spilling the leaping text from the page. At six he reappeared, covered with a motley-from-horror stubble that had bubbled up in this short time, and announced that in the absence of the institution of vice-president in Russia, power was transferring to the Provisional Presidential Council, which they showed: twelve people sitting in a row, slightly separated from one another. Two were wearing gold general's uniforms and had gloomy, constrained faces; the woman from Women of Russia, wearing a baggy green suit and a short conservative haircut that stuck to her temples, was firmly pursing her tragic mouth; a former television commentator and deputy who had been in an endless number of congresses of various organs of power was looking at the journalist with goggly bare eyes that had no eyelashes whatsoever. Before they had even begun to act, these people looked simultaneously wound up and terribly weary. History seemed to have struck them simultaneously, like an infectious disease that had been produced by medics everywhere. Just how this had happened, the Chairman of the Provincial Council, former health care minister and academician Karenin, probably could have told them. But he himself looked infected. A lean and ungainly old man with a cloud of gray hair on his high aluminum skull, Karenin had never before been the focus of so many TV cameras and now was looking into them in turn, like a researcher looking into microscopes set up by his lab assistants. Under this piercing look, Krylov felt as if he could be seen straight through, like a transparent microorganism. Tall, lop-sided, his empty jacket slipping onto one shoulder, Karenin's look alone suppressed the journalists' chirping as they tried to get out questions about preparations for democratic elections and the reasons for declaring martial law in the capital. Anyone looking at him resting his straight bunched fingers on the stack of scribbled papers could tell that everything that was happening was the truth.

"I hope we don't forget something because of that raven of a scholar," Farid muttered as he returned to packing the backpacks.

The night passed in Krylov's attempts to drift off, to get through the muffled hours when no one could call anyone. Opening his eyes, he saw to his right, on the stool, a glowing dial where the pressure of time was measured, mounting as the rickety minute hand took little jumps. He greeted the European dawn in the darkness, lying with his feet facing the ghost of a window. At that time a snowstorm was sweeping over the corundum river. Snow milk was flowing weightlessly from the cliffs, and the thickening river water was sticking to the icy edges in soft, seemingly warm patches. The black forests gave off a white smoke. In the freezing shroud a four-meter female silhouette could be made out just barely. The Mistress of the Mountain's bright, faceted eyes were wide open, and a frozen pink fur coat that stung like a brush hung on her stone shoulder. Broken suitcases lay open at the feet of the richest woman in the world, on the snow-speckled boulders, and delicate women's dresses fluttered, turning to ice.

Right then, Menshikov, who had been shot and whose dull pain kept him awake, went out to smoke, which the attending physician had strictly forbidden. Down the empty hospital corridor, slipping ridiculously on tiptoe so as not to click the heels of her short boots, a petite woman was moving toward him. She'd probably been sitting up with a relative, a brother or a husband, and now was hurrying home to get a little rest. There was something inexpressibly touching about her young neck, the soft brush of hair on her round nape, and the red ladybug of a cold sore on her upper lip.

"Tell me, please, what's your name?" the brash Menshikov asked when the stranger, who had nearly come even with him, stopped to switch her heavy package from one arm to the other.

"Nadia, let's say," she replied cautiously, looking stealthily with her clear golden eyes. And she immediately asked, unable to restrain her curiosity, "And yours?"

"Viktor, let's say," Menshikov responded, delighted, feeling a burning desire to throw his arms around this warm creature of the night right then and there.

★ ★ ★

Krylov awoke with sore joints and an aching heart, at half past nine in the morning. In the kitchen, Farid was eating a dried-out potato turnover as he recounted the money.

"Here, take this." He separated a good third from the plump packet of thousand-ruble bills. "Go see your mother today. Give it to her. I'm going to the station for tickets."

In a dark funk because the phone, which had been silent through the night, was going to be left untended, Krylov headed out. Unwilling to risk the four stops on the Metro, he made his way through back alleys, which were sometimes completely deserted, sometimes thronging with the local population. Long-haired old men were strumming cracked yellow guitars, torturing the strings with their arthritic fingers; young men were perched on the backs of well-trampled benches, some of them with scarlet ribbons fraying on their satin quilt jackets. One time, some rosy-cheeked men who smelled appetizingly of watermelon and vodka started shaking Krylov's hand and calling him comrade; then he saw ten or so saddled horses, stocky and worn, with manes like old ladies' hair. A dashing Cossack with a short forelock peeking out from under his cap was playing holographic Tetris and watching after the horses. Krylov zigzagged between stuck cars as he passed through—there were lots of people on foot walking in the middle of the street, as if it were a metallic mirrored river.

At home, as always, the half-witted electricity was on in the middle of the day; the glass jars that constituted a turbid mountain in the vestibule had accumulated all kinds of dust and dried insects. His mother emerged at the noise from her unaired bedroom, where even when it was light outside the air was like the darkish water you rinse your watercolor brush in.

"Oh, it's you." Over her robe his mother was wearing a thick, fluffy shawl, curly with age. "None of the radiators are giving any heat. There's snow outside, and they're not giving us heat. You should put on some kind of jacket, too."

"I'm just here for a minute. I'm going to Novosibirsk on business," Krylov lied, as if his mother and Tanya would try to find him in Novosibirsk, if anything happened. "Here. I brought you some money."

"Money, money. Where's that money of yours now?" His mother turned away in anger and shuffled to the kitchen, shaking her dead-looking chignon, which looked like it was made of cat hair, and dropping bobby pins on the floor.

Distraught, Krylov trailed after her. Almost all his life he had asked himself why he couldn't pity this stranger, who did give birth to him after all and who had been through so much. Over that business with his aunt? Over the fact that he had nothing to talk to her about? Or because in the *inauthentic* world her sufferings were a sham? Today, as always, Krylov had no answer. At least, in the end—because he might well be seeing his mother for the last time—he wished he could feel something. And all of a sudden he recognized the felted clump pinned to his mother's head. A long time ago, rummaging around in search of scissors, he thought, he'd seen it in the pier-glass drawer—the same drawer where he'd stolen his aunt's photograph from and scattered it to the wind all those years before. The dry, motley tresses, which looked like they'd been drawn on with first a soft and then a hard pencil, was the very loss that his mother had stored away in a yellowed newspaper as she'd lost her hair. At the time Krylov had been stung by the thought that you see hair like that in a coffin; now all of a sudden he realized his mother was trying to do everything she could not to lose herself, to collect herself and *keep it as a memento,* the way people keep the cherished lock of someone dear to them. For some reason today she had decided to spruce up and pin on the little chignon; there was something so vital and human about this that Krylov suddenly felt at peace.

In the kitchen his mother was stirring something in a babbling pot; the black and white cat was washing her cunning face with her paw, as if checking just in case for a torn ear on her round head.

"The police were here," his mother said without turning around. "They asked about you, but I wouldn't let them into the house without a warrant. Regular policemen, sparrows in glasses. As far as the money goes, I'll tell you this. You shouldn't have left everything to your Tamara. You were a real crook, after all, the kind that ride around in those super fancy cars, covered in gold. Your father and I were so worried about you. At least you got rich, but then you went and threw it all away!"

Krylov plunked down on a stool in astonishment. So this was what his mother had been thinking all this time!

"What are you laughing at?" His mother sat down at the table, took her knotty crocheting out of her pocket and from the other pocket, which bulged with a ball of something, pulled a smooth thread. "And you're going to Novosibirsk in such troubled times? Is it something profitable?"

"Yes, Mama, very profitable!" Krylov assured her earnestly.

Right then he realized he hadn't lied but had told her the God's honest truth. And in a way this spoken truth let him feel that he might even return. His mother's toothless, dropsical face smiled almost like a baby's, and it occurred to Krylov that she had in fact performed the main purpose of an adult's son's mother: on the threshold of the unknown, she had made him believe he would come home.

"All right, then so be it," his mother said, gravely straightening her holey shawl on her shoulder. "Go, and put the money in the parlor. I haven't straightened up here."

His mother hadn't straightened up in Krylov's room, which she called the parlor, either, but it wasn't as gloomy thanks to the gangly plant, once as imperceptible and barren as an old wire, which had suddenly put out a striped bell of a flower that looked pinned on. Everything here was crammed in, as always, and the dusty things, if you happened to look right at them, got lost in the clutter. Krylov looked around, trying to decide where to put the envelope of money so it didn't drown. First he decided to set it on the pier-glass, but that was so heaped with curly clumps of loose wool that he was afraid to touch it. Then Krylov cleared off a corner of his ink-scratched desk; there the white envelope stood out distinctly and could be seen right from the door. When he turned around, the layout of the place was drawn in his mind with uncommon clarity: the desk was the "mailbox."

Krylov came running back to Farid's, puffing and panting.

"No one called?" he shouted from the threshold as he pulled off his raincoat.

"Pavel," Farid replied, coming out into the corridor. "He's taking his family to Losinkovo today; he's got a house and garden there with potatoes. He told us, when we come back, not to go to town but straight there." Farid paused, holding onto the doorjamb, and added, "It's started in Moscow."

In the back room the television was on, its dying audio turned all the way up. A crowd was slowly pushing forward, down thronging Tverskaya, toward the Kremlin towers, which loomed like New Year's trees. Its slow movement scooped up the White Guards in their battered caps and the Red Army soldiers in their pointy helmets equally; overhead, like a sailboat moving into a deadly storm, red, black, and tricolor flags and banners rose crookedly, bowed, and fell. Sitting on the equestrian monument to Yuri Dolgoruky, like a child getting his picture taken, in front of the blind metal prince, was the capital's mayor, his bald head like a puffy dandelion, his hands full of proclamations that he couldn't bring himself to fling from that dangerous, fall-threatening height. In the side street teenagers wearing blue Soviet kindergarten caps were taking a running job and kicking and turning over squawking foreign cars. A hunched monk with fine hair that looked like the wind had sucked it out, was mincing along, his bony hands raised, toward a snub-nosed machine-gun poking out of an SUV. On Lubyanka Square, a resurrected Dzerzhinsky was observing the thousand-fold rally, which when seen from above was as enigmatic as the dark yearly rings of a thousand-year-old tree. At the Duma, the dictator Karenin, clutching the official tribune like a stevedore clutching a crate, was croaking inflamed speeches into the microphones, but the focused men sitting in front of him in the hall of state were not for the most part deputies. Once again the TV cameras took the viewer out onto the streets. The TV commentators—not the venerable, fame-lacquered ladies and gentlemen who read the news on the main channels but obscure girls and guys, disheveled in their dock-tailed tweed coats, with trembling lips smeared with lipstick and the cold—were each shouting on a backdrop of clanking tanks grinding up the Ring Road.

Nonetheless, this did not look like a popular uprising or a military coup. Moscow resembled a huge train station overflowing with troops and refugees where everyone was searching for their relatives. Those who didn't have a Red or White army uniform had still left their buildings—and the virus of History, which you'd think had been suppressed long ago and barely existed anymore, was spreading freely through the civilian crowds and the police and army units. Once he caught the disease, no one was what he had seemed or looked like or considered himself to be before. Each person could now be someone else, with a surprising destiny and indeterminacy in each tomorrow. No quarantines now could hold back the events that threatened—without logic or benefit other than the logic and benefit of historical movement itself—to shake up civilization. The epidemic of History was spreading through Moscow, and people were searching for their near and dear, hoping to gather once more before being sent off into the future, listening to contradictory announcements, and not knowing the train schedule.

"We can't go that way in any case," Farid spoke calmly, squinting at the screen. "I got us two berths on a train in transit from Kazan. Tomorrow, at eleven thirty."

"We may not come back to the country we left," Krylov noted, restraining a shudder.

"Why don't we check the medicines and provisions one more time?"

★ ★ ★

Strange though it may seem, Krylov got an excellent night's sleep before their departure. He woke up clear-headed and immediately realized that he was now utterly free of everything other than the long-appointed encounter on the corundum river. The final assembly took half an hour. Then Krylov and Farid sat quietly for a moment before departing, each looking at his own sturdy, tar-coated boots, and then abruptly harnessed themselves into their backpacks.

After the door slammed shut behind them the telephone twittered. It scraped in the curtained, stagnant half-gloom for at least twenty minutes, but who was trying to reach them and from where remained a mystery.

Destiny was at hand. Solid ranks of special squads were marching down empty Ascension Avenue to a rock-and-roll tread; friable snowflakes, like tiny white inflorescences, were melting on their taut, honed faces. Marching in step, the woolen army units were drawing toward the center of town; snow was sprinkling on them as if they were evenly plowed rows of vegetables. The low white sky slanted. The demolished TV tower, barely visible as a blurry, almost colored shadow, was broadcasting. On the incline of the dam that dumped beery water into the soft icy flab the freshly repainted sign—"There is no God"—was tilted, like a lure or a runway sign.

Out of the streets and side streets, straight and crooked, that led to Ascension, snow-flecked civilian marches poked their heads out, testing the air with their damp flags. Only one demonstration, which was dragging a small piece of pathetic red cotton, was moving behind the special squads, seemingly even following the elite unit at a distance of a kilometer. These were the old men and women in their shaggy wet coats, granddads in quilted camouflage and worn, plywood-like coats; some were hobbling like ungainly birds that for some reason had decided to go on foot. These were people from a bygone era who had not forgotten the genuine, salty, scorched taste of History. Pensioners, sellers of newspapers and counterfeit phone cards, petty swindlers, commuter train performers, decrepit shysters, home-based counterfeiters, and criminals if only because they continued to exist and remind people of another, otherwise-arranged world, they stubbornly dragged their stiff legs, and their faces looked like rumpled pockets turned inside-out. At the head of the demonstration were the flag-bearers, two men. Under a real velvet flag, worn at the folds to its pink fabric, marched two old geezers, shuffling as if their feet were searching for their house slippers, wearing uniforms from World War II: an infantry private in a porous rusty helmet and a rusty-brown waterproof cape; and a tank lieutenant who, in his helmet and outfit, resembled a fly with its wings torn off, and who had glossy, unaging skin on his left burned cheek. Because there were only two of them—perhaps in all the four-million Riphean capital—and by some other cryptic but unmistakable signs, you could tell at first glance that these weren't maskers: they were the real thing. The two old men were exactly what they were dressed up to be and what they appeared as at the head of their march of invalids—and this felt like a direct blow of *authenticity*.

That morning the wet snow that stretched white nets over the streets and trickled off the sticky russet leaves never did let up. Many people were trying to leave the city, and many were dragging cumbersome, haphazardly crammed luggage, dragging children too tightly wrapped up by the hand, flagging down passing cars, and besieging the ticket offices. In the dense crowd no one paid any attention to the two men—the dry old Tatar and the other, younger, with a stony mouth and a pointed hood pulled right over his eyes—who were striding evenly under enormous, well-packed backpacks. Destiny was seeing them off, stepping across the snow barefoot. It safeguarded them from an encounter with the drunken Cossack patrol that was firing their long-nosed Mausers at ravens and citizens and quickly dragged them through an intersection where a Young Communist blew up an army truck with a grenade five minutes later. Their tickets had been purchased in advance, and they reached their destination safely.

There was no one at the station to see them off.